THE GHOSTS
OF MAO

IAN LOOME

DEDICATION

To the survivors out there.

PART ONE

1

OFF THE COAST OF NISHINOSHIMA ISLAND, SEA OF JAPAN

TODAY

The sea two miles off coast was calm, but the fisherman's eyes were wide with surprise, nonetheless.

In his thirty-seven years on the job, Minato Fujiwara had seen a great many things, some quite wonderous, others too incredible to believe. The latter, he had to admit, were often due to consuming too much Saki in the hot sun. Fishing can be a lonely occupation at the best of times when it's not from a multi-crew vessel, and for all his statements while drinking among others about how much he enjoyed solitude, sometimes it went better with alcohol.

It was only on the rarest of occasions that he saw something truly frightening.

He had once been just a few miles from a giant wave, only to see it miraculously dissipate into violent-but-survivable swells before reaching his tiny one-man skiff.

He had fallen overboard once and found himself surrounded quickly by tiger sharks but managed to cover the few yards to his vessel and climb back in without attack.

He once caught his foot in the anchor line and only just got it free in time to avoid an impromptu amputation.

None of these worried him as much as what he had just witnessed.

It had been a black dot on the horizon, and he assumed at first that it was an airplane.

Then, it changed course, rapidly shooting to his left, then his right. It was so far away that he couldn't make out details, likely dozens of miles. But it flitted back and forth in the air like a fly avoiding a swatter.

Then it got closer. First, it lost some altitude. Then, it shot almost straight up. Then it started to descend again and move in his direction. It was big enough now to have a shape; it was so far off, still, that he assumed it was an out-of-control airplane.

The sea was relatively calm, and just the odd spray traversed the lip of the wooden boat's hull. The water lapped against it quietly.

If it was a plane, he assumed, it had to have a radio. That meant there should be ships on route, maybe another plane or rescue chopper.

But the horizon was empty in all directions, the sky an undisturbed blue-white. And he'd never seen a plane change direction so quickly.

Perhaps his aging eyes were playing tricks upon him, Fujiwara decided. Perhaps it was just a bird or a bug, its size making it seem like a large object rendered tiny over distance. The nervous sensation creeping up his spine was foolish, he told himself.

The object seemed to have settled just above the horizon line, as if hovering above the water. But it was getting larger, or...

It was approaching, he realized, not far above sea level. The water began to churn ever so slightly, the swells picking up, his boat beginning to bob uncomfortably. Another swell hit, this time larger, as if a series of waves was building up strength. The

sun peeked through the clouds long enough for
Fujiwara to shield his eyes with a hand visor, but the
boat was rocking heavily, and he grabbed both sides
to stable himself. He said a small prayer that
whatever it was, it would see him and halt or pass by
undisturbed.

It was within a few miles now, and he could tell
that it was round, or perhaps a long cylinder...

Fujiwara felt the same chill down his spine once
more. He'd seen large rocket-style missiles in movies
and on television. But it was markedly different to be
staring one down. And yet that's what he thought it
had to be: a missile flying so low that it was creating
a jet wake in the water.

His family had fished the waters around
Nishinoshima for generations and the topic of a
possible North Korean attack on Japan had come up
many times. The islands were, in some respects,
Japan's first line of defense. Like most of the island's
residents, however, he had long since resigned
himself to worrying about things he could actually
change.

He rose from his bucket bench and moved
quickly to the rear of the sixteen-foot skiff. He primed
the outboard motor, then pulled the starter chord.

Nothing. It whirred back into place.

He looked to his left, where the black dot had
grown to the size of a small radio speaker. The boat
bobbed more from his movement, water slapping the
hull, sloshing. It had to be large, he knew, nothing
like the small missiles he'd see on the wings of
military jets that sometimes flew by. He pulled the
chord again, and again, and once more. The motor
made a wet, squelching sound.

Flooded. He'd flooded the engine. He looked
desperately to his left once more, where the black
nose cone of the missile was the size of a large ship,
and just a few miles away. If it passed right
overhead? He didn't know. There had to be a jet
wake, he knew, and this was some sort of small
rocket, judging by the size.

There was no time to wait for the motor to clear. He moved back to his bucket seat and reached down to each side, finding the boat's oars on the floor, then slotting them into their oarlocks, the small metal hook-like guides on port and starboard.

He began to row, trying to maintain his calm, the oars arcing through the water as he pulled with all his might. Despite his advanced years, he was wiry and strong, without an ounce of excess fat, and he had decades of experience; nonetheless, he was nervous, the tension etched across his leathery face. The boat began to move north, out of the missile's path.

But it wasn't fast enough, he knew. He gazed to his left again and this time, thought he could hear it over the rush and hiss of the roiling waters. He pulled the oars frantically; the hissing of the ocean spray was overwhelmed by the roar of the rocket's engines growing ever louder. He pulled the oars and prayed, prayed that he'd make it back to shore, prayed that he would see his wife and pregnant daughter again.

It began to turn... toward his vessel, a sliding arc that made Fujiwara think it was tracking his small boat. Instead, the nose cone suddenly jerked to the right, a trail of blue flame and smoke visible for a second; then it jerked to the left, hard, the nose veering upwards, the sheer size of it obvious to the old fisherman in the moment. The rocket began to sputter, the flames cutting in and out, smoke billowing from its tail as it roared past, perhaps fifty yards from his vessel. The wake from the jet created a cresting of high swells, and for just the barest of moments, Fujiwara expected the boat to tip over. Instead, before he could regain his balance and look around, he heard the crashing rush of the gigantic weapon as it smashed into the ocean.

His boat started to accelerate on its own in the direction of the crash, the rocket's rapid descent into the water creating a vortex behind it, like water going down a drain. The old man grabbed the oars once more and pulled with all his might. It had gone in at least a hundred yards away, but it was still all he could do to control the small boat, and he prayed once more that he would make it home that night.

2/

KOWLOON, HONG KONG

It was just before midnight, and the count was short.

Tony Lo was a Deputy Mountain Master and had been a Red Pole before that, an enforcer for the White Crane Triad. He usually stood to one side of the faux wood table and watched the procession that occurred on the second-to-last day of every month, while the administrator, a bald and bespectacled man in a blue suit, sat behind the table and handled the count.

But he had been watching over the handling of tribute for a decade, whether in this broken-down, empty apartment or one of a dozen like it, each ideal for keeping foot soldiers away from people's places of business; and when Siu Fen, a young soldier from the docks, placed his bundle in front of the administrator, Lo didn't even have to ask for a recount.

'You're short,' he said. He left it simple, to give the kid a chance to explain. Soldiers – or 'forty-niners' – like Siu never had the balls to simply hold back cash. Lo was a huge man, his chest more than fifty inches across. In his dark-blue silk suits and black dress shirts, he was a menacing presence to even those on his good side.

'That's... what they gave me,' Siu said. His eyes danced around the room. Lo had been on one side of this discussion before with others and knew the kid was probably terrified.

'Who did the count? By my estimate you moved... how much, administrator?'

The administrator, or 'White Fan', turned to his

left slightly so that he could tap on the laptop keyboard a few inches away. 'Six kilos, deputy'

'You moved six kilos. There should be at least fifty grand more in there.'

'Deputy, I...'

'Explain,' Lo demanded.

'I cannot,' Siu said, lowering his eyes to the floor. Then he raised his head again, looking determined. 'But I can find out.'

'What is the ten oath, Fen?' Lo demanded. 'The tenth of the thirty-six oaths we all swear?'

He lowered his eyes again. 'I shall never embezzle cash or property from my sworn brothers. If I break this oath I will be killed by myriads of swords.'

'Someone in your district has stolen from his brothers,' Lo said. 'Find him. Find him and bring him to me. But be sure, because even if it is one nearest and dearest to you, no brother may break his sworn oath to us. You know the consequence of failure.'

Fen bowed quickly, keeping his eyes raised so that he could watch the room, gauge whether he was, in fact, being given a second chance. He backed away and then turned, leaving as quickly as he could.

'That's the second this week,' the administrator murmured.

'A poor precedent if they are not both quickly dealt with,' Lo said. 'The longer we both do this, the more I worry that honor is truly a thing of the past.'

The administrator barely smiled, but he chuckled slightly on the inside. The old guard, guys like Tony Lo, just didn't understand how much times had changed. They still had soldiers handing out envelopes of 'tribute' instead of just transferring the money electronically, via encrypted account. And the hierarchy in the gang was still so top-heavy that those at the bottom were left with scraps. No wonder they stole.

Either way, honor had never had much to do with any of it. 'Just keep in mind that leaving a messy trail of messages attracts the wrong attention,' the administrator reminded his younger associate.

Lo snorted slightly. 'That is why you are a White Fan and were never a Red Pole, my old friend. You were always too squeamish.' Lo knew it was also the reason he would eventually inherit the mantle of Mountain Master; the leader had to be seen to be strong and potentially ruthless, and a number cruncher would never fit the bill.

Lo's deputy had taken a call in the kitchen but walked into the living room with a concerned look on his face. He studied the three men waiting to drop off tribute envelopes then went over to his boss and leaned in. 'You have a visitor on his way up. A Charlie Pang? He says it's urgent and you go way back, but I don't know the name.'

The larger man's eyes widened. 'Charlie... Gods, it's been years.' Charlie had been a foot soldier as a teenager before his parents had moved him to a private school in the Philippines. The last Lo heard, he'd been working for the government in some capacity. But they were brothers from early childhood, in spirit if not blood.

The front door opened and the guard leaned in to announce him. Lo waved a hand to acknowledge the request. A moment later, Charlie walked in. He was twenty years older and maybe twenty pounds heavier, his shoulders broad. But he still looked like Charlie.

Lo got up and met him halfway across the room and the two embraced. 'Little Tiger! I thought you were long gone from these parts.'

'Nearly twenty years,' Pang said. He eyed the crummy apartment. 'It doesn't look like much has changed... except you're behind the table now.'

Lo smiled. 'I've come up in the world. You should have stuck around; maybe you'd be here beside me instead of Pei...' he said, nodding toward the administrator.

'Things got pretty weird after Manila,' Charlie said. 'Can we talk alone?'

Lo nodded to the White Fan. 'We're going to talk

for a few minutes. Yell if you need me or we get any shorter counts.'

In the kitchen, Charlie sat at the small, square table while Lo got them each a coffee. 'After we moved to the mainland for my father's government job, we were set up in this big old colonial mansion from the British days in Harbin. My father was being rapidly promoted and the prestige and acquisition was swift.'

'Sounds great.'

'It was,' Charlie said. 'And then I met this guy, this old-time player from back in the day, from the seventies.'

'The bad old days.'

'You don't know the half of it. He had a story to tell. And I believe it was one that could be worth a great deal of money to both of us. I spent the last five years trying to find out enough to actually do something with it, but if we can get just a little more proof, it will make us both very, very rich.'

'I'm already rich,' Lo said.

Charlie shook his head. 'Not like this. This... this is information everybody wants.'

Less than fifteen feet away and through the plaster wall to the next apartment, CIA field agent Adam Kwok listened to the patter from the two men who'd just entered the kitchen.

He'd been annoyed at drawing short straw on the stakeout, taking the tap on the west side. Each relied on a thin fibre-optic line for sound pickup, inserted through a pin-sized hole in the wall, so small as to be near invisible to the naked eye. But the east side tap was directly into the living room, and that was where all the action had been for two days.

It wasn't that he hated the assignment; Tony Lo was a major player in the Triad's smuggling operations into the U.S., and he did business with everyone from white slavers to spooks. It was the first time in years they'd had a solid location more than a few hours before tribute, and with the talk being of modernization, perhaps one of the last chances for a while to have both high-ranking and low-ranking guys in the same room as dirty money. The National Security Agency

I couldn't get anything off regional signals intelligence partners and there was bound to be important intel discussed, stuff that could lead to actual shipments and real, tangible progress.

But the kitchen tap had been silent for two days, a procession of footsteps over to the coffee machine every hour or so the only sign it was even picking up sound.

Until today. Today, Kwok quickly realized, something big was going down.

As soon as they started talking in muted tones, he knew it was important. For one, he recognized Tony Lo's voice right away, and Lo didn't take people aside for chats over nothing, even though the second voice was completely unfamiliar. He picked up his walkie talkie, left on the secure channel, and hit up his partner in the east-side apartment. 'Starling to Raven, over.'

'Go ahead Starling, over.'

'You get any of what was said before Lo left the room for the kitchen over?' he whispered.

'Yeah, something about a visitor,' the voice came back quietly. 'Guy named Charlie Pang familiar to you, over?'

'Never heard... shhh, gotta go.'

Lo had finished pouring coffee and gone back to the table, his footsteps faintly audible through the wire. Kwok pushed the headset tight to his ears and craned his neck forward, as if it might help the clarity.

'... realize there's no way for me to confirm any of this without spending serious money,' Lo said. The wire was inserted next to a picture, on the wall behind the breakfast table. The pickup was suddenly clear and strong, as if both men were seated right there.

'I get that,' the odd-man-out named 'Charlie' replied. Kwok took cramped, pencil-scribbled notes as a matter of veteran habit, even though multiple digital recordings were running. 'But we're talking about making it back a hundred times more with Project Legacy.'

There was brief pause. 'How much are we talking about?' Lo asked.

'Eight figures. Maybe... depending upon the entirety of it and what we can get for the various intelligence agencies... maybe nine.'

'Nine fig...' Lo let the thought hang there. A hundred-million dollars for what amounted to information?

'Surely that's not possible...'

'Really?' Charlie said. 'Think of the consequences. Untold lives lost, untold billions gone...'

Kwok felt his heartbeat increase as the digital recorder and laptop nearby recorded it all, his adrenaline rising. It was something big. And who the fuck was this guy? Tony Lo took him seriously and Lo was a major player. And this guy was talking about something worth that much money?

This was an immediate priority. He needed to...

The blast thundered through the apartment and the fibre optic connection like a cannon shot in a bus shelter; Kwok tore the headphones off and grabbed reflexively at his ear drum, the rumble subsiding to a high-pitched whine. A few seconds passed and it, too, disappeared. He grabbed for the walkie talkie but before he could press the button to talk, heard shouts and voices.

Someone was taking down the apartment.

He rose and grabbed the clip-on pistol holster from his makeshift workstation, the top of a short-but-wide chest-of-drawers in the apartment's rear bedroom. Another crime family? No, there would be gunfire, and plenty of it. This had to be police.

Goddamn it. Now things were going to get harder,

just when something big was shaking loose, something important and deadly. He opened the apartment's front door and peeked out into the floor's corridor. Tactical officers from the HKPD armed with assault rifles were pushing waiting tributes down to their knees, a line of young gangsters with their hands behind their heads, envelopes on the floor in front of them like some grotesque mockery of prayer. Police streamed into the apartment, commands screamed at the men inside, telling them to get down, to drop their weapons.

Kwok ducked back inside quickly and closed the door again. He radioed his partner. 'Starling to Raven.'

'Come in, Starling.' The voice was hushed, nervous and breathy.

'This place is way too hot; the locals are going to go nuts if they run into us. You clear out at first opportunity; maybe they'll say something else about this alleged intel before the local PD haul Tony Lo in for...'

The call was effectively interrupted, drowned out by three loud machinegun bursts of fire, then three more. And then it was silent, the walls of the small apartment enough to hold out the normal sounds of the day, absent breach blasts, and battering rams, and screaming tactical officers.

Shit.

He wasn't sure if the shots had taken down his surveillance targets or if Tony Lo was singing like a bird in the next room. Either way, there was every chance he could be discovered in short order. But he had to know what was going on. Kwok hurried to the back bedroom, grabbing the headset and listening frantically.

He turned up the volume on the small blue gunmetal preamp box that sat next to the wall, until the emptiness of the sound from the kitchen devolved into a static hiss. In the background, he could just faintly hear someone talking from the next room.

'... were resisting and had to be taken down. Do we have an escort to intake yet?'

Kwok listened for the static of a walkie talkie response but there was none. *A mobile call?*

Twenty seconds passed. 'Sure, a quick sweep. We'll know...'

The door to the apartment exploded inward, the frame wood splintering under the impact of the police battering ram.

3/

Superintendent Winston Chen had been on the job for three decades and was long past the point of being surprised by the pitfalls of bureaucracy. Cops that didn't talk to one another were more common, he'd found, than those who did. So crossed wires at a stakeout or bust weren't that uncommon.

But the man seated across from his desk, though Chinese American, was most definitely not police. Chen leaned back slightly in his office chair and pursed his fingertips together like a church steeple as he studied Adam Kwok.

'What to do, what to do...' Chen muttered in Cantonese. 'Mr. Kwok, you have diplomatic papers identifying you as part of the American consulate security staff here in Kowloon. And yet you were discovered next door to a major gang member who belongs to a Triad with broad American interests, with recording equipment and a fiber-optic tap.'

Kwok said nothing. A veteran field hand, he followed a series of protocols for capture that included volunteering as little as possible.

'Of course, Hong Kong is somewhat more... enlightened, shall we say, in the latitude we have when dealing with such matters.' Chen threw the idea of co-operation out there early; he didn't expect the American agent to bite, just perhaps start thinking that the superintendent might be marginally more sympathetic. 'If you were even just to share unofficially your reasons for such a specific interest in the White Crane gang...'

Kwok remained silent. Chen was beginning to suspect the man would say nothing at all unless provoked. 'You should be aware that your recording materials were accidentally destroyed during the raid and therefore cannot be returned to you,' he said. 'Additionally, you will not be allowed to contact your consular colleagues immediately.'

'Why?'

Finally, a response. 'Why? Because you were engaged in espionage activities, Mr. Kwok, and in China, such activities are punishable by methods up to and including execution. Your diplomatic immunity extends a privilege to you with respect to criminal activities. But espionage is a state security matter, not one for the criminal courts.' It was a bluff; Chen himself had no pull in the intelligence community and he doubted the HKPD would have any say in what happened to their guest. On past experience, there was every chance they'd be ordered to return him to the American consul, which would then be politely asked by the government to transfer him out of China.

Had it worked? Chen saw it for just a split second, a glimmer of nervousness, the slight widening of Kwok's gaze, the tip of the younger man's tongue darting out for a split second, then a piercing stare as the diminutive, unassuming agent began working out options. 'I have nothing to say without a representative of the United States diplomatic service present,' Kwok intoned.

The veteran officer knew if Kwok had anything useful on Tony Lo, he had to get to it relatively quickly. The intelligence service was already on route to question the American, and there was every possibility that once that happened, he would be unavailable to local law enforcement. That meant everything on the taps would wind up in Beijing, being handled by some government spook, instead of feeding valuable and potentially life-saving information to Hong Kong cops.

'My detectives inform me you recorded two days' of Tony Lo's activities. Of course, you had no authority to do so.'

'What happened to him?' Kwok asked.

'We'll get to that,' Chen said. It was an opening. 'What do you know about Project Legacy?'

Kwok hid his surprise. There was no way they'd

gone through all of the recordings in just a handful of hours since the bust; they must have had ears inside, maybe even someone undercover. But the fact that Chen was asking meant they had no idea what Lo and Charlie Pang had been talking about.

Or...

They'd been there for more than just a proceeds-of-crime bust, which meant Chen's real goal was to find out how much Kwok already knew. 'Ask your inside man,' Kwok bluffed. 'I'm sure he can give you a first-hand account.'

Chen maintained his pleasant demeanor, smiling gently. In an earlier age, when he was a younger and more competitive man, he would have enjoyed the prospect of jousting. But at fifty-seven, it merely made him tired. He did not intend to show it, however. He still had that much pride, at least.

'I'm certain you are aware, Mr. Kwok, that we at the Hong Kong Police have a far more tolerant reputation than the people from Chinese state security. Unfortunately, I'm quite certain my department has been thoroughly infiltrated by them, as you might expect. We have no secrets from them, and you have already been in custody for two hours. It is two o'clock in the morning, which works to your advantage. But regardless, it means we do not have long to reach a more congenial accord...'

Kwok ignored the implied threat. 'Did one of your men shoot Tony Lo?'

Chen got up to pace slowly, for dramatic effect. He wanted it clear he was in control, that Kwok's decision to ignore his interrogation tactics had no impact. But he was tired; it had become harder and harder at his advanced age to pantomime a commitment to the dance, to the passion that makes men sing for their souls, or at the very least merely their safety.

He stopped next to the American's chair and leaned down to speak softly, unsure of who might be listening in, even in his office.

'Mr. Kwok, it is entirely possible, as you have no

doubt been instructed many times, that should the intelligence service spirit you off to Beijing or Chongqing, your family will never hear from you again. In very short order, you're going to need a friend, and a good one. I've never claimed to be a politician or to have any great ambition except being a good cop. But I promise you, if you give me nothing, I shall see no reason to raise a word in your defense, and you shall disappear to some nasty, greasy shithole work camp in the back of beyond. The man Tony Lo met with is a gangster from Hunan, but a connected one, with friends high in the party. It seems more than coincidence you were staking out that apartment – and there are signs you had some help – unless you knew Charlie Pang would be there. So talk to me; help me now, and let me make this easier.'

It was new information; that meant it was worth keeping him talking, keeping him trying, Kwok thought. He had nothing to offer, really. But Chen didn't have to know that. 'How long have you known they were planning to meet?' he asked. The officer shot him a short, sharp look, but Kwok held up both hands in protest. 'Hey, information is a two-way street. I mean, if you can tell me that at the very least, I know if I have something that can help you.'

'The clock is running, Mr. Kwok,' Chen said. 'You know that much must be true...'

Kwok was enjoying the joust. He'd been stuck with the impersonal duty of various wiretaps for most of his two years in Hong Kong; it felt like real work for a change. 'Inspector let's not kid ourselves: any decision about what is to be done with me will be made well above our pay grades. Given how hard your team hit that apartment, it's clear you're aware of the implications of Legacy already. It's clear you know why a guy of Charlie Pang's repute would want in.'

Was he fishing? Chen recognized the signs, each question ducked or responded to with one in return, building on things he'd already said but offering absolutely nothing back. It had been naïve, perhaps, to expect someone with intelligence training to roll over easily. 'The potential for embarrassment for your nation over this incident is, of course, considerable. Those in authority will, in return, look for a scapegoat. If you help me now...'

'You'll what? Protect me? What happened to Tony Lo and Charlie Pang, superintendent? I heard the shots. I didn't see them come out with the rest.'

Chen looked down at his desk. He'd been told by his deputy chief that an officer on the scene had been surprised by both men upon inspecting the apartment kitchen, and had returned fire, killing both.

'They are being interrogated as well, Mr. Kwok, and so far, they are being far more helpful. But then, their involvement is direct, while yours appears to be merely observing. Again, I accept that. The intelligence service will not.'

'You've got Charlie Pang in one of these rooms?' Kwok gave the officer his most doubting look, as if he couldn't believe the gall. He still had no idea who Pang was, but if Chen knew he was a gangster from Hunan, he might know more.

'You find that hard to believe?' Chen said. As far as he could tell from the network, Pang was a mid-level player peddling muscle and girls. His file had suggested he was from Kowloon originally, so perhaps he'd known Lo from earlier days. But their man inside hadn't heard much else of the conversation – just a snippet or two about Project Legacy while hovering by the kitchen door.

'I find that hard to believe.'

'Because Legacy is too big for a small-time player?'

'Sure. And, like you said, Tony Lo is a major figure, superintendent. Why would he...'

'What?'

'... why would he discuss something that important with a nobody?' Kwok stared the older man down as he asked the question.

'Billions of dollars...' Chen said. In reality he had just the two snippets of information from his inside man.

'Millions of lives...' Kwok retorted. 'Why didn't HKPD take this to a higher level earlier, given the ramifications? I didn't see any outside agencies represented at the building.'

'That doesn't mean...'

'If they'd been watching, they'd be here already, picking me up.'

Chen took a deep breath. Kwok was working hard; given how little information the superintendent truly had, it almost suggested the agent knew nothing of Pang's presence. Had the Americans really just been there for Tony Lo? 'As you say, Mr. Kwok, I suspect they won't stay away for long. And the decision will be made high above our pay grade on where you go from there.'

The superintendent took out a packet of cigarettes, withdrew one and lit it. 'Totally off limits in the office, of course, but when you're on nights, nobody's paying much attention. Anyone working is usually out, or burrowed in an office trying to kill time until morning, or to finish a mountain of paper work. It's usually just me and my deputy roaming around.' He blew out a plume of smoke, then flicked the ash into the small office garbage can beside his desk. 'Would you like one?'

'Never been my thing. But apparently I'm going to share yours...'

Chen's eyebrows rose. 'Really? An indignant and politically correct spy?' He exhaled again. 'What is the world coming to? You make me feel old, Mr. Kwok.'

'Keep smoking,' Kwok said. 'It'll pass.'

- chuckled a little at that. 'My wife says the same. She smokes too, but she's full of self-loathing about it. She's younger than me, you see.'

He took a deep drag from the cigarette. 'When you talk about her, do you get the urge to smoke?' Kwok asked.

THE GHOSTS OF MAO

Chen's eyes went cold, his mouth grim. 'I am attempting to be cordial, Mr. Kwok.'

'It's all you have control over, at this point,' Kwok said. 'Either they do as you suggest, and I disappear, or they make me go home, and I'm on the beach in San Diego in a few days. Either way, I'm already done in Hong Kong. I have nothing that can help you.'

It wasn't really contempt, Chen understood, just the ruthless realism of youth.

Even though Kwok had also concluded neither knew anything else about Project: Legacy, it still struck him as part of the job to walk away with the upper hand, to let this local policeman know he worked at a higher level. He was still going places, after all.

Or at least, that was how it felt. Kwok eyed him, expression neutral, neither happy nor sad, a picture of analytical poise. 'Perhaps they won't come until tomorrow...'

'Unlikely.'

Chen knew he was right. And part of him wanted to bare his teeth, challenge the younger man, prove to him why and how he'd survived so long in law enforcement. But he was tired, and it was the dead of night.

There was a tap on his office door.

'Well. That resolves that question, I suppose.' Chen held up both hands. 'Any last requests? Anything else to share before...?'

'It has been nice meeting you, superintendent.'

'Come in,' Chen said loudly.

The door swung open and a young man with dark hair leaned in. 'Superintendent Chen?'

'Yes?'

The man stepped into the room, his movement so deft and deliberate that neither men had time to react as he raised both arms, a different pistol in each hand, both suppressed. He shot Chen three times in the chest and Kwok three times in the chest with the other hand, their bodies snapping and convulsing, the recoil muffled to a loud popping, like New Year's firecrackers. Then he methodically shot each man once in the head. He placed the pistol from his gloved right hand into Kwok's open grasp, closing the dead agent's fingers around the grip and slipping his forefinger into the trigger guard, before repeating the procedure with Chen, then letting his hand slump naturally off to the side of his chair, the gun falling realistically to a spot beside him.

The young man in the dark suit left the office and closed the door behind him, turning off the light. The deputy superintendent, a lithe man with a wispy beard and prominent front teeth, was standing in the center of the common area, near the empty detectives' desks, one hand on his pistol holster. It wasn't a big station, but the late hour accentuated how deserted it seemed, with just the two of them there.

'It's done,' the young man said. 'The security camera file?'

'Dealt with,' the deputy superintendent said. 'How long...?'

'Just wait until I'm out the front doors. Longer than that isn't necessary. After all, this is a matter of national security, deputy. No one will see this for any more than it appears.'

'What about Const. Wu, the undercover officer...?'

'An unfortunate accident at his apartment. A gas leak. The other American has also been handled.'

The deputy stared down at his feet. He knew where his loyalties truly lay, but he had been with the department for a decade. These people were colleagues and friends.

'Your exemplary service will be noted,' the young man said. He turned on his heel and headed for the main doors, leaving the deputy alone with the shadows of the long turn toward daylight.

Less than a city block from the station house, in the back of a hole-in-the-wall bar, a thirty-something Australian signals intelligence officer arrived coffee in hand. He had no expectations from yet another shift in what was quickly turning out to be a terrible career move, and he was hungover, finally accepting the advice of his colleagues from Britain and Canada, that being posted to Sig Ints in Hong Kong was about as valuable as a hot beverage in the outback. Take advantage of the expense account, they'd said; eat, drink and say bugger it to the home office, they'd said.

He sniffed deeply as he closed the office door behind him, his sinuses still hurting from the mild dehydration. He walked over to the plain wood-grain office desk and moved the mouse, bringing the computer screen to life; he was technically relief, but he was late, and the officer on the evening shift had long since gone. It was no big deal; no one paid much attention to Hong Kong Station.

He sat down and put on the pair of headphones; the station was tasked with the most basic of signals intelligence: direct interception, using equipment stationed near government offices and police stations. It was broad-scale intelligence gathering, but everyone did it; countries that routinely co-operated and shared intelligence also spied on each other and looked for every advantage they could get, in trade, defense or whatever suited the policy requirements of the day.

That was mostly over the young officer's head. He sat down and put on the headphones, then started taking meticulous notes. He didn't expect to hear anything, so the first series were just observations, conclusions about how little of use was floating out there in the Kowloon ether.

It took two hours before he reached the digital recording from the shotgun mike just a few blocks away, at HKPD Station House Six. He'd set it up, along with the other police mics, in the hopes of shaking something loose on smuggling or drugs, something that would impress the higher-ups back in Canberra. It angled from an opposite rooftop, directly through the front window of Supt. Winston Chen's office.

The agent fast-forwarded through hours of silence before there was a blip on the computer screen's sound wave form, a few peaks and valleys suggesting conversation. He backed up the recording slightly and hit play.

After a few moments, his eyes widened; he snatched for the phone as if his life depended upon it.

4/

DAY 2

WASHINGTON, D.C.

CIA deputy director Jonah Tarrant was in full flow by seven in the morning, and he paced the carpet of the National Security Council's narrow corridors with a purposeful gait, like a golfer trying to stay ahead of the next foursome. Senior Agent Brandon Mah was having trouble keeping up with him as they headed for the main conference room.

'What do we have?' Tarrant asked.

Mah was looking over a traditional paper file, printed off from an encrypted report by his assistant an hour earlier. 'What we have is a pretty solid stream of information coming in from our Australian friends. They've been running a ground tap for some time in Hong Kong, and it hit on something last night. We're fairly certain in turn that it relates directly to what the authorities there are calling a murder-suicide involving a part-time U.S. consul security officer and a police superintendent.'

'One of ours?'

'Yes, Adam Kwok, an agent assigned to the consular staff. He was keeping surveillance on a gang house when all hell broke loose. He was picked up by Hong Kong PD and they're claiming at some point made a go for his arresting officer's gun, if you can believe that. In the hours after that happened, there was a flurry of intelligence traffic coming out of the mainland, and from what our monitors could pick up, Chinese intelligence is in a heck of a state about something called Yichan, or Project Legacy. From their heightened state of excitement and a few stated fears, we're left with the impression that it involves a high-ranking or highly placed operative within the United States.'

They passed the busy central hub of the office, where staff officers were already hard at work poring over data, analyzing it, looking for value. 'So what's the gist?' Tarrant asked. 'Give me the broad strokes.'

'Those were the broad strokes,' Mah said. 'We know nothing about it other than what we've learned overnight from Hong Kong. Kwok was almost certainly a professional hit, along with the cop. So, it's someone or some group with contacts and money. Maybe the Chinese; certainly, we have no idea who might be involved or what any potential targets might be. It's just too early.'

'Then why the excitement?'

'Two reasons: first, we believe the North Koreans launched an ICBM toward Japan this morning.'

'Jesus H.'

'It was a test for their latest guidance program. Satellite evidence suggests the missile ditched just off the coast. Whether that was deliberate, to keep this to a provocation while suggesting it could have reached the mainland, or another failure of their tech is unsure.'

'What now?'

'The President has a battle group steaming to the Sea of Japan and our NSC liaison with the forces suggests he's not kidding. He wants to send a message.'

Tarrant shook his head. 'That's a hell of a start to the day. What was the other reason? '

'A sig ints officer picked up a conversation in a police station prior to the alleged-murder suicide. It sounded like our guy stumbled onto something of significant magnitude,' said Mah. 'Statements like 'America's economy collapsing' and 'billions of dollars lost'. And this on the same day as the North Korean test? It doesn't seem coincidental.'

'That's bad.'

'It gets worse. The tap picked up what sounded like both our man and the police superintendent he was talking to being executed.'

Tarrant stopped walking for a second, just to absorb it. He kept his game face on as they resumed their pace. 'Do we have anything official from the Chinese yet?'

'We have an official denial of any knowledge of any such operation, yes. We don't believe it for a second.'

'Why?'

'Too much traffic, and too much of it vociferous. Along with the Australian report, we've talked to our other overseas partners, and they're hearing the same things. Again, all very vague, but targeted here.'

They reached the conference room. Mah pushed the double doors open; the rectangular office space had just one set of furniture, an eighteen-foot-long conference table and chairs, and the entire south wall was covered by a series of flat-screen monitors. Five of the chairs were occupied.

'Good morning, ladies and gentlemen,' Tarrant said. 'Agent Mah tells me you've been briefed. The situation is extremely fluid and we have limited intel at this time.' He sat down at the head of the table, Mah to his right. 'We've been reaching out to our contacts in China as well, and so far have nothing, except a sense of great impetus on their part. There's been some hyperbole about it being an operation with a major potential impact on both human life and capital. There's no suggestion of a North Korean connection, other than the test timing. But we're a long way from any sort of clear and present danger. I'll take suggestions.'

'Fuck the North Koreans,' said his lead analyst, Edward Currie. 'They're always pulling this stuff. But this Hong Kong situation is out of left field. And we've got the heaviest stake in this. We're down two good men in Kowloon...'

'Priorities, Eddie,' Tarrant said. 'We can worry about payback once we figure out what we're dealing with and whether the two incidents are connected.

For now, we need to figure out what to throw at this.'

'Well, the language on 'Legacy' suggests a sleeper of some sort,' Currie said. 'They've used 'activated' several times, but there's also confusion, like they're not sure what they're looking for.'

'That's encouraging,' Tarrant said dryly. 'So it could be a Korean Spy or it could be a WMD, or it could be a Mountain Dew machine. Are we hearing anything on the domestic front? John?'

John Wrexham was the NSA's senior liaison to the CIA. 'Nothing like this. What should we be looking for? Do we have anything on the actual nature of the threat?'

Tarrant shook his head. 'We know a gangster from Harbin tried to sell information on it to a colleague from Hong Kong, and that as soon as the designator 'Project Legacy' went active, a select number of senior Chinese officials went batshit. Then the North Koreans launched a missile. If this is China's party somehow, it's incredibly hushed.'

The fifth man, the scholarly and slight Dr. Roland Massey, had been quiet to that point. As a key presidential adviser on international affairs, his interest was insulating the commander-in-chief when issues were unlikely to have a candid upside. 'Who are the heaviest hitters, in terms of chatter?'

'Yan Liu Jeng, undersecretary of the security and intelligence oversight committee. Chan Man Wei -- or 'David Chan' to those familiar with his business holdings -- the chairman of the security and intelligence service. Wen Xiu, the Interior Minister,' the CIA's Currie said. 'We're just seeing traffic, mind; it's all encrypted six ways from Sunday, so we can't see what they're actually talking about.'

Tarrant thought about it. They'd been on it for twelve hours already and it amounted to a whole lot of nothing. 'Brandon, do you have any ideas on where we can take this?'

Mah nodded. 'I have one. There's a freelancer we turned to a few years ago; he's suspended right now from the available list for insubordinate behavior.

But he's active in the academic community over there and has the Chinese intelligence contacts, if he isn't irreparably burned.'

'Where is he?' Tarrant knew they needed to be up and running quickly; any knowledge that a plan was leaked might push the Chinese to speed up their agenda, causing something to happen before they could uncover and counter it.

'In Macau,' Mah said. 'But there's a problem.'

'Of course there is!' Tarrant muttered. 'What, exactly?'

'He'll only speak with his last handler.'

'Who is...?'

'Joseph Brennan.'

'Ahhh... Hell,' Tarrant said.

BEIJING, CHINA.

Yan Liu Jeng's morning felt like navigating a minefield.

The undersecretary of the security and intelligence oversight committee had not expected his own rapid ascent through the ranks; at forty-six, he was one of the youngest senior officials in the party. But he knew he did not have the experience to survive the constant politicking that surrounded him without help, let alone the judgments of his elders in the powerful central committee. And he relied on his trusted confidantes to ensure he had the right options when problems arose.

This, however, was a unique situation, and no one, so far, was taking the bait; no one was taking the initiative and suggesting concrete action, which was what Yan really required.

He knew what he wanted, but he wanted the idea to come from someone else.

He sat at the head of the semi-circular table and studied the members of the overarching State

Security Committee as their assistants delivered them information germane to the day's discussions.

'Gentlemen,' he said softly into the microphone. The dozen other members quickly turned to pay attention, with no need for gavel banging or theatrics. 'As you are aware, we have credible intelligence that Legacy has been activated and that, despite the long-held belief that it was a myth, we must now face the potential of a catastrophic attack against the United States by agents believing they are acting on our behalf.

'The timing of this has been unfortunate, to say the least. We have reached out to our partners in North Korea and expressed our... extreme dissatisfaction.'

Toward the end of the table, one of the men was quizzical. 'Could the two matters be tied?'

'I do not believe so,' said Yan. 'We have already taken steps to examine every piece of stored data that may have survived from the period immediately prior to and during Jiang Qing's incarceration. As you are aware, this is a massive volume of information, but if there is something useful, a pearl among that ocean of history, we shall uncover it; however, it seems impossible for a program from that era to have predicted or had any role in the peninsula's nuclear capabilities.

'In the meantime, our agent in Macau has found a former intelligence asset who is now teaching there and may have something for us. He interviewed Jiang during the prison years, on several occasions, and stayed in contact with some of her supporters. It is possible that, in her periods of manic fanaticism, she mentioned something important to him about her intentions.'

To Yan's right, state security chairman Chan Man Wei -- known as David Chan in the west for his many business investments -- looked typically thoughtful; despite a public persona as a successful entrepreneur and investor, he was known within the Central Committee as an intelligence executive imbued with foresight and reason. 'Is there any reason yet to assume that the Americans know Legacy even exists?'

'Unfortunately, yes,' Yan said, glad the question had come from someone like Chan, who was less inclined to turn it into an attack on his competency. 'They are... showing an active interest in Hong Kong, due to the loss of an agent.'

'An agent?'

'CIA, we believe. He was running surveillance on the Red Pole. Perhaps that's why, for reasons of public confidence, they seem inclined to work with us. To what extent, given the potential political ramifications, we are as yet uncertain.'

At the far right end of the table, Interior Minister Wen Xiu raised a cautious hand. 'Chairman So... as the other committee members will attest, our staffs have been able to find little-to-no information on this purported project, even in the context of something mythological, or a party legend. And yet we are taking this all on faith that...'

Yan interrupted. 'It is somewhat more than that. The criminal who was able to determine Legacy existed and that it has, indeed, been triggered is believed to have met just prior to his death with a loyalist to the Lin Biao and Jiang Qing Counter-Revolutionary Clique,' he said. 'The threat is credible and the Americans know we are pursuing it. They also seem aware, according to our agent in Macau, that it involves a sleeper or sleeper cell... and that we have lost track of it.'

There was a collective groan around the table. The old days were gone; most of the committee members had substantial investments and holdings in the United States. China as a national entity held much of the U.S.'s long-term debt. There was nothing to be gained from some absurd Maoist propaganda attack.

'Gentlemen! Gentlemen!' Chan called out, re-establishing control. 'Please... let us see how our agent makes out. It may yet prove to be a minor concern, and as things stand, the Americans concede they know of no specific threat. We may all yet walk away from this with reputations unscathed.'

The drive back to his impressive four-bedroom home in ChaoYan District shouldn't have taken Yan more than fifteen minutes, but terrible traffic and a driver he'd already decided was witless had combined forces to stretch it to nearly a half hour. When his wife Mai greeted him at the door, he ignored her attempt to peck him on the cheek and walked past her to the butler, who took his coat.

'I'll be in my office,' he said perfunctorily. Mai watched him and felt ignored, which was nothing new. She was not accustomed to her husband slowing down just because he'd come home. Or explaining himself.

Yan followed the short entry hallway to the vast American-style kitchen and living room, with its wall of windows overlooking the lights of the city's downtown. Though he'd been raised in Hong Kong and educated in England, he felt an affinity for all things American, at least in matters of style and aesthetics. He turned right and walked straight through the room to another short corridor, taking the first door on his left.

The office was the size of a studio apartment and along with his broad oak desk and floor-to-ceiling bookshelves also featured a small lounge for a reading area. The wall between the office and corridor was nearly covered with a one-hundred-inch projection screen. Yan reached for a switch by the door and dimmed the lights; then he walked over to the desk, took out his government-issued phone and placed it in a metal box. He opened the top drawer and withdrew another phone, turned it on and paused for a moment. Speaking with the leader always unnerved him.

He dialled a number. The big screen on the wall sprung to life as the conference call connected.

The man on the screen was front-lit, shrouding him in shadow and anonymity. When he spoke, his voice was filtered and modulated as part of the transmission's encryption.

'Yan.'

'Sir, my apologies first for not calling you privately in advance of the committee session...'

'It could not be avoided.'

'The situation is fluid, but the central committee is inclined to send an agent to Macau, where there is reportedly a source of intelligence on Legacy.'

'Are we in control of the North Korean operation?'

'We are not.'

The man was thoughtfully quiet for a moment.

'Are we still in control of Legacy?'

'We are.' Yan knew he dared not show weakness.

'And our next step?'

'To cut off the source and take care of the official response with one single stroke.'

'The Americans will hear of it.'

'But they won't be able to stop it or get involved until it's too late.' It seemed unlikely, anyway, Yan thought. It had been many years since the Americans had a firm information footing in the region.

'Unless their existing intelligence has already pointed them to a source from the time,' the leader warned. 'Do not take this threat lightly, Yan. As you are doubtless aware, Legacy relies on absolute discretion. That's why the approach is so... unconventional. Do we have the assets in place to achieve this 'single stroke,' as you put it?'

Yan nodded. 'We do, sir.'

'Who is the Macau source?'

'We believe it's an English college professor named Stanley Lawson. He's been in the area since he was a small boy, just after the Second World War. His intelligence connections are extensive but his gambling and drinking habits preclude him being taken seriously any more within the community. He did some work for us two decades ago and we think worked for the Americans as well.'

'How much is he likely to know?'

'I assume he knows the Dorian Fan story or, at the least, the version that was floating around Harbin twenty years ago.'

'That alone will not take him anywhere."

'No,' Yan said, 'No, it won't. But it may well lead him to another source. And another. Eventually it would prove catastrophic.'

'And?'

'I have an asset in mind. We merely await your word...' Yan felt a surge of adrenaline, secure that he'd taken the right approach with the people he feared and respected the most.

'Deal with Mr. Lawson,' the man in the shadows insisted. 'Demonstrate your worth to me, and cement China's glorious future.'

5/

DAY 3

JACKSON HOLE, WYOMING

The old sheep ranch had been in the Bernard family for more than a century. It wasn't much as farms go, with a pen for the shrinking flock and a few paddocks of lush green grass for grazing, as well as a few dozen acres of arable land. But it was picturesque. They'd repainted the house red with white trim a few years earlier, to match the color scheme of the bigger barn's aging, peeling walls. Eventually, it would get a new coat too, when there weren't greater priorities. Which, as is the case on most farms, there always seemed to be.

It was set in a small valley surrounded by emerald foothills winding their way to the horizon, where they seemed to suddenly shrink in the presence of the Teton mountains' towering crags and peaks. The sun was still hanging around a hazy sky. A slight breeze rustled through the leaves of the forests of white pine and poplar that dotted the hillsides.

Joe Brennan stood on the back porch of the farmhouse, watching his nine-year-old son and his twelve-year-old daughter play volleyball against the Bernard's grandkids. Josh's hair had turned from blonde like his father's to a reddish-brown, like his mother's. He was a happy kid, Joe figured, at least most of the time. His life was uncomplicated, regimented, protected by his loving parents. Jessica was another story; she was twelve going on nineteen, maturing so quickly it terrified both of them. Carolyn kept muttering things about finally understanding why they used to send girls to convents. Her daughter's latest preoccupations were smoking cigarettes and swearing, although she continued to get straight 'A's and to embarrass her teachers intellectually whenever possible.

It all worried Joe, but it didn't surprise him. Not in the slightest. She had a little of her mother's ambition and her father's rebellion, but was smarter than both of them. There were things about her that reminded him of his late friend Myrna, an Agency analyst who'd passed a few years earlier in the line of duty. Myrna had been savant-level brilliant, but also socially withdrawn. That made him feel both blessed and doubly terrified.

On the plus side, she had no idea what her father had done for a living for most of his adult life. She knew her mother used to work for the CIA and was now with the National Security Agency. And she knew her father spent a lot of time on the road. And that was about it. Some sort of sales job, she used to tell her friends. Totes boring.

There was a slight creak to the door spring on the screen door behind him. He glanced over his right shoulder as Carolyn joined him. She handed him an open bottle of Michelob. 'How are they doing? I figured after the hike they'd be tired and wanting to crash or watch movies or something...'

'What? You figured we'd actually get a night of peace to just hang out with Mike and Vicky? Maybe drink a little too much vino? Maybe smoke some of that 'medicine' of Mike's?'

'Yeah, I know... Loony Tunes, right? Crazy notion.'

'If they're down by nine o'clock we'll be lucky,' Brennan suggested.

'If Mike's still conscious at nine it'll be a miracle.'

Carolyn wasn't exaggerating. His agency mentor had been pounding back drinks since the morning. Brennan turned slightly so that he could look back through the sliding door to the living room, where

Mike and Vicky were watching the news. 'He wasn't always like that. You know his background.'

'I do. It's one of the reasons we need your retirement to come through officially. The old man signs those papers...'

She was far more enthusiastic about it than he was, Brennan had to admit to himself. It had taken his wife a year of solid lobbying, but he'd finally agreed to not just quit the agency but to get out of covert operations entirely. No insanely-well-paid-but-risky merc contracts; no freelancing; no protection details or bodyguarding; nothing that involved the imminent risk of a bullet to the head. He'd noticed how, over the week prior, she kept maneuvering them into positions where he'd get a prolonged view of the kids playing. Carolyn was tenacious, but she'd never exactly been subtle.

She was also right, he told himself. His kids deserved a father who was around, not one who used the spectre of honor and duty to his country to skip out of town whenever he felt the itch. It wasn't right, he knew. He had a duty to be there for them, as well.

The patio door slid open again. 'When was the Agency ever there for you, Joe?'

Mike knew how to make an entrance, Brennan figured. But then, that wasn't unusual: the dramatics usually got ramped up a little after the tenth beer.

He turned to face him. 'Chief. Is it that obvious when I've got work on my mind.'

They'd known each other so long and shared so much that the two men had a strange bond that Brennan's wife had never quite understood. Carolyn looked uncomfortable. 'I'm going to go see if Vicky needs a hand with the dishes,' she said.

Mike waited until she was inside. 'The question stands.'

'There are a lot of different answers to that one.' The drunker Mike got, the more bitter he got about the past. 'I guess the one that suits me most is that I never really did anything for them, either. I did it out of a sense of responsibility.'

'So… always in the wrong place, but for the right reasons?'

'Yeah, something like that.'

The rancher slugged back half his beer in one long swallow. 'You know that old line from the movies about spies never retiring? It's only true if you let it be. If you let them, they'll use you up and toss you out. You're just a means to an end to the Agency, Joe. One regime ending today; another person's life ending tomorrow. But where does it end for you?'

Brennan suppressed an urge to sigh. 'You got out….'

'I got a buyout from a full-time staff gig as a trainer, and only then because I'd been off for a year on stress leave.'

Brennan nodded. He didn't want Mike to start debating health choices; his old friend was mentally fragile enough as it was. 'How has that whole thing been going, anyway?'

Mike shrugged. 'Before we invited you guys out for the week I told Vicky I was going to stop talking about it for a while; but with the date coming up…'

It was a big part of why Brennan had snapped up the invitation. He knew Mike needed comfort every August and had for a decade; his friend would fixate on Sara Evans, one of his most promising recruits. She'd thrown herself into the Potomac, or at least that was the official verdict. He'd never believed it, never see in her intense nature the strain that must have lain underneath the cool exterior, the pain that swept her away with the river's current, never to be found. They'd located her belongings on the riverbank, along with a suicide note. The agency's best experts had been unanimous that it couldn't have been a forgery.

Eventually, Mike had had to face it, and the internal inquiry that said she'd pushed herself to dangerous levels of stress. All to score well in his training course and qualify for covert operations. And then the grief had kicked into high gear, and it had never really left. He'd gotten past denial to anger and occasional bargaining, his wallowing fed by self-loathing, a tragic attempt to keep an emotional connection to a girl who, in truth, he hardly knew, and in doing so, avoid thinking about her as being gone forever.

The self-loathing led to drink, to make the edges blurrier. The drink led to depression. The depression led to more self-loathing, and the cycle repeated itself. Worst of all, they all knew it, everyone staying at the house, an unspoken understanding that a man as smart and well-educated as Mike was either going to bottom out and deal with his demons, or...

And that was the road no one really wanted to go down; instead, they avoided the matter entirely. 'Eventually,' Brennan had told Carolyn on their first night there, as they talked in their guest room, 'people are going to make their own damn fool decisions.'

But they all loved him; he'd been like an uncle to the kids and, along with the late Walter Lang, had been a fixture at their Annandale home over the years. They all felt the same anxiety, distress and guilt over his decision to slowly drink himself to death.

'You're still seeing someone about it?'

Mike snorted at that. 'Doesn't that just sum life up right there? We're all so damn uncomfortable about our feelings that we have to make her death and me seeing a shrink sound like a trip to a specialist about a pesky mole.'

'Avoiding the question. Was that interrogation training kicking in?'

'No, I just genuinely find it ridiculous. That okay with you, Joe?' He took another long pull, finishing off the can of beer.

He crushed the aluminum can with one hand and was about to toss it toward the corner of the deck when he saw the look of concern on Joe's face. 'Ah... give it a rest, will you?' He put the crushed can down on the deck fence rail instead. 'I mean, how many goddamn times can I cover the same awkward ground with another headshrinker? Just... just do me a favor, okay? When they give you that call to come in and see the old man and he offers you that hearty handshake, make damn sure you take it. Then turn around and walk out of there, and don't ever look back. After everyone we've both lost, that's the smart play, Joe. That's the percentage that keeps you sane.' He gestured toward the kids playing volleyball. 'And you have two exceptional reasons. I hardly know my son and I'm lucky as hell that I get to see my grandkids twice a summer. All so that I could devote more time to...'

'Mike...'

'Nah, skip it,' he said. 'You're here on a family vacation, not to listen to my whiny bullshit. You want another one?' He nodded toward Brennan's beer. 'Kids don't look like they're going to let up any time soon.'

Brennan shook his head. 'I'm good for now.' He wasn't so sure the game would continue for much longer. The sky had gotten hazier, the clouds almost grey, a storm brewing.

6/

DAY 4

Brennan woke early, rose and showered, and pulled on his jeans and a sweater while Carolyn slept soundly, just a few feet away. He'd become an expert over their years of marriage at moving around the house without disturbing anyone, a necessity in his periods of insomnia. Maybe the same nervous itch that kept him alive in the field also kept him awake at home, he'd always figured. Maybe it was response to his addiction: as profoundly controlling as Mike's issue, but adrenaline, rather than alcohol.

He watched his wife sleep, the sunlight of the new morning cutting across the dimly lit room and shining through the strands of her golden hair. She looked so peaceful and innocent just then; he was uncomfortable with how wrong that felt. He knew her as a force of nature, a rapidly rising star since transferring to the National Security Agency, still able to use her minimal time off to help raise their kids. But he had to admit to himself that the discomfort stemmed from his desire to be with her softer side, from before she had a career. He missed the woman he'd married, and he knew that was unfair. He'd brought her new life about, constantly exposing her to national interests, tension, the hint of excitement accompanying danger.

In the still of the morning, before life cast them onto the mouse wheel of daily routines and expectations, he wondered if he'd ever meet that person again, then wistfully realized that she no longer existed.

The sunbeam had stretched just enough to catch her barely fluttering eyelid, and she woke, using her left hand to shield her eyes as she turned toward him but went immediately back to sleep. He smiled at that. She could go on four hours a night for weeks, still, if needed. But when they had downtime, it was like trying to wake the dead.

There was a light tap on the door and Mike leaned his head through and into the room. 'Everybody decent? Good.' Then he saw Carolyn still sleeping and modulated to a whisper. 'Oh, hell. Sorry about that! There's a call for you, Joe. It sounded official. You want me to tell them to take a long walk off a short pier?'

'No, that's fine.' Brennan was puzzled. He wasn't expecting anything important; no one else knew he was there and he hadn't had an assignment in eighteen months. He pulled on his sneakers and followed Mike out of the room and down the hall, to the large sitting room. The phone sat on the coffee table.

'Joe Brennan.'

'Joe, it's Jonah Tarrant.'

There was silence between them for a few moments as Brennan collected his thoughts and tried to figure out what to say.

'You know you're a son of a bitch sometimes, right?'

'I can understand why you'd feel that way, Joe...'

'You left me in the middle of a hostile riot in Jakarta without any support.'

'It was a snafu, we've admitted that...'

'Three broken bones. One bullet wound to my thigh -- thank God it didn't nick an artery. My credit cards stolen from my room in the meantime and racked up before the embassy could get me out of that dung heap that passed for a hospital.'

'Like I said... we've admitted mistakes were made, we paid an agreed upon settlement and you know I didn't personally call off your support team...'

'No, that was your lapdog Adrianne Hayes. To protect a deputy ambassador who'd flown out two hours earlier. Why in hell did the old man hire her for your old job, exactly? You weren't qualified for it, and you make her seem like... well, no, scrap that, neither of you has a clue.'

This time, it was Tarrant's turn to go silent. Brennan needed to vent. He'd expected that. It was human nature. 'You about done? Are you remotely curious...'

'Yes, damn it, of course. Why are you calling me, Jonah? You know I put my papers in, right?'

'Sure. Of course, officially you don't exist, so that's a pretty flexible situation...'

'Jonah...'

'Your country needs you, Joe.'

'My country has had twenty-two years of me.'

'A lot of lives may be at stake.'

'Probably so. And they always will be. Let the next guy handle it. I have to think about my family.'

'I don't see Carolyn scaling back her time at the NSA.' Tarrant knew it was a low blow, but it was true. Plus, she'd stabbed the old man in the back by leaving.

'That's none of your business. I put in my time.'

'I need you specifically. We've got a witness we need debriefed in Macau.'

Brennan frowned. 'I only know one guy in Macau and he cheats at poker. Plus, I have to figure he'd be dead by now.'

'If you're talking about Stanley Lawson, he is seventy-eight years old. From your vetting, your file suggests you first met him when you were still in the navy, then used him a decade later to transfer a message for you to the daughter of a Tong boss. Sort of 'off the reservation' on that one again, weren't you?'

'The job got done,' Brennan said. 'What does Stanley have that you want?'

'We have no idea,' Tarrant said. 'But we know it's something big. The intel says it's an operation that will 'strike at America's heart'. It may be the Chinese; or it may be the North Koreans. Or it may be both.'

'That's pretty goddamn vague, Jonah, even for you.'

'And we know someone put out a call yesterday

to several freelancers in the region, a contract on Stanley Lawson's life. The problem is, he doesn't believe us. He has information he knows we need, and he thinks this is a negotiating tactic. Now, as far as we know, no one has accepted the contract yet. So maybe we can get to him first. You do this, you might save a man's life and prevent a catastrophe.'

Brennan stewed gently on the other end of the phone line, cooking like a grenade with the pin pulled. *Goddamn you, Jonah,* he thought. Training gave him the restraint to keep it to himself, but just barely. *Goddamn you, Stanley Lawson may be a poker cheat but he has grandkids, a daughter who loves him, and you know that.*

'You know,' he said calmly, 'if I were in DC right now, I would punch you really hard in the face, right?'

'Yeah,' Tarrant said, 'Yeah, I get that. There's a ticket booked for you on a commuter shuttle out of Jackson this morning. Call me when you get back to D.C. and we'll go from there, okay?'

The line went dead. Brennan stared at the phone for a moment, then at Mike, who was standing a few feet away with an uneasy look. 'My wife's going to kill me; you know that, right?'

He shrugged. 'And I keep telling her divorce is so much easier.'

'Thank you.'

'You're most welcome. You going to tell her now?'

'Why?'

'I want to get out of range.'

7/

MACAU AUTONOMOUS REGION PEOPLE'S REPUBLIC OF CHINA

Tommy Wong was crestfallen. He looked at himself in the public washroom's mirror. The white linen suit and black dress shirt were custom tailored and ideal for a stylish day at the races; but to Wong, the image that reflected back at him was cheap and tawdry.

'You are a coward, Wong,' he told the reflection. 'The tip was good. You could have won a fortune. And instead, you bet the favorite.'

What had his grandfather always said? 'Let luck be with you, and you shall turn iron to gold.' Instead, his cynical nature had gotten the better of him.

It wasn't that he needed the money, of course. His bank accounts were flush with cash. And his lifestyle in the Chinese gambling mecca was under no constraint; he had all the good food and women he could shake a dollar at. He had an elegant condominium apartment up above the city, overlooking Nam Van Lake. By all of his typical markers, Wong's life was idyllic.

Except, of course, that it wasn't. Perhaps, he told himself, it was just the boredom of having gone for so long without having to work. He'd made more than four million dollars in the year prior, and suddenly found himself battling laziness, a desire to sit back and relax on his well-earned laurels. Wong cursed his own indolence and vowed to stop taking it so easy.

He turned on the tap and splashed his face with cold water. The day was moist, with humidity tipping ninety-six percent, and the racetrack was busy. Even in the open air, all of those people increased the sweltering temperatures that much more. He pulled a long sheet of paper towel from the dispenser and dried his face and hands, then balled it up and tossed it into the trash can.

Outside, the long boardwalk that headed to the main grandstand at the Macau Jockey Club teemed with people; he looked both ways, trying to decide where to go. He could head for the parking lot, instead of likely throwing good money after bad. Or he could head back to the ticket windows and stay for the sixth and seventh races; he didn't know any of the horses on the card, but there were two heavy favorites.

They wouldn't make up for the forty-to-one shot he'd just blown, a tip from a friend in Hong Kong.

Wong had a love-hate relationship with gambling. He loved the risk and the rush of a reward but hated that it conflicted with his generally cautious nature. You couldn't live in the world's gambling capital without some self-restraint, it was true. But he had concluded that as he got older, the risk of losing some of his nest-egg seemed to outweigh any potential reward. It made him feel cowardly, but secure, and he was torn.

His phone rang and he immediately hoped it was something that would take him away from having to decide. He took out his phone. The number was unfamiliar but that was typical.

'Tommy,' he said.

'Good morning, Mr. Wong.'

The voice was synthetic, a computer simulacrum. It still managed to be familiar, and strangely comforting. Each time it called, the number was different, part of its exceptional misdirection security that bounced the original signal point around digital phone systems around the world. It stated a single number and if Wong replied in the affirmative, it sent an email to his laptop; the email, in turn, was honey-trap encrypted with a version of the software Twofish that split the message into more than a dozen 256- and 128-bit strings of data. If someone tried to crack the data strings, any failed attempt would spring the "honey trap", a data dump that included thousands of pages of illegal pornography and a particularly nasty root kit virus. The virus lay dormant until the individual's computer was rebooted. Then it would wipe and rewrite the target drive and flash the individual computer's bios, changing its power settings and causing a motherboard overload.

As far as Wong knew, it had never been triggered, or defeated. If it had, he assumed, the hacker in question probably deserved whatever they could figure out from his messages. Typically, they included a name, a photo headshot, and a date.

'One million U.S.,' the computer voice intoned.

'Yes,' Wong said. He ended the call and returned the phone to his breast pocket, then walked the boardwalk back toward the parking lot at a brisk, even pace. The track was always busy, even when the mercury climbed. He tried to avoid bumping anyone with his shoulders. It wasn't that he was particularly large or wide at a fit, trim five-foot-nine inches. He was just excited and inclined to rush as a result.

A few minutes later he was ensconced in the light-tan leather driving seat of his Aston Martin DB9, a low-slung sports sedan in battleship grey. He reached under the passenger seat and pressed a fingerprint-encoded button. The tray drawer released and slid out. Wong withdrew his laptop and opened it. It booted to his mail and he placed his thumb on the pad by the keys while entering the twelve-digit string. The screen went black for a split-second. His email browser opened and he clicked on the new message.

The photo was of an elderly white man with a silver-grey bowl cut and a shaggy grey-and-black beard. He wore steel rimmed glasses. Behind them, the skin under his eyes was wrinkled and bagged from age.

'Stanley David Lawson, Local.'

'ASAP.'

He deleted the email and shutdown the laptop before returning it to the drawer. He would wait until he got back to his apartment. He could get out of his three-piece suit and into a martini, relax before planning how to kill the old man.

8/

DAY 5

WASHINGTON, D.C.

It had taken some rapid-fire diplomacy to arrange a video conference call so quickly with his Chinese counterpart. Now Jonah Tarrant just had to convince the man that whatever they were hearing from Asian listening posts was important enough for them to co-operate.

'Thank you for your time, Chairman Chan,' he said. David Chan was a well-known entity in the capital. Tarrant supposed they'd chosen him because he would make an unfamiliar American more comfortable; but he knew there could be any number of reasons. Chan wasn't exactly a lightweight. Perhaps they knew something serious was afoot; or maybe they just wanted to impress him.

'Deputy director Tarrant. National Intelligence Director Wilkie was not available, I assume? A function of his age, no doubt.'

It was a direct shot. Everyone knew that Nicholas Wilkie had been relatively old when appointed. Too old, in point of fact. A former three-star general, he'd spent most of the prior six months in and out of hospital rooms.

Tarrant's instinct was to return the broadside, bring up Chan's country had some sort of mess on its hands. Instead, he was deliberately diplomatic. It would have the double impact of being both effective and annoying, he knew. 'As you've doubtless been informed, one of our men was killed in Hong Kong on Monday.'

'Adam Kwok, a field agent.'

'A consular attaché. A glorified security consultant...'

'...who was no doubt using all of that fiber optic

cable to help Tony Lo fix the terrible holes in his apartment building's walls.'

'You're speaking of the raid in the adjacent apartment? Coincidence, I'm sure. Obviously, however, it's of great concern to us that he appears to have been slain while in the custody of the Hong Kong Police Department, and the night before a missile launch from China's partner...'

'We have many partners.'

'...North Korea.'

'It appears your intelligence in this regard is also mistaken,' Chan said. 'We know nothing of this latest incident with our neighbors. And your officer was in fact found with the gun in his hand that took his life, and that of one of our fine Hong Kong police officers. It is a most regrettable incident, given his diplomatic status.'

'And it's part of the reason why I felt the need to contact you personally and offer our help with respect to this other matter,' Tarrant replied.

'Other matter? Whatever could you be referring to, deputy director?'

Tarrant kept his tone matter-of-fact, as if everyone knew. 'Well, obviously this whole 'Legacy' project, chairman. My apologies, I assumed you were of sufficient rank to have been briefed.'

'If there is something of significance for us to discuss, deputy director, I assure you I am fully aware of it. Perhaps you could be a bit more specific. After all a "legacy project" is a fairly common term.'

Tarrant wanted to smile but he remained stoic. Playing 'who can say less' with Chan was fun, but it was clear neither wanted to make the first concession. 'This would be the one involving your agents striking at America's heart. That one. The one over which you appear to have little-to-no-control.'

'We have no such operation,' Chan said. 'Certainly, if there is any intent on the part of individuals to attack your country, it is not done with the endorsement, guidance or authority of the People's Republic of China.'

'For a non-existent operation, it's receiving a startling amount of attention right now from your various agencies. It has a lot of people thinking that perhaps the North Korean launch was a dry run of some sort. While the United States would obviously never violate the sovereign communications of a nation such as China, some of our foreign partners tell us your various intelligence agencies are talking about almost nothing but; and your own technical surveillance department seems most interested in everything we're talking about. So maybe we should all try getting along on this thing...'

Chan shook his head as if slightly bemused. 'What 'thing?' As I said, deputy director, we have nothing to share. And we do not appreciate obvious violations of our privacy. If there is an internal matter that is receiving the lion's share of our attention, you may rest assured that it will remain private.'

'Isn't this something we should get out of the way now, before your premier and our president meet in a few weeks to discuss limiting the North Koreans? I'd hardly suggest a potential international incident is the ideal backdrop to diplomacy.'

'Mr. Tarrant,' Chan suggested, 'I have no idea what you could be referring to.'

The committee session had not been scheduled until the following day, but Chan wanted everyone aware of the Americans' involvement. He'd given them a recap of the conversation with Tarrant. They sat around the semi-circular conference table awaiting his recommendation.

'It is clear, at this moment, that the Americans are fully aware that Legacy exists and that its purpose is malevolent. The true nature of it, I suspect, eludes them. Our priority now must be to shut it down as quickly as possible. Even if its individual components are not in place or we are not aware of them, we must not allow a decades-old fable to be used as justification for a terrorist attack. Our holdings in the United States are far too extensive, and the risk of retaliation is significant.'

Wen Xiu was concerned that Chan Man Wei was holding information back. They had sparred numerous times over the years. Xai was also a more traditional communist, seen as more aligned with the interests of the State than business. He knew his broad and openly held opinions were often unwelcome among his silent-but-ruthless colleagues. Still, it had been several days already without concrete action.

'At this time, what options have we? We have no idea who is responsible or where they are located. We have few connections known to still exist to the Gang of Four that might be of any use. Then what do you suggest, chairman? We cannot simply wait for intelligence to come in...'

'Obviously,' Chan said. 'We are facing talks with the Americans right now with respect to the North Koreans' test; an incident of any magnitude could ruin them before they begin.'

Wen had done his homework. 'There's one lead. We have information that there's a man in Macau who may know the location of the original source for Charlie Pang, the gangster from Hunan who died in the raid. If we can follow that back, the connection to Jian Qing may become more apparent.'

'We need to find this man immediately,' Chan said. The territory's enforcement autonomy was no more than a formality anymore. 'Who do we have in Macau right now?'

MACAU

Daisy Lee didn't really need the flop. The table was down to her and the Swede, Magnusson, and he didn't have the stomach for it. He'd held three cards but given away that he was bluffing with one of his legion of tells, in this case flaring his nostrils every time someone else had drawn a card.

She'd studied tape of all of her opponents before the match, and had already played most of them several times anyway. Throughout the Poker Gems Invitational Texas Hold 'Em tournament, he'd flared those nostrils every time he'd been full of hot air and this was no different.

But just for good measure, the dealer flipped over a Jack of Hearts, giving her a full house, threes over jacks. Unless she was reading him wrong -- and Daisy was not known for blowing a read -- Magnusson was done.

'I'm all in,' she said at the dealer's nod. She pushed her chip stacks forward far enough to solidify intent.

Magnusson could see the steel in her eyes, the complete lack of concern or remorse for his position. He sighed visibly and tossed his cards into the center of the table. 'I fold.'

They were almost done, then. He barely had enough left for the ante.

Her phone rang. Not the phone in her clutch purse; the one she kept on her person at all times. It looked like an outdated flip phone but had built in satellite relaying, letting her stay in contact anywhere on the globe.

Not now, she muttered to herself. *Not when I'm about to finish this arrogant Gwai Lo off in near-record time.*

Magnusson smiled. 'Do you need to take that?'

She returned the pleasantry. 'A moment, please...' She reached into the inside pocket of her toreador-style half-jacket. Lee took the phone out and checked the text message:

'Your presence is required immediately. Report to this address within the hour.'

She knew the location in nearby Tanzhouzhen. It was an office of the Liaison Department, the branch of the Army responsible for psychological warfare.

Critically, she'd forgotten about the game while reading the message, and to hide her annoyance behind a poker face. Magnusson was wearing a toothy grin; he'd recognized that she was under a time crunch all of a sudden and he motioned to the dealer. 'We're allowed to request a short break in the final, aren't we?' He asked. 'I certainly could use fifteen or twenty minutes to freshen up.' He looked back at Daisy and smiled more demurely this time, like a satisfied cat.

Daisy stared plaintively at the dealer but he had to shrug his shoulders. 'Players in the final are allowed to request one recess of up to one-half hour,' he said.

She let her head tilt back in frustration. Lee pushed her million-and-a-half dollars in chips to the center of the table. 'Player concedes,' she said.

The Swede's jaw dropped open.

TANZHOUZEN, A SUBURB OF XIANGZHOU CITY, PEOPLE'S REPUBLIC OF CHINA

A half-hour later Daisy was seated before an official with the Liaison Department. He was young but nearly bald, with a wispy beard and round, steel-rimmed glasses.

'You are Li Daiyu, commonly known as Daisy Lee?'

'Correct on the first attempt. Admirable,' she said dryly. 'Surely your future within the party will be paved with success. Can you perhaps explain to me why you chose to ruin my tournament after weeks of preparation?'

The stone-faced officer ignored her insolent tone. 'Your cover as a professional poker player is of little concern to my department. I believe you were informed by your handler with State Security that you were to acquiesce to all of my requests and give your complete co-operation.'

'Why am I here? Get to the point.'

'In three hours, a man named Stanley Lawson will attend a work retirement party for a university colleague at Wing Mei, a wine bar near Fisherman's Wharf. Lawson knows the identity of a foreign operative who, in turn, has collected something we need.'

'Better timing?'

'Most amusing. No, he has intelligence on a program initiated within the Liaison Department more than thirty years ago, but quickly dismantled and expunged from the official record.'

'And he has the 'unofficial record'. Is he blackmailing the department? Surely no one is that stupid.'

'Quite the contrary. Despite having been on our payroll at various times, Mr. Lawson sold this information to a gangster, who in turn was killed before it could be retrieved. But enough of it leaked out in the process for us to determine that the program involved a strike against the west.'

'So? Back in the day I understand they developed plenty of strange schemes to prove the decadence and weakness of America.'

'This one has been set in motion by players as yet unknown. What we do know is that the project was called 'Legacy' and it was believed to have been established by loyalists to Jiang Qing and the Gang of Four.'

Everyone in China was familiar with recent history and the purge of Jiang Qing, the former wife of Mao Tse Tung known in the west as 'Madame Mao'. Her Counter-Revolutionary Clique had set China back years via a "Cultural Revolution" that purged intellectuals. But she had died in prison in 1991. 'Again, no one in their right mind...'

'We do not know that these are people 'in their right mind',' he said. 'We do not know anything about it at all, except that, according to signals intelligence on the gangster who obtained the plan, it would cause a major international incident and involves a terror attack of some sort, likely in America. And Stanley Lawson knows the man who has the key.'

She opened the file folder on the table. An 8x10 glossy of an elderly man with a beard stared back at her. He had imposing, bushy eyebrows that were still mostly black.

'An electronic copy has been sent to your account. We want you to extract Lawson from the party, debrief him and then terminate.'

She frowned. 'Why, exactly? All he's giving us is the name of the man with the actual information.'

'That data is well above your pay grade,' he said. 'You are to follow through with your orders and assist us in all requests, as per your supervisor's demand. We cannot be sure what Lawson himself has learned, and this is a matter of utmost national sensitivity.'

'You mean political sensitivity.' She regretted the words as soon as they'd left her mouth; after all, there was no role in public life in China that did not rely in some way on the machinations of politics.

'Your counter-productive attitude shall be noted for the official record,' said the bureaucrat. 'Return to Macau and complete your assignment, then contact me here.'

'And my regular handler?'

'He has been reassigned and has returned to Beijing. All of this is in the electronic file. Study it carefully. We would prefer Lawson's death to look like an accident.'

'Or maybe a heart attack?' Daisy suggested. 'Perhaps in five-to-ten years from now?'

The man did not smile or even blink. 'Most amusing,' he said.

MACAU

Lee risked another speeding ticket on her way

back to her hotel, where she kept a suite as a player-in-residence for the casino downstairs. It wasn't that she was in any particular hurry, because the party didn't start for three hours. She just liked the rush of cutting her Nineteen Seventy-Two Porsche 911 in and out of traffic at twice the speed limit.

She checked for messages at the front desk but there were none. She took the first in the bank of five high-speed elevators up to her room on the twenty-second floor.

At the door, she paused. As an old habit, she'd left a strand of moistened hair on the door, across the crack, just to be sure no one visited when she was away.

But it was out of place.

Lee took the QSW 06 five-point-eight-millimeter pistol from her shoulder holster. She stood away from the door then reached over and pushed it slowly open. The entrance looked clear; the light was on in the bathroom and the door open and she turned to face it as she passed, keeping guard for someone coming out, then taking another hesitant step to her right, toward the suite proper.

'There's really no need for the gun, Ms. Lee. At least not yet.' He squinted at the gun, slightly confused. 'A suppressor? A bit much for a poker player, isn't it?'

She recognized the man sitting on her sofa, and the two bodyguards perennially by his side. 'Jackson Chu. You're aware it's illegal to enter someone else's suite...'

He waved both hands in a mock show of innocence. 'A misunderstanding, I would have to claim. The owner of the hotel is an old friend, so I assume it won't be too much of an issue.'

'And to what do I owe the unique pleasure?' As far as she knew, Chu was still an enthusiastic medium-market money launderer through his five betting parlors. He had no intelligence profile whatsoever.

'I believe you owe me some money, Ms. Lee.'

'I... think I'd remember something like that. You're sure you're not looking for someone else named Lee who plays poker? There are about a billion of us.'

'Yes, but they didn't just cost me a six-figure payout by walking out on a world-class poker tournament with more than a million in chips still on the table.'

She looked wistful. 'Yes... unfortunate, to say the least, but something came up.'

'Really? That's your explanation? You were interrupted?'

'That's what happened. Not that it's any of your business, Mr. Chu, but I have other life responsibilities other than just winning at cards.'

'From an outside perspective, it could be construed that you walked away and threw the match deliberately. Certainly, I imagine your poker league's authorities will ask no less than I am asking; and they probably lost a lot less money.'

'Yes, but I have an agreement to speak with them about such matters; and they're a poker league, not the International Olympic Committee. They don't care that much what I do, if I'm being honest. You, on the other hand, shouldn't be laying downside bets on games in which you are not involved.'

'Ms. Lee...'

'And your two gigantic helpers should learn that if the intent of bringing a gun to hotel room is to intimidate someone, it's a good idea not to leave that gun in a shoulder holster.'

One of the bodyguards began to take a step forward, but Chu shushed him and held out an arm, blocking the man's path. 'Are you quite sure that's the attitude you'd like to take, Ms. Lee? My man Harold here seems quite intent on demonstrating his lack of requirement for a firearm.'

'Let him demonstrate his proficiency,' Lee suggested.

Chu admired her conviction and smiled inquisitively. He removed his arm, and the six-foot-plus guard took two steps her way, then threw a deceptively quick round house punch. Daisy arched over backwards like a limbo dancer, the fist sailing just over her head.

'He only gets one swing. The next time, I hit back,' she said. 'Okay?'

Chu shrugged. 'As long as this conversation ends with you paying me my three hundred thousand dollars, I don't really care what you do.'

'Well, that's not going to happen.'

'Then I'm afraid we shall have to let Harold make up his own mind on the matter.'

Not wanting to be shown up by a slip of a woman, Harold charged at Daisy, intent on overwhelming her with his sheer size. She dropped low then drove her fist upwards with perfect timing. The guard's expression shifted to one of shock and he stopped dead in his tracks, the shot to his testicles so painful that he dropped to his knees, a stream of drool flowing from one corner of his mouth, eyebrows furrowed. Daisy used one dainty, heeled foot to push him over onto his side. 'Next.'

Chu frowned. 'Jerome?' he said, looking up at his other guard.

Jerome wasn't messing around. His hand quickly slipped inside his jacket and withdrew his pistol. But before he could train it on Daisy, she'd pirouetted in a blur, a spinning round kick sending the guy flying across the room.

'Try again,' she said, raising her chin to the thug defiantly.

Jerome looked at his empty gun hand, then back at Daisy. He sneered angrily and threw a straight right hand at her head. She stepped aside adroitly, then spun three-quarters of the way around, as if gliding down the back of his arm, until she was back-to -back with him. Her heel came up hard between his legs, catching Jerome as violently as his partner. His hands shot down to his balls to protect them from another kick. She took another quarter-turn to his side and her elbow flashed out, catching him in the temple and stunning the much larger man.

He collapsed to his knees, groggy and concussed, trying to remain conscious. A few feet away, Harold continued to writhe and cup his damaged groin.

Chu hadn't moved but he looked worried. 'That was particularly vicious,' he said.

'Thank you. That was actually the 'no permanent damage' version. Unless you count having kids.'

'I rather suspect from the ease with which you accomplished it that you could have beaten both men without reducing their chances at producing offspring.'

She shrugged. 'True. But this way, the next time they see me, they'll think twice before trying to hit me. And the world will be better off without them as parents, anyway.'

'Are you going to do that to me, as well?' Chu asked.

'Are you going to accept your good fortune and leave quietly?'

'I'm beginning to think there might be more to you than your public persona suggests, Ms. Lee,' he said. 'I shall take my leave while my family jewels remain intact, thank you.'

'And will I be hearing from you again about this, or shall we both go about our respective business as if the other does not exist?'

'I am practically a ghost and this conversation never happened,' he said. He rose carefully, keeping his eyes on her throughout. 'Come, Harold. Jerome....' He gave Jerome a gentle kick with the toe of his Italian leather boot. 'Shake it off, Jerome, we need to make haste.'

Jerome shook his head vigorously, trying to clear the cobwebs from the elbow stunner to his temple. He rose uncertainly, shaky. He shook his head again and looked at the diminutive woman. 'You hit harder than you look.'

'Thanks... I think,' she said. 'Now, everyone out. I've had a long day and fairly soon, I'm going to lose my temper.'

'We shall doubtless meet again, Ms. Lee,' Chu said. 'Perhaps next time...'

'Perhaps next time I will be less charitable, Mr. Chu, and afford you the same treatment as your underlings. As things stand, I assume my charity affords me good standing with the Black Cranes?'

Chu studied her with hawkish intensity. 'You most certainly are full of surprises, Ms. Lee. I wonder how far that goes.'

Lee said nothing; better to let him wonder. As they closed the hotel room behind them, Daisy walked over and sat down on the edge of the bed, irritated. The Black Crane Triad was a major operator in Macau, with ties to a vast Black Society in Harbin. The last thing she needed was to get on the gang's bad side and be constantly looking behind her.

She rose and walked over to the full-length mirror on the bathroom door. Her bullfighter's jacket and blouse with jeans wasn't going to do for a party. She still had nearly two hours and there were some nice clothing stores in the adjoining shopping center. What did one wear to a debriefing and assassination? Maybe something black, off the shoulder?

9/

DAY 6

MACAU

The going-away party was an hour along and
Stanley Lawson was beginning to feel his age. While
most of the university staff either danced or chatted
at one of the large round dinner tables, Lawson
found himself a quiet spot at the bar and nursed a
fourth gin-and-tonic. He felt slightly drunk and
slightly left out; it wasn't as if people had ignored
him completely, it was just that he didn't often take
part in staff get-togethers, and he was at least twenty
years older than the next oldest man there.

Still, he told himself, it beat another night with
his book or watching television alone. The bar was
done up in bamboo, reeds and tikki torches, as if
attacked by a Polynesian decorator. The school was
picking up the booze tab; and there were free cab
rides home.

He turned on his stool and looked at the room.
Although there were a dozen or more from the school
there for the going away, the bar was still open to
other customers and fairly busy. He caught the eye
briefly of a fifty-something blonde and wondered if
someone her age could still find him attractive. He'd
been told he looked like the late English horror actor,
Christopher Lee. That had to count for something.
He'd expected his urges to diminish as he aged and
they had, to an extent. But he still spent time
wondering if he'd ever actually manage to pick up a
woman again just for the night.

He turned back to the bar, his impaired vision
blurring slightly as it tried to keep track. When he'd
worked for British Intelligence, years earlier, there
had been lots of women. Probably too many. His
'lifestyle' had been cited during his dismissal, a

'compromising feature'. That, and the unfounded suspicion that he was serving more than one paymaster, a political maneuver in a field replete with them.

'You like this woman?' a man's voice said from the next stool over.

Lawson gave the man his attention. He was Chinese, dressed immaculately in a white linen suit and black shirt.

'She's pretty,' Lawson admitted. It was someone to talk to.

'I can get you a girl much prettier and younger,' the man said. 'All you have to do is tell me.'

Wonderful. A pimp. 'No, thank you,' Lawson said. 'I'm actually here with the group...'

'Ohhh,' the man intoned. 'You think I'm selling girls. No, not at all! Not at all, Mr. Englishman. I just know a very pretty girl who has a thing for older guys, that's all.'

If he'd still been with MI6, Lawson would've assumed he was being honey trapped. As it was, he suspected, it was probably just a shakedown. 'So, I go with you to meet this girl and then when we're alone somewhere, I get robbed. Maybe I should call the manager...'

The man appeared taken aback. 'Not at all! I thought you look sad that's all, so I try something nice for you.' Then he looked irritated. 'What? You think I'm a pimp? That's pretty racist, man.'

Stanley took a sip of his drink, then said in perfect Cantonese 'Whatever it is that you're after, I can't help you.' Just to be safe, he repeated it in Mandarin and Hakka.

The man looked impressed and held out a hand to shake. 'Tommy. I don't think I've heard a westerner speak that fluently before' he replied in Mandarin. 'Your Cantonese is better than mine.'

'Stanley. And like I said, I'm just here for a quiet drink while my work colleagues get drunk.'

The man looked surprised. 'Stanley? Stanley Lawson? The language professor at Macau

Polytechnic?'

'Yes. I presume we've met?'

'I saw your lecture last year on the development of Standard Chinese. You didn't have a beard then.'

It was true, Stanley recalled. The school put a picture of it in the monthly alumni newsletter online and he'd heard nothing but jokes about his unshorn mug for a week.

'True,' Lawson said. 'Then... you're a student.'

Tommy shrugged. 'My English is still not so good. But I'm working at it.'

'Better than many,' Stanley said diplomatically. 'This young female friend of yours: is she here tonight?'

'No, but she's staying in the hotel. And she isn't pricey; she'll just want a gratuity of some sort, a little cab fare.... you know. She's only nineteen.'

Lawson's alarm bells were still ringing but it had been so long since he'd had sex. The offer was enticing, even if it was probably incredibly stupid. Really, really stupid, especially now that he was back in the game. Sort of. She was practically a child, and he was old enough to be her grandfather – or great grandfather, even.

Still...it had been so long.

'The hotel here, connected to this building?'

Tommy smiled. 'This hotel.'

It was beyond foolish, Stanley knew. Even if the offer was real, he didn't have any sort of protection. Of either sort. And he was drunk, never the condition in which to make important decisions.

The bathroom. The bar had a condom machine in the bathroom. 'Well then, perhaps I should like to meet your friend. Would you excuse me for a moment while I visit the loo?'

He rose and crossed the room, skirting the busy dance floor. The DJ was playing a remixed version of 'Dance Hall Days' by Wang Chung, an old pop song he actually remembered. The bathroom door swung open heavily. It was gloomy inside, the walls painted a dirty yellow/tan shade. Lawson walked up to the urinal and unzipped.

'Hello Stanley,' a man said -- in a familiar tone, but just barely. 'It's been a long time.'

'I know that voice.' Lawson looked over at the man who'd taken the stall next to his. 'Joe? You must be joking. They actually dug you up just for me?'

'They did. You owe my wife an explanation, assuming either of us lives that long.'

Stanley zipped up. 'All they wanted was a name. It can't be that serious. I just thought I could tighten the screws a bit. It's expensive living here.'

Brennan joined him and both men walked over to the line of sinks to wash their hands. 'Let me put it this way: when I say 'if we live that long', I'm not talking about a trip to the U.S., I'm talking about getting out of this building.'

Stanley's face sank. He stood there with a pair of soaking wet hands. 'What?'

Brennan leaned over to turn off Stanley's sink tap.

'Your friend Tommy out there is a renowned professional killer. If you'd left the bar with him, you'd have been dead in under an hour.' He turned off his own tap and then hit the large button for the automated hot air blower.

'What do we do?' It had been decades since Stanley's last serious involvement in gathering intelligence. His nerve, his training, had long abandoned him.

'I thought you were a full-time agent, once upon a time.'

'Decades before you were born. When you hit your ninth decade, my lad, memories from that long ago begin to run together somewhat.'

'Tommy's going to have eyes on the door. Either he'll be casually leaning on the bar and half-turned this way, or he'll be watching it in the reflection of the mirror. So I can't walk out with you. You came in before me, so you have to leave first, head on back over to him, and then draw him outside.'

'Where?'

'There's a staff parking lot around the front right corner of the building and down the small alley. Tell him your car is there. You need to take a pill before you meet his lady friend.'

Stanley kept the lamentations from his prideful side silent. 'All right.'

'He may try to steer you back onto his course by telling you she has all sorts of erectile dysfunction medication, or something like that. Tell him you need yours because it's a prescription, due to your heart condition.'

'Then what?'

'Then I'll probably have to kill him. He's smart, so he'll be wary. When I come at him, I'll come hard and try to finish it quickly. Get down or better yet out of the way completely. But if you try disappearing on me, Stanley, I'll find you. We still need to have words about your gangster friends.'

'All right. I shall endeavour to remain as cordial as possible.'

'He may also suggest you finish your drink before you go. Don't.'

'What harm...?'

'He's probably dosed it six ways to Sunday by now. It'll either knock you out or kill you where you stand. Tommy Wong isn't known as an intelligence asset; he's strictly here to end your life.'

Brennan gave it a twenty-count before he walked out of the bathroom and back into the stifling volume of the nightclub. The party goers were getting down to 'Uptown Funk', the bass speakers making the floor vibrate slightly.

He scanned the bar area quickly. Stanley was heading for the exit with Tommy Wong a half step behind him and to his left. If he was anticipating trouble, he clearly thought it would come from out in front of them, likely as they walked outside.

He waited until they'd cleared the doors before following. At the double doors he gave it a five-count, knowing Wong's second move would be to check their six, given that no one had made a try as they left. Brennan caught some luck; a young couple walked in from outside, and he ducked out behind them as the doors swung closed.

On the street, he turned right until he reached the building's corner, then toward the laneway. Shadows from the nearby streetlights clung to the base of the wall and Brennan sought concealment there, moving cautiously so that he could be motionless and difficult to spot if Wong looked back once more.

Twenty yards up, the laneway opened into the parking lot proper. Stanley was almost there, his new friend checking back occasionally, Brennan holding tight to the wall, out of sight. The professor took a half-step into the lot and Wong pivoted quickly, the pistol drawn from the speed holster clipped to the back of his belt. The suppressor reduced the usually loud retort to a series of dull cracks as he peppered the alley behind them with bullets. Brennan was almost caught flat-footed, but he threw himself back up against the wall.

Behind Wong, Stanley began to run -- and was acquitting himself well for a man of his age. Wong turned back his way and let loose two shots that missed their mark; Brennan used the respite to sprint forward, closing the gap between them. Wong heard the steps before he could get Stanley properly sighted and turned again, firing blindly in Brennan's direction.

Brennan slapped the pistol down with an open-palm right hand and attacked Wong's knee with a short kick. The pistol clattered to the ground but the assassin managed to turn just enough to protect the joint, taking the strike to his calf.

He countered with a swinging backhand followed by a rapid strike to Brennan's solar plexus. Brennan covered up, crossing his forearms to block Wong's rapid advance, catching the killer with a quick elbow strike when he came in too close, then a quick shot to the face.

Wong took the impact of the blow and used its force to drop low, rolling his right shoulder forward so that he could swing his right leg around, striking hard for Brennan's ankles. Brennan anticipated the move and leaped straight up, coming down on the ball of his right foot so that he could quickly execute a spinning jump, out of the other man's range. Wong strode forward and executed a string of snapping high kicks before surprising Brennan with a low reverse scissor, sliding in with both feet and using them to catch the agent's ankles. He went down hard and Wong was on top of him in instant, his thumbs on Brennan's windpipe, about to crush it.

The standing outdoor ashtray crashed into Wong's skull, swung with surprising force by a woman in a black evening dress. He crashed to the cement, stunned.

Before Brennan could thank her, he was rolling sideways, ducking another forceful shot from the oversized ashtray. When he was a few feet out of range she flung it toward him with all her force and Brennan timed a side kick perfectly, deflecting the object away. She slammed a front kick into his chest while he was still perched on one leg, sending him careening backwards. Brennan reacted instinctively, tucking up and taking the momentum, rolling over backwards and coming up perched on his feet just as she followed up the initial kick with a string of punches. He blocked each methodically, his hands a blur of positions.

From the corner of his eye, Brennan saw Wong stumble back to his feet and down the alley. He blocked a slapping back hand and saw Wong reach back, the gun extended to fire wildly in their direction even as he sprinted after the professor.

'Down!' Brennan said, slipping Lee's punch to free up his right hand so that he could push down on the woman's head and duck simultaneously. The bullet whizzed over head and thudded into something solid.

'Thank you,' she said as they both rose.

'You're wel...' Before he could finish, she unloaded a right cross, staggering him to one knee, then turned to sprint after the assassin and his target.

Brennan shook off the impact of the punch and took pursuit.

A few dozen yards ahead, Stanley Lawson was terrified and running for his life.

But age made it difficult. After nearly nine decades of battling to get the most out of his time on Earth, he was fitter than most octogenarians, but still plagued by pains, aches, weak joints and creaky bones. He exited the alley to the bright light and bumper-to-bumper traffic of Estrada do Istmo, idling and low gears creating a dull background rumble, pierced only by horns and stereo systems that could raise the dead.

Stanley stumbled between the cars and across the road. There was a busy restaurant on the other side of the street. Perhaps the man would not pursue him into there...

Perhaps, perhaps, perhaps. He looked back and could make out Wong, nearing the alley's end. *Why?* Stanley asked himself. *Why couldn't I have just been content with a professor's salary?* It occurred to him that he might never see his grandchildren again. He reached the front stairs and climbed them hurriedly.

At the front door, he pushed past the maitre'd, eliciting calls for him to stop. Shocked diners and those waiting at the bar for tables watched him stagger through the room toward the kitchen opening. He gestured at a waiter. 'Please... a phone? I need the police...' His past be damned, Stanley had decided. If they wanted information, he'd sing like a canary if it meant protection. If Brennan failed...

And it appeared he had. As he reached the back of the vast dining room and the corridor to the rear exit, Wong burst through the main doors. Diners instinctively retreated from the front of the room at the sight of the man with the silenced pistol. Wong raised it and Stanley realized just in time that his assailant didn't give a damn about their surroundings; the former spy ducked and ran down the hallway toward the exit sign as the slugs thudded through the drywall behind him.

At the end of the hall, he pushed hard against the emergency door latch bar.

Locked.

He turned back, still in a crouch. Tommy stood at the end of the hallway, looking profoundly irritated. He raised the pistol and Stanley threw up his arms in a subconscious bid for self-protection.

The woman came out of nowhere, flying full-force into Wong with her shoulder buried in his ribcage. Even though he was much larger, she moved so quickly and struck him so perfectly that he left his feet, their momentum smashing both through the drywall and into the kitchen beyond.

Stanley gingerly crept back up the corridor toward the restaurant. He was almost to the hole in the wall and could hear metal-on-metal, the pair still conscious and brawling. He peered through as he passed. The woman in the cocktail dress was using a pair of frying pans to block a series of strikes from a pair of Wong's butterfly knives. Stanley stood there for a moment, transfixed by the fluid, rapid strikes and parries.

He was there a moment too long. Whether she'd seen him and was worried about him escaping or was just trying to take him out, the woman in the dress sacrificed one of her makeshift shields, flinging the frying pan sideways without turning her head, the heavy object catching Stanley in the temple and knocking him to the ground, unconscious.

THE GHOSTS OF MAO

Brennan rounded the corner, expecting to find one or both of his adversaries standing over Stanley's body.

Close enough. The professor was lying in front of a gaping hole in the drywall and he could hear the grunts and blows of a fight from the other side of the wall. He knelt down and checked the old man's vitals, then slapped him gently. 'Stanley? Stanley, wake up.'

In his periphery, he saw the knife just in time, a glint of light on the steel blade from twenty feet away. He rolled backwards and to his feet as it thunked into the wall beyond him. He anticipated an immediate follow-up attack but Wong, who'd thrown the blade as soon as he'd seen Brennan out of the corner of his eye, was still tied up by the string of kicks and punches from the woman in the dress.

In the kitchen, the assassin backed up and absorbed the blows, passing steel prep tables and still-cooking food on the adjacent stove burners as she assaulted him relentlessly. The staff had fled through a back entrance. Brennan climbed through the hole and raised his pistol at the woman. Her back was to him as she fought Wong, an easy kill shot.

Brennan hesitated. His finger was curled on the trigger, but he couldn't bring himself to pull it. She was after his objective, and she'd hit him twice, but he wasn't going to shoot her in the back. Instead, he rushed up behind her and slammed the butt of the gun into the nerve cluster at the base of her neck. The woman went down hard, badly stunned. Wong reacted first, reaching back just a few inches with the knife, intent on plunging it into Brennan's throat. But he trained the gun at Wong's eye level and waved a finger on his other hand.

'Uh uh uh, Tommy.'

'You could have shot us both when we were

fighting. If you didn't then, you don't have the nerve now.'

'I've seen your file, Tommy. I'm game to find out if you are.'

Wong raised both palms in a show of surrender. 'Hey, I'm good, but I can't dodge bullets.' As the words left his mouth he was on the move, closing the few feet between them, then spinning his body like a top as Brennan squeezed the trigger, moving out of the path of the bullet and coming around at speed, a backhand sweeping toward the American's temple. But Brennan was unfazed, coolly professional in his focus. The move left the assassin's chin unguarded; Brennan slammed the butt of the gun into it with a short jab, the hard metal connecting with the nerve. Wong slumped to the ground, his eyes lolling back in his skull, his breathing suddenly even and short.

He heard a click, the sound of the pistol behind him far enough away that his only option was to turn and face the music.

The woman in the cocktail dress had recovered. She was young, perhaps in her late twenties, her black hair falling just short of her shoulders but cut close and layered, styled by a pro. She was Chinese and pretty, with high cheekbones and dark almond eyes; her makeup was light, sparingly applied. The dress was torn at one thigh slightly and scuffed with dirt but obviously elegant, and at some point, she'd kicked off her heels and gone barefoot.

And she had Wong's silenced pistol in her left hand.

A southpaw, Brennan thought. *I always have problems with southpaws.* 'You could've just shot me...'

'But I'm offering you a chance to walk away,' she said. 'You saved me in the alley, and you could have shot me first here. You didn't, which is honourable. However, I cannot allow you to interfere with my assignment.' She extended her pistol hand. 'So, what will you choose? Stay and die, or go now?'

In point of fact, Daisy Lee had a problem: the

dossier had explicitly stated that if she encountered any Americans after her objective, she was to observe and attempt to avoid engagement. The subtext was that she was to avoid an international incident...such as outing an American asset and killing him publicly. In Macau, the state media did not exert the same control as in China proper, and it would not be able to explain the narrative.

'Hmmm....' Brennan said, squinting as he studied the gun.

'What? If you're trying to guess the pull weight on this trigger, I can guarantee you Wong is enough of a pro that you don't have time to close on me.'

'Nope, that's not it. I was just thinking about the last time I played Blackjack. You see, I'm trained to count the number of shots fired from a particular brand of gun and clip size, so that I'll know when an enemy combatant is out of ammo. And if I was smart, I could've used that skill to count cards at Blackjack, and maybe not lose so much darn money.'

The inference was obvious; but rather than ask the question, Lee flung the gun toward him with a lightning-quick sidearm, as if tossing a throwing star. Brennan tried to duck it but it caught him in the side of the forehead, stunning him for long enough for her to follow up with a spinning round kick that caught him flush, staggering him to one knee just as her foot crashed into his chest, sending him flying onto his back. She ran forward, flipped head over heels, her buttocks coming down hard on Brennan's chest, pushing the air from his lungs. She rolled to one side then slammed a fist back toward him, the winded agent unable to block it, the strike just missing his throat and catching his collarbone.

She pushed her grounded torso backwards slightly then rolled back over, catching his head between both knees, her rounded calf muscles flexed and choking the air from his windpipe. Brennan ignored the instinct to reach up and try to pry her thighs loose, his training kicking in.

Instead, he reached down to her bare feet ...and

snapped her left toe bone.

Lee grunted and choked down a shriek, the pain excruciating. She rolled off him and Brennan was up quickly, his breathing back to normal, his adrenaline in flow but controlled. She was prone on her back, trying to scramble to her feet. He aimed a well-timed kick that caught her on the chin, putting her lights out. He fought back a momentary sensation of guilt at having kicked a woman in the face and looked back at Wong. He was still unconscious, which wasn't good. It had been at least a couple of minutes, which meant he was probably...

The hitman stirred, his body jerking for a few seconds spasmodically as his nerve processing kicked back into gear. He began to shake his head to rouse himself and to push himself up onto his elbows. Brennan's boot crashed into his face a split-second later, and he was out again.

Brennan could hear a police siren, which meant the authorities were already there. Outside in the hallway, Stanley staggered to his feet. Brennan ran over to the hole in the wall and climbed back through. 'Come on, we've got to get out the back here somehow.'

As they ran toward the rear exit, Stanley said 'No, no, I've already tried this door. It's...'

Brennan opened fire with a volley of at least six shots from the Smith and Wesson, the door frame around the lock hasp disintegrating in a cloud of splinters. In one smooth motion, Brennan kicked the door open wide and they ran out into the street. It had begun to rain in the torrential fashion common to humid climates, the water coming down in near-blinding torrents, and both men were soaked instantly.

The police squad cars were there before either man could react, dazed and damaged as they were. The cars squealed to a halt in front of them, their lights spinning, and four officers piled out, guns drawn. The streetlights were blinding white.

'Macau Police! Drop your weapons!'

Brennan raised his hand and dropped the dangling pistol from his forefinger. It clattered on the wet, dirty asphalt.

PART TWO

10/

DAY 6

LOS ANGELES

Zoey Roberson was in love.

It wasn't the mild infatuation that springs from a first meeting or a first date, and it wasn't hero worship. It wasn't just about sex this time, or making rent, or having someone to protect her. In fact, given her past, there were a lot of things Zoey was glad her relationship wasn't.

This time, it was real. This time, he loved her as much – or even more, maybe – than she loved him.

This time was different.

It hit her like a ton of bricks again as she watched Ben from across the dinner table, oblivious to her attention and chewing a mouthful of green beans. It was that warm sense of belonging and attachment, the knowledge that they had found each other, and that she could depend upon him. She'd never felt truly loved before, growing up in a single-parent home with a mom who drank herself insensible and didn't even seem to care if she was there.

She had the urge to go around the table and mount him; to pull open that dress shirt, pull off those studious glasses and run her fingers through his tight dark curls. To wrap her thighs around his waist...

But that was the old Zoey, and things were better now. The quick rush from satisfying a bad boy was still a lure, a pull she felt any time she drove through the wrong neighborhood, with the wrong bars. The weird mix of satisfaction and shame was still familiar, lurking in the background. But loving Ben had helped her gain control, to focus her affection on someone who deserved it.

And the shame was gone. Zoey knew she probably still looked odd to some people on the outside, with her pale white skin and tattoos, her black-and-blonde hair and her nose ring. She'd always been proudly loud about not caring what they thought, but it had always cut her to the quick when she was sure someone was making fun of her. And the idea of feeling good on the inside had seemed almost ridiculous for so long...

Ben looked up from his food, realizing they hadn't spoken in a few minutes. Zoey was gazing at him with a wide-eyed, distant look. 'What? Do I have something...?' He felt around his lip for stray food.

She shook her head in small, quick motions, leaning on her hand and smiling. 'It's just... this is nice, you know?'

He nodded. 'Good casserole,' he said, turning his attention back to the plate.

In a way, the scene seemed surreal, Zoey decided. Just months earlier, her life had been the same disaster it had been since childhood. She'd been dancing at a club in Mid City, barely scraping by on a few nights a week, her life a mess of bad men, bad drugs and no prospects. The club's owner was trying to pressure her to turn tricks out of the back rooms, and she owed enough on her credit card debt that quitting wasn't an option; besides, dancers and staff had been the closest she'd had to family for nearly a decade, since dropping out of high school as a sophomore.

Consequently, it hadn't occurred to her that six months later she'd be sitting across from a forty-year-old Jewish plastic surgeon from Ohio, wondering if he'd eventually pop the question and turn her fairy tale into reality. Or that he'd be so wonderful that nothing from her past would matter.'

He took another forkful of food and raised it to his mouth, then noticed she was still staring, not eating. 'You don't like it,' he said. 'You don't like the tuna casserole...'

'No, I do, really!' she said.

'But you're not eating. Is this like the monkfish, where you don't want to make me feel bad after cooking...?' he began to ask.

'No, no, no. I'm... It's just...' She leaned across the table slightly and held out a hand and he took it in his. 'I'm just happy, that's all. It's just nice to look at you.'

Ben blushed. His parents had long passed, but when he was a kid, the Levitt clan had never been especially touchy-feely. Zoey had so much affection for him – so much of it physical -- that at times he felt overwhelmed. It wasn't always sex; she also liked holding hands in public, and hugging him, and spooning with him in bed. He wasn't sure why, or how, but she seemed as infatuated with him as he was with her. When he looked in the mirror, he saw a five-foot-eight guy with a paunch, a balding head and hair on his back. Zoey, however, could look right past all that.

He knew they didn't really have much in common; his friends figured he'd tire of her eventually, like the rest. But Ben wasn't so sure.

Then again, he hadn't been sure with Wendy, or Jill, or Danielle, or...

'You want to head over to the pier tomorrow, see if we can catch some fish?' she asked as he finished the last mouthful of casserole. 'Or we could call Ginny and Mark and see if they want to get brunch?' Ginny and Mark lived in the condo below them and were the closest thing they had to 'couple friends.' Despite her fears, they'd also seemed underwhelmed by Zoey's appearance, or when she fiercely announced early on in their friendship that she used to be a dancer.

'Contemporary or modern?' Ginny had asked.

'Naked,' Zoey had replied.

Ginny had just shrugged. 'Beats an office gig,' she'd said.

They'd gotten along well after that and Zoey was eager to preserve the union. 'We can see if they want to go for dim sum,' she suggested.

'Sure,' Ben said, smiling back. He'd already fallen in love with her; he knew that much. Mark had warned him off, saying Zoey was all trouble, the kind of crazy girl who'd cheat on him at the first opportunity. But it hadn't taken long before she seemed just as infatuated with him. He knew it didn't make any sort of sense from a normal social standpoint; she was the most beautiful woman he'd ever seen. The guys at the racquet club had been all over him about her tattoos and miniskirts, to the point where he'd almost gotten into a fight for the first time since grade school. And he knew the life she'd led, what she'd done to make ends meet.

It didn't matter. He was sure this time that his wandering eye had finally set upon the right woman for him. They'd moved in together after just a few weeks. It didn't matter that his friends disapproved – and boy, did they disapprove – and it didn't matter that his colleagues thought he was having a midlife crisis. What mattered was that at the end of the day, after stitching up countless wrinkled, Botox-laden widows from the Hills, he got to go home to her.

His phone rang. He took it out of his suit pants pocket and answered.

'Benjamin Levitt.'

Zoey watched as he nodded his head once. Then he put the phone down on the dinner table and got up, walking out of the open-plan condo's dining area and down the hall toward the bedroom, saying nothing.

'Sweetie?' Zoey asked.

He ignored her. Zoey stared at the empty opening to the hallway.

She sat and waited for a few moments. 'Are you okay?' she called out. 'Because you got up awful sort of sudden there.'

No response.

Zoey got up from her chair. She grabbed their empty plates and carried them over to the black marble kitchen counters, where she set them above the dishwasher. 'Was it work? I thought that always went to your service after hours...'

She waited for a reply but there was only silence. 'Sweetie?'

She walked the short corridor to the bedroom and pushed the ajar door open. 'Ben?' she asked.

He had a suitcase on the bed and had already half-filled it with folded clean clothing. Beside the suitcase was a black attaché case. He ignored her presence as he unfastened the catches and opened it. The suitcase was full of money, stacks of bills held together by slim strips of paper. There must have been tens of thousands of dollars there at least, she thought. Then he reached into the lid pocket of the case and withdrew a small black pistol, which he secreted into the inside pocket of his suit jacket.

'Ben, what the hell...' she said. He continued to ignore her as if she wasn't even there, transferring the rest of the money from the attaché case to the suitcase pockets. Then he took his wallet from his back pocket and began to throw credit cards and ID onto the bed, emptying it. He reached into the suitcase pocket again, withdrawing a small Ziploc plastic bag. There were two credit cards inside, a driver's license, other documents.

She walked over and knelt next to him, beside the bed. The driver's license said 'Paul Joseph.'

'Sweetie... what are you doing? I didn't know you owned a gun...'

He ignored her and said nothing, as if she wasn't even present, finishing up his packing and zipping the big brown suitcase closed. Then he rose, picked up the case even as she walked beside him, and headed into the dining room. He picked his phone back up off the table, then moved to the front room.

A wave of fright crept through her, a sense of lost control, an old familiar feeling, out of place. 'Ben, you're scaring me; why are you packing? Why aren't you saying anything to me? Ben! What's going on?'

He walked to the hallway closet and took out his dark grey wool topcoat, the formal coat he wore over his suit when they went to Temple. He closed the closet door and fished his car keys from a bowl on the adjacent end table.

Was he walking out? Zoey was confused. 'Bennie, please... you're not acting right....' It seemed obvious he was about to leave, so she hurried up the front entranceway ahead of him and stood in front of the door, next to the kitchen entrance, blocking the hall.

'Tell me what's going on,' she said. 'Please! You're really scaring me, Ben.'

He took a step toward her, then withdrew the pistol from the inside pocket of his jacket and pointed it toward her. Zoey's eyes widened and she instinctively threw herself sideways, out of the path of the shot as he pulled the trigger, the bullet plowing through their front door.

'FUCK!' Zoey yelled, scared and shocked, her ears ringing.

His route unimpeded, he walked to the front door and opened it, ignoring her as she lay three feet away, breathing hard and frightened by the near miss. He picked up his suitcase, walked out of the apartment, and closed the door behind him.

Zoey lay on the cold faux-wood tile of the kitchen floor, trying to compose herself. What had just happened? One second they'd been eating dinner, and then it was like he wasn't even in the same place as her. She got up and walked over to the hallway. The door had a bullet hole in it, right at the height of her forehead.

'He tried to kill me,' she said to no one.

It didn't make any sense, any of it. She went back over what she'd said during dinner, anything she might have mentioned that could have deeply hurt him or offended him. But there had been nothing remotely close and his behavior was nothing like normal. She rose cautiously and went over to the door, intent on chasing him, then realized it would be futile; he'd taken his keys and would be out of the building before she could even reach the street.

She paced back and forth nervously, trying to figure out what to do. He'd left his phone in the bedroom, so trying it was a waste of time. He'd left his license, his credit cards... She realized she had no way to contact him.

'What do I do?' she asked herself. 'I can't call the cops. I guess I could tell them about the gunshot and maybe...' She thought about her own record, a solicitation bust from one of the few times she'd had to turn tricks to make rent. Cops didn't listen to the girls; they never listened to the girls. She'd worked at enough nightclubs to know that.

Who else did Benny know who could help?

Mark.

Zoey went out into the hallway and closed the door behind her before taking the elevator down one level. She knocked on 6 C, and a few moments later Ginny opened the door. 'Hey kiddo, what's up?'

'It's Ben,' Zoey said. 'I think he might be in trouble.'

Mark had taken another half-hour to get home, during which Zoey filled Ginny in on the sudden exit and gunshot. After Ginny had explained it to him, he'd hung his coat in the hall closet, a serious look on his face. 'What about his phone?' he asked, as they waited for him in the living room.

'He took it. Everything else he tossed before he left. None of his own ID, no credit cards – I mean, not his normal ones.'

'What?!?'

'He had a couple stored away in a plastic bag.

They looked new; I think one of them had a few years left before expiring. I'm telling you it was freaky; it was like something from a movie or something. He had this sort of focus.'

'So, like... 'crazy calm'? Like they talk about when someone disconnects and ... you know, does something terrible?' Mark asked.

'Yeah.'

'Mark?' Ginny asked, watching him ponder the issue.

'I'm thinking,' he said. He walked over to the couch adjacent to theirs and sat down.

Ginny suggested, 'Maybe he's in witness protection or something. You know, like, from the mob?'

Mark gave her a withering look. 'He's a Jewish plastic surgeon whose family is from New Boston, Ohio. That's about as far from the swamps of Jersey as you get.'

'And it wasn't like that,' Zoey insisted. 'It wasn't rage, or anything. It was like he didn't even see me, right up until I got in his way, and then he shot at me. He just...' She trailed off, still not able to really believe it.

'We can call his family,' Ginny said. 'I mean, he must have told someone what's going on. If he didn't think he could tell Zoey, maybe he told his mom.'

Zoey looked downcast. She was thinking about the gunshot, wondering how he could have even thought about hurting her. She felt confused. 'I don't have a number. I've never met them.'

Ginny looked surprised. 'After six months?'

'They live across the country. We were planning on visiting eventually but Ben just had things come up. Oh... damn. I'm so frightened.'

Ginny put an arm around her shoulder. 'I know, sweetie. But maybe this is nothing, just some midlife crisis thing. I know Benny and there's no way he'd ever hurt you. There has to be an explanation. We'll probably get a call from him in a few hours saying he's at some motel in Malibu pondering the direction of his life or something, and the gun wasn't supposed to go off... or...'

'Hmmm,' Mark said. 'Sure.'

'What?' his wife asked.

'Well... it sounds like he really did try to shoot her. It just doesn't sound much like Ben, that's all.' He turned to Zoey. 'You know what he's like. Is there anything that suggests he was unhappy...?'

'No, nothing,' Zoey said.

'I think we should just call the cops if he isn't home by the morning,' Ginny insisted. 'Just to be on the safe side. Or like I said the first time, his parents.'

Zoey didn't have a number for them. 'He talked about them a lot. His father is the longest-serving OB-GYN in the greater Portsmouth area, or something.'

Mark snapped his fingers. 'His service. If he's an OB-GYN, he'll have a call forwarding service.'

'Then we just need to find his clinic,' Ginny said. "Come on, let's go up to your place, you can show us where everything happened."

A few minutes later, they gathered around the small computer desk that sat at the back of the living room and Zoey brought up a browser window. New Boston was a village within the city of Portsmouth and well-served medically. They spent several minutes searching, to no avail.

'I don't get it,' Zoey said. 'There's not a single reference online to an OB-GYN named Levitt in New Boston, or even Ohio.'

'And there are four clinics and two hospitals within twenty minutes, and there's no one named Levitt on staff at any of them,' Mark said.

'He must have retired,' Zoey said. 'What about people named Levitt in New Boston?' She brought up a white pages for Ohio and typed in Levitt for the Portsmouth area.

There were two pages of listings, including Leavitts, and Lovetts. But there was no one named Levitt listed in the area.

'Must be unlisted,' Zoey said.

'Uh huh,' Ginny said. She didn't sound as certain. 'It's a pretty small place, right?'

'Yeah, looks it.'

'Then perhaps we can find another doctor there, after-hours. If Ben's father worked there for years, they'd at least know about him. Who knows, maybe they'll have a forwarding address.'

Mark had wandered over to the front door and was fingering the bullet hole. 'It sure looks like the real deal.' He turned to his wife. 'You hear a shot, hon?'

Ginny shook her head. Mark frowned, his uncertainty sudden and stark.

'I'm not lying to you,' Zoey said. She held her arms across her, feeling defensive, that familiar sensation of feeling less than worthy, of knowing it must have somehow been her fault. 'That wasn't Ben. I looked right in his eyes and it was like there was nothing there. He was just ... blank. Like he was acting on instinct.'

Mark nodded sagely. 'We know. We know you wouldn't lie about Ben, right Hon?'

Ginny smiled, and it felt genuine. 'But you're going to have to go to the police if we haven't heard anything by tomorrow, and if we can't get hold of his father.'

Zoey's head dipped. 'I guess, yeah...'

Ginny moved over to her and put her arms around Zoey, then drew her close in a tight hug. 'Don't worry, sweetie. You know what a great guy he is. Whatever happened to make him freak out tonight... I'm sure we can figure this out. It's...' She looked at her watch, '... eight-thirty now. I'll stay here with you until bedtime, and then in the morning, we can go to the police together. Okay?'

Zoey wasn't so sure. Every instinct told her the police were the enemy; the only type of cop she'd ever dealt with either wanted to bust her, or take advantage of her, or hit the club up for bribes. 'Okay,' she said, unsure of what to do next.

Come morning, there was still no sign of Ben. Zoey woke with the sunrise, a habit she'd been trying to build for months, a new way of starting her day after years of late nights. She didn't need time to think; she'd decided the night prior that there was no way with her record that she was getting the police involved until she'd scoured the city and was damn sure she couldn't find him.

Ben Levitt was the man she loved, the key to her happiness; she wasn't going to tell them he'd taken a shot at her. There was a good chance Ginny would dial nine-one-one anyway, as soon as she woke up and realized Zoey had gone looking for him on her own – or caught a dose of Mark's paranoia and assumed she had something to do with Ben disappearing.

But maybe by then, Zoey figured, she'd have tracked him down.

Something was wrong and Ben was in trouble. She felt it in her bones. After a decade of being used, abused, pushed around and tossed away, Zoey had had enough. She got out of bed and went over to the walk-in closet, opening it and taking out her small suitcase. She was tired of life kicking her in the teeth, tired of everything being overcome with drama and crushing her spirit. Nothing she'd done in the past had seemed to matter, and any control over her own destiny seemed illusory.

Benny had changed that.

And she wasn't giving him up without a hell of a fight.

11/

DAY 7

LOS ANGELES

It took Zoey less than an afternoon to discover that, though she loved Ben and was sure he loved her, she didn't really know that much about her boyfriend.

She knew he went to the gym and so she had started there but was rebuffed by the counter staff. The guy at the comic bookstore was more helpful and recognized Ben from his description... but hadn't seen him in two weeks, at least. After that, her options were more limited. She'd seen a country club membership in his wallet once but hadn't asked about it and he'd later told her it expired; Ben was pretty humble, and she figured if he went to a snooty members' only place, it was for work reasons only; plastic surgeons had to network in a certain financial sphere. He was fascinated by urban planning, but that mostly consisted of visiting environmental groups' websites on how best cities could use space.

She was left with a single option: the train station. He'd talked about how much he loved it there, how he'd grown up wanting to take the train across the country. He knew the names of all the locomotives and the carriages and the companies, and he'd told them all to her at one point or another, each going in one ear and out the other, because... well... it was trains.

But after three hours of alternately walking the station's marble-floored hall, browsing the magazine shops and people watching for any sign, she slumped onto one of the passenger benches, her head in hands. She took a deep breath, then let it out.

What had she said to him? What had she done to set him off? He'd never acted like that before, never been violent. It was like someone had thrown a switch...

The phone call.

It had been so short that she hadn't really thought about it, but he took a call right before he freaked out. She tried to remember his side of the conversation but was pretty sure there hadn't been more than a few words spoken. Whatever it was had driven him over the edge.

Had someone threatened him? That would explain the gun but not why he took a shot at her. That was a Ben she didn't know. She gazed around the train station; a working girl near the stairs was greeting arriving passengers with offers and hadn't yet been shuffled off by the police officers who periodically patrolled the hall. For a moment, she caught Zoey watching her and a smile crept across her lips, like she knew something, something deeply personal about the ex-dancer, a flaw that wasn't easy to see, but was always there, something they shared. Zoey averted her gaze, feeling a flush of embarrassment.

Whoever had called Ben hadn't had time to get out more than a sentence or two. So it had to be someone he knew, and it had to be either expected or so distressing it took over his ability to think straight. She wondered if she'd made a mistake by running, instead of letting Ginny and Mark take her to the police. Their neighbors' intentions were good; but she'd had her fill of the law while working at the club. And they'd take one look at her record, she knew, and that would be an end to any serious interest on their part.

But... she had no idea what else to do.

'You having troubles honey?'

Zoey looked up. It was the hooker who'd been standing by the platform steps a few minutes earlier. She shook her head. 'It's nothing, really. It's fine.'

'You've been crying,' the other woman said. 'Here:' She reached into her purse and took out a tissue. 'You should wipe your eyes carefully, or that mascara's going to run. Believe me, I know: occupational hazard.'

Zoey smiled wanly. 'Thank you. I'm just a little upset.'

'Uh huh,' the woman said. 'And what's his name? 'Cause every time I seen a girl that upset, it's over some guy.'

She had to smile at that, because Benjie so wasn't like those guys... but he was still the reason she was crying. 'You're perceptive.'

'It's not that I think they're all preoccupied with the opposite sex,' the woman said. 'It's just that men are mostly stupid. If it's something stupid enough to make someone cry, there was probably a man involved.' She realized Zoey wasn't sure how to respond and added, 'You taking a train somewhere hon? You've been walking around an awful long time.'

'No. I thought maybe he was here.'

'Ah. He took off on you, huh? I'm Valentyna, by the way.'

She held out a hand and they shook. 'Zoey. But he wasn't himself.'

'Let me guess: he was all sweet while you were just knocking booties, but now he gets mad at the drop of a hat? He a mean guy? He try to hurt you?'

She shook her head vigorously. 'No! No, it's not like that, really. Thank you, though.'

'Oh...' The prostitute got the sense that maybe she wasn't needed and took a few hesitant steps away. 'Well... okay then... I guess I'll get on about my business.'

'Thank you for asking, really...' Zoey said.

The woman stopped. 'Then what is it? It's okay, you can tell me. I've seen and heard it all.'

'He just... became a different person. One second he was Ben, the next he was pulling out a suitcase full of cash and credit cards and...'

'What?' The look on Zoey's face was obviously pained.

'He took a shot at me. With a gun. He shot at me.'

'Oh no!' the older woman said. 'No, no, no. That is not okay, sweetie! You have to go to the police on him. Or else next time...'

'No! I mean... I can't; I have... I have a lot of baggage in my past. No cops.'

Valentyna put a hand on Zoey's forearm, a gentle touch. 'It's okay. I know a guy, a vice cop. He works mostly missing persons, he'd know what to do. He's a different sort of guy, you know? He won't treat you bad. He might even be able to help. When I had a p... when I had a manager, he used to get tough with me sometimes, and Norm would have a word, and things would get better.'

'I don't know.' Zoey's uncertainty was obvious. 'I mean... even if he wanted to help, I don't know what I can tell him. I don't have any idea what's going on.'

'Just tell him what you told me,' the street walker advised. 'Tell him about the money and credit cards and the gun, all that stuff.'

The distraught young woman's eyes widened. 'The credit card,' she said. 'I saw a name on the credit card.'

Valentyna smiled. 'See? Now things are looking up already.'

But the optimism didn't last long. Valentyna's exasperation was written across her face as she leaned in and tried to get the desk sergeant's attention one more time. The waiting room at the Burbank station was full, and the line to make a complaint went back to the stairs near the main doors. 'Please, Sgt. Ohler, even if I could just leave Detective Drabek a message...'

The elderly sergeant shrugged. 'Miss... what is it again? Vixen? Something like that...No! Don't tell me!

I don't want to know. Miss, whatever problem you're having with your pimp or a john, Det. Drabek is a very busy man with a very heavy caseload of things that are important to the people of Los Angeles. Next, please!'

'You can't just refuse to help us!' Valentyna demanded. 'I have a right to contact Det. Drabek...'

The sergeant pointed to the far corner of the waiting room. 'If you'd like to call him and leave a message, there's a payphone right over...' Then he looked over and realized how much time had passed since there had actually been a payphone there. 'Oh... right. Anyway... respectfully, sweetie, this line is for serious complaints, and we've seen you a few too many times. Next please!'

'Oh no you did not just dismiss me!' Valentyna exclaimed.

Zoey pulled on her arm. 'Come on, let's go.'

Behind them, the next man in line was getting anxious. Valentyna wagged a finger at him. 'Y'all just cool your jets.' She turned back to the sergeant. 'Now just because a woman has a few scrapes with the law does not mean that she is not entitled to its full protection. And that's the truth! Now I'd like to know what you have to say to that!'

Thirty seconds later, they were standing on the steps outside the station, Valentyna sporting a sullen look. 'Y'all could have stood up for us a little more,' she sniffed at Zoey. 'You basically let him throw us out of there.'

'It was a police station and he was a cop. I think that was pretty much his call from the get-go. Besides, you were going to get us arrested.'

'We need another plan,' Valentyna said. 'If I had his card or something, we could just call him, but if we dial the station, we're just going to get the same run around.'

'Do you know where he lives?'

'As a matter of fact, I do. What? You figure we go over there, break in and wait for him?'

Zoey peered at her new friend quizzically. 'No. No

that's definitely not what I was thinking. It's late afternoon...'

'So?'

'So he has to go home at some point. There must be some place nearby we can wait until then.'

L.A. Vice Detective Norman Drabek was curious; the two women had followed him for half a block, from outside his condo building to the nearby Horseshoe Tavern, where they were sitting at the far end of the bar, occasionally whispering things to each other.

He thought he recognized one of them, the black girl. But at fifty-eight, his eyes were going, and he'd taken off his glasses. He put them back on again and squinted. Yeah... a prostitute who worked the train station downtown and the subways in North Hollywood and Burbank. What was her name again? Vesper? Vixen? Valentine. That was it. No... Valentyna, with the 'a' at the end. He'd helped her with that piece of shit Denny Thorn, the Iranian pimp who'd changed his name and had his hands into half of the city's pies. Drabek's fingers twitched subconsciously for a cigarette as he reminisced. He'd quit two months earlier, but the habit was still there, still picking away at him.

A short man with brown hair, a pinched rat face and beady brown eyes, Drabek had grown up in Burbank. When she wasn't trying to get jobs on movies, his mother owned a salon near the airport and her rates were good. She had quite a few working girls come through and he'd known all about their harsh lives long before he had any other interest in them. Drabek's mother had believed in toughening her son, exposing him to the realities of the world early enough to dispel any childhood delusions he might have had about the world being a sweet place. Becoming a cop had just seemed a natural extension of her desire to see him grow up giving a damn.

He hadn't wanted to move to Vice after twenty-two years in Homicide. But it hadn't really been up to him. A DEA informant named German Rojas had been holed up in a safe house awaiting his testimony in a case against Sergio Rincon, a Peruvian drug smuggler, people smuggler and generally all-around bad dude. But someone had dropped a dime on Rojas, likely someone in the department, and they'd been ambushed. Drabek was the first responder, and that was all it took to make him the scapegoat. He'd eventually been cleared, but he'd been told the 'optics were bad' for him staying in Homicide, where he had one of the best closure rates in the city but was seen as having an insubordinate attitude, and general authority issues.

Drabek would've explained it differently. Saddled with back-to-back captains from the politically expedient side of the promotion track, he'd pissed off one too many sticklers from political correctness, one too many old-school guys who judged him a disrespectful troublemaker without so much as a conversation first. But he got things done, and usually by the book, even if he wasn't always polite about it. That was what they didn't seem to get.

He drained the last of his eight-ounce glass of draft and held it up to Micki behind the bar. 'Hey Mick! Another one over here!'

Micki was thirty going on two hundred. Her father had owned the place going back to the fifties, when it was mostly a restaurant for blue-collar guys, meat-and-potato types. Over the years it had slowly morphed from Ralph's to Ralph's Bar, and then -- during a phase throughout the city of Irish pubs springing up -- the Horseshoe Tavern. Drabek had been on the same stool every other night or so since the late eighties. Early on, there had been a bunch of beat cops who lived in the neighborhood and also made it their haunt. But they'd mostly moved upward and onward, and now it was just the same regulars, people knocking back boilermakers, shooting the shit about work and maybe watching the pony races on the flat screens.

Micki came over with the draft. It was weak as horse piss, Drabek knew, but he'd developed a taste for it, and it was still only a buck for each eight-ounce glass. Technically.

'On the house, as always,' Micki said.

'Not acceptable, put it on my tab, as usual,' he said. They went through the same routine every time. The compromise was that she hadn't asked him about the tab in at least five years.

Two stools over, a young dockhand Drabek barely knew -- Dan? Don? Something like that -- watched the exchange with bemusement. 'Hey Norm,' he said, because everyone there knew Drabek, whether he remembered them or not, 'how come Micki won't ever let you pay?'

Drabek took a healthy swallow of his draft and savored the bitter, tinny taste. 'Some nonsense from way back. Nothing interesting.'

From behind the taps, half a bar away, Micki yelled back to be heard, 'He always says some humble bullshit like that because he knows it forces me to explain. Then everyone gets to hear what a hero he is and all. Because he's Mr. Humble.'

Drabek cringed a little. 'It was genuinely nothing, a kid with a sawed-off.'

'And Drabek 'heroically' dove in front of my father and saved his life,' Micki said. 'Although it turned out it was just rock salt in the gun and Drabek took it in the butt. Didn't you, Drabek? Take it in the butt?'

The dockhand giggled at that.

Laugh all you want kid, Drabek thought, *but I get the free draft.* He drained the rest of the glass in glacial silence.

'Det. Drabek?'

The two working girls. He'd gotten thinking about the old day and gone and forgotten all about them. 'Valentyna, right?'

'And this my friend Zoey. We just met today but

she needs your help.'

Drabek fished a business card from his pocket. He avoided eye contact. He didn't want them getting any ideas about his level of interest. 'This has my cell on it. Call me during the workday and I can probably help.'

Zoey took the card. 'Thank you.'

'Don't mention it.' He kept staring ahead, waiting for them to leave. He slugged back most of the remaining draft in his glass.

'This is sort of urgent.'

Drabek put the glass down. Of course it was. When wasn't everyone's problem urgent? 'Okay, shoot: what's troubling you?'

'My boyfriend has disappeared.'

Drabek cringed internally. 'When?'

'Yesterday. From our condo. I mean, I was there when he left...'

'Then, he left, he didn't disappear.'

'Yeah, but...'

'It's not the same thing.'

'Yeah, but he wasn't himself. I mean, I know that sounds lame, but he was acting like a different person. He was violent; he had a gun and a big suitcase full of money.'

Drabek turned his head slightly to look her over. Miniskirt, tattoos, piercings, black streaks in the suicide platinum hairstyle. He got the feeling that maybe the boyfriend had a history. 'He ever hit you, this guy?'

'What?! No! Ben is a plastic surgeon. He belongs to service clubs. He likes Bonsai...'

'Bon-what?' Valentyna asked.

'Japanese ornamental tree trimming,' Drabek said. He had to admit she was starting to catch his attention. 'Service clubs?'

'You know: Rotary, Knights of Columbus...' Zoey proffered.

'Yeah, yeah... I know what a service club is.' It just didn't gel with the women standing next to ... Or, maybe it did. 'Is 'Ben' also married?'

Zoey's expression turned sour. 'No, and I'm not like that,' she said.

'Apologies.' His eyes shifted to Valentyna. 'I just sort of assumed...'

'Assumed what?' Valentyna snorted. 'You assumed because she was with a hooker that she must be a hooker too? You think I don't got no normal friends, Det. Drabek?'

He held up both hands in a show of mock surrender.

Zoey came to his rescue. 'I think maybe he was drugged or hypnotized or something,' she said. 'One second he was eating dinner at our place, the next, he was storming off into the bedroom to start packing. When I tried to interfere, he took a shot at me with a gun I didn't even know he owned.'

'A shot you say? While inside the condo?' That was something verifiable.

'Then he just took off. I've tried everywhere...'

'Does he have family in the city?'

'It gets stranger...' She told him about their fruitless search for the Levitt family in Ohio.

Drabek's intuition suggested Ben Levitt may be a double-family type and that this was the girlfriend, the one who didn't know about his wife and kids. He might even have been using a cover story with her the whole time. It wasn't unheard of, although he'd never run into one before personally.

Zoey could see the fatigue in the man's eyes, how he kept trying to look away, how he was fighting to retain interest. 'Look... detective: I know what people seem to think of me. I've always looked or behaved different and now that I'm older not much has changed, I suppose. And maybe when I was younger, some of what they said was true. But I've been trying real hard to change my life. And Ben is the only person who has believed in me the whole time. I need him, and right now he needs me. And I need your help, because this is serious. Ben's the only person who had faith in me, but I need you to have faith too, detective.' She felt like she was going to sob, and instead held it in. 'Because I don't even know where to start.'

Drabek knew fear when he heard it, and she was genuinely afraid, and that wasn't okay. He turned on his bar stool to face her properly. Then he softly nodded his head. 'Okay then,' he said. He nodded toward the street. 'Let's go back to my precinct and I'll get a file started. We'll get started on this tonight, and tomorrow we'll see where it takes us.'

Zoey smiled broadly and felt a tear well up in the corner of her eye. She pursed her lips to avoid chewing on them. 'Thank you. You don't know what this means to me.'

'Yeah... well, don't thank me yet. We haven't done anything, and you haven't met my partner yet. Compared to him, I'm the charmer.'

LOS ANGELES

Det. Jeff Pace felt his frustration building. He sat at his desk at the Fifteenth Precinct with his phone cradled between his cheek and shoulder. His left shoelace had a knot and he'd been trying to use the wait to pull it apart. He'd been on hold twice, talked to three different attendants and still hadn't received an answer.

The precinct was busy, and the vice detectives' bullpen looked like a steno pool, with a series of burly policeman in cheap suits taking typed statements from women in hip-high mini skirts, and from bookies with varying degrees of male-pattern baldness, as well as witnesses ranging from shrieky ginger-haired hipsters to silent, nervous victims.

It was always a madhouse, and Pace had learned to let it all fall into a uniform background din of noise. It was the only way to get anything done.

'Hello?' A woman picked up the on-hold line.

'Yes!' Pace said too enthusiastically. 'Yeah, hi! It's Det. Pace from the LAPD Detective Support and Vice Division. I was put on hold?'

'Regarding?'

He inhaled sharply and held it, then counted to five silently. 'As I mentioned to three of your colleagues, I need a credit card trace and recent use report on a client named 'Paul Joseph'.'

'Ah. The time-waster,' she replied. 'I'm their supervisor. They had a concern that this might be another waste of our time. You know... what with the other three times you called being about someone who isn't a client. And wasted our time.'

They'd tried to check Ben Levitt's recent credit history and purchases only to discover that his accounts had been paid out in full and closed a week before his disappearance. 'Ma'am, have you ever handled a missing persons credit request before?' Pace asked. 'Is there someone...'

'I'm the someone,' the woman said. 'So you're going to have to deal with me on this issue, sir. There is no other someone. And I shall ask again: is this another time-wasting matter?'

From across a few desks, Det. Norman Drabek watched his partner's slow boil with amusement and sympathy. The public had the impression it was easy for police to get co-operation on minor issues like a credit check, or a security tape. Instead, it was a continual debate about inconvenience, or privacy, or both, usually with someone who had no idea what the laws and rules were around gathering that sort of evidence.

He'd been told clearly by his captain that the case wasn't a priority, and that any time spent on it better not come out of other investigations. Which was fine. It wasn't that uncommon a request, either, sort of a form of time management by threat. He called over to Pace as the latter got off the line, still looking aggravated.

'How's it going there, partner? You still with us?'

'I tell ya, Normie, there better be something to this. Because the lovely ladies at the credit bureau and the credit card company are stitching together little Detective Pace voodoo dolls as we speak.'

'You're doing good work, remember that. If you hadn't gotten on them three times, we wouldn't have found out he closed that account. We'd have been left with a denial that he even had one.'

'Not that that's helping us figure out where the guy has been for the last three days,' Pace said. 'You sure this girl's not just kidding herself? I mean, maybe he took off back east or something.'

'Nah, nah... like I told you, there is no 'back east'. That's the weird part of it. I checked what she told us and it's true: his family doesn't exist. I mean, other than that and shooting at her, this guy has the cleanest record I ever saw. When he pulls up at parking meters, they must spit quarters at him, he's so clean.'

Pace went back to his call: 'Hello? Yes. Paul Joseph, in the area of North Hollywood or Burbank. Then maybe outward from there... no, I understand. I understand, but this isn't a fishing trip...'

He began scribbling notes, which got Drabek's attention. A moment later he hung up the phone. 'We've got a hit, potentially. There are a dozen Paul Josephs living in LA right now with the same type of credit card. But one of them set off a suspicious purchase hit yesterday at an electronics store near Burbank and Lankershim, and we have a home address on the genuine card holder. Chances are he bumped into this guy at some point...'

'You up for a quick ride over there?'

Pace nodded. 'Sure. Sure, let's go see what we can find.'

Paul Joseph lived in a small wood a-frame house just a few blocks from the store on Burbank Boulevard. It wasn't exactly fancy; the paint was peeling, and the front lawn had died. Like most of its neighboring homes, the place was small, perhaps eight hundred square feet.

They knocked twice on the fading red wooden

door, then tried the bell without luck. But there was a car parked in the driveway. Drabek leaned around the front edge of the building to see if there was a gate to the backyard.

Along the wall was a large air-conditioning unit, humming away at full tilt. A rear window was wide open.

'Hey partner, check this out.'

Pace looked around the corner as well. 'Either someone's home or someone's been visiting.

'You don't usually open the window when you're cranking the AC,' Drabek said. 'Let's see if there's a back door to this place.'

They followed the whitewashed wall to the back fence. Both men hopped it, Drabek taking his time. He tried to stay fit but recognized his middle-aged limitations. The backyard was also dead. A barbecue sat on the stone back patio, which ran up to the screen door.

The inside door was ajar. Drabek drew his service weapon, then knocked on the door and stood away from it.

There was no response. Pace held the screen while Drabek pushed the door open gently. 'Hello? LAPD, is there anyone home?'

As soon as the door was fully open, the smell hit them, a sweetly noxious, gassy concentration of decay and death. Both men covered their mouths and noses with their handkerchiefs. The backdoor opened into a kitchen; the sink was full of dishes and the tap dripping slightly, the monotonous sound their only accompaniment. At the back of the kitchen a doorway led to a short corridor past a bedroom and bathroom. Drabek leaned into the bathroom and took a look.

The corpse in the tub hadn't been dissolving for long, but the lye had done a job. The man's head and neck had yet to sink below the reddish-brown surface. There was a bullet hole through the middle of his forehead.

In movies, police officers who find a body nearly

always make a wise-crack, gallows humor to diffuse the shock of the moment. But both men were too experienced to be shocked, and too smart to remove their handkerchiefs. Soon, the medical examiner's office would be there, and the real work would begin.

12/

MACAU

Brennan sat silently in the stark white interrogation room and watched the one-way mirror for signs of life he knew were there, just out of reach. On the other side of the room, a Macau policeman in a short-sleeved pale-blue dress shirt and black ballcap sat right by the door, his arms crossed. He looked bored and hadn't said a word in an hour. To him, Brennan figured, shifts like this were just an exercise in figuring out what he'd missed on TV that night.

He wondered what Carolyn and the kids were doing. *Probably perforating my voodoo doll with large needles.*

The door swung open and Captain Peter Chen entered. He was middle-aged with white flecks in his hair and he appeared less than pleased.

'Mr. Arthur,' he said. He walked over to the interview table and sat down then placed a small file folder upon the tabletop and rested his hand on it. 'Or should I call you Mr. Joseph Brennan, late of the Central Intelligence Agency?'

'Over to you,' Brennan said. 'It's your party.'

'You have a watch list file with every intelligence agency in Asia. It seems strange that American intelligence would send such a less-than-ideal representative here on business. I must assume this has something to do with Professor Lawson, and, given that we have a record of you visiting Macau multiple times a decade ago, that the two of you are personal associates. I must assume he asked for you personally. Therefore, I must assume he has information that America needs.'

'You got 'they know each other' from this already? What, the two of us stumbling out of a half-trashed restaurant riddled with bullet holes didn't give that away? No? Maybe the two unconscious killers in the kitchen?'

'We found no one inside the building.'

'Fantastic.' Joe knew the standard procedure would be to demand consular assistance and leave it at that. But he was irritated; the heat on Stanley Lawson should've been in his intel. He expected an easy package retrieval, and instead he got a John Woo flick. 'Have you called my people yet?'

'No. We are... reluctant to have Macau dragged into whatever this is. Rarely in cases involving espionage do we find that the interests of the territory are paramount or even considered, and this almost certainly had something to do with China. We called our associates in Chenzhou. They were most happy that we did, although they also did not seem interested in elaborating on Professor Lawson's sudden value.'

'They can be like that, I've heard.'

The captain flashed a smile rapidly enough to make it clear he wasn't in a joking mood. 'Mr. Brennan, I have been a policeman in Macau now for thirty-two years. In that time, there have been numerous occasions in which two foreign entities wished to loom over us and squabble, as if the government and residents of Macau were not even present, as if they were two adults arguing in front of a child they choose to ignore.'

He leaned forward on the table and arched his fingers. 'And do you know what I have found to be the best approach to dealing with these incursions? To get the individuals involved out of Macau as quickly as possible, and to let them do their squabbling elsewhere.'

'And how do the Chinese feel about that?'

'Of course, that is a significant complication in this particular case. Technically, Macau has authority over all local legal matters. They would like me to simply hand over Professor Lawson; but he has done nothing illegal, as far as we can tell. On the other hand, if I release him, he believes he may be assassinated by a third party. If I release him with you, in order to expedite your departure, the Chinese will be most upset indeed. And if I refuse to release either of you, the Americans will be angry, and there is substantial investment here.'

Brennan could tell he'd like Chen if they met in other circumstances. The man was cool and calm, polite, and totally aware of the difficult position in which he found himself. 'And do you have a resolution to that diplomatic quagmire, captain?'

Chen allowed himself a small, contented smile. 'Simple.' Then he turned and looked up at the camera in the upper corner of the ceiling and nodded. 'Just ensuring our privacy for the next few minutes. Professor Lawson has a heart condition. He requires medication for this condition, and he does not have any on him. Well, not anymore. Were his paperwork to be ...misprocessed, it's quite possible he might die in a holding cell before anyone knows what he had to offer. On the other hand...'

'We've heard about the stick,' Brennan said. 'Here comes the carrot.'

'...were both parties to agree to talk to Professor Lawson together, here, under supervision and the agreement that you both leave when the conversation is completed...'

'Then all of your problems disappear.'

'As I said, Mr. Brennan, we would prefer you take your squabbling elsewhere.'

'Do I get a choice...?'

'No.'

'Do I get a phone call...?'

'No. We're going to bring Professor Lawson into the room, and then your opposite number from the People's Republic. You'll have a little chat, under the supervision of Const. Tan, and then we'll see you both off to the airport. Good? Good.'

Captain Chen rose and walked to the door. 'You have one half-hour.'

'It'll probably take five minutes. Just keep an eye

on 'my opposite number,' as you called him.'

'Her.'

Chen opened the door. The woman from the restaurant walked in. She'd changed into a business-like dress and blouse with a pair of flats.

She shot a stern stare at Chen. 'My employers will be somewhat upset at this accommodation,' she said.

'Doubtless. But this is Macau, not China. And as long as we still have jurisdictional authority, it seems a most fitting application. Sit, please...' He gestured toward the chair opposite Brennan. 'I would make the introductions formally, but I'll leave it up to the two of you to decide how much you wish to chat. Constable Tan, if either of them attempts to harm the other or Professor Lawson, shoot them.' He turned and gave them a nod. 'Good day to both of you. I shall send him in momentarily.'

Daisy kept a cool exterior, but her nerves were shaken. Yan Liu Jeng would be apoplectic over Lawson's arrest, and only the more reasoned intervention of Chan Man Wei would prevent Yan from recalling her.

In the interrogation room, she had a chance to limit the damage. Getting the information was paramount; killing Lawson was a secondary objective but was pointless if the American was also allowed to live.

But she'd studied his file. They'd shipped her a dossier on Joseph Brennan and his past operations, both rumored and confirmed. It wasn't impressive so much as it was terrifying. Lee's cover as a professional poker player got her into elevated financial circles around the globe and allowed her to gather rich intelligence; and she was trained as a full-cover operative. But Brennan appeared to be the kind of 'black ops' killer she rarely encountered. The last time they'd fought she'd caught him by surprise.

She didn't appreciate her odds of a repeat.

She sat down opposite him. He peered at her as if studying a portrait for a previously unseen flaw.

'I know you.'

'I... don't think so,' Daisy said. She'd learned English at Oxford and private school, and she retained a clipped English tone. 'I'm quite sure I'd remember...'

'Daisy Lee. The poker player.' He grinned. 'You must really be in trouble. A cover like that blown over Stanley Lawson? You'll be lucky if they don't have you on guard duty in Altai by the end of the week.'

Aside from the obvious attempt to gain a psychological advantage, what he was saying wasn't entirely false, Daisy knew. Still, he didn't need to know that. 'My my, Mr. Brennan, you are confident for a man whose career has been hanging by a thread for the better part of two decades. My reading of your situation suggests no one would let you guard anything. Aren't you 'out to pasture', as they say in your country?'

'Yeah, I wish...'

'In fact, it's our understanding you're only here because you have some prior association with Professor Lawson, indicating he will only speak with you. Or deal with you, as is more likely the case, given his history of selling intelligence.'

'Why, Ms. Lee, what could possibly be so important that they'd need to haul an out-of-commission old hand like myself out of semi-retirement? Something about a rogue covert ops project, perhaps?'

'Do tell.'

'Oh please, let's not kid ourselves Ms. Lee. I'm sure you're quite versed on Legacy.'

Really? We're doing this? 'Of what, specifically? I'm quite sure the CIA wouldn't have sent someone with your particular... skillset if it wasn't vital.'

Brennan frowned a little at that.

He's thinking the same thing: that as much fun as

this is, it's a waste of time.

'We're going to be questioning him together,' Brennan said. 'If we outlay what we need answered now, we can avoid treading on toes and get as much out of this as possible...'

'Not a chance.' She didn't like the idea of explaining to Beijing that she'd given up a tactical advantage.

'Oh sure... because of course, this is a Chinese fuck up to begin with,' Brennan said. 'So naturally you have all the details already.'

'Your effort to rattle me is trite and beneath you,' she retorted.

The door opened and both turned their heads that way for a split second. Then they looked at each other, both realizing that one had to be the first to...

'Stanley!' Daisy bounced to her feet and over to the elderly man. She switched to Cantonese. 'I'm here to help. My name is Li Daiyu. Are you okay? Are you hurt in any way?'

Brennan answered for him, his accent poor but his use of the language perfect. 'No, he's not -- no thanks to State Security.'

The professor gave her a perturbed look and backed away until he was standing adjacent to Brennan's chair. 'Is that true Joe?'

'She's a Chinese spook.'

'Oh dear.'

'You really stepped in it this time Stanley, my man. You still feel like negotiating terms? Or maybe I should just turn you over to Beijing?'

'I'd really rather you didn't.'

'So tell us about it.'

'About what?'

'Stanley...'

'You mean... Legacy?'

Lee could have sworn she heard Brennan release a slight sigh of relief, as if thankful someone else had finally said it.

'Yes,' she said, conceding at least that. 'Tell us about Legacy.'

PUBLIC SECURITY HOSPITAL, BEIJING

JUNE 14, 1985

It was not the time for displays of strength and authority. As such, Fan King Wen was not his usual brash and confident self.

Two guards escorted him down the concrete main corridor of the prisoner wing. The staff at the hospital were not merely an assortment of doctors and orderlies and nurses, but also a full compliment of highly trained guards and a cadre of psychiatrists whose sole responsibility was extracting information.

Their patients? Political prisoners and dissidents, spies and celebrities; the castaways of China's high society and assorted other enemies of the state. If he didn't play his cards carefully, Fan knew, he could be a patient there himself one day.

Such was the strength of a destructive rumor in the air-tight confines of the party. Officially, he had denounced Jiang Qing at the time of her arrest. 'Madame Mao', as she had come to be known in the west, was reviled by the public and seen at best as the avenging fist of her late husband. At worst, she was the architect of a reign of terror that killed hundreds of thousands and purged the ranks of the nation's intellectuals and creatives.

To Fan and others like him, she represented something much more, the last gasp at holding onto a dream for a simpler, more egalitarian society, where the sheep were led by shepherds such as himself and protected by guard dogs like Jiang Qing. Even though he had followed her direction and separated himself from her supporters a year prior to her arrest, he had read her court testimony each day, and he believed every word. He knew full well that she had only acted at the Chairman's behest, that she represented nothing more than his priorities, the same priorities that had built the party to greatness over the four decades prior. The notion that those in the courtroom had laughed at her, ridiculed her, filled him with rage.

Fan was no political reactionary. He came to his opinions over years of consideration and eventual fealty to the notion of the purest Maoism. But he had been an Olympic athlete once, competing in gymnastics, training under an eastern European coach in a time when it was a rare step, gaining a following as an international athlete under the Anglicized name 'Dorian Fan'. As such, he had profile, influence. He was a star, a potential up-and-comer. And Jiang Qing recognized that if he was to be of any real use to the movement, he could not be associated with the Gang of Four during their most dire hour.

Thus, his visit was not that of a former apostle returning to his master, but a functionary trip by a party bureaucrat, charged with helping to decide whether she should be moved to house arrest or returned to prison once healthy. Many in the party remained convinced she was a suicide threat and that it could prove politically difficult if she was martyred by hardliners. Still others felt she might even try to push for a pardon, for release and another attempted rise to power. He was there to assess, to question.

And unbeknownst to his masters, to receive instruction.

At the door to her room, one of the guards unlocked it, then pushed it open. There was no deference to privacy, no hollered request to see if she was decent. Just entry.

'Leave us,' Fan said to the guards. 'Remain outside within earshot.'

He waited until the door was closed.

Though there was a hospital bed and an array of equipment, the room looked otherwise like a typical eight-by-ten cell, complete with cinderblock walls and musty, rank smell. Jiang Qing sat on the thin mattress of the cot, her chin raised defiantly. 'Fan. A most unexpected visit.'

'I had to come now, while you were in the hospital. As soon as they return you to your cell, there will be no opportunity for privacy.'

'And your 'official' rationale for being here?'

'I am to help decide your fate.'

She smiled. 'You are coming up in the world.'

'There is a position open in state security administration. I understand I am to be recommended. Likely there will be no actual time left to pursue it, but...

'Good. Excellent, in fact. Fortune smiles on the just, Fan King Wen. And the program?'

'The program continues. From the reports of Administrator Shou, the results have been nothing short of astounding. However, I intend to see for myself.'

'Is that wise?'

'It's necessary, I believe. We are seven years in, and they will be reaching the point where self-rationalization and problem solving makes indoctrination more challenging.'

'And the next step?'

'According to Dr. Park, they will move soon to the sensory deprivation and night sequencing stage. He believes that of the fifteen subjects, this process will prove too severe for at least seven to ten to take. The ones who make it out with their sanity intact will be ideal for our purposes.' Fan adored the direct precision of her questions, the lack of pretense. As an athlete, he'd seen time and again the concerted strength of a well-honed team, and he knew to the core of his soul that Maoism -- pure, proper idolatry of the communal unit -- would establish China as the dominant world power. To the young and faithful bureaucrat, Jiang Qing might as well have been the chairman himself brought back to life.

And she appeared pleased. 'Remember, we will not be able to speak after this, potentially ever, without you receiving undue attention. I may never be able to communicate to you my fierce pride at your ideological strength of purpose, or to congratulate you when Legacy's task is fulfilled.'

He wanted to ask her when that would be, but he knew there was not, as yet, an answer. Legacy was a failsafe, an option put into place in case the worst came to pass and the toxic seeds of capitalism took root in the nation. Neither expected that to occur soon, but the stage was set for moderation, a betrayal of the chairman's dream. Her arrest and the denunciation of her efforts was proof enough of that.

'One day, they will speak your name in hushed and reverent tones,' Fan said. 'And I will tell them of your ultimate sacrifice for the cause of the worker. I will tell them of your serene grace in the face of your persecution. You will be the mother of us all.'

She studied him, and he felt a flush of embarrassment to be her center of attention. He knew that she could be utterly ruthless, as required, but that her heart was filled with love for the chairman, and for China. He swore to himself that he would not fail. The legacy of the Paramount Leader and Jiang Qing would be preserved.

Fan had returned to his apartment with the intent of an early night. He had a flight the next morning to Chenzhou. But he slept fitfully, tossing and turning in bed as dreams of Jiang Qing's demise tormenting him. He was not old enough to have known her when she was a desirable actress, rather than an aging revolutionary, but he loved her, nonetheless.

His phone began to ring. He looked over at the Russian-built clock radio; it was just shy of midnight. He snatched the phone from the receiver, irritated. 'What?'

'Fan? It's Mah Xiao.'

'Mah? It's almost midnight. Couldn't this have

waited until work tomorrow?'

His younger associate sounded nervous. 'I checked with your secretary. You are travelling to Chenzhou tomorrow. She booked you a ticket.'

Damn. 'I have a few things to take care of at the office there. It's nothing I need your help with...'

'I've been looking at the books.'

The comment stopped the conversation cold. Fan tried to think of a quick explanation. 'Yes, I imagined that would come up eventually. It's something for the party, something off the record.'

'Respectfully, sir, I need to know about something like that if I'm going to audit accurately,' Mah said. 'I looked back, and there are similar expenditures in past accounts going back twelve years. Only the first had any sort of notation, and that was just the word 'Legacy'. What's this about, Fan?'

'It's complicated.'

'I've been here with you for three years and you know how much I value your guidance.'

Fan suspected the man was homosexual and attracted to him. He had cultivated a flirtatious relationship with him to garner Mah's absolute loyalty and it had worked well to that point. If it was being questioned, the scope of the financial misappropriation had become obvious.

It had to be dealt with. 'Xiao, old friend, don't worry: I can explain it all easily. Let's meet. Say, the Double Ox bar, on the south side?'

'That's a long way from downtown. Why not just somewhere near...'

'I like to drink in peace. Besides, that way we can talk... you know, privately, and too many people at the bars near the office know my face...'

'Well, it is a very nice face,' Mah said. 'And you are gaining more authority by the month, it seems. Good looking and powerful is an enticing combination.'

'As ever, flattery will get you everywhere,' Fan said.

The Double Ox bar was in an ornate concrete building on a block where most of its neighbors dated back as long as one hundred years. It had a painted glass window advertising food and beer specials, and four tables on the sidewalk outside serving as a patio. All of the tables were taken, old men playing chess and mahjong, smoking cigarettes and drinking baijiu from whiskey tumblers.

They'd found the most private booth at the very back of the old bar, which had been around since the days of the British, and Fan spent ninety minutes getting Mah drunk and listening to him prattle. One beer had turned to two, then four, then six. Or, Fan had made it appear so. They'd talked briefly about the file, though nothing specific, just enough for him to learn that Mah had the only copy in his vehicle.

Now the younger man was whispering to him. 'Just one kiss? We could go back to my place...'

Fan looked him deeply in the eyes. 'Is that what you really want?'

Mah nodded solemnly, his intoxicated gaze glistening with affection and wonder.

Fan gestured toward the nearby back door to the club. 'Come into the alley with me.'

Mah's eyes widened. 'Right here?'

Fan smiled. 'You have a better idea?'

They got up and Fan looked around to ensure no one in the front of the bar was paying attention. They were alone.

Outside, the night air was sticky and humid, the temperatures hardly cooled from the heat of day.

Mah played the aggressor, confidently looping an arm around Fan's neck. 'You're making me so happy right now, I can't even remember why I called you.' He leaned in to kiss the soft tissue around Fan's ear.

'Legacy,' Fan said. He extended the stiletto with a button push, then drove the blade forcefully into the base of the younger man's neck, severing the connection between his spinal cord and brain stem. The man fell backwards, every bodily function instantly paralyzed, his eyes wide as the air slipped slowly from his lungs.

13/

TODAY

MACAU

'And that is as much as I can tell you,' Lawson concluded. 'They believe Fan met with Jiang Qing to set the groundwork for something big. They believe Fan was responsible for killing a senior government bureaucrat to cover this up. And then...'

'And then?' Lee repeated.

'And then he just disappeared,' Lawson said. 'At the time, word got out pretty quickly in the intelligence community that a high-ranking party member had vanished and the Chinese were looking for a bunch of money. The opportunity to turn him was too tempting for the British or the Americans to turn down, and they put considerable time and money into finding him.'

'And?'

'Nothing,' Lawson said. 'Fan disappeared off the face of the Earth. I know from some of my Chinese colleagues that in the years following, his government tried to establish the terms of the meeting between Fan and Jiang Qing, but the closest they ever came was that it was an intelligence project named 'Legacy.' Last week, according to my sources, new information came to light.'

The generic nature of Lawson's data wasn't helping, Brennan thought. 'What kind of information? Are we talking operational intelligence?'

'From the anxiety levels in Beijing, I'd say this was definitely a mission in progress,' Lawson cautioned. 'But my source wasn't that specific.'

'We need a name,' Lee said. 'Give us the source and you'll walk out of here in one piece.'

Lawson took umbrage to that. 'From what the police tell me, local jurisdiction means I'm walking out of here no matter what I tell the two of you...'

'The question you should ask yourself,' Lee retorted, 'is how much you want to annoy the government of China, considering that the Macau police will not always be there for you.'

That made Brennan smile a little. 'Stanley, I've known you a long time. You've never been what anyone would characterize as a morally upstanding individual, and as good as you have it with this teaching gig, your past can catch up to you. It almost did tonight. But if you help us...'

'What? You'll look out for me? Don't make me laugh,' Lawson replied.

'However much you fear this individual, professor,' Lee said, 'I suspect they are not as thorough in their approach as my employers.'

Stanley's expression said he knew he was between a rock and a hard place. 'Fine. But it didn't come from me.'

'The name, Mr. Lawson,' Lee insisted.

'It's Raymond Pon. Professor Raymond Pon.'

The name wasn't familiar to Brennan. If it was to Lee, she didn't show it.

They separated, and Brennan returned to his hotel room with more questions than answers. The room was untouched save for the open suitcase on one bed.

He used a secure channel to contact Langley but was still surprised when Jonah Tarrant took the call personally. 'Joe. This is a quicker turnaround than we anticipated, or are things getting complicated?

'Not complicated, just vague,' he replied. 'Stanley gave us a name...'

'Us?'

'Chinese intelligence decided to send a representative over to Macau to keep me company.'

'How did they know...?'

'They didn't. They were following Lawson and we stumbled into one another. Or, more to the point, Lawson stumbled into a local hitter named Tommy Wong.'

'I assume it's been dealt with?'

'To a degree. There was a confrontation, some egos were bruised. I think he's gone to ground, at least for now.'

'And the name?'

'Someone named Raymond Pon, another academic. Lawson said he was...'

'We're familiar with him. He had some shady dealings and fell out with the government. He's been working in Mexico for a few years, something to do with graphene technology.'

'We have another complication,' Brennan added.

'Yes, you said the Chinese are involved...'

'As you'd expected. They've got a deep cover agent named Daisy Lee causing me problems. Can you find out whatever you can about her? It might come in handy if she pops up again.'

'Will do. Check in once you're on the ground.'

'Roger. Jonah... you know you owe me for this, right? I expect you to honor that when I get back, and I expect you to talk to Carolyn about how important this was, and about how I didn't have a whole lot of choice.'

'I'm not a marriage counsellor, Joe...'

'Really? Because you're pretty good at splitting them up, as far as I can tell. The situation in New York State wasn't my cross to bear, but I dragged you out of it. Look, you owe me for this, you owe me for Walter, you owe me for a lot of things.'

'I know, Joe, I know. Just... leave it with me, okay? I'll talk to her. We have to brief them anyway...'

'NSA is in the loop on this?'

'Whatever 'Legacy' is, it's a threat to national security. Everyone is in on this, if we need them. I should tell you that our Australian friends are monitoring a ton of traffic from the Chinese. I'll pass them the agent's name.

'And Raymond Pon?'

'Do whatever you need to do. Just... don't kill him, okay? He has some interesting friends. If you could avoid an international incident for even one week, that would be good.'

'And the woman? The Chinese agent?'

'She'll likely show up again. Don't kill her either, whatever you do. The last thing we need is for the Chinese to have an excuse, an international provocation a few weeks before their premier visits D.C.'

LOS ANGELES

Zoey felt ill at ease the moment she walked into the city morgue building, and the sensation hadn't let up. The two detectives, Drabek and Pace, were both there as well and offered some comforting words. But inevitably, she knew, she would either see what was left of Ben, or go back to wondering what the hell had happened to him.

The fluorescent tube lighting and the extremely low temperature accentuated the room's sterility. Along the wall to their right sat a series of sinks and workstations. To their left, the wall was covered with a bank of refrigeration drawers. One was already open toward the back of the room, its slab extended, the body on it covered with a sheet.

'You okay?' Drabek asked.

She nodded curtly. 'Let's just get it over with.'

Drabek gave the assistant medical examiner the okay, and she pulled back the sheet, just as far as the man's chest. The lye had dissolved half of his chest cavity. The slash across his throat was open but dry, like some plastic anatomical model in a biology class.

She shook her head. 'It's not him. It's not Ben. They look sort of similar, but it's definitely not my Ben.' Then it seemed to click in, and she realized what she was looking at. Both hands came up to her mouth, as if they might help her catch her breath.

The examiner covered the man up again and Drabek put an arm on her shoulder, guiding her away. 'That's it. We had to know for sure; since it's not Ben, we're left with one other pretty solid option on who this man is.'

Pace had been talking to the assistant medical examiner, and he caught up with them as they walked the corridor toward the elevators. 'Of course, if that's Paul Joseph back there, then we know who probably...'

Drabek cut him off abruptly. 'Not now.'

'What?' Zoey asked, looking over her shoulder at the younger cop. 'Solid idea of what?'

Drabek punched the elevator button. 'Don't worry about it. We should get back to station and see if there's a birth certificate on Ben yet. Maybe we can figure out this whole Ohio nonsense...'

She got into the elevator behind him, followed by Pace. 'Don't change the subject,' Zoey said. 'He said we know who probably... Probably what? Are you suggesting that Ben killed that man? Because that's a bunch of...'

'With respect, ma'am...' Pace said, '...he's using the man's credit daily, they look just like one another...'

'It's not the issue at hand,' Drabek said. 'Not for us.' It was true; homicide would be all over Ben as a suspect, but in the immediate, their job was just to find him. They didn't need to complicate things for the girl any more than already was the case. 'We just need to reunite this young couple so that they can get their lives back together.'

'And Ben isn't like that,' Zoey interjected as the elevator rose toward the ground floor. 'He's a gentle person. At Rosh Hashana last fall, he volunteered to serve the elderly from his Temple at the big dinner they have. He fundraises for heart and stroke...'

Pace was about to say something, but he caught Drabek's glare out of the corner of his eye.

'We'll get it all sorted,' Drabek said casually. 'We'll get it all sorted.' He could feel Pace glaring back. The second they told homicide, he knew, they'd be officially off the case and the kid would be back to square one. There was zero chance of Ben Levitt getting a pass as a suspect. Zero. And that meant the girl was a material witness.

His shift was technically over, so Drabek took Zoey back to his favorite bar to break the news to her over a free bite to eat. He wanted her to understand he wasn't going to give up, but that her life was probably about to get a whole lot more difficult.

After the shock of seeing Joseph's body had worn off, she'd realized that meant Ben was still alive, and a sense of optimism had set in.

He was going to ruin that, Drabek knew, which was par for the course in Vice.

They grabbed a two-person table near the back and each looked over the one-page vinyl-wrapped menu.

'Thank you for buying me dinner,' Zoey said. 'You didn't have to. I have money.'

'Yeah...' They'd freeze Levitt's assets the next day, he knew. And he couldn't tell her. Technically. 'You might want to take out any money you think you're going to need for a while. You know... just in case.'

'I don't like to carry around extra.'

'Yeah... listen, what Detective Pace said at the morgue...'

'Uh huh.' Her head dropped. 'I'd been thinking about that.'

'You said yourself, he wasn't acting anything like normal. If he could shoot at you...'

'Yeah...' She couldn't hide her fear that it was true.

'Look, the boys in homicide will be looking to pick him up for this. And they're going to have a lot of questions for both of you.'

She looked puzzled. 'Me? I haven't done anything...'

'You're a material witness to his state of mind and his behavior.'

'When...?'

'They'll have assigned two detectives to work it already; when I go home tonight, I'll turn my phone back on, and there will be a bunch of messages from them about why Pacey and I were at Paul Joseph's house in the first place. And I'll be obligated to tell them.'

'Why are you telling me this?'

'I want you to know what's coming. It won't be easy. They aren't going to express a whole lot of concern for Ben's health or your relationship. Whenever this happens, there's a lot of stress, a lot of pressure. You might hear or learn things about Ben you didn't know, things that are hard to hear...'

'Things I didn't know?' Zoey took a swallow from her drink. 'Right now, I'm not sure I knew him at all. I mean, it was always a whirlwind romance kind of thing...but Ben isn't exactly Mr. Excitement. It's one of the things I love about him...'

'Anyway,' he said, getting her back to the present, 'I'll be taken off the case, almost certainly. I don't have a lot of champions inside the department anymore, and they won't see this as a missing persons case.'

The woman hardly knew him, Drabek told himself. She didn't need his help. She needed a lawyer and a sympathetic girlfriend. But the look on her face said different; it said she trusted him, and it felt as if he was about to break that trust.

'So... you can't help me anymore?'

'Not officially, no.' He heard the words come out and cursed inwardly. He should've just said no, Drabek knew.

'Officially?'

'I can't work it as a file, but there are still leads to follow...' He didn't know why he was offering.

Maybe the kid reminded him of his daughter, Nicole. Maybe he'd met too many vulnerable people to just let her walk out alone.

Her face brightened somewhat. She grabbed his empty bottle and her glass and stood up. 'I'm going to go over and get us each another,' she said. 'Okay?'

He nodded. 'Sure.'

Drabek watched Zoey walk back up to the bar. If he had any sense, he told himself, he'd just walk away from this before hackles were raised and noses put out of joint. *She's really just another street kid. There are a million of them who need help, former and current. You can't bring Nicole back by helping this girl. And you can't help enough people to change anything.*

That was the little voice inside. Drabek smiled as he watched her get them drinks. He'd made a habit out of ignoring that little voice.

14/

WASHINGTON, DC

Jonah Tarrant was playing a waiting game. The CIA deputy director was meeting with his new number two, Adrianne Hayes, who'd come over from the NSA with a reputation for getting things done. In a month, she'd managed both to establish a half-dozen solid ideas and to thoroughly undermine him at every turn.

He'd called her into his office to discuss the China situation, and just how much should be shared with the National Security Council given the fluid nature of Joe Brennan's investigation. The White House had reached out to the Chinese, and to discuss North Korea; once the initial contacts were concluded, they would pursue broader talks; if the NSC's political players felt Brennan risked tipping the apple cart by offending the Chinese, they might demand he be pulled before they had a solid sense of what "Legacy" was, or its objective.

Instead, he was having her sit quietly in front of his desk while he finished 'reviewing a file', which really just meant making her wait; the purpose was simple: establish that she had a complete absence of control in his presence. Leave her wanting more. The best tool to accomplish both ends, Tarrant had found over the few years prior, was to just be silent and let her fill that void contemplating as many theories about his purpose as possible. Adrianne had been nothing but ambitious; but if left to her devices, she'd avoid any necessary risk that might hurt her politically. That could include curtailing Brennan's assignment.

After about five minutes, he expected, she would

interject, and....

'Excuse me, Jonah,' she said. 'I know you need to...'

He raised a finger without looking up from the document and shushed her. 'Just a second.'

Then he went back to silently 'reviewing' the document while she seethed and squirmed slightly in her chair. When five full minutes had passed and she looked about to climb out of her skin, he put the folder down and arched his fingertips on the desktop.

'Now.... China.'

'Yes! China. There's...'

'There's a real risk,' Jonah said, cutting her off. 'There's a real risk that Brennan won't find out what's going on before they agree to sit down. With the way things are headed, we expect those talks to be led by POTUS. What I need from you is this: a complete dossier on what we know to date about both Legacy and existing security protocols for diplomatic visits as laid down by Homeland Security and the Secret Service. Also, we need to talk to the bureau and D.C. police. We need to fill them in that we're working on something without letting their feet in the door.'

She waited for the right moment to speak and when he didn't continue made a point of it. 'Can I say something now? Good...'

'Well... that is why you're here, Adrianne, because I value your advice.'

'My advice would be to pull Brennan off of this right now,' she said, obviously eager to get to her key talking point. 'I know you respect Joe's history...'

'Especially the parts you don't know.'

She was startled by that and couldn't hide it. 'Excuse me?'

'Much of Brennan's file is classified from anyone below the deputy director level. That likely doesn't leave you enough of the picture to make a solid decision on his role. But I do value your input, obviously.' He was basically telling her to keep her nose out of the operational end of things and stick to logistics. He didn't expect her to listen. Hayes had been the director's pick to take over Tarrant's old position when he was promoted. Like most of the purely political appointees in similar roles, Tarrant sensed, the director was inclined to favor ambitious young women.

'If he causes some sort of international incident before we can get the Chinese to agree on security protocols for the meeting with the President, the potential escalation could mean a new cold war... or worse,' she said. 'I don't need to remind you how important....'

'No, Adrianne, you certainly don't. What you can do, however, is use your formidable reputation for running a tight ship and clamp down on any leaks. I'm making it your responsibility to guarantee any negotiations aren't impacted by this.'

He saw the slight flare of her nostrils, the barely perceptible widening of her eyes as she recognized the implication: everything she'd wanted to use against him politically was now her responsibility. And yet she had no control over Brennan's operation whatsoever.

'Then we won't be pulling him out?'

'I see no reason to,' Tarrant said. 'He's on route to Mexico now and making progress. In fact, I'm quite sure he has things well in hand.'

DAY 7

MERIDA, MEXICO

Brennan hung suspended by a single hand grip from the balcony ledge, the city a blurred backdrop of rooftops, mostly lower than his precarious locale.

He tried to tense his muscles up for just a moment, to center his weight and stop his body from swaying side to side, deadly asphalt beckoning from hundreds of feet below.

He looked back up to the ledge, every sinew in his body straining against his own weight.

Of course, it wasn't supposed to have gone that way. He'd ziplined to the large balcony from the neighboring building's roof, nine storeys up. As his feet set down upon the concrete, the balcony door to the apartment in question had opened and Brennan had flung himself over the rail to avoid detection.

But he'd missed with his right hand and had to hang on with one arm; then the two guards in question had opted to smoke cigarettes, and after two minutes, Brennan's arm was rapidly tiring. The point of going down from the rooftop had been to get in quietly and undetected, to find his target and either question or extract. Now, he was either going to have to make some noise and attract enough attention to be shot before he could right himself... or fall to his death a few hundred feet below.

It wasn't as if anything had gone smoothly since Macau. He'd flown back to the States, then from New York to Merida, a grand old city in the middle of the Yucatan jungle that had its heyday in the art deco/French colonial architecture era. That was back when the region's staple crop, henequen, was the base fiber for rope. Use of sisal overtook it, and the city that once housed more millionaires than anywhere else on Earth went slowly broke. Decades later it had recovered somewhat, but much of its grandeur had wilted under the humidity and mildew.

It was over a hundred degrees Fahrenheit in the shade; the airport was crowded, tourists coming to town at the worst time, unless they liked ninety-nine percent humidity and torrential rain. Merida had a thriving community of gringo ex-patriots, taking advantage of the lower cost and the peaceful Mayan culture to set up new roots.

Brennan had everything he needed in his carry-on; anything operational would be waiting for him at his hotel or provided later.

Outside the airport doors, the heat and moisture

felt like a wet blanket. He hailed a cab and rode it to Centro, where the boutique hotel hosted visitors in a converted mansion, complete with eight bedrooms and Romanesque columns surrounding the central courtyard pool.

His room was spartan but elegant. There was a small flat-screen TV on the wall behind the door, a bookshelf full of paperback loaners and a queen-sized bed with bright yellow linens.

His phone rang.

'Brennan,' he answered.

'The package is amenable.' Jonah Tarrant didn't identify himself.

'Where and when?'

'He wants a public intro. There's a restaurant in the Centro district, La Chaya Maya. Tortillas in a courtyard setting, that kind of thing. More entry points than you'd like but we've got you a corner table with decent sight lines.'

'So what's the plan? I buy him a few pork-and-cilantro specials, pick up an extended bar tab, and ...?'

'He whispers sweet stories about Chinese spooks in your ear, we figure out what they're up to, you fly home. That's the general idea, anyway.'

'And then what?'

'Then what? That's not part of your task, Joe. It never is. You know that.'

'Just being curious. A few days ago, you were talking about this as if it was something really heavy; now I'm wondering what you plan to do with the information. There are talks coming up...'

'That's above both of our paygrades. Really, Joe, let's not go there; we've got the possibility of this being just intel, sure; but more likely, there's a real threat here. The Chinese wouldn't be nearly as anxious if they didn't stand to take the blame for something. I'm not jerking your chain for some politician.'

Brennan had long ago learned not to take assurances on face value, but also not to tip his own hand. 'Okay. Are we expecting any resistance? Did you get any sort of make on Daisy Lee?'

'The analysts have already run her playing schedule for the last four years, and they match up with a pattern of tradecraft incidents involving the Chinese.'

'Color me shocked,' Brennan said. 'She could throw a heck of a right cross, I'll tell you that much.'

'We've touched base with our Mexican colleagues and there's no indication of Lee entering the country. We feel you're probably good to go.'

'So why the public place?'

'That was the professor's choice. He's working on some pretty hi-tech stuff, I guess, and we dropped this on him basically overnight. I think he's worried you may not be legit.'

'They have any cartel problems down here, any locals I should worry about?'

Tarrant snickered a little. 'In Merida? Are you kidding? No. He's probably just being paranoid. It's a different vibe in the Yucatan. It's hot as hell, so people are more laid back. They get along to get along, and it's generally safer than here. Like I said, you don't have anything to worry about. Trust me.'

15/

DAY 8

The restaurant was popular with locals, which Brennan figured was a sign the food was decent. Nestled in the grid of narrow two-lane downtown streets, it was a pink-pastel-shaded building with a bright-yellow central courtyard, an old full-sized carriage resting in its midst as an art piece. Around it, the surrounding shaded nooks and crannies were occupied by four-person wooden tables, each with a centre piece and candle. In a few spots, they'd been pushed together for larger parties.

Most of the families appeared to be Mexican, with the men in short-sleeve dress shirts and trousers, the women in light blouses. But there were quite a few tourists as well, inevitably wearing knee-length shorts, sandals and sunburns. Almost everyone was eating fresh tortillas. A few were drinking wine or beer, but it was a family place, not a party atmosphere.

Pon was by himself at a two-person table in the far corner, adjacent to a street exit. He was aging, perhaps in his sixties, with a small, frog-like face and thinning black hair, streaked with grey. According to his dossier, he'd been jailed for four years during the cultural revolution, prompting his eventual exodus to the west. In the ensuing years, he'd become one of the world's foremost experts in the production of graphene, a new ultra-strong material produced at the molecular level. *Score another one for Madame Mao's contempt for the intellectuals*, Brennan thought.

He approached the table. Pon saw him and put down his water glass. 'Excuse me,' Brennan asked, 'didn't we meet at the Mall of America?'

Pon looked around furtively. 'In the sporting

goods section?'

Brennan pulled out the chair opposite the man and sat down. He didn't like having his back to the courtyard. The heat was stifling, the humidity proving itself in the beads of sweat along his brow. 'I bought a tennis racquet, remember?'

'Slazenger, wasn't it?'

'Donnay Borg Pro.'

'You're Brennan?' Pon asked.

'I am.'

'Good. Are we eating?'

'I hadn't planned on it.'

'Also good.' But he was staring over Brennan's shoulder, surveying the room avidly.

Brennan checked his six but there was nothing out of place. 'Are you expecting someone else?'

'That depends. Would it sound paranoid if I told you I think someone has been following me?'

'Not really. The last professor I met over drinks ended up with a hitman on his tail.'

'Comforting. Merida's not the sort of city where you find trouble. It's one of the reasons I like it here. Then I get a call from your Mr. Tarrant and he sounds genuinely concerned about Legacy.'

Brennan checked the room again quickly. 'Maybe keep it down a little with that stuff, eh Prof?'

Pon looked bemused. 'Look, I don't know how to tell you this, and I tried to convey this to your boss, but the whole thing is crazy. Even if we assume it was ever real to begin with, it's a thirty-year-old plan, and its architects are all long dead. And like I said: that's if we assume it was real, and I don't think it was.'

'Then why so worried?'

'I have... local business interests who are growing impatient. After I left China, I needed help establishing my company and laboratory here. We've made a lot of money for both PonTech and Santerra's company since then, but he wants the return of his original investment post haste, due to a downturn in his own business.'

'Which is.

'Wholesale methamphetamine delivery to the illicit international market, I believe.'

'Fantastic.'

'Yes, well... financing is difficult to obtain when you're a relatively unknown dissident Chinese refugee. My limited contacts in Taiwan came up with Ramon Santerra, a real estate developer.'

'And meth dealer.'

'And meth dealer. But he sells a lot of homes, and he sells a lot of meth, and Graphene sheets are incredibly expensive to produce. Prohibitively, for practical purposes.'

'So why is he interested if it's such a money sinkhole?'

'Because he likes the chase.'

'The chase?'

'We're all chasing the same thing, you see, which is a cheap and consistent method to produce graphene sheets. Whoever comes up with that first and patents it will have a license to print money that'll make the old robber barons of the early oil age look like paupers in line at a soup kitchen.'

'But he's got meth problems....'

'And he may have had a change of heart about how soon it will be before graphene is financially commoditized.'

'Eh?'

'He read an article in *Newsweek* saying it may yet be decades before graphene is an everyday household sort of thing. I'd suggested a shorter time frame.'

'Such as?'

'By next year.' The professor took a long swallow from his water glass.

He wasn't looking over his shoulder for the Chinese, Brennan knew. He just thought his investor might show up guns blazing. 'Smooth.'

'It's been more than a decade since I arrived here, to be fair.'

'So you gave him an estimate years ahead...?'

'Well... no. Initially I gave him a three-year window, and then that came and went, and then we extended it to seven, and then ten years. He was angry after ten years, I remember, but I met his wife at a gallery show and managed to talk her into a further injection of funds...'

'Problematic. And you know someone was following you because...'

'Because I recognized him. He's one of Santerra's bodyguards. I think he was figuring out what it would take to get past my building's security. I thought initially that your boss's call was an attempt to draw me out, but a few checks with colleagues in the States confirmed his legitimacy.'

'You were glad to meet with me, not because of what you could tell us but because you figured I could what? Protect you? That's not how this works, professor. I need some incentive, as in some real information.'

'I'll tell you what I can.' The waitress arrived and Pon waved off the menu. 'I'll just have a cup of green tea, please.' He gestured toward Brennan. 'And my colleague?'

'A bottle of Perrier,' Brennan said. The waitress scratched it down on a pad.

He waited until she'd left. 'You were saying...'

'Yes,' Pon continued. 'Project Legacy.'

Then his eyes widened.

'We have company.'

Brennan half-turned in his chair but knew instinctively it was going to be too late. Both men had drawn pistols with suppressors attached. They had dark suits on, and dark glasses, and they meant business. They took aim at the professor.

The woman seemed to come out of nowhere. One moment she was seated at a table, only her long black hair and the back of her blue silk dress visible from Brennan's vantage point; the next, she was rising and turning in a single motion, pirouetting into a position between the two men, her hands coming up from behind them to slam their heads

THE GHOSTS OF MAO

together.

Brennan saw her face clearly.

'Daisy Lee.'

Pon was on his feet immediately and, even in his sixties, was spry enough to head for the patio's rear exit. Lee saw him and ran to intercept. Brennan slipped out of his chair and grabbed its back in one smooth motion, hurling the four-legged projectile at her. Lee didn't break stride, batting it to one side with her right arm even as she closed on Pon. But Brennan was a step ahead; the second that the chair left his hand he was taking a half-step into a crouch followed by a long, low leg sweep.

It caught her flush across the ankle, at speed, and she went head-over-heels, her back slamming to the patio. Across the courtyard, Brennan saw two more gunmen enter. 'Go!' he yelled at Pon. 'Find a crowd!' Lee was recovering, spinning her legs like a coffee grinder and pushing off with both hands simultaneously, the momentum pulling her up to her feet. Brennan's hand had gone to the inside of his sport coat and the Sig Sauer concealed in his shoulder holster; but she struck quickly, darting in with a punch to the nerve cluster in his shoulder joint, deadening his arm, then following it with a hard, quick kick to the side of his knee that he just managed to slip. He threw a wide arcing elbow and caught her in the side of the head, following it with a pair of punches that she blocked ably.

She wanted to face off, it seemed. Brennan looked behind her; both gunmen were training their weapons toward the pair, without regard for the threat to customers or staff. He shook his arm to regain some of the feeling.

Behind him, he could hear Pon rattling the door, which was clearly locked, or...

'I think they've barred it from the other side,' Pon said.

Brennan nodded toward the carriage in the center of the courtyard. 'Get behind that and hide. If you see an opening behind them, head for the front door.' Then he looked back at Lee. 'We don't have time for this,' he told her. 'The guy who is chasing him has more men here than even you can handle.'

Lee turned around in one smooth motion and released the two throwing stars she'd secreted in the folds of her sash. They were unerring, whirring through the air and thunking into each man's throat, both gunmen clutching wildly at their weapons as they collapsed.

'You were saying?'

Customers were screaming, running for the doors, staff bravely shielding them and helping them escape. Pon ran out amongst them.

'Aside from the spectacle,' Brennan shouted at her, 'it's not the ones in here I'm worried about.' He nodded toward the back wall and exit. 'It's the ones out there.'

On queue, a gunshot resounded from somewhere outside. Lee looked at him and then back at the two men and the rapidly emptying restaurant. She seemed to be spoiling for a fight, Brennan thought, but torn. She turned in the moment and sprinted for the door.

Brennan followed her, barely able to keep up with the lithe woman, who had kicked off her shoes during the encounter. She ran out into the suddenly busy street, Calle 55, and looked both ways. Pon was running east, toward a small park.

'Professor!' she yelled. 'Please! Wait!'

As he turned to look for the source of the call, an old tan Renault compact screeched to a halt next to him. The back door opened and a pair of beefy arms grabbed Pon by the jacket, pulling him inside.

She turned back toward Brennan, an angry look on her face, her fists clenched. But a siren sounded nearby, and she looked past him. He braced himself, expecting her to charge him, as she'd done in Macau. Instead, the sound of the nearby siren had given her pause, and the poker player known as Daisy Lee quickly blended into the crowd and disappeared down the side street.

16/

DAY 9

WASHINGTON, D.C.

Stoicism can carry one far in a world filled with conflict. Secretary of State Robert Tully knew he could look cool and calm standing in the middle of a forest fire, which he had no doubt had been a large part of his corporate success, prior to getting into politics.

In business, it made him seem indispensable. No matter how grave the circumstance, he appeared to be the one man in the room who was afraid of nothing. To a president focussed on the economy, he must have seemed ideal to bring into the fold.

The truth was, he was terrified.

In his nine months on the job, he'd followed the mandate handed him by the president: keep the economic wheels greased and keep us out of trouble. That hadn't been difficult, given that it had been followed by month-after-month of meetings with staunch allies and fawning would-be democracies.

Nine months without needing to address significant conflict or terrorism was unheard of in modern diplomacy. Tully had ridden it to a shift in public perception from 'wrongly appointed corporate toady' to 'honest effort, learning the ropes.' Keeping the momentum positive meant diplomatic wins, not taking on thorny issues like North Korea and extremism.

And yet that was clearly what was about to happen. Even before the Chinese reached out and asked for the video conference, Tully was receiving security briefings on North Korea's latest missile test, and the likely reaction from the largest of few allies.

He was in deep, and he knew it.

To his left, his deputy was reviewing notes. 'As we suspected and discussed in the briefing, you're going to be speaking with Zhao Fuhua, the deputy foreign secretary. We expect he will take their usual brusque initial tone, dismissing any notion of American interests in the region.'

They'd also discussed his approach. Tully was to be forceful, reiterating the President's perception that North Korea was, in effect, China's responsibility. If China decided to shirk that responsibility, the U.S. would have to shoulder the burden, up to and including military intervention.

'We expect him to focus on North Korea's sovereignty and the inherent danger to South Korea in insulting the Dear Leader. Although we have no doubt that the North now has the capacity to destroy Seoul, this line of approach is a bluff on the Chinese part; it is a detente situation, with North Korea well aware that any strike on South Korea or Japan would result in a global exercise in regime change.'

Tully's Texas drawl was more pronounced under stress. 'And then I lean heavily on the fact that China's economic interests and ours are so heavily tied that they'll suffer as much from this as anyone.'

'Exactly. You'll do a fine job, as always, sir.'

'Let's hope so, Bobby. Let's hope so.'

A voice came over the room speakers. 'We're going to connect you now sir,' a technician's voice said.

The lights went down. On the wall ahead of them, the sixty-inch flat screen flared to life. A middle-aged Chinese man appeared unaware the camera was on for a moment, then gestured with a quick nod to someone off screen. 'Secretary Tully. It is good to speak with you finally.'

'Well now, the feeling sure is mutual,' Tully said. 'I want to thank you for being willing to talk at what must be a rather busy and difficult time. And the hour, of course, isn't favorable in your part of the world.' It was just after one-thirty in the afternoon

D.C. time, but that was three-thirty in the morning in Beijing.

'You are most kind,' Zhao said. 'Of course, we are concerned that America feels a need to dialog about this at all. North Korea is a sovereign nation, after all, and its decisions are its own.'

Tully smiled, revealing perfectly capped teeth. 'The United States understands and affirms that position. We also recognize that there are important talks about increased trade and co-operation about to take place between our two leaders. Having said that, North Korea's continued unwillingness to step back from increased militarism in the region has begun to somewhat force our hand. Just as the People's Republic of China has assets in the United States that are vital, America has allies in the region who are valued and vital. And they have reason to be nervous. The missile test...'

'The missile test was ill-advised, but there was no technical threat,' Zhao said. 'We are informed its payload was disarmed and that this was merely a guidance experiment.'

'If you don't mind my saying so, Mr. deputy secretary, it was a pretty spectacular failure. The Japanese are incensed, as they have every right to be. One of their citizens nearly lost his life when that missile ditched, and many others are now terrified.' Tully tried to add some concern to his tone, as if the worries of the Japanese were his own.

'Regrettable,' Zhao said. 'Nevertheless, that is a matter for discussion between Japan and North Korea; there is no need for an American battle group to be anywhere nearby.'

'We have allies to protect,' Tully said forcefully, 'and the President has directed me to be crystal clear that we will do so to the utmost of our ability. China can go a long way to ensuring that doesn't happen by ensuring its partner knows the implications of attacking the United States or an ally. And with the session coming up between our two leaders, it's imperative these implications are considered...'

'Implications are a two-way street, Secretary Tully,' Zhao argued. 'As there may be implications for North Korea, so too will there be many for the South. It is much closer to PyongYan than Japan is, after all.'

Tully tried to flash a paternal, forgiving smile. 'The President is well aware, Mr. Zhao, that North Korean intelligence will have analyzed the likelihood of military intervention in the region and, recognizing the sheer number of potential opponents after the fact, will have dismissed a nuclear option out of hand. The North Koreans know something I learned myself years ago, down on the farm in East Texas.'

'And what is that?'

'It's one thing to bait the bull, Mr. Zhao. It's another thing to try to grab it by the horns.'

'China will not sit idly by if the United States intervenes,' Zhao stated bluntly.

'Then let's hope it doesn't come to that,' Tully said. 'Let's hope we can get this all sorted long before that happens.'

MERIDA, MEXICO.

Brennan paced his hotel room and was fuming by the time Jonah Tarrant answered his private encrypted line. 'Do you have any more useful intel for me? Maybe something ticking ominously that we can shake?'

'What happened?'

'The professor was grabbed, potentially by a local crime lord named Ramon Santerra. We would have gotten away together, cleanly, but our friend from Macau decided to show her face again.'

Tarrant cursed inwardly. 'At least she didn't grab him before us. How much trouble is he in?'

'He owes a local meth dealer a bunch of investment capital. He's been selling graphene tech as snake oil, cashing in on the fact that it's years from market.'

'Uh huh. It's not hard to see how this guy ended up in a Chinese prison. Do you think he's as advertised?'

'Hard to say,' Brennan replied. 'We'd only just started talking about Legacy when the guys with the guns showed up. Again, do we even do proper background work anymore?'

'We were sending you in on a day's notice. Look, we can still get the horse back into the barn. Find out where this Santerra guy has him holed up and whether you can snatch Pon back. Try not to engage the locals; but I highly doubt the Merida cops will cry too many tears if things get messy.'

Get the horse back into the barn? The longer Tarrant spent in the deputy director's chair, the more he'd begun to act exactly like the men above him, Brennan figured. It was like he'd forgotten the pressure of three years earlier, and the near-miss, and his boss's betrayal.

'I'll do what I can,' Brennan said. 'What about Daisy Lee?'

'The same rules still apply. The North Korea situation is... tenuous, at best. We need relations to resemble something cordial, at the very least.'

'So don't kill her and don't hurt her. Got it. If she tries to brain me with another right cross?'

'Duck.'

It had taken a few hundred pesos tipped to a pair of cabbies to find Ramon Santerra's building, an office block in the south of the city. It was one of Merida's taller efforts at a dozen storeys, topped only by the Hyatt and a couple of other hotels. The men in blue blazers hovering around the front and back doors suggested he controlled the whole place.

Brennan had already circled the building from across the street, getting a general lay of the land. There was a cafe with a sidewalk patio to the south of the place, and it gave him a perfect view of the doors. He gazed up and across from the building to its neighbor due west. It was at least four stories lower, although there was what appeared to be a patio about eight stories up.

The sports bag under the table at his feet contained a grappling hook. Technically, it looked possible to cross the gap between the two buildings and enter the building via the balcony. But even at night there was a severe risk of being spotted; and there had to be an easier way, he knew. He just needed a day to get plans for the building, an idea of the guard rotations...

Across the street, a taxi pulled up to the front doors. The driver got out and opened the back door hurriedly, like impressions meant something. Then he held out a hand to help his passenger out to the sidewalk; the woman wore a black evening dress and elbow length gloves, as if headed to a formal dinner. She tipped the driver and turned her head slightly as she did so.

Daisy Lee. And judging from the way the guards at the door parted to accommodate her -- and opened the front door -- she obviously had an invite.

'Well doesn't that just beat everything,' Brennan muttered.

A waiter approached his table. 'Sir, would you like to order?'

'Just a cup of decaffeinated coffee please. Black.'

Her arrival took the decision out of his hands. He couldn't storm the back or front doors, the ground level windows were covered six ways from Sunday and they already knew both his appearance and to expect him. That meant a vertical approach. He looked back at the other building wistfully. So much for the best-laid plans.

He waited until an hour after dark. She'd been in the building for nearly three hours, and from his perch atop the adjacent building he could see both exits clearly. The balcony was slightly lower, perhaps seven or eight feet below his rooftop. There was no sign of any regular guard rotation or even a camera above the door to the broad ninth-storey patio.

Brennan loaded the grappling hook into the gun and used the rail on the side of the roof to brace it for precision. The pneumatics punched the grapple and wire through the air in a long lazy arc. They clattered onto the balcony and he pulled until the hook caught the balcony railing. He peered over the edge at the toy-sized traffic. No one appeared to have noticed anything. He tied the free end around the chimney behind him then tried the line for tension. Satisfied, he threw the two-handled leather slide over the line and propelled himself across the divide.

He slid quickly down the line, careful to turn his shoulder to take the brunt of the impact as he thudded to a halt against the side of the balcony wall. The wall was flush with the balcony floor and there was nowhere on the outside to stand; he moved his hands close together and pulled upwards so that he could grasp the leather slide with one hand to support his weight, and the balcony railing with the other. Then he quickly swung his other hand to the rail and used the momentum to swing one leg up and over.

Brennan saw the men through the long glass wall that fronted the adjacent corridor, about ten feet before they reached the balcony door. He knew they couldn't be allowed to see the grappling hook, or he was done. He reached over and detached it, letting it swing across the street and clatter into the opposite building. The door opened. He dropped over the side, reaching to grasp the rail with his right hand as well as his left, but missing. He hung there, his left arm taking his full weight, the men who'd just noisily exited to the balcony unaware of his presence.

He heard one light a cigarette. A few seconds later, he smelled American tobacco burning. They were close, maybe just a few feet away.

'We don't have time for this,' one of the men said

in Spanish. 'We're supposed to be downstairs for his big speech.'

A man took a loud drag off the cigarette. He blew out the smoke contemptuously. 'You go then, guard the man while he preens, like a child in a school play.'

'He pays the bills.'

Brennan gritted his teeth; he was flexing his shoulder and neck muscles, trying to take some strain off his arm. But it was a painful exercise.

'So? Like I said, go without me.'

'Just take another drag and put it out for now and let's get the fuck out of here, okay? If you piss of Santerra, you know what happens. You'll be lucky if he doesn't throw you off this balcony.'

The other guard took one more loud puff, then exhaled. 'Fine.'

Brennan heard steps. Then the roof door clicked open, and a moment later, it swung shut. Brennan pulled up with all his might, but his arm felt nearly numb. Instead, he relied on his grip strength, swinging himself gently, first right, then left, then right again, until he had enough momentum to reach the rail with his right hand, his left wrist feeling like it might break. He pulled up with both arms until he could hook an elbow over the rail, then swing his left leg up and over.

He collapsed on the tile floor, the effort exhausting. He took a few deep breaths to reoxygenate his blood then rose to his feet.

Not the smoothest start, Brennan told himself. *But we're on the ninth floor; here's betting they didn't even lock the patio door...*

He opened the door and peeked down the neighboring hallway. Halfway along, near the ceiling, a security camera panned slowly back and forth. He waited until it began to turn away from his direction, then followed the wall, flattening himself against it once he was under the camera. As it panned down the hall toward the balcony, he moved quickly to the next corner. There were more cameras, this time at each end of the hall. Trying to avoid them all was going to prove impossible, he knew, but the less time on camera, the less chance there was of him being spotted by a bored guard at the front desk, tasked with watching multiple switching feeds all night.

At the end of the hallway was a door. Jonah wanted things handled quietly, Brennan knew. He withdrew the six-inch tube from his belt pouch and loaded a dart into one end. A guard circled back and passed in front of the entrance. Brennan blew hard into one end of the pipe, the dart finding the guard's neck unerringly. The man looked surprised, irritated. His hand drifted to his neck and he snatched at the dart to remove it, the powerful sedative kicking in at the same time, the effort spasmodic. He collapsed to the floor unconscious.

Brennan moved to the end of the hall and checked the man for his phone and electronic key card. There was at least one more guard, he knew, likely in the suite, and then the men in the lobby to be handled. He doubted he could talk Pon into rappelling down the side of the building. He reached into the waist pouch and withdrew a second dart, before loading the blow pipe. He swiped the key card against the door lock with his other hand and turned the handle on a green light.

He pushed the door open quickly, anticipating a professional, alert to danger. He crouched as he did so, lowering his target profile and surprising the guard. The man had been standing just beyond the door and was still trying to pull the pistol from his shoulder holster when Brennan's dart found its mark.

In the room were a pair of queen-sized beds, a floor lamp and bureau, like any hotel room. Pon was sitting on the end of one of the queen-sized beds. He rose, a surprised look on his face. 'I thought you'd been killed.'

'Not this week. Are you hurt?'

'No. Santerra is busy with something but was going to be visiting me shortly for a discussion, I was told. I took it to mean some sort of ultimatum. Or perhaps he simply planned to kill me.'

'Is there any point in lecturing a man of your... advanced life experience on how dumb it was to borrow money from a gangster?'

'Probably not. I'm acutely aware of how much trouble I'm in.'

'Are you acutely aware of a route we can take out of this building? You don't look like rappelling would be your strength. But it sounds like Santerra is tied up with some sort of dinner.'

'I noticed an emergency exit sign on the other doors by the elevators. Maybe there are back stairs?' Pon suggested.

'Okay, that's a start. If they lead to the back door, we might have minimal opposition other than the building's rear guard. Lead the way, professor.'

Pon rose and led them both out of the room. 'The elevators are the end of this corridor,' he said.

The lobby in front of the elevators was perhaps fifteen-by-twenty feet square, like a small room, with a door on the far wall. Pon nodded toward it. 'That's it.'

The elevator shuddered slightly as it came to a stop. The door pinged and slid open, and Brennan turned to face it.

His eyes widened.

17/

LOS ANGELES

The computer screen was blurry, a photo increased in size and resolution artificially, details slowly being filled in by a piece of software that cost more than Drabek's apartment.

'What am I looking at here, Vic?'

Sgt. Vic Ady, the officer tasked with learning to use the arcane application, looked over his shoulder at the detective and beamed proudly. 'That, my friend, is your suspect, coming out of an electronics store on Brentwood, taken by the security camera in the lobby of the apartment building across the street. But that's not the best part.'

'Which would be?'

'Watch the birdie.' Ady pushed a button and a sequence of photos played out in a rapid-fire slideshow. A blurry Ben Levitt crossed the street and got into a nineties-model Jeep Cherokee. Ady stopped the slideshow on the final panel, then zoomed in on the license plate. 'Stolen off Hollywood Boulevard two days ago.'

'Maybe he knows his Paul Joseph credit cards are compromised,' Drabek said. 'Vic, you know how many cheap motels there are within two miles of that store?'

'A whole shitload,' Ady said.

'Eloquently put as always. Exactly. A whole shitload.'

Ady looked back at him again. 'You know I have to send this up to Cummins in Homicide, right Normie?'

Drabek clapped a hand on his shoulder. 'Just don't mention that I saw this already, okay? The speed Terry moves at, I might have a chance to sweep those dives and find this guy before he complains to the captain.'

Ady swivelled in his computer chair. 'Why're you so hot on this guy anyway? He stopped being your problem as soon as he iced somebody.'

'Yeahhh.... it's complicated. There's this young lady...'

'Ohhh...'

'No, it's not like that. Really. She's younger than...' He'd been about to say Nicole. It had been four years since his daughter's heroin overdose but he still thought of her in the present, as if he might wake up one morning and find it had all just been a horrible dream. 'She's thirty, tops. Her man went missing, she's freaked out, and she had a hard life.'

'Ah. That makes more sense. Norm Drabek, detective with a soft spot the length of the San Andreas fault.'

'Yeah, well, she's had a rough time of it. This guy was her white knight, and... I don't know, Vic, there's just something weird about this one, something interesting.'

'You are intrigued.'

'I am.'

'You have to keep digging into it.'

'I do. You know how it is...'

Vic had been Homicide for a decade before becoming a desk sergeant. 'Oh yeah. Still have the itch occasionally.'

'How do you handle that?'

'I keep a little bottle of formaldehyde in my desk. Every time it comes on me, I take a little sniff and get reminded of all the trips to the morgue.'

'That'd do it.'

'Oh yeah. You think you'll find this cat before Cummins?'

'I hope so.'

'It's going to break your young friend's heart, you realize.'

'Yeah... yeah, Vic, it will.'

Zoey watched the electronics store from the front passenger seat of Drabek's unmarked squad car. He'd been in there for nearly ten minutes, which didn't surprise her. He'd seemed nothing if not methodical. But the place would soon be closing. How many questions could a guy ask, anyway?

He'd also taken on a grimmer look most of the time, and Zoey was a good judge of character. He was trying to put off talking to her about Ben, she knew, about the fact that he was being hunted for murder, and that maybe her life with him wasn't going to go back to what it had been.

She knew all of that already. She was telling herself, still, that it wasn't entirely true, that there had to be some other rationale. She'd spent the night prior on Valentyna's couch crying herself to sleep, so angry at him, for lying to her, and for loving her in the first place, or pretending to. She couldn't really believe it, though. There had to be some explanation, some middle point they could come to in which everyone came out of this okay.

Everyone except Paul Joseph. She leaned on her right fist, elbow against the passenger side window and frowned, thinking back to the horrible sight of the decomposing body in the morgue. But maybe... maybe there was another explanation, some natural cause of his death, with Ben only getting involved after the fact...

Oh God, sweetie, give your head a shake, she told herself. *For everything that was right about him, just like everything else in your life, this has gone wrong.*

She felt her anger rise again; if nothing else, this time she wanted an explanation. For once in her life she'd made all the right choices, said and done all the right things. And again, she'd been saddled with a bad guy.

But Zoey wasn't taking it lying down.

She looked over at the store again. Drabek sure was taking his sweet time. She opened the glove box, bored and curious. It was stuffed full of paperwork and more than a few citations, of both the speeding and parking variety. She smirked at that and wondered if Drabek would blame Pace. They seemed to have a good partnership that way, easy going, respectful without being uptight.

She almost didn't notice the small patch of dark brown plastic between the car documents. She moved them aside.

The pistol was large and clipped in a half-sized speed holster. She let it sit there for a moment and contemplated whether to pick it up at all. Doubtless Drabek had either forgotten it or hadn't planned on her nosing around.

She reached into the glove box hesitantly and picked it up. It was bulkier than she'd expected, and she bounced it slightly in her palm to judge the heft.

'I like to be an optimist and assume I won't have to use that.'

The voice caught her by surprise, and she juggled the gun back into the glovebox. 'Norm! I mean, Detective...'

He got back into the car.

'Norm is fine. Don't mess around with those things, you hear?'

'Yes! Of course! I apologize for even picking it up. I was just...'

'Bored. Yeah, I've done my share of stakeouts in cars over the years and the longer you have to sit, the worse it is. We used to order pizza to the car sometimes. But believe me, fifteen minutes is nothing. You ever think maybe you've got the attention deficit thing there?'

'I think it's just the circumstances,' she said. 'I've got a lot on my mind.'

'True enough. Apologies for the remark,' he said. 'Anyway, the clerk said Ben came in and picked up about twelve hundred dollars worth of stuff the day after he skipped out on you. The kicker is he said he'd be back for more in a week's time and wanted a couple of other things ordered.'

'Then we just wait for him?'

'No. He used Paul Joseph's credit to pay for that stuff. If he's returned to Joseph's house and seen us there, he knows the card is compromised, which means he can't come back here, either. But if he was planning on doing so, his motel or borrowed space is probably near here.'

Zoey felt a flutter of anticipation. Near here? That meant the police might find him soon, which might give her the answers she was looking for -- although probably not the ones she wanted.

MERIDA

The taxi driver opened the rear door, a pair of Bruno Magli pumps stepping out into the hot evening air.

Daisy Lee's black cocktail dress showed enough leg to get attention, not that it was really needed. She already had a date for the evening. Santerra's underling had been bribed to arrange his escort via one of numerous agencies owned by the People's Liberation Army intelligence department.

Santerra had a taste for Asian women. Lee had no intention of honoring the string of perverse requests his handlers had left with the agency; but getting close during Santerra's dinner party would make him as vulnerable as he could be. If necessary, she supposed, he would gladly let Raymond Pon loose in order to save his testicles.

The building was tall by Merida's standard, one of a handful of towers grouped together in the north central district, mostly hotels. Santerra's extensive intelligence file suggested he owned it outright. His equally extensive history of precursor chemical shipments from Asia suggested he paid for it with methamphetamine.

She scanned the street quickly before

approaching the front door guards. She didn't have to say anything and was obviously expected, as the doors opened ahead of her without a word.

A serious-looking man with busy grey-white hair, a blue blazer and gold cufflinks was sitting at the security desk. Lee approached him with a smile.

Before she could say anything, he gave her a perfunctory smirk and then pointed toward the pair of elevators. 'He's on the twelfth floor in his personal quarters.'

In the elevator, she was tempted to check on the pistol strapped to her thigh or the knife and shuriken secreted in her sash. But wary of security cameras, she stuck to her character.

Daisy couldn't get Macau out of her mind. It had been years since she'd fought someone other than her instructors who could ably block and counter with her. But the American had done it with relative ease. She suspected it was only his hesitancy in hitting a woman close to a hundred pounds lighter that had given her an edge. Daisy had no great desire to hurt anyone, let alone someone just doing his job. If they met again, however, she knew she could not show mercy.

The elevator doors pinged and slid open. Santerra's apartment was grandiose, filling the top floor. Outside the rosewood front door, a pair of hulking guards stood at ease. Along with those in the lobby and outside the front and back doors, she counted at least a half-dozen protectors, and there were probably more. The ministry wanted things handled quietly; the North Korea situation practically demanded it.

One of the guards gazed over her from head to toe then smirked sleazily before buzzing the door for her with his proximity pass card then holding it open.

The man on the other side of the door wore a white linen suit; it matched the furniture in the gargantuan living room, as if by odd design. On the wall adjacent to the front door was a flat screen television. He turned it off with a remote control, took a sip from the whiskey glass in his other hand, then nodded her way as if they were old acquaintances.

'Ah, you must be Lucy,' he said in Spanish. 'You are even lovelier than your picture.'

He was squat and overweight, with a wispy brown beard and moustache. A gold Rolex dangled from a loose bracelet on one wrist, and his other hand featured several rings. 'I'm very pleased to meet you, Señor Santerra,' she said, offering a hand for him to kiss.

'Charming,' he said. 'Such poise! You will be a most elegant dinner date tonight my dear.'

'I look forward to it, Señor.'

'Please... Call me Ramon.' He walked over to the bar along the opposite wall and poured himself more scotch. 'A drink?'

'White wine?'

He smiled. 'Of course. An elegant drink for an elegant woman. This... thing tonight, the party. It is not important. But the people who come to these things think they are, and it is for business reasons that I must put my best foot forward.'

'I understand.'

'Be as social as you like, just don't say anything controversial.'

'Certainly, Ramon, it will be my pleasure.'

He approached her, placing one thick, stubby hand around her waist, running it from the small of her back down until it was cupping one of her buttocks. 'We'll get to that part later,' he leered.

Lee had the urge to headbutt him between the eyes and break his nose; instead, she merely smiled. 'I shall give you a night you will never forget,' she promised. 'Is there anyone particular you would like me to focus on during the dinner?'

'Jorge Gasol, the politician. He's old and smells of mothballs, but he's also a complete letch, a self-appointed Don Juan. He sits on the police commission and could be of value to me.'

'Of course.'

'When we get downstairs, I will be seated at the head of the table. Take the chair directly to my right. The one on the left is reserved for Martino, my head of security.'

'Will he join us there?'

'No, he'll accompany us down from the apartment.'

Damn. Lee had counted on isolating Santerra for long enough to get Pon's location out of him. Dealing with a bodyguard would necessitate a change of plans. 'Perhaps we should spend some time in your bedroom before the dinner -- to ease some of the pressure of the night.'

But Santerra didn't like that suggestion. 'No no, everything is set. Do not involve yourself in my affairs while you are here.' He appeared stern for a moment, then softened. 'Come, I'll show you where the powder room is so that you can splash your face.'

The half bathroom was just down a short hallway from the living room, on the way to what Lee presumed was Santerra's master suite. She didn't need the refresher, but Lee appreciated the moment of peace to figure out her next step. The bodyguard was unlikely to be anything special. It was possible she could even turn it to her advantage. She removed the pistol and suppressor and checked its magazine and chamber.

She flushed the toilet for sound effect, then followed the marble-floored corridor back toward the living room. Before she could reach it, she heard a man's voice.

'.... I tell you about bringing in these girls without talking to me?'

'Martino, she's just a whore. Will you relax, man?'

'Do you know how many enemies you have in this city right now? Whose agency? Who owns her?'

'Eh? I don't know. She's just a whore. My God, you see a conspiracy around every corner...'

'And one of your competitors probably pays her.

Think about that for a moment, please, patron. Did you even have her searched?'

The drug lord sounded exasperated. 'You're being paranoid now. Goddammit, Julian...'

Lee hung back from the end of the corridor to listen for a moment. 'I'm being practical. A little paranoia amounts to taking thirty seconds to search someone. What? You think she'll be offended? Like you said, she's just a whore.'

She'd heard enough and strolled back into the room casually. 'Who's just a whore?' she asked pleasantly.

'You,' Martino said. 'Get over here, now.'

She swung her hips as she sashayed over to him.

'Ay ay ay,' Santerra professed. 'If something's going to kill me...'

Martino shot him a disappointed look. Lee looked him over and smiled.

'Are you planning to search me?' Lee asked demurely. 'You have such... big hands.'

He approached her, unimpressed. Lee ran through the variables and likely outcomes of her limited options. There was a high probability he'd insist on searching her, and would find the pistol; and if they came to blows and he was prepared, his size advantage was considerable: the mustachioed protector was over six feet, probably close to two hundred pounds, and packed with muscle.

'That's exactly what I'm...' Before he could finish the sentence, Lee sprung forward, rising up from beneath his chin and hammering the palm of her hand into the bridge of his nose, driving it backwards into his brain. Without a pause, she quarter-turned then used the extra momentum to drive the side of her hand hard into his windpipe, crushing it. Martino collapsed face first to the floor, stone dead.

Santerra was so shocked by the sudden explosion of ferociousness that his mouth dropped open and his cigar fell out. Before he could move, Lee had removed the pistol and suppressor from her thigh holster and trained it on him. 'Now you and I are going to have a little talk, señor, and then we're going to take a little walk.'

'You won't get away with this, you little bitch. I have men all over this building.'

'Yes. But most of them are downstairs in the conference hall waiting for your big birthday dinner. Now, while I cover you, you're going to lean out of the doors to this place and tell the two guards to go downstairs for the event, and that Martino will escort us down. Do it confidently, because I'm not sure at this point how much I even need you in order to accomplish my objective.'

Santerra's head slumped. 'The scientist. I should have known he would be more trouble.'

'He has cost you a lot of money. If I were you, I'd be glad to be rid of him,' she suggested.

'Not before I get some of that money back,' Santerra said. 'You know how many armed men I have in this building? Across this city? You won't survive the night.'

'Where is he?'

'Why should I tell you?'

'Because if you don't, I'll start breaking limbs, starting with your fingers and toes.'

He appeared to believe her. 'The ninth floor. But you won't get past the guards.'

'That's where you come in, Mr. Santerra. You're going to come along as my date for the evening and get us past any trouble.'

'So maybe I refuse. Maybe I'm not afraid of dying and don't like being used.'

'Okay. Then I shoot you in the head now, and go look for myself.'

He shrugged. 'When you put it that way...'

She walked behind him, one arm hidden so that she could keep the pistol pressed against the small of his back as they made their way to the door. 'Keep in mind that if I have to shoot you in this position, the bullet will go through your spine. You won't die, but I doubt you'd ever walk again. Or order any prostitutes.'

They opened the door. Santerra leaned out. 'You two, go downstairs and get drunk with the rest. Martino will bring me down in a few minutes.'

Lee could just barely hear the footsteps as they made their way over to the elevator. A few seconds later, it pinged and she heard the doors slide open. She waited thirty seconds. 'Okay, let's go.'

They waited for the elevator to return.

'Whatever they're paying you, whoever's behind this... I'll double it,' he said.

She ignored him. The elevator doors slid open. 'Inside,' she said, pushing him forward with the tip of the barrel. All of the guards would be downstairs except for those on the ninth floor. The trick was going to be getting a second of advantage. They'd move directly to the elevator when it stopped, she knew.

'When the doors open on the ninth floor, I'm going to kiss you,' she said. 'The pistol will be pointed at your internal organs, so nothing tricky, please.' The idea was simple: the doors would open, the guards would see them embracing and drop their guard in surprise, and she would eliminate both.

The simplest plans usually worked best, Lee had found.

18/

LOS ANGELES

'You wanted to see me, Cap?' Drabek closed the captain's office door behind him.

'Norman.' Capt. Forrest Dean was in full dress uniform, as usual, an irritated expression on his face. 'You know why I'm calling you in here, right?'

Drabek played dumb. He raised both hands in an expression of befuddlement. 'You got me.'

'Really? So, you haven't been stepping all over a homicide investigation for the last couple of days because of some missing persons bug you have up your backside?'

'Oh, that.'

'Oh that, indeed. Detective Cummins tells me you've ignored his emails asking for updates on whatever angle you're working.'

'Well... not ignoring exactly; I just don't check email that often...'

'It's a new century full of new technology, Detective Drabek. Please do us the courtesy of catching up to the rest of us.'

'Yes, cap.'

'And send everything you've got to Cummins tout suite. You got it?'

'Sure.' Dean wasn't exactly his biggest fan, but he wasn't a ballbreaker either. He played it straight. 'Anything else?'

The captain's gaze narrowed. 'Norman, do you have anything else you'd like to talk to me about?'

'I... don't think so,' Drabek said uncertainly. What was he getting at?

'Look, this is the third missing person's in the last six months that has quickly become someone else's file, and each time, I've had to get involved to tell you to stick with your own case load and let it go. You're a great detective, Norman, and you know we think the world of you. I can't help but think this relates to your daughter's passing.'

Drabek just nodded a little at that. 'Uh huh,' he said. 'Uh huh.'

'I know that prior to her body being found she'd been missing for several weeks, and we accepted that it may have been part of your motivation for asking to come over to Detective Support and Vice.'

'Sure.'

'But you can't hang on to every missing kid like it's your personal responsibility to fix humanity. Do you need more time to speak with a professional...?'

Drabek waved that off. 'No! No, no, absolutely not. Look, I get it cap...'

'The Los Angeles Police Department is a team...'

'A team. Absolutely.'

The way the officer looked at him, Drabek knew he wasn't convinced. But he didn't have to worry about that. He just had to send his file up to Cummins by email. Of course, if he spelled his name wrong in the email address, which can happen, it might get delayed by a few days.

And surely everyone would understand that.

MERIDA

The elevator doors slid open abruptly. Brennan's eyes widened. The couple were deeply embraced in a lip lock. He knew the woman: Daisy Lee. The man looked a little like the mugshot he'd found of Ramon Santerra, only shorter than he'd imagined and about a hundred pounds heavier.

The woman's right eye opened in mid lip lock and spotted him, widening in surprise. She pulled back from the shorter man slightly, then used her right hand to slam his head into the side of the elevator car. Santerra crumpled to the floor. Lee took three steps forward and launched into a high snapping kick that Brennan blocked with crossed forearms. She was on him in a split second, following the move with a flurry of blows that he blocked with precision, before finding an opening and returning a punch of his own, catching her hard.

Lee went down and Brennan tried to pin her so that he could rain blows down, finish the fight quickly. But she managed to sweep her feet up and around his neck, yanking him over sideways and onto the floor then following it with a hammering side fist to the solar plexus. The spy felt his wind go out.

Before he could roll away, she spun on one hip and rose to a crouch, the silenced pistol emerging from her thigh holster. Lee had the winded American in her sights. She squeezed the trigger... and then the lights went out, and Lee found herself dreaming, floating through a dark space, her unconsciousness sudden and complete.

Brennan wheezed his way back to breathing. Prof. Pon was standing over Daisy Lee's prone body, a large standing ashtray in both hands. There was no sign of blood, which suggested maybe he hadn't killed her.

'I didn't know what else to do,' he said.

'Don't worry about her,' he said as he got up. 'She doesn't deserve it.' Brennan looked back at the elevator doors, which had closed. 'Come on, we've got to move.'

They crossed the atrium to the stairs. Brennan was about to yank the door open when he saw the elevator doors slide open again. Santerra stumbled out, a pistol in his right hand and a groggy look on his face. 'You sons of bitches!' he said in Spanish. He raised the gun, but before he could squeeze off a shot, Brennan had closed the gap between them, a stunner blow to the wrist forcing the gangster to drop his weapon. A sharp kick to the side of Santerra's knee forced him down to the ground. Brennan threw a hard uppercut, and the fat man went down again, his body spasming slightly as it fought to regain consciousness. Brennan kneeled beside him and removed the two zip ties from his pouch. He looped one over Santerra's wrists, another around his ankles, then pulled them tight.

They took the concrete stairs to the first level. 'I've got a car parked across the street from the backdoor,' Brennan said as they approached the emergency exit to the rear corridor. 'Chances are good there are still exterior guards, but they're looking for people coming in; they won't be wary of anyone leaving, which gives me a few seconds to act. When that happens, you hit the deck.'

The older man nodded. 'If anything happens, I would like you to know...'

Brennan shushed him. 'Save it, professor. I'm just here for information, I'm not your savior.'

He opened the door slowly. There was a guard immediately to his right. Brennan grabbed him quickly by the shirt collar and pulled him through the door into the stairway, his left arm snaking around the man's neck to choke off his air while the other hand covered his mouth. The guard pulled at his arm and kicked for a few seconds before passing out. Brennan reached into the small pouch at his waist and took out duct tape and a steel-reinforced zip tie. The tape went across the unconscious man's mouth and the zip tie around his left wrist and right ankle.

'I don't understand...' Pon said as he worked. 'Why don't you just leave him? Why did you stop to tie up Santerra?'

As he said the words, the man's right leg began to spasm involuntarily, kicking slightly. Then his eyes opened and he looked surprised, kicking hard at his shackles.

'That's why,' Brennan said. 'In the movies, they stay unconscious for hours. In real life, you get maybe a minute, if you're lucky.'

Pon looked over at the closed door. 'Then your

lady friend will be right along, I imagine. There was another door at the end of the hallway...'

'That's where we're headed.'

They walked the length of the hallway to the back door. 'I expect two more guys standing outside of it. If we're lucky, neither of them is Einstein...'

He reached the door and gently depressed the latch button and pushed it forward just enough to hold the lock mechanism in place. Then, with the door resting ajar, Brennan kicked it as hard as he could. The door flew open a few feet then smacked resoundingly with a thunk that sounded a lot like a grapefruit hitting pavement. Brennan charged forward, lowering his shoulder to barge the door open again. This time it flew mostly open, once again hammering someone standing behind it. Just ahead of the steps, on the sidewalk, a second guard was fumbling for his pistol. Brennan raised his suppressed Smith & Wesson, the angry shot muted but still loud, the bullet striking the man between the eyes. He dropped his weapon as he fell to his knees before pitching face forward on the cement.

Brennan turned to the dazed other man, the side of his hand travelling in a quick arc, hammering the man in the face, smashing tooth and bone. Traffic passing honked their horns at the sight but didn't slow down. The guard went down to one knee and Brennan followed with a hard kick to the jaw that knocked him senseless.

He nodded across the street to his rental. 'That's our ride.'

The darkness and fog of unconsciousness gave way to sound, and light, and the creeping reassertion of self. Lee shook the cobwebs out and looked around, squinting against the migraine headache that had resulted from the blow to the back of her head.

Damn it. She'd had the better of the American

again and someone else had snuck up on her. The professor? Probably.

'Hnnngh...' Someone was groaning a few feet away. She shifted her view to just in front of the elevator doors. Santerra was trying to pick himself up. That wasn't going to help anyone. She rose to her feet and walked over to him, then took a healthy backswing with her leg, before kicking the gangster hard on the chin once more. His eyes rolled back into his head and he slumped back down to the ground.

The door on the other side of the lobby clicked and began to swing open. Lee sprinted toward it, arriving just as a guard's head poked its way into the room. She continued in full flight but leaped forward, spinning head over heels in midair, the overhead kick striking the crouching guard on top of the skull, his body clattering to the ground and propping the door open. Before the man behind him could react, Lee sprung back to her feet, a fist flying into the open gap, catching the second guard in the solar plexus and driving the wind out of him. He heaved for breath and clutched at his chest, opening him up for a series of hard shots to the face. He slumped down to the cement in the stairwell.

She grabbed a proximity security card from one of the men, then clambered over them and took the stairs down toward the rear exit. Perhaps she'd gotten lucky and the American was still within distance.

At the top of the final flight of stairs, Lee heard a commotion below and slowed to a halt. She peered around the corner; a man in sunglasses and a short-sleeved dress shirt was trying to drag an unconscious guard into the building. The back exit made the most sense; doubtless Brennan had already passed through, with the professor.

She quietly made her way down the final flight. The man saw her once she was all the way down, and even while concerned for his friend and crouched at his side, his hand immediately went for the gun inside his coat. He was quick, quicker than most, and he had it clear of the holster for just long enough to have Lee launch a spinning side kick that knocked it from the gangster's hand. He smiled, reaching into his coat pocket and withdrawing a butterfly knife, spinning its two sides apart and together again so that the long, sharp blade was exposed.

He ran forward, swinging it in a pair of wide arcs, Lee backing up to the opposite wall. She looked around for a weapon; seeing nothing, she pulled the long strand of white pearls over her neck, bunching them at one end for a handle then swinging them like a short lariat. The guard smiled wickedly, noting his advantage, then thrust quickly for her stomach with the tip of the blade. Lee dodged sideways, slapping the pearls toward his knife wrist, the strand wrapping around it and the baubles tangling up so that he was snagged. She yanked sideways, the knife flying from his hand and his arm pulled away from his body, exposing his face; Lee rose onto her right heel and delivered four rapid, sharp kicks to the man's face and throat. He collapsed, and at the last second, she let the pearls go, the strand breaking, the little white spheres cascading across the concrete floor.

Thank goodness they were fake, she thought. *At least, I think they were fake. I hope to hell they were, or that was expensive.*

She opened the back door slowly.

The guard was trying to rise from the parking lot asphalt. He was young, she figured, barely twenty. He scrambled for the pistol nearby and Daisy drew hers from her thigh holster, both turning at the same time, guns trained on one another but the guard still down on one knee, beaten and frightened.

His hand was shaking, the gun vibrating visibly.

'What's the point?' she said directly. 'At worst, we shoot each other. At best, one of us walks away. Santerra won't give a shit either way. Drop the gun and kick it over and I'll let you live.'

The young man ignored her, saying nothing. But

his hand continued to shake, worsening by the second.

'If you try to shoot back at me right now,' she said, 'you could miss me by ten feet based on how much the muzzle is moving. Whereas my hand is stable, calm, and I will kill you if you don't drop the gun.'

The shaking increased. He leaned up onto one elbow and used his other hand to steady it. Then he frowned and looked right through her, as if there were just bigger matters to consider. He let the gun drop to the asphalt and timidly raised both hands.

Twenty yards past him, a taxi pulled up across the street to let out a passenger.

Timing is everything, Lee noted.

At the hotel, Brennan squired the professor to his room. Both men were nervous, but the old colonial building was dark, quiet and private.

Brennan gestured for him to take one of the two guest chairs. 'Okay, professor. This better be a hell of a story after all of that.'

Pon relaxed a little. 'It was believed to be the pet project of Dorian Fan, the high-ranking committee member who disappeared in the Nineteen Eighties whilst under investigation.'

'We know that much already.'

'What you don't know is that after he murdered his colleague, who was charged with auditing his expenses, Fan travelled to Harbin where he met with Master Yip Po, the former head of intelligence training for the People's Army. Yip was under house arrest at the time and, as you may already be aware, later disappeared completely. The feeling at the time was that he was smuggled out of the country by Jiang Qing loyalists. But first, he met with Fan and they discussed Legacy.'

'Okay, but what is it? I mean, operationally?'

Pon shrugged a little. 'Vague. Initially it involved

placing sleepers into dozens of different American communities, but the logistics were apparently too haphazard, and the methodology was experimental. It fell apart.'

'So then...?'

'As I said, it's vague. But the authorities were sure Fan had used some of the millions he stole to procure elements of the plan.'

Brennan wasn't buying it. 'Where would he find dozens of sleepers able to adapt to American life and disappear? That doesn't seem feasible. Getting past the recruitment aspects, and that there would be little point in pursuing this without trained agents, there's the fact that this was thirty years ago; surely they'd have long since exposed themselves or gone home.'

'As I said, the methodology was innovative, but shaky,' said Pon. 'They were going in quite a different direction. They used Americans.'

19/

PLENTY, MONTANA
MAY 3, 1984

THE GIRL AND THE BOY HELD HANDS and looked up at the stars in the clear night sky. It was rare for the sky to be so clear, the clouds hiding as if doing them a favor, gracing them with the sheen of a million twinkling dreams. Their hands felt warm together and they were both smiling, and happy, and content in the moment. At eleven years old, neither would want to call it love, not without making icky faces and sticking out their tongues, as if poisoned with double helpings of liver.

Neither had anyone else, not really. They had their parents, and their teachers, and their school leaders. But they only trusted one another.

'You think there's anyone out there?' asked the girl. Her name was Amelia, but everyone called her Amy, and she hated both names completely. She like Mia, but it had never stuck, and the other girls at school had mocked her for trying to make it so.

'I think there has to be,' Chris said. He was shorter than Amy, by at least three inches. She'd already had a growth spurt, but both were still blissfully short of their teens, and had yet to start worrying about even the most mundane things. 'I think it would be a damn arrogant thing, to say it was only us out here, floating around alone in the universe; that all of that is just a show.'

She drew her attention away from the stars for long enough to glance at him and smile. 'That's a nice way of looking at it.'

'Thank you.'

'You're like that, seeing the good in things.'

He smiled but was embarrassed and didn't know what to say back. So he blushed a little... then punched her in the upper arm with the side of his fist. 'You're stupid,' he said.

She hit him back. 'No, you are!'

He tried to grab her and put her in a headlock, but she snatched his hands into hers and they wrestled for a minute, before the girl forced him down onto his back and pinned him. 'Give!' she demanded.

'No way!'

'Give, or you get a wet willie!'

'No!'

She put her knees over his upper arms so that he couldn't move then used her free hand, wetting one finger in her mouth, then jabbing it into his ear. 'Wet Willie!' the girl yelled. 'Wet...'

The siren sounded loud and clear, a blaring klaxon just audible from their position a half-mile from town, like an air raid warning. It only sounded once, but that was all that was required.

'It's time,' she said, getting up, then offering him a hand to his feet. 'We have to move! Quickly!'

They hurried down the moonlit hill, the grass brown and yellow, dried out by the summer heat. The school was only two minutes away, the town's biggest building by some measure. It was bigger than six houses put together, Amy figured, and was home to a hundred students, so by most city standards it was tiny. But it had a gym with a stage, and it had four classrooms.

And, of course, there was the basement. The thought of it caught her, and she slowed down, fighting her own momentum from the hill until she was standing there with a dazed look in her eyes. Chris saw it and called out. 'Hey! Hey, Amy!'

She looked over at him, her distraction broken. 'Sorry. I ... I was just thinking about how this... about the last time.'

He folded his arms self-protectively and looked away, intent on showing no weakness. 'You have to be tough. You know that.' He frowned, remembering a mantra. 'We must be proud, of ourselves and our country. We must be strong, as strong as steel forged in fire. We must be clever, as guileful and contradictory as a trap baited with petals. We must be firm yet flexible, like a mighty river that cuts through barest rock.'

She looked past him at the school, the trepidation still there, the anxiety fluttering in the pit of her stomach. Then she looked at Chris again, so strong and so sure of himself. And then she felt an onrush of positivity, a peaceful ease settling in. Soon, the session would be over for another week, and another lesson would be learned, and they would both be closer to the next stage.

But first... first, there was the basement.

A few dozen yards from the building's front doors, just down the main hallway, students were lined up from the top of the stairs to the bottom floor, waiting to enter the session room. Mr. Shou and Principal Anders looked on sternly.

'Principal looks upset,' Amy whispered to Chris. 'Do you think the first three went poorly?'

'It wouldn't matter. They're always serious.' Then he noticed how worried she looked. 'Why? What's wrong?'

She didn't wish to show weakness, even to Chris, and she hesitated. 'It's nothing,' she said. 'Nothing to worry about.'

But he could tell she was bothered. 'Let me guess: more nightmares?'

She nodded. 'I think it's the drug. It only happens after Session, like it's trying to stick in my head or something, even when it's supposed to be gone.'

'They told us, remember? It builds up in your blood...'

He was trying to solve it for her. She hated that. He never just listened. As much as she liked him, he was still a boy, still always trying to take charge. 'I know that. It's just... look, just forget it, okay?'

She felt an elbow dig into her back, just below her last rib.

'Surprise, surprise: Amelia's scared!'

She turned and gave Donny a shove. He was a heavier boy, known for bullying his peers and delighting in tormenting them. He shoved her back and she bumped into Chris, who in turn bumped the child ahead. 'Hey! Watch it!' the kid admonished.

'I'm not scared of you, Donny Taylor!' she declared, her little fists balled up and ready. 'You better quit it, or I'm telling Principal Anders!'

'Shhh!' Chris muttered. 'Both of you better shut up or we're all in trouble.' He glanced at the principal and saw he wasn't paying attention. 'Next time we might not be so lucky.'

'You're scared!' Donny whispered to her. 'You're chicken. I heard you asked to skip...'

'Did not!' Amy said. 'That was Becky.' Becky was her little sister, three years younger and wide-eyed, always clutching her teddy, Jack. They'd said she was too young to take part, but the principal and Mr. Shou had intervened personally. Becky had a big heart, they'd said, and needed special attention.

But she feared Session, that wasn't in doubt. Amy realized she hadn't seen her all afternoon. She frowned, trying to think what Becky had said to her that morning at the breakfast table, when she hadn't really been listening. It wasn't coming. She scanned the line behind them, looking for the girl. There were only twenty people waiting, to be split into the usual two groups of ten, then taken in one at a time. It would be nearly midnight by the time they finished.

She couldn't see her. Amy pulled on Chris' sleeve.

'What?'

'She's not here. My sister... she's not in line.'

He glanced up at the mesh-covered clock above

the doors. 'She has three minutes.'

They both knew the potential consequences of being late. The punishment would be harsh. Amy's eyes widened as the realization set in that she might not make it. 'We have to go look!' she insisted. 'Maybe she got distracted somehow...'

Donny snorted. 'Huh. Maybe she's just chicken like her big sister and her boyfriend.'

'Uh... Amy?'

The voice came from near the back of the line. She leaned out to see who it was. Jimmy Palmer's little head leaned out as well, further back. He was a small, timid boy, his black hair always a little mussed and the bags under his eyes deepening by the year. Jimmy seemed perpetually worried, as if he knew something about the future lost on the rest of them.

'Shut up, Jiminy Cricket!' Donny demanded. 'Or I'll beat your little ass again like last time.'

Jimmy quickly ducked back into the line. But a second later he popped his head out again and blurted, 'I saw her about ten minutes ago by the old oak, along Second Street.'

That was a solid five minutes from the school. Amy looked up at the clock again.

Two minutes.

'I have to go up and look,' she said.

'You'll lose your place in line,' Chris warned.

'You're not going to come?' Her voice seemed almost desperate and Chris felt an unfamiliar wave of guilt wash over him.

He looked around quickly. The teachers weren't paying attention. He knew his father would beat his ass if he found out he'd risked missing Session. He'd probably be okay about him losing his place in line, and he might even forgive him not taking advantage of the girl's weakness. But risking lateness was unforgivable. His butt would be tanned black and blue. Chris couldn't imagine how stricter parents -- like Amy's or Donny's -- might react.

'I'm going,' she said, pulling out of the line and

striding up the stairs, to the gasps of her classmates.

'Amy... wait!' Chris said. He followed her, cursing losing his place for the first time since the sessions began, when they were in preschool.

They ran up the stone steps to the main level, both educators watching them, hands in pockets, seemingly non-plussed by the last-second decision. Chris made it to the front doors first and flung them open. The wind had picked up and was gusting, the sky darkening, leaves rustling in the trees along Main Street, torn free, cascading onto the pavement below.

There was no sign of her.

'She's never going to make it,' Amy worried. 'I should go look for her.'

'She only has a minute-and-a-half,' Chris warned. 'That's probably not long enough to...'

Before he could finish the sentence, Amy grabbed his bicep with both hands and leaned in. 'Is that...? It's her!'

A few blocks away, a tiny figure had just turned a corner onto Main. The little girl wore a red sweater and blue shorts. She had strawberry blonde hair in natural curls that fell just below her shoulders. She must have seen the time on the nearby church steeple, because she began to sprint for the school, the clock counting down silently.

'Come on, Becky, run!' Amy screamed. 'They're going to close the doors! Run! RUN, BECKY! RUN!'

The wind rose and gusted, dust and dirt blowing off the road. Leaves filled the air, blowing across the street. The girl was just a block away and had seen them, but she was tiny, with barely nine-year-old legs. She charged ahead with all her might, as haphazardly as any small child on the run, stumbling, almost losing her balance.

Behind them, Principal Anders leaned in and wrapped fingers around the door handle. 'You both know the rules.'

Chris shot a glance at the clock, the second hand counting down. 'Thirty seconds!' he gasped.

'FASTER, GO FASTER!' Amy screamed, thunder rumbling through the clouds, the wind gusting, leaves swirling around the fluttering base of her sister's dress. 'FOR GOSH SAKES, RUN!'

The girl barreled ahead as fast as her tiny shoes could take her. She made it to the steps. She ran up one, then another... and then she tripped, her knees slamming into the concrete. 'Aahhh!' she cried out, both hands cupping the skinned knee, her task momentarily forgotten. She rubbed at the wound gently, tentatively, as the seconds ticked down and the rain began to spatter the concrete.

'No!' Amy's eyes widened. She checked the clock, the second hand approaching the hour. 'No, Becky, get up!' There was no time left to decide. Amy pushed past Chris and out the door. She bolted down four steps to the smaller girl, grabbed her by the collar and pulled her to her feet, stumbling and reluctant.

Principal Anders began to push the door shut.

'No! No... please...' Chris said, panicked, terrified at what would happen to them if they didn't make it. 'They have...' He looked at the clock as it counted down the final few seconds. Four... three... two... one...'

The two girls burst through the door together and stumbled to the ground as the principal pushed it closed. 'Barely, Miss Sawyer,' he said, staring down his nose at Becky. 'I do not need to remind you of what might happen if you missed Session. I think we all remember a certain young sinner named David Webber and what happened to him. Hmmm?'

Becky looked terrified. David Webber had disappeared months earlier and the school had made it known to parents that police suspected a sexual predator. They had been warned not to expect him to return alive. He'd been on his way to Session and late when he was taken.

'She won't make any trouble again sir, I promise!' Amy declared, hauling her baby sister to her feet. 'We'll just get back in line now...'

The principal nodded. 'The back of the line. And

Christopher... you go last. You didn't need to help them. They could've coped without you. It was a bad decision.'

Chris hung his head. 'Yes, sir.'

It took three more hours before Amy's turn came. She grasped her little sister's hand and gave it an affirming shake. 'Don't worry Becky, it'll be fine. It always is.'

The little girl pursed her lips, trying to be a big girl and not cry. She hated going through Session, even though she knew it would be good for them in the long run, just like her parents said. The wisdom of the Elders was unerring, a multi-generational pledge to follow the traditions of Plenty's residents. Amy smiled at her one more time, then pushed her way into the room.

The door swung closed behind her. The chamber was dark, the size of a small changing room or large doctor's office, barely lit in shades of red by bare crimson bulbs. Against the back wall, a cylindrical metal tank in the shape of a pill capsule sloped forward and down to the ground, a porthole-style circle of tempered glass three quarter of the way up.

Electrical leads and wires led from the back of the tank to a control panel and computer display, the letters green-on-black, resting on an adjacent metal table.

Mr. Shou stood beside the tank. 'Disrobe,' he said dispassionately. 'Have you taken your dose of the treatment?'

She nodded as she got undressed. She was glad she didn't have to speak back. She hated speaking to them, even though Master Yip told her she was gifted.

Amy had gone through the process twice a week since her fourth birthday, seven years earlier, and her modesty in front of the grown man had long since disappeared with clinical detachment. She hated the drug, not just because of how it affected their memories, but because it upset her stomach, just like milk. But her father didn't believe that, either, and the last time she'd tried to turn down breakfast cereal, he'd beaten her with his belt until her bones hurt.

Even the session was better than that, she reasoned, better than being in the house with him. At least... it had to be. She didn't remember much more than Chris or anyone else. There were nightmares, but they were fleeting, abstract images that she immediately forgot when she awoke each morning.

She put her foot on the first metal step alongside the apparatus. The tank would be cold at first, then near freezing, the water and gel solution covering everything except for her nose and the attached breathing apparatus that hung suspended from the tank door. Within minutes, she would lose all sensation in her body, and the drug would kick in. After an hour, the complete absence of sensation coupled with the total blackness of the tank would cause her mind to detach from reality, being taken to the place where answers lay, the place of universal truths and divine instruction.

The next day at school had been difficult. Principal Anders' morning sermon at assembly had been on the virtues of commitment and hard work, and he'd made a point to emphasize being timely, before staring twice at Becky with pointed disdain.

Amy made sure to keep an eye on her younger sibling through the day. After lunch, she tracked her down in the playground, where the younger children hung from the jungle gym and watched some of the boys play touch football. Becky wasn't paying attention, alone in the crowd, a vacant look on her sad little face.

'Don't worry, Sis... it's like Mr. Platt says in civics class: 'all things pass.'

'I don't get it,' the younger girl said.

'It means you won't feel like this forever. They'll have forgotten by next week that you were late, so long as you don't do it again. Do you get that?'

The girl nodded vigorously. She was only nine, and Amy knew it would be some time before she could give up the role of protector; Lord knew their father wasn't going to do it.

Jimmy Palmer sidled up to Becky. He was nine or ten, two classes below Amy and picked on by some of the bigger boys. But he seemed nice, and was always trying to be optimistic, to make the best of living in the small town. 'Don't worry, Becky!' he enthused. 'I've been late twice, and I'm okay! It's how hard you try next time that they care about.'

She glanced his way. 'You think?'

'I know for sure,' he said. 'It's going to be okay.'

The shove landed squarely between his shoulder blades with a powerful thump. Jimmy flew forward face-first into the ground. 'Shut up, Little Orphan Useless!' Donny Taylor insisted.

Jimmy rolled onto his back. Donny was beefy, with red hair and freckles. He stood over the terrified smaller youth. 'I ought to whup your little weirdo ass. What makes you so happy, huh? I ought to beat that smile off your face.'

'Please... Donny...' Jimmy implored, trying to skitter away on his backside.

Donny laughed at him. 'Look at this loser. I guess that's why your mom left your family, right Jiminy Cricket? Because she couldn't stand living with you and your old man? What does he do again? Oh yeah: he makes computer programs. Your father is a dweeb, Jimmy, a four-star nerd.'

'Leave him alone.'

The voice came from Donny's right, toward the school. A handful of students were milling around watching the display, bored. Chris stood in front of them with both fists clinched.

'Or what, Platt? I'll whup your ass too, just as easy...'

The boys marched toward each other with

homicidal purpose. They met in the middle, Donny trying to stare down the smaller student, Chris looking up at him with a gaze that suggested he intended to give as good as he got. 'Yeah? Bring it on, fat boy,' Chris offered.

The bell rang, a piercing clang. Both boys looked up at it simultaneously. They knew the rules about ignoring the bell and what would happen if they didn't immediately go in for afternoon classes. They knew it wasn't worth it. 'We'll fight later,' Donny said.

'Be there or be square,' Chris said. His father had told him all about his war-hero grandfather, a Golden Gloves boxer before the Big One. He'd trained a little, and as big as Donny was, Chris figured he deserved a pop in the mouth. As they walked back to the main building, he made sure not to glance at the windows to see who was watching. He didn't want to show any weakness.

After school, Amy walked home alone. Chris lived next door but was nowhere to be seen. Becky got off an hour earlier and it was just a few blocks. It was the kind of small town, people said, where kids could be safe strolling the tree-lined streets on their own. The disappearance of David Webber hadn't changed that. People put it down to a drifter, a one-off occurrence. They weren't going to let it change the joy of small-town living, they'd all agreed at a town hall meeting.

Their house was boxy and serious, she thought, just like the Platts'. The difference was that the Platts kept theirs in nice condition, while her father and stepmom didn't seem to care. The dark blue paint on the Platt house was pristine and even. The white siding on the Sawyer house was sagging, the paint peeling. The lawn was a mess, her sister's toys scattered about among the ever-lengthening blades of grass. She felt a little ashamed each time she returned. Since her mother's death two years earlier and the introduction of her father's girlfriend, his tempers had gotten worse, his drinking more commonplace. She knew he lied and faked his reports to the Town Elders.

But she also knew if she said anything, he'd probably kill her. Or worse, take it out on Becky. She took a deep breath to prepare herself, then opened the rickety wooden gate and walked the short paving stone pathway to the front porch and door. She pushed the door open slowly, hoping it wouldn't squeak too loudly and attract attention. The last thing she ever wanted from her father was attention.

She could hear the television playing Dan Rather and the Evening News, something about America's moral failings. The usual background noise. Amy crept through the kitchen to the stairs, then up the two short flights to the landing above.

The floorboards creaked and groaned under her feet and she stopped short, her breath shallow, trying to listen past it for her father. The TV droned on, a commercial for something, the newsman's voice replaced by a higher pitch, just audible. She exhaled, then crept the last few steps to her door.

'AMELIA!' He bellowed it like an accusation, and a moment later Art Sawyer's worn boots were tromping across the Kitchen and up the stairs.

Amy ran into their room and closed the door. Becky was on her bed reading but she dropped the book and her gaze filled with fear at her sister's expression. 'Hide!' Amy demanded. 'Get under your bed! Don't argue, just do it!'

Becky scrambled to comply, the bedroom door flying open a moment after she'd disappeared into the shadowy recess.

'WHERE THE HELL WERE YOU?' her father demanded. He began to take off his belt. Unbuckling it, then sliding it through the loops in one tug, then wrapping it around his fist. 'I won't give you the buckle this time if you're honest with me.'

'I had a study session with Mrs. Carrier, our French teacher. But Daddy... I told you about it...'

His face turned red, then purple, the veins in his

neck and forehead bulging in tandem with his eyes, his balding pate the same angry hue. 'ARE YOU TALKING BACK TO ME, YOU LITTLE BITCH?!? GET OVER HERE.'

Under the bed, Becky covered her ears and shut her eyes tight. She knew it wouldn't be enough to shut out her sister's tortured sobbing.

It never did.

He beat her for nearly five minutes. He'd be careful, avoiding her face so that she had nothing to show the teachers or Elders. When the sound had finally subsided and Becky was sure he'd left, she uncovered her ears.

Becky wouldn't talk to Amy about it. She knew that was a mistake. The last time, she'd cried on her sister's shoulder only to be rebuked and slapped across the face. 'You're pathetic and weak,' Amy had said. 'You need to be made of stronger stuff if you're going to be my sister.'

So instead, she stayed under the bed, curled up in the shadows, until Amy went to the bathroom to clean herself up. Then Becky climbed back up onto her bed and under the covers, pulling them up tight over her head and wishing it all away.

The three days until the next session were long and warm, and Chris spent most of the evenings on the hill with Amy, looking down over the school and the town. His anxiety was getting worse, and he wasn't sure why. He knew he couldn't talk to her about it, that she'd be compelled to turn him in as unstable.

Then, the nightmares had begun.

It was a Monday, the session two days earlier, and Chris found himself sitting alone during recess, trying to remember the latest. He'd been caught in a maze, then cornered, then fighting for his life. The faces had been unfamiliar, the dream non-linear and jumbled. But he couldn't lose the unsettling feeling that he'd done something terrible. As the other students milled around the playground, he sat on top of the double-sided park bench with his knees up to his chest, wishing he was home in his room, alone.

'You okay, Chris?'

Chris snapped out of it. Jimmy had his hands thrust in his shorts pockets. He had pale blue t-shirt on that said 'Detroit Dodgers' in florid white-and-red text. 'Yeah... I mean, yes. Yes, I'm fine.' Then he scowled at the younger boy. 'It's not healthy to worry so much about others.'

'I know,' Jimmy said glumly. 'I guess I'm in my own head too much. That's what they tell me at Session. They get pretty mad with me.'

Another reason to stay away from him, Chris thought. Then he caught himself, a feeling of guilt settling into the pit of his stomach. 'Yeah... I guess that's kind of tough, right?' Then he stopped, frowning.

Jimmy turned to see what had caught Chris' attention. Donny Taylor was striding their way, looking as angry as ever.

'Hi.... Ah, hi, Don,' Jimmy stammered, attempting to defuse anything before it occurred.

The bully was having none of it. 'Did I say you could talk, pipsqueak!?' he spat. Then he punched the smaller boy in the shoulder. 'Sad little Jiminy Cricket...'

Chris jumped down from the table. 'You leave him alone, Donny. I warned you already.'

'Yeah?' Donny countered. He leaned in, a good four or five inches taller than his classmate. 'You sure talk a good game... faggot.'

Donny reached to push him, but Chris was expecting it. The bully did the same thing every time, using his bulk to force other kids down. He grabbed Donny by the lapels, falling backwards, letting his own weight and Donny's momentum take them both down, reaching up in mid fall to boot the bigger boy in the stomach. His foot acted like a tiny catapult, hurling the boy over his head. Donny slammed to the ground back-first.

Both boys struggled to their feet, Chris winning the race. From the corner of his eye he could see two of the instructors on the edge of the playground. They were nodding and gesturing his way. It was the throw, it had to be. Chris smiled. His judo practise had paid off and he'd found favor.

Donny wiped some blood from a skinned elbow. 'You can use all those wimp judo throws all you want, queerbo, but I'm still going to...'

Before he could finish the sentence, Chris stepped forward two paces and threw a left jab, catching Donny square. His nose snapped, then blood began to stream out. The bigger boy's eyes teared up completely and he tried to stop the blood flow with both hands. He looked around in a hazed panic, then ran toward the blurry school building, unaware of the critical onlookers. Donny hadn't gone eight feet when Jimmy stuck his foot out; the bigger boy still couldn't see and he tripped head on, his chin smashing into the playground asphalt, teeth breaking and coming loose.

There was a pause as the murmured shock of the moment rippled around the crowd like a slow-building avalanche. From the bench at the back of the yard, Chris saw the bigger boy raise both hands up to chest height, pushing up off the ground until he was on his knees. Then he pulled his t-shirt up to his mouth to wipe away the blood and broken teeth, before turning his head slowly to look back at Jimmy with an expression of abject rage.

He was interrupted by the whistle, a two-tone blast loud enough to carry for miles. Everyone turned to the source. Principal Anders and Mister Yip, the physical education instructor, had been taking notes on clipboard paper.

'Mr. Taylor, you shall refrain from retaliation,' Principal Anders said. 'Your performance today has been most disappointing already. We don't wish to compound it, now, do we?'

Donny looked madder than anyone Chris had ever seen, madder even than Davy Webber's father the night he disappeared. He stormed off toward the schoolhouse with his hands still balled in fists.

'Mr. Platt,' the Principal said. 'A commendable job of defending yourself. Mr. Palmer, once again you require someone else to fight your battles for you. We are nothing, Mr. Palmer, if not demanding of independent problem solving. This sort of continued dependency on those stronger and cleverer than you shall not be tolerated any longer. Am I making myself absolutely and entirely crystal clear, Mr. Palmer?'

Jimmy looked like he might cry, but he bit his tongue and distracted himself enough to hold back the tears. 'Yes... yes, sir.' He said. 'Thank you, sir.'

'Don't thank me, Mr. Palmer,' the principal admonished. 'Thank Mr. Platt. Mr. Platt, though I congratulate your skills at self-defence, I cannot help but think that this is the second time in three weeks you've stepped in to save someone weaker. Let's hope there is not a third. I foresee big things in your future, Mr. Platt. Don't prove me overoptimistic.'

'Christopher, you haven't touched your peas.'

The comment didn't really register. Chris had his elbow on the table and his fork suspended as he daydreamed, committing at least three cardinal sins in the Platt household. 'Huh..? Sorry, what?'

'You need to go to bed earlier if you're this tired this early,' his mother said. 'I said you haven't touched your peas, little man. You finish those all up. There are kids in India who would literally kill their own parents if they had to for those peas.'

His father had been circumspect about his dazed behavior all night. Finally, he asked, 'Son, is there something in particular bothering you, something you'd like to share with us?'

'I...' He looked up at their expectant, supportive faces. 'Aw, heck... it's nothing.'

'Is it about the fight today?' his father asked. 'I heard you beat up the Taylor kid pretty good.'

'Yeah...'

'So you should be proud of yourself,' his father said. 'You stood up to a bully and acquitted yourself well.'

'They didn't like that I was defending Jimmy Palmer.'

His mother dabbed at her mouth politely with her napkin, then placed it beside her plate. 'Well, son, when someone makes a judgment like that, you know what you do? You make sure and you learn from it. Because Jimmy is weak. And when we coddle the weak...? What do we say?'

'We carry the weight," Chris repeated. "I know, Ma, I know...'

'And you don't want to be a weakling, do you? Now, we all know that it's true, and that he's not someone you want to hitch your wagon to, so to speak, at least not unless you're told to do so. The work is just too important for you to be dragged down with him. You hear me?'

He looked anxiously at his father, the school's teacher of the year – as voted by the students – for three years running. His father grasped the boy's smaller hand in his own, like a preacher leading a prayer. 'You listen to your mother, son,' he said. 'The next time something like that happens, you help them beat that boy's head in. You hear me?'

If his parents said it, Chris knew, it had to be so. Every kid in Plenty knew that rule. 'I did tag Donny pretty good though,' he said, eager to regain their favor.

His father grinned, then mussed the boy's hair playfully. 'You sure did, son. You sure did.'

20/

But the next day was no better.

Despite his parents' assurances, Chris had woken feeling glum and not looking forward to anything. That wasn't abnormal during the school term; but it was worse on this day, a gnawing sensation that he was not heading in the right direction, that all the advice was wrong. That his own parents did not have the best of intentions.

It was unsettling. He'd remained distracted through classes. At lunch, Principal Anders had stopped at his regular table to ask if he was okay. Then the principal had congratulated Becky for getting to school early, leaving the little girl beaming.

After eating his snack, Chris had ventured outside into the sun to wait for lunch period to end. Uninterested by the other kids on the playground, he wandered around the building, daydreaming, until he found himself at the rear parking area reserved for teachers. He heard the voices before he rounded the corner. Principal Anders and Mr. Shou were addressing someone.

Chris peeked around the edge of the building.

'You were made to look the fool, you had to have dental work and the other boys no longer fear you,' the principal was saying. 'The question is whether you are willing to fight to regain your position as a favored subject.'

Donny nodded vigorously. 'Yes, sir.'

'Good! Good. Then what we need you to do is to prove that worthiness by ridding the sessions of Jimmy Palmer's incompetence.'

The boy's eyes widened.

'Are you ready for such a task?' the principal asked. 'Are you committed – I mean, really, really committed – to the doctrine?'

'YES! Yes, sir, absolutely. You have no idea how much I want this...!'

'Now, Donald. Calm yourself. We're not going to

let you just go wild. This must be done properly, within the parameters of school policy. Tonight, before Session, we will make an example of his indolence and distraction.'

Chris pressed his body to the wall. A few seconds later he heard the crunch of shoes on gravel, then the heavy rear emergency exit door slamming shut.

He spent the rest of the day trying to find Jimmy to talk to him, but he wasn't in any of his classes. He stopped by his house after school, but the gate was locked and the lights off.

Amy met him on the way back to the school and they walked together. She had a long-sleeved shirt on again despite the heat. 'Hey,' she said, falling in stride.

'Hey... you see Jimmy?'

She shook her head, unsure. 'I... don't think I saw him today at all.'

'Yeah. Look...' He stopped walking. 'I think he's in a lot of trouble.'

'I don't get it.'

'I mean, I think he might be in trouble like David.'

They'd both known David Webber well. He'd been performing poorly in Sessions, just like Jimmy, and other people had to repeatedly stick up for him. The teachers talked about him holding everyone back. Then... there had been an incident. The details were hazy, for all of them. They knew he'd been at school the day prior, then there had been an assembly before Session. That was when everyone stopped remembering him being there, and when, it was assumed, he wandered off and was taken.

That was also the start of Chris' anxiety, like he knew more about it than he could remember. Like there was something hidden from him, just out of reach, something dark and desperate.

By the time of the assembly, twenty minutes later, the gnawing sense of loss was still with him. There were just the eleven kids left in the advanced program that night, which meant Principal Anders wanted to talk about Session, or something related. The assembly hall was two-thirds empty.

Amy met him at their regular seats in the front row, saving a chair for Becky. Chris kept the seat at his end of the row open in case Jimmy showed. The smaller boy wasn't a friend, but he still felt a need to reach out and protect him. Or... something. He wasn't sure what he felt. There was a fear there, a real fear that they were going to hurt him, accompanied by a strange compulsion to see it happen.

Donny Taylor snuck into the last empty seat, at the other end of the row next to Becky, getting there just as the principal entered from the rear offices, to the left off the stage and dais. The children stood in unison. He strode up to it and placed his ledger down.

'Be seated,' he said sternly.

Chris cast a quick glance around the room but couldn't see Jimmy anywhere.

'Today we have a grave duty to perform,' Anders said. 'Today we purge the program of a failure. This is not the first, and it will not be the last. Ideally, it occurs right before Session, allowing a learning experience for you, and a teaching one for us.' He glanced back toward the side door. 'Bring him out.'

Mr. Shou paraded Jimmy Palmer out through the door. His hands were tied behind his back, a black scarf tied around his eyes to blind him. The teacher led him to the center of the stage, then down the steps to the top of the aisle. Shou pushed the boy down to his knees.

Then he turned to Donny, withdrawing a chrome revolver from inside his coat pocket. He flipped the gun around so that he was holding it by the barrel and chamber then handed it the bully.

Donny stared down at the gun like a bad choice. 'I don't... I don't get it,' he said, even though he did, and his fears were warranted.

'Donny, it's time,' Anders said gently.

The change in the boy was immediate, his eyes

wide but dead, so unmoving as to seem lifeless, as if he was looking through everything ahead of him. Then his arm came up, the weapon held straight ahead, his other hand raised to brace the butt of the grip as he looked down its iron sight at Jimmy.

Amy tried to remain calm, her breathing shallower. She could hear a sharp intake from her little sister as the weapon came up.

'No!' Chris said. 'This isn't right. This isn't... this isn't what... this isn't right...'

'Fire, fire burning bright...' Mr. Anders said.

Donny cocked the hammer of the pistol.

'Don't do it!' Chris implored his nemesis. 'You know it's not right, Donny!'

The bully's hand began to quaver and shake, his trigger finger flexing. He tried to steady himself, regain his composure. The shaking became worse, his forearm practically vibrating, his breath short and fast as he tried to commit the deed.

'Fire, Mr. Taylor,' Anders demanded. 'Shoot him, now!'

The boy's face scrunched up as he tried to push through his misgivings. A few feet away, Jimmy wet himself, a puddle forming across the front of his trousers.

'Don't do it, Donny!' Chris insisted. 'Don't let them make you kill someone. It's not right, darn it!'

'Aahh...' Donny made a whimpering sound as he lowered the gun, then lowered his eyes to the floor.

The principal looked unimpressed. 'Mr. Taylor. I am most disappointed in you. Your position as the program's prime will bear serious review at his moment. In any event, we require...'

Before he could finish the sentence, the gun was snatched from Donny's grip, smaller hands raising it unsteadily, the trigger yanked, the gun exploding with sound, momentarily deafening all nearby. The concussive sound made Chris wince and shut his eyes tight, although only for a moment.

When the whining sound subsided, Becky stood with the gun outstretched, quavering from its weight, her eyes wide and vacant, a thin contrail of smoke drifting from the revolver's barrel. A few feet away, Jimmy lay on his back, the blood pooling around the top of his head. The thirty-eight-calibre bullet had struck him in the middle of the forehead, right between his eyes.

Principal Anders smiled. 'Well. Well, well. You see, children? This is the kind of commitment that makes us proud to be your teachers. Well done, Becky Sawyer! One day, you may be as effective as your sister. Or even Mr. Platt.' He turned his head slightly as he said it, the way a vulture might crane its neck toward a new lunch prospect.

Chris stared him down. 'I would never...'

'Oh, but of course you would, Mr. Platt. You're our number one student. We'll go into it during Session tonight. We'll go over the efficiency with which you executed David Webber, whether there was anything upon which you could have improved. Air drifts.'

The words triggered a release, the memory flooding back, of the Webber boy kneeling in the same exact spot, in front of the dais. And of pulling the trigger not once, but twice, making sure the job was done.

His eyes glazed, Chris stared at the front of the room, unthinking and unfeeling, waiting for instruction.

Amy got home later than allowed, ten minutes after her seven o'clock curfew. The lights were out upstairs in the home, and she supposed her parents were asleep. She closed the back door quietly and put her coat over the back of the kitchen chair, rather than on the hook, as her mother preferred.

The stepmother usually didn't feel well by the evening and, as was her habit, had gone to bed early. Amy peeked her head around the corner of the door as she passed it in the hallway. 'I'm home.'

Her stepmother was middle-aged, wrinkled, with

recently dyed red-brown hair. She wore the same white cotton gown every night, and had settled into bed with a book, *The Water Margin*. 'How was it?'

Amy shrugged nonchalantly. 'Nothing special. You know; it's always the same. A few questions, a few tests, a few bad jokes from Principal Anders. It's the session. The session is the session.'

Why did adults always ask the same dumb question? Amy wondered. They'd all been young once. They'd all gone to the session. They'd all taken the advice, learned from the Elders. That was life, after all. School was school.

'Did you learn anything new?'

'Uh huh. Some stuff about nutrition and keeping fit. They kept Chris and Donny Taylor and me late for it again. I think it was like one we already did.

Her stepmother's sudden tension was palpable. 'They... repeated lessons?'

What was the matter with her all of a sudden? 'It's not the first time.'

Amy's stepmother already knew that. It was why she was nervous. But the girl was too young to understand. 'Really?'

'Uh huh. There was one a few months ago, about building a lean-to. We'd heard that one before too. What's got you so worried?'

Her stepmother smiled thinly. 'It's nothing sweetie. It's just that moms and dads get worried when there's a do over. It usually... times poorly. There's always some other neighborhood worry to handle when a lesson is repeated. We like to avoid... negative consequences from the sessions. They can be... problematic.'

Amy nodded. She didn't really understand, but she knew that when her stepmother became nervous for confusing reasons, the Elders were usually involved. But it didn't matter. 'Obey one's Elders,' Mom would say if she asked. 'That's the most important thing one can do.'

Amy smiled but didn't reply. She didn't like discussing the sessions; none of the kids at her school did. She guessed it was probably the same for kids everywhere.

She headed to her room to study. It didn't seem fair that they still had homework after a night of Session. But Amy knew instinctively that it wasn't up to her, that as long as she followed the guidelines, did the course work and showed up on time, everything would be okay.

The desk lamp was too bright, hurting her eyes. She tilted it away slightly as she sat at her desk and looked out her bedroom window at the house next door. The town was small enough that people had decent-sized lots, and she couldn't quite see in well enough to know if Chris was awake. She supposed he was doing the same work.

She wondered how long they'd been in Session. They were never told; that was part of the arrangement.

Becky passed the door. 'Hey,' Amy asked. 'How was your Session?'

The younger girl shrugged. 'Stupid. We studied birds and electricity.'

'Hey! That stuff is important,' Amy said. 'If you want to stay in the program you have to remember all of the lessons perfectly. That's one of the rules.'

'Yeah... I guess. I'm going to go to bed now.'

Amy nodded as her sister wandered off down the hallway. Then she frowned. She didn't think Becky would make it. Her sister had the fight in her, no doubt. But the interest and intelligence weren't there. She wasn't bright enough. She couldn't learn the skills, wouldn't read enough. That's why it was even more important to look out for her.

Then she caught herself. That was defeatist talk. If Becky failed, she would do so on her own, without being propped up by her big sister, she decided.

Amy felt her tummy rumble. She'd missed dinner again; her stepmother had tired of trying to teach her the importance of getting home early on those nights. Usually there was something left over in the fridge, though. She headed downstairs to the kitchen to see what she could put together.

The inside of the fridge was sparse, but there was a half-bottle of milk and the leftovers of a roast chicken. All she needed were some vegetables...

Out the corner of her left eye, she noticed the light to the basement stairs was on, just past the front door. Her stepmother was always nagging her father for forgetting it; he had a little workshop down there.

She closed the fridge and walked over to the door. She reached to the switch at the top of the stairs and was about to flick it off when she heard something, a muffled noise of some sort, low and grunting, followed by a high-pitched ticking. She crept down the stairs cautiously. The ticking sound got louder, morphing into a sharper, slapping noise. Her foot hit the third-to-last step and it creaked loudly.

The noises stopped. She heard someone whispering something. 'Shhh. You hear...' she caught, with the rest being too low. Amy took the last three steps and leaned around the corner, hanging onto the edge of the wall like it was a shield.

Her father was on the sofa, naked, and on all fours. Another man -- Mr. Craig, the local butcher -- was kneeling behind him and also naked. Both men were sweating profusely, and her father was red-faced.

'Amy... please...' he implored, as if there was enough explanation somewhere for what she was seeing.

She frowned and shook her head gently. 'Homosexuality is a perversion that can only be used against you,' she said. 'You should know better.'

'Please, Amy... don't tell your stepmother...'

'I shall report this to Principal Anders. This is unacceptable,' the little girl said, her tone lecturing the middle-aged man.

'Please... sweetie...'

'There is no other way,' Amy said. 'You're just going to have to learn.'

They would be hard on him, she knew. She would probably never see her father again. But it was a matter of principle. And she knew that, beyond anything, she had to follow direction and correct the record. She had always suspected from his harsh treatment that he was wicked.

Now, she was certain, and she would turn him in.

There was no room for mercy in Plenty.

21/

JUNE 18, 1985

In the dark of the evening, Dorian Fan felt physically uneasy. It was a different sort of discomfort from the nervous tension of possible discovery, and he was past that. This was purely a matter of being thrown into an uncomfortable scenario and feeling like a fish out of water.

As he kept his eyes on the road ahead and his left hand on the wheel, he tugged at the collar of his dress shirt with his right. It was foreign clothing and although it had been cut perfectly to fit him, the material felt wrong. Not itchy, but noticeable, and anything that is ever-present can become just as irritating as something obvious.

But it was part of the procedure. Everything had to be perfect, without a thread out of place to make him appear from China. The car was equally foreign to him, a modern sedan, built in Detroit, Michigan a year earlier, complete with wood-grain finish on the dash, tilt steering and auto-reverse cassette deck. The Pennyloafer shoes pinched his feet as he pushed down on the accelerator.

It was not going to be an enjoyable trip, he knew. He had spent enough time during college in the United States to know that he did not care for western mores or customs; the food was bland and banal, the discussion and debate near-non-existent, the people reliant on personal Zara and the joy of acquisition to relate to one another. And from what he'd read in Master Yip's dossier, there was nowhere on the planet more American than Plenty.

It was his first trip to the town. He knew basically what to expect and that it was just a quick assessment, an assurance that everything was on schedule. They had three years left until deployment and there was no time to spare. And just as Jiang Qing had sacrificed herself for them, he knew he would soon have to disappear from public life and his increasing authority. The financial matters would be discovered, they would be traced to him. The money would not be found, nor any physical hallmark of Legacy. But were he to be questioned, they would have ways to pry the information from him. Steps to prevent that had to be taken.

The road was shrouded in night, the car's high beams cutting a wide swath that illuminated just enough of the periphery to see the fields of corn, a wall of crops that set the scene permanently. He checked his watch, a battered Casio digital with a built-in calculator. It was just after ten o'clock, and it couldn't be much further.

On his right, a sign appeared, the white letters in a flowing, stylized font against a pale blue background. 'Welcome to Plenty!' Underneath, it stated 'Home of Matilda, the World's Biggest Bison'. Pop: 1,412.'

If Yip's information was as accurate as always, the sign was about a thousand souls optimistic, even into its second generation; but appearances were important. There would be a gas station coming up on...

There. To his left, he saw the '76' logo and the white pumps. He was curious and still had time. He wasn't expected for another forty-five minutes, but had gotten an early start.

He flipped on the car's turn signal, muted orange flashing across the asphalt, and pulled into the lot, parking a few yards from the wooden steps up to the gas station's store. Fan got out and climbed the steps; there was an old screen door on a spring hinge, the paint peeling. He pulled it open, then pushed open the main door behind it, a bell ringing to announce his presence.

The place was brightly lit with fluorescent tubes. A tall man with grey-white hair stood at the main counter, directly ahead of the entrance. To his left was a small store with racks of magazines, video cassette tapes and snacks. To his right, a long lunch counter. There was no one there, and the Formica counter was pristine. Behind it, along the back wall, were a handful of soda fountains and a milkshake machine, along with a slot window that likely led to the kitchen. There was a row of tables opposite the counter, along the front windows.

'It's pretty quiet tonight,' he said to the attendant in English.

'Yes sir.'

'You do not get many customers at this time of night.'

'Not normally, no. We close in an hour.'

'Would you mind if I get a hamburger?'

'Kitchen's closed already. But we've got sandwiches in the refrigerator there that you can heat up in the toaster oven. Little subs and such.'

Fan shook his head. 'No, that's fine. I just had a desire for a hamburger.'

'Uh huh,' the man said. His look suggested Fan's accent unnerved him.

'Anything going on in town right now?' Fan asked. 'I am just passing through for a day or so.'

'Well...' the man scratched his chin. 'They got a prayer vigil on right now for little David Webber, the boy what disappeared last fall. But I don't suppose that's what you mean. There's the bowling alley. That's always good for killing a few hours, I guess. If you want to wet your whistle, the bar at the Veterans Hall is open until one. There ain't much to look at, other than buildings. You probably know about the ordinance, and such..."

"The nuclear regulatory commission order."

"Uh huh. Folk from here got to stay here, on account of the exposure levels; so when a visitor comes through it's always a nice change, but get some folk nervous, too."

'I'm supposed to be staying with a local family, the Taylors...'

'Oh yeah... yeah, Jed and the boys. Real shame about Marcy, of course.'

'Yeah, terrible.' According to the dossier, the wife had been horribly raped and murdered the summer prior. 'I can't imagine what that does to a man.'

'Especially... well, you know. With what his boy could've done and all. I mean, if he'd had any guts.' Then the man looked down at his shoes, as if slightly ashamed to be sharing that discussion with a stranger. 'But I guess it ain't none of my business.'

Fan gestured back toward the door. 'Well, I'm going to head on into town then.'

'You have yourself a good one,' the man said. 'Don't mind me and my nonsense. It gets kind of boring out here at night. Ain't a whole lot to do and I get a bit stir crazy.'

'Understood,' Fan said. He walked back to the door. 'Good to meet you.'

A minute later, he was driving down the main route, tuning his car radio to 580 AM KKPZ, the Voice of Plenty. 'It's another perfect night in America's safest town!' the DJ intoned with just the right touch of overzealousness. 'In fact it's so nice tonight, I feel it's my civic duty to remind everyone not to go too crazy out there, to obey your parents and to do your share! And hey, those of you coming home from the Davy Webber vigil, let's keep some perspective on who's really to blame here, okay? And we all know who that is...'

He switched off the radio so that he could concentrate on the street signs. The Taylors lived in a grey house at the intersection of Freedom Avenue and Washington Boulevard, a Cape Cod style with upstairs dormers and a full-width front porch.

The town looked like it couldn't have had more than three or four wide blocks to the entirety of it. The main street had a handful of businesses with unassuming signs: a bank, a gun store, a drug store, a furniture place, a small grocery, a liquor store. The next block over featured the town hall, the car wash, one of two churches and, on the corner, the Rendezvous Motel, known locally among the teenagers as the 'Randy View.' There wasn't a car in sight, nor traffic lights. At every other corner was a four-way stop.

It took less than two minutes to find the Taylor residence, a blue-and-white ramshackle wood-frame home in farmhouse style. There was no driveway and no fence between it and neighbors, just a path to the front door made up of functional grey concrete slabs. He parked at the curb and looked around their part of town as he slammed the sedan door. There were curbside trees, other wood craftsman homes, a line of them in different shades and shapes, the only commonality the single bulb burning above each front door.

Before he reached the front steps, the door opened. Jedediah Taylor was tall and broad-shouldered, his hair nearly gone on top but strategically covered with an oily combover. He had on blue denim overalls over a red-check work shirt. His two boys were shorter, their hair thicker, but otherwise their father's sons. Each shared his glum expression.

'You Dorian?'

'Mr. Taylor. Thank you for allowing me to stay with your family.'

'Ain't nothing. Since Marcy went to the Lord we've been working real hard to make penance for whatever we done what made the Lord so mad at us as to take her.'

Without notice, Fan switched to Mandarin. 'That's an exceptionally thick accent. I can barely understand you.'

The man squinted, puzzled. 'Whuh...?'

Fan wanted to be sure and continued in his own tongue. 'You don't understand a word I'm saying, do you? And you've lived here for twenty-three years?'

'Mister... look I don't want to sound rude or un-Christian or nothing, but I don't understand your lingo none.' He looked over his shoulder. 'Boys, you know any of this ching chong stuff?'

They both shook their heads vigorously.

Fan switched back to English. 'My apologies, I was reciting an old Chinese proverb, blessing your family with Good Luck.'

Taylor grinned out of one side of his mouth, like a man who likes his plug of tobacco. 'Well, all right then! That's sure nice to hear, because we sure could use some. Donny, get the man's case.'

The taller of the glum children reached over and took Fan's suitcase from him.

His father took a half-turn toward the house. 'We got you in the back bedroom on the bottom floor. It ain't much fancy, but it should do. Used to be Marcy's sewing room, but we took to renting it.'

'And my food requirements?'

'Yeah... we got that list. Mr. Shou had to supply most of it, 'cause the grocer here in town, he ain't got what you'd call the broadest selection. I'd have cooked some of it up for you, but we had to go over to David Webber's vigil at the school.'

'Ah yes... a boy who went missing, I understand.'

'Uh huh. Taken by a remorseless predator, is more like. Well, we're going to deal with that the way it's supposed to be dealt with.'

'And how is that?' Fan asked. The man had developed a fanatical air.

'Well, we all know it got to be a government agent what done it. Government is the ones what got us stuck in this town, due to the testing. No one likes an agent. So, we're going to find him, and we're going to kill him.' He glanced over his shoulder at his two sons. 'Ain't that right boys?'

After making himself dinner in the Taylor family's modest farm-style kitchen, complete with wood stove, Fan took his bowl to his room, where he dug the dossier folder from his suitcase and tossed it onto the single bed. He opened it to the section on the Taylors, who had gathered in the family room to watch *Miami Vice*.

The father was an exceptional subject, he decided, the perfect parent for their needs.

So far, he'd passed every suitability test like a

duck takes to water, and his righteous fervor at the notion of hunting down a child-killer had been positively chilling.

Like all of the parents, he was an orphan child of missionaries -- or missionaries and locals -- one of more than three hundred originally obtained by agreement with their sympathizer, a high-ranking administrator in the Lutheran overseas movement. Fan reminded himself to compliment Administrator Shou on the precision he'd observed, honoring the man's meticulous preparation.

The boys seemed a little too numb, perhaps a bit dulled by months of going through the process. Donny, the older one, was clearly stronger than other children his age would normally be, visibly muscular at just twelve years of age, a perfect bully foil for one of the younger lead candidates.

Matt, the youngest child, exhibited the same vacant-yet-piercing gaze Fan observed in the older subjects who'd failed, those identified for sociopathic tendencies. That wouldn't do.

There wasn't much point in spending years identifying and grooming individuals if they failed during the toughest stages.

The boy would be removed, he expected. Something natural, of course: a car accident or illness. Compared to some of the machinations Shou had had to engineer, it would be nothing too challenging.

Perhaps they would use him for ideological entrenchment exercises, as they had with the Webber boy.

22/

TODAY

MERIDA, MEXICO

'So, Fan travelled to this town in Montana; and it had something to do with the recruitment effort, I know that much,' Pon said. 'But I don't have any more details. That was as much as I was told.'

Brennan fetched the bottle of whiskey from the top of the chest of drawers by the window. The story was far-fetched at best, but Pon seemed to think it was true. 'You need a drink?'

'Please,' Pon said. 'I'm still shaken from... well, from everything tonight, I guess.'

'Are you rethinking your business arrangements?'

'I suppose I'll have to.'

'When you said 'as much as I was told...'

'Yes?'

'By whom?'

Pon frowned. 'I'm not really at liberty to share that information.'

'And I'm not really supposed to take you back to Ramon Santerra and his men, but that's what I'm going to do if you don't tell me the name of your source.'

That embittered him. 'It's nice to know that the people helping me live through the night actually care about my wellbeing.'

'I'm not here to judge you one way or the other,' Brennan explained. 'You're just a means to an end.'

'A pawn.'

'Exactly. That's what happens when your investors are very bad people.'

'I was fleeing China...'

'It's just my job, professor. In the story...

'I don't know anything else.'

'I understand that. But you mentioned a 'Master Yip Po' as being involved.'

Pon's head dipped slightly. 'And?'

'You tell me, professor. When you mentioned his name, you smiled a little, as if he was someone you knew.'

'That... is observant of you, Mr. Brennan.'

'Is he your source?'

'My source has my word that his name will not be revealed. And that is very important to me. As such, I would never confirm that Master Yip Po of the Black Cranes Society is my source. Never.'

'Would I be far wrong if I went looking for the individual that I named in a Black Crane city, like Changzhou or Harbin?'

It was just the slightest expression; the very tip of Pon's tongue darted out for just a split second to moisten his top lip as he averted his gaze. But it spoke volumes. 'As I said...'

'Yeah, I know: you won't compromise your source. You know the woman I fought with at Santerra's?'

'I do not.'

'Her name is Daisy Lee. She's a Chinese spy.'

'Ah.'

'She'll probably come after you again if she can find you. From the fury she demonstrated the last two times I've met her, she'll probably kill you. Unless, of course, we protect you.'

Pon stared hard at him for a moment, as if weighing the man's inner character. 'You already have your answer, Mr. Brennan,' he said.

'So... then Master Yip Po?'

'As I said...'

'... I already have my answer, yeah. Okay.' Brennan drew in breath sharply, warding off some rising tension. *Why the hell did I agree to this?* he asked himself. *And why can't anything ever just be easy?*

DAY 9

BEIJING

The Committee for State Security was known throughout the party as one of its most sober bodies, capable of rational debate and second thought, and typically populated with some of China's best and brightest. Lessons had been learned from history, hard lessons about how power should be controlled and what would happen when too much of it fell into too few hands.

As such, it had become David Chan's preoccupation. A long-time technical industry CEO and senior party member, he had assumed the chairmanship because he was unanimously seen as having the most insight into how the west viewed China.

But, as with anything serving the party, he had to get the job done. And Yan Liu Jeng had come before the committee bearing bad news, the type of news that might stain his reputation.

'As you requested,' Yan told the chairman, 'our agent pursued the source of the Legacy leak to Mexico. However, she was unsuccessful in her approaches and it appears the package was picked up by our American friends.'

'Your agent failed,' Chan said, removing any notion from the equation that he bore part of the responsibility. 'The question now becomes how we can catch up.'

From the end of the table, a voice piped in, 'With respect, Mr. Chairman, I believed you approved of that decision as well,' said Wen Xiu. 'Perhaps it would serve the party best if we concentrated on where to take this from here.'

Yan nodded his way gratefully. Wen had been his biggest supporter in fending off Chan's attacks. 'Thank you, Comrade Wen. It seems likely that the target, Professor Pon, has gone to ground with aide from an American agent, the same man who was in Macau.'

'Do we have a possible location?' Chan asked. 'Would it be possible for us to remedy the situation?'

'The American will have sent any information he obtains back to his people long before we find them,' Yan said. 'That is the unfortunate reality of it.'

Wen looked crestfallen. 'Then the Americans will inevitably uncover everything. We are exposed.'

Chan frowned. 'Not necessarily. At least, not from a publicity perspective. There is a possibility we have yet to consider.

Yan appeared doubtful. 'I am, of course, open to suggestions.'

'Have we considered working with them?'

The dull roar of murmured doubt flew around the committee table as all eighteen members discussed the statement.

Wen Xiu looked doubtful. 'Chairman Chan, I am not sure I quite understand. You are aware that this would put the Americans in a position to gravely harm our reputation internationally...'

'At the expense of our assistance,' Chan said. 'And at the risk of further offending us when they are already looking for our support with respect to North Korea.'

Yan smiled. He had always respected Chan, even when he didn't have his backing. 'This is quite true, chairman,' he said. 'I shall make note of this.' Then Yan had a clever notion. 'You recently discussed the situation on the peninsula with your opposite number at the CIA, did you not?'

Chan wasn't sure where the younger man was taking the discussion. He had to tread carefully. 'That is true, yes.'

'And I believe you mentioned in your report to the Central Committee that the Americans' preferred course of action was for us to stay silent and out of the matter. This supports your contention.' Yan turned to look at the other members around the semi-circular table, to each side of the chair's position. 'I would like to nominate the chairman to re-establish this relationship, should the Central Committee approve.'

Chan risked losing face if he backed out. If he did, the preferred protocol would be to hand the matter over to the undersecretary ... Yan Liu Jeng. Yan would either resolve the matter and look like a hero, or fail and it would appear as if he'd been set up for it by Chan. 'As you suggest,' Chan replied. 'I would be happy to take direction from the Central Committee to ensure this matter is handled with the appropriate skill and tact.'

'Of course, we shall need to act quickly,' Wen said. 'The American battlegroup will be anchored just off North Korean sovereign waters within a day. At that point, the odds of a conflagration grow exponentially. After the meeting between our foreign ministers, we had hoped the Americans would back down. The American President seems disinclined; and yet we need to use Legacy to convince his administration to do just that; because if Pyongyang decides to obliterate Seoul in a mushroom cloud, the world will still believe it was with our tacit approval.'

'And if we can't shut down Legacy,' Chan said, 'North Korea might be the least of our problems.'

WASHINGTON, D.C.

The waiter was hovering suspiciously with a menu in hand, even though Carolyn Brennan had told him she was waiting for someone. She smiled at him as graciously as possible, then went back to her phone and her emails, in an attempt to make it clear she wasn't going anywhere, he couldn't have the table, and she wasn't ready to order.

He bowed his head and averted eye contact, then moved along. She went back to her texts.

'Did I just see you give the waiter a nasty look? It showed from a distance. I could see you glaring from the entrance.' Adrianne Hayes had on a lawyerly navy suit and white blouse.

Carolyn gestured to the opposite chair. 'He was hovering. Please...'

'What are we drinking?' Adrianne asked as she took a seat.

'Virgin Mary, unfortunately,' Carolyn said. 'I've got a meeting with the chairman this afternoon.' She'd filled Adrianne's old job as deputy assistant director of information security. It was a thankless and exhausting role, but she was loving it.

'I had a small ulterior motive in inviting you,' Adrianne said. 'I'm working on a file involving your husband right now.'

Carolyn's mind whirred over the possible questions, but the one that jumped immediately to mind was automatic, procedural. 'Are you supposed to be telling me this? And here?'

'Oh, nothing too specific,' Adrianne said. 'But I did think it would be helpful to get your opinion on how suitable you felt it was to have him out and about, as it were, rather than back training the youngsters.'

'Why? Are you worried about his performance for some reason?' She'd been in the trade long enough not to show overt concern for Joe's safety. But her first thought was that something must have gone wrong.

'Nothing of the sort, don't worry,' Adrianne said. 'It's just that as you're no doubt aware this particular matter came upon us rather suddenly and I don't know him from Adam, and yet am tasked with handling the fallout. It's not the most comfortable position in which to find oneself. Have you heard where he is right now?'

'We... haven't really been keeping in touch while he's away.'

'Ah.'

Carolyn suppressed a small smile. She could

smell Jonah politicking from ten miles outside the Beltway. 'Well, don't worry; if there was any chance that Joe would be any less than stellar, I wouldn't have let him go. We were in the middle of our first family vacation in three years.'

The older woman looked pained. 'Sorry about that, really I am. So given his preference, he wouldn't be handling this one?'

'That's fair to say.'

'The devil is usually in the details.'

'Sometimes. These days, that's a pretty normal response for him.'

'Then he hasn't complained about any specific issues?'

'No. Like I said, we haven't talked much recently. But Joe takes his sense of duty pretty darn seriously. If the gentlemen upstairs want him somewhere, off he goes.' What was she playing at? She didn't expect her to indict her husband, did she? Then Carolyn silently chided herself for being so cynical; Adrianne had recommended her for the NSA position and championed her in the first few rough months.

'They can be tough,' Adrianne said. 'I know better than most; but you and I are both proof that the old boys' club isn't the future of either agency. Maybe when we have a woman in charge, we won't see stressed-out agents being forced to leave their families back home.'

She wasn't going to overtly agree, but Carolyn had felt exactly that way about Joe's career since prior to Walter's death and the nuclear incident. It felt good to have an ally for a change in the briefing room. 'That would be good,' she said. 'Adrianne...'

'Please... it's Adi to friends.'

'Adi... thank you for this. For inviting me today. I really needed this, to get away from the office and just let off steam.'

'You and me both, sister.'

23/

LOS ANGELES

The schedule seemed solid. The man known publicly as Benjamin Levitt was calm as he looked down the shelves in the corner grocer's refrigerator cabinet for the two percent milk.

They'd discovered the first safe house too quickly for comfort, but he knew that was a possibility. The handler had drummed it into his head, along with every other detail of the operation. The second base was two miles from the strip in a fleabag motel, and he had no reason to believe they knew his appearance. He had no motive to kill Paul Joseph, other than their physical similarity and his need for a place to work, so there was nothing to connect them. And no one had seen him leave the man's house.

There had been the girl he'd shot at, right after activation, but there wasn't much he could do about her. He assumed she'd been integral to his cover, but there was no way to be certain. And that was Malibu, miles away.

He paid the young Korean clerk for the paper bag's worth of food and supplies and began walking back to the motel, a block away. It had been nice to find food so close to his room, he decided, so that the he could walk in the sun without any real risk of being spotted. After so long in the dark, it made him feel close to whole again.

Not that that would ever be possible. He knew time had passed since his last activation -- years, potentially. But the concept of time itself was abstract to him, no longer part of his central programming. His life had long ago ceased to be his own.

The street was nearly deserted, a residential row a few blocks off of Sunset Boulevard. The motel was on the next corner, a ten-unit brick joint that might have been nice at some point before the Second World War. Its small parking lot was almost empty; most of its inhabitants were month-to-month, and without the means to afford transportation.

He'd parked his stolen station wagon horizontally at the curb by the office, so that the plate wasn't easily seen from the road, and his eyes naturally travelled there, keen to ensure it was undisturbed.

Then he stopped short.

The man looking at the car was middle-aged, maybe a bit older, in a grey business suit and tie. He was taking notes with a pencil and small pad of paper.

A policeman? Probably. Maybe he'd made the plate as stolen. Levitt looked up and down the street, but there was no other traffic, no one watching. It had to be connected to his objective. The man was too well-dressed to be a car thief. He reached into the side pocket of his coat and gripped the stiletto, then began to cross the street, walking at pace.

The man's back was to him, his pencil tracing swift passage across the notepad page. He wasn't a big person and appeared middle-aged or older, a veteran. He wouldn't have the reaction times to prevent what was about to happen, Levitt knew. He closed the gap between them and began to slip the stiletto out of his pocket. He walked quickly, heel to toe, so that there was no noise. His target put the notepad into his pocket again and looked at the building. With his head tilted slightly back, the timing was perfect...

A car pulled into the lot and Levitt paused. It slowed to a crawl, its path running between the stalls, parallel to the road, as if it was looking for the right room number or something. Levitt wasn't sure what to do; he couldn't jeopardize the operation by taking the man out, but if he was discovered again, the chances of finding an easy third bolt hole were slim-to-none. Police would be looking for him everywhere.

He swallowed hard, his eyes shifting from the slow-cruising car and back to the presumed plainclothes policeman. If the man turned around, he would have to explain the bizarreness of standing in the middle of the road fifteen feet behind him, staring at his back.

The car reached the end of the lot, but instead of turning left to park in one of the stalls fronting the long building, its right-turn signal lit up and it pulled back out onto the street and departed. The policeman didn't even lift his head from his examination of Levitt's stolen station wagon. The missing man's eyes refocused on his objective and he crept up slowly behind the curious note-taker. He was five feet away, the knife about to come out of his pocket so that he could slide it into the man's basal ganglia, the clump of nerves between the spine and brain...

The motel's front door opened. 'And if you can believe it,' a large woman said as she and her husband walked out, 'he claimed the air conditioning never works in July. July!'

Behind the car, the policeman looked up at the couple emerging from the office. The risk had become too great, the couple witnesses. He slid the knife back into his pocket and was about to turn and walk away when the policeman headed toward the front door.

Levitt watched him until he was inside. The motel was no longer secure, and neither was the car. He had to assume Paul Joseph was no longer useful as an identity, as it might have been how they'd traced him. He grimaced ruefully at so much cover work going undone. But it couldn't be helped. It probably wasn't going to matter anyway, as the next phase was almost upon them. He turned and headed for his room, the last unit. He had a few minutes while the policeman followed procedure and questioned the motel manager to gather his things and move on.

The man at the front desk had wild, greasy black hair and smelled of sweat. There was food caught in his moustache, which drooped to either side of his mouth like remorse. His string t-shirt was stained with food and perspiration, and his brown skin had a greasy sheen to it from the broken air conditioning.

He didn't look up when Drabek entered.

'Air conditioning's out for everyone. You people, you gotta stop asking...' He turned the page on the magazine that sat open on the counter ahead of him. 'I gotta... I gotta do everything 'round here.' His round, nasal tone made him sound simple. 'I gotta run the whole show, the whole shebang.' He turned another page, caught up in the glossy celebrity pictures. 'That's why Mister Herrera says I'm a smart guy, 'cause I can run the whole shebang.'

Drabek walked up to the counter. The office was a relic from the Seventies or earlier, with yellow wallpaper and cracked tile floor, the wall sconces populated by dead flies. In one upper corner of the room, an old tube TV sat on a wall bracket, its screen spewing out Family Feud in an analog blur. 'Top one hundred people surveyed...' the announcer drawled, the volume down just enough to be barely audible.

'Excuse me,' Drabek said.

'We don't got no air conditioning!' the man exclaimed. 'I told the others that. The old lady and man. All wrinkly.'

'That's okay I'm not here for a room. I'm with the police,' Drabek said.

'No police!' the man exclaimed, looking hurt and a little frightened. 'We didn't do nothing wrong, I swear!'

'I'm not here for you,' Drabek said, keeping his tone deliberately soft and gentle. 'You have someone staying in number one?'

The man frowned. 'No.'

'Are you sure?'

The clerk looked back at the keys on the hooks along the wall behind him. 'Yeah, uh huh. Only number twelve right now.'

Maybe Levitt was staying there but had parked in front of a different unit deliberately, Drabek figured. The place was anonymous and unkempt, unlikely to attract much attention. Whatever he was up to, he was working hard to keep a low profile.

'Number twelve?'

'Uh huh. One guy, staying in number twelve. Nobody else. Air conditioning is out again.'

'This guy here long?'

'Since two days, I don't know, something like. He paid cash. Only cash, no checks! No cards or checks!'

'He say anything you remember?'

'He asked for a room.'

'Yeah, aside from the room.'

The man squinted, puzzled. 'I don't get it.'

'Did you hear him say anything else, other than asking for a room?'

The man squinted again, then shook his head. 'Nah, he didn't say much. People...' He looked puzzled again. '... People don't talk to me so much.' Then he found some resolve. 'Mr. Herrera... Mr. Herrera says I'm smart. So I run the whole shebang.'

'He sounds like a smart guy. Did you see this man from number twelve today at all? Or see him go out?'

The big clerk nodded quickly. 'Sure. Sure, he went out both days. He was in the lot, by his car, and I could hear him...'

'By his car?'

He nodded toward the small window under the television. 'Through the window, when I turned to see Feud.'

'Yesterday?'

'Uh huh. Steve Harvey got all up in this girl's face, 'cause she was flirting with him. He was speaking funny on his phone, like a Chinaman.'

'Eh?'

'The guest. You know, all 'ching chong ying yong'. Funny. Like a Chinaman. He said some stuff in American, then a few words of ching chong ying yong talk.'

That didn't fit at all, Drabek thought. Zoey hadn't mentioned languages or anything like that. More likely, the clerk had the wrong person. 'Did this guy sign a register or give you a credit card?'

He nodded. 'He paid cash. We only take cash, no cards! Machine's broke!'

'Uh huh. Let me see your register book.'

The clerk frowned again. 'Mr. Herrera, he said... Mr. Herrera said if police come I'm not supposed to talk. Just call me, he said.'

The veteran detective suppressed a sigh. Whatever else the owner was up to it probably didn't compare to Paul Joseph's remains in a tub. 'He's not in trouble and you're not in trouble, so you don't have to call anyone,' Drabek advised. 'Just let me see the book and maybe I can get out of your hair.'

Gingerly, the clerk proffered the vinyl ledger. 'Okay, I guess, since you're police.'

Drabek flicked through to the date. There was only one name on the registry.

Paul Joseph. Room one.

Drabek nodded to the clerk. 'Dial 911. Tell them 'officer needs assistance, then hang up.' He made for the door quickly, unclipping the butt of his pistol on route. He peered outside cautiously. Across the lot, at the far exit, a man was walking out onto the sidewalk with a small gym bag over his shoulder. He was medium height, brown hair, well dressed, glasses. He looked exactly as he did in Zoey Roberson's photos.

He turned his head and saw Drabek. Then he began to run.

'Levitt!' Drabek yelled. 'Stop!'

Drabek barged out of the office and jumped the three steps to the pavement, the jarring concrete shaking his aging bones. His dress shoes clattered on the asphalt as he crossed the lot to the street and tried to make up the distance. He reached into the pocket of his coat as he ran, withdrawing his phone and keying the built-in walkie talkie mic at the same time. '10-99 Officer... Needs... Assistance...' he intoned breathlessly, trying to hold pace. 'Suspect is code 417... north on Gardner between Fountain and Sunset... male, medium height, brown hair, blue dress shirt, tan slacks, sneakers... wanted for homicide, answers to Benjamin Levitt. He's running. Recommend... air ... support.'

He could hear the call being acknowledged and the static-filled sound of a reply, the all-cars going out; but Drabek concentrated on keeping his breathing steady. Ahead, the man was picking up pace, the distance between them growing. He cut right suddenly, running between two walk-ups.

It took Drabek another eight seconds to get there. He cut behind the building and found a long six-foot-high wooden fence. He clambered over it, the old structure swaying, and tumbled to the ground on the other side.

Drabek found his feet and sprinted out to the street. He looked both ways quickly, then turned his head slowly, his eyes searching for movement.

But Levitt was gone.

24/

WASHINGTON, D.C.

By the time the video conference call was ready to roll, Jonah Tarrant's palms had begun to sweat. Never the physically fittest of men, he was carrying extra weight after falling off his fitness regimen; he blamed the time devoted to his new job and responsibilities, but deep down he knew it was a matter of more willpower and less pizza.

He told himself that none of the eating was from stress. He'd shot and killed his own boss just three years earlier, then received a hero's commendation and a promotion. He'd also had nightmares ever since. But that wasn't this, Tarrant decided. That was separate. That could wait until things settled down.

When he got nervous, the extra weight exhibited itself as flop sweat. He wasn't worried about appearances; the giant sweat circles under his armpits wouldn't be visible through his suit jacket, and he was careful to have a fan placed on the table to keep his brow from beading. So he wasn't concerned about the Chinese representative gaining confidence at his discomfort; it was just sticky and distracting. It would get more so, he was sure, if the conversation with David Chan was anything like their last.

The screen flickered to life on the wall ahead.

'Chairman Chan, good of you to speak with us again,' he said.

'Deputy director Tarrant. Doubtless you wish to discuss the cold file you raised the last time we spoke. Project Legacy.'

'As I recall, you seemed in a difficult position, unable to really discuss it.' Tarrant wanted the man to feel as if he could change tack without losing face.

'That... would be an accurate description, yes,' Chan remarked. 'However, the situation continues to develop.'

'Mexico.'

'Yes, Mexico. That ended poorly for us.'

Tarrant shrugged. 'I did offer a path to us working together when we last spoke. At that time, as I recall, you had absolutely no interest. That suggests to me that you must be concerned with how this is all progressing, and I do realize the politics of the day can have substantial impact on how these issues are handled.'

'Concerned, certainly, but not alarmed,' Chan suggested. 'We are quite in control.'

Sure, Tarrant thought, *and I'm the late King of Sweden.* 'Of course, chairman, of course.'

'I merely felt that given America's concern over North Korea's sovereign exercise of its right to self-protection...'

'Is that what we're calling an out-of-control ICBM these days? A defensive countermeasure?'

'Given America's aggressive stance on North Korea's military and testing regime in the past...'

He'll do anything to frame this as our fault at this point, Tarrant knew. *But maybe I can use that.* 'Certainly, chairman, the United States respects the considerable influence that you can exert over North Korea's sovereign affairs and the cordial relationship your two nations have. Perhaps China can help keep us from stepping in it along the Korean peninsula, if we in turn help you round up this pesky Project Legacy situation.'

'What are you suggesting?'

'Tell us what you know about Legacy and we'll see if we can unravel it before any talks begin. The last thing we want is to see our respective countries debating the peninsula with a potentially explosive disruption in the offing.'

'Just like that?'

'Just like that.'

'You wish our help...'

'We want to help you to help yourselves,' Tarrant said.

'And?'

'And if we share resources we have a far better chance of uncovering what Legacy was all about. Our man needs to follow a lead in China...'

'Absolutely out of the question,' Chan said. 'It is one thing to share intelligence with you, it is quite another to allow an American agent onto Chinese soil.'

'That's not very helpful, chairman...'

'Oh come now, Mr. Tarrant, surely you don't expect me to believe you would allow Chinese agents...'

'We already do, tacitly. They're all over the country, because we already let people in and out more easily than you do. We just keep a good watch on them, that's all.'

'I would never get it past the committee,' Chan said. 'The best I can offer is to have our field agent on this matter pursue whatever lead it is you think is so important...'

'There's a man rumored to be in Harbin, a former intelligence academy instructor named Yip Po...'

'The venerable grandmaster. He was declared missing many years ago.'

'We understand he was a captive at the time.'

'Under house arrest; due to his stature with high-ranking party members he was afforded leeway.'

'Smooth move.'

'Deputy director...'

'Oh... don't sweat it, David. We've done dumber things; Snowden didn't exactly make us look like a tight ship; and look at the Brits with Philby and Blunt.'

'Your reassurance aside, we have had no luck locating Master Yip in many years and I'm not sure why you think that would change because of a decades-old rumor.'

'Nonetheless...'

'Certainly, we will try.'

'What else can you tell us about his role?'

Chan knew the question would come. He knew he needed to sound as helpful as possible. 'Yip was a trainer at our recruit school in the Nineteen Seventies and Eighties. A master of multiple fighting styles, a former intelligence agent during the Korean crisis. He fell out of favor during the purge of the Gang of Four and their supporters, due to his loyalty to the Chairman's widow.'

'Jiang Qing. Madame Mao.'

'He was a staunch protector, a former teacher of hers; and his sense of honor prevented him from abandoning that political perspective even after her death. If he is even still alive, he would be ninety-six years old, according to his file.'

'And his connection to Legacy?'

'We are...still uncovering the fullness of his function,' Chan said.

Tarrant suppressed a chuckle and remained stoic. Experience told him that mocking Chan for a politically correct 'we don't know' gained them nothing.

'And when you're certain...'

'We will take whatever steps best suit resolution of the problem. My hope is that I will be able to openly share with you whatever I can.'

Tarrant wasn't sure he'd get much of a better offer. It was almost co-operative; almost. 'And the agent who has twice interfered with our efforts?'

'That is none of your concern, deputy director, and an internal matter for the People's Republic of China. But... for your edification, I shall note that she has been recalled. Two failures suggest she is not suited to this portion of the assignment.'

Tarrant didn't really care. He just wanted to be able to tell Brennan whether she'd be an issue for a third time. The Chinese wanted to appear open, co-operative. But Chan had revealed absolutely nothing of any real value, and the CIA had no existing assets in Heilongjiang province.

'And what about Dorian Fan?' he asked.

'What about him?' Chan replied. 'He disappeared nearly three decades ago. Surely you don't think he's involved in this in any respect? It's a myth. A legend. The man is long dead.'

Tarrant doubted the Chinese had given up the notion so easily. 'Yeah, but you don't know for certain. And I have to believe a man with a reputation for meticulous care such as yourself would have that at the back of his mind.'

'True. And in the meantime?'

'We have more to investigate. Our source...'

'The professor.'

'Yes. He told us Legacy involved American sleepers, potentially recruited from a small town in Montana. But the story is problematic.'

'How so?'

'Well for one,' Tarrant said, 'the town of Plenty, Montana doesn't exist. And it never has.'

PART THREE

25/

DAY 10

DETROIT, MICHIGAN

The light wasn't good, but it was sufficient to keep watch, and Paul Gessler was certain that his neighbor was up to trouble. He peeked through the front hallway window from behind the curtains, his eyes wide, his breath shallower than normal. A tall, balding man with a crown of red hair, Gessler's nostrils flared with contempt as the man climbed out of the aging grey Honda Civic. He had a couple of grocery bags in his right hand, as if he'd retrieved them from the passenger side.

It was dark out, but the light above the neighbor's garage door cast just enough of a glow to cut through the gloom.

What was he up to? *He's an A-rab, that's for goddamn sure. Probably one of the Muslims. Probably going down to his basement to work on his suicide vest.*

Gessler hated how foreigners had taken over his town. They were everywhere, speaking languages they knew nobody American could understand. This one had shown up two months earlier, renting the house from the son of Mr. Laughlin, who'd passed six months earlier. Every so often, another raghead or sand monkey would show up and stay for a few hours. The guy had some sort of routine, leaving every morning at the same early hour, before Gessler was normally out of bed, but consistent enough for his neighbor to eventually spot it. He got back late as well, after dark sometimes, especially in winter.

What are you up to, Mister Muslim? You come to blow up my town, kill God-fearing Americans? You go out in the day and train with your crazy, shitbag brothers, pray to Mo-hammed to destroy us? Is that what you're about?

The neighbor reached his front door and retrieved his house keys from his left pocket, before opening the door and disappearing inside. For a few quiet moments, Gessler just stared at the front door in apprehension, fearful something terrible and tragic might occur at any moment, his hatred for the man swelling. Gessler's father had been a brutal man, a lifelong John Birch Society member who believed in beating the sin out of his wife and son. In his father's America, Gessler believed, a clear danger to the public like this man and his religion of death could have been shot on sight, and no one would have complained.

He turned back to the hallway and walked the few feet to the living room doors. His wife of twenty-one years, Mary, was sitting on a fading striped sofa, knitting and watching television. 'It's a fucking travesty,' he said roughly.

She didn't raise her head.

'Do you even fucking listen to what I'm telling you?' he barked at her. His face was contorted with contempt. 'God, you're pathetic. Our country is being slowly taken over and it's because of people like you, sheep who can't think for themselves.'

She wanted to talk back to him, to yell in his fat, ugly, angry face. But she knew what Gessler was really like, and what he was capable of; and she was afraid.

'What's for dinner?' he demanded.

'Liver and onions,' Mary replied quietly. Gessler had lost his job at the construction company a month earlier and they were on a tight budget, although he still seemed to find enough money to buy booze and rifle cartridges. He should've been out looking for work; instead, he was collecting unemployment insurance and stewing, standing at that front window and judging everyone he saw pass by. At least on the weekends, when he was training with his militia, he was out of the house.

He squinted at her with revulsion. 'Liver again? What is wrong with you, exactly? I come home after looking for work, trying to find a way to keep us fed, and this is the shit you serve me? You can't even cook it good, you useless piece of shit. Fuck this noise: I'm going to Eddie's.'

Eddie's was Gessler's regular bar, where he'd had the same stool for two decades.

He grabbed the car keys off the adjacent telephone table. She knew he'd already had a few, and would have a lot more before he came home, and that he shouldn't drive. But she didn't say anything; behind her tired eyes and pale skin there was much anger, and she secretly hoped he would crash and die, and rid her life of his toxic, painful presence.

Cliff and Ronnie and Dave were all at Eddie's, each with a pony jug or two already put away by the time Gessler showed. The place was old and familiar, with faded salmon pink walls and carpet that smelled of old cigarette butts. The counters were all cheap vinyl, the tables equally so. The Michelob clock had a chunk of glass that had been missing since the late seventies, but the mirror behind the bar -- fronted by rows of bottles no one ever requested -- was whole and intact.

He nodded to Jerry, the bartender. 'Boilermaker and a pony of Bud,' he said. He pulled out his cigarettes and lit one, ignoring the local bylaw and Jerry's signs. Jerry had known Gessler for twenty years and he also feared the red-headed demolitions expert. The other patrons probably didn't like it, but Gessler had never much given a damn what other people thought of him.

He took his bar stool. 'Fucking ragheads,' he muttered.

'What's that, Paulie?' Ronnie asked.

'Fucking ragheads, Ron. They're everywhere in this town now. You know that old place next to mine? I've got one renting it. Like he fucking belongs right under my nose. Fucking travesty.'

He dropped the shot glass into the beer and knocked back the boilermaker in four long swallows. Then he wiped the profusion of beer from around his mouth with the back of his hand. 'And you know what? I think this fucker might actually be up to something.'

Cliff snorted slightly. 'Come on, Paulie, what are the odds...'

'Shut the fuck up, Cliffy. I'm telling you, boys, there's something up with this little Muslim guy. He's up to something. He gets up and leaves in the earliest hours, when no one else is up yet, he doesn't get back until nightfall...'

'I got it!' Cliff said. 'Maybe he has...'

'Yeah?'

'... A job? You know...'

Gessler wagged a finger in his face. 'You think you're funny, but you're about to get a slap...'

'Seriously, Paulie, what the fuck are you yammering about?' Ronnie asked.

'Just that this guy freaks me out. He's young, Muslim, lives on his own, has visitors at odd hours, usually other young Muslim guys...'

'Yeah, well, if you ask me, Paul's got it right,' Dave interjected. 'You can't trust none of the ragheads. We learned that real quick in Kandahar. We're building fucking schools and roads for these people and they're trying to blow us up with IEDs.'

'Am I right or am I right?' Gessler said. 'One of these days, I'm telling you boys, I'm going to follow that fucker in through that front door, and when I find out what he's up to...'

'You do what you gotta do,' Dave suggested,

tipping his drink in Gessler's direction like a toast. 'More fucking power to you, if it'll make things back the way they used to be.' Dave's father had worked on an auto line for most of his life but it had been twenty years since his last regular job that paid anything. Dave was on disability and an army pension, after taking shrapnel in his thigh from a grenade.

'You're a crazy man, Paulie,' Cliff suggested.

'Shut the fuck up, Cliffy,' Gessler barked. He didn't need advice from the smaller man, or any of those guys, Gessler told himself. Ever since he was a boy, in the orphanage in Baltimore, he'd known he hated Arabs, and niggers, and spics. The older boys, the black ones, had beaten him regularly, taken his things.

Then he'd been taken out of there and thought things would get better, only to find himself in Detroit, cold and alone. The orphanage was barely a memory now; it had been nothing compared to the lickings he'd taken from his foster father, Mr. Gessler, any one of which should have disqualified him from raising children. When he was still working, a decade earlier, the union had paid for a head scan. He couldn't remember what it was called, some set of initials, something stupid. They said his headaches were caused by the blows he'd taken as a child, and he'd lied and told them he'd ridden motocross, ashamed at what he'd let his father do.

But it had forged his hatred, and for forty years, it had grown until it was sometimes damn near overwhelming, ready to break out at just the wrong moment. Maybe, he told himself... just maybe, when he got home, he'd go looking for the sand flea, and then squash him like the bug he was.

26/

WASHINGTON, D.C.

The view from the fifth-floor corner office window was panoramic, a sweeping vista of city lights at night, double dots of locomotion filling the roads, the night too cloudy for stars. Brennan held the vertical blinds slightly apart to take it in. For all of his time with the Agency, he'd spent very little of it in either Langley or D.C. Or, at least, not enough. He liked D.C. and had close friends there with whom he hadn't recently spoken. When he wasn't working, he lived less than an hour away.

But every time he was in town, it was for work. And the longer he stayed on, the more unpleasant it felt.

'Surely you've thought the logistics of this through,' he said, turning back to the room, where Jonah Tarrant sat behind his desk, pensively waiting for a reaction. In front of the desk, Adrianne Hayes sat quietly next to an analyst whose name Brennan couldn't recall. 'You must have a half-dozen assets on the mainland, all of whom have better language skills than me and look a lot more local.'

Tarrant shook the notion off. 'Not at all. We have some regular sources, yes, but no one who can run an operation. And even our sources are, in general, known to the opposite side, or suspected. As Chinese nationals, most of them take a heavy risk in passing information to us. Asking them to handle field work is out of the question.'

'But you have no problem asking me, even though you know I'm trying to get the hell out of this business, right?'

'I have no real choice,' Tarrant said. 'We have no

one with your combination of skillset and deniability. This has to be completely off the books.'

'I got you Raymond Pon...'

'And that was a fine start. But you know full well that we don't have enough from what he told us to find Master Yip Po. We've got some tacit understanding with the Chinese that if they can locate him and figure this thing out...'

'So they don't know what Legacy is either...'

'Not beyond what we know, that it's a sleeper cell and that it used Americans. Problematically, Pon's story begins to fall apart right around that point.'

'Why?'

'Because the town in which they were allegedly recruited and trained, Plenty, Montana? It doesn't exist. The description is as American as apple pie, but the place is fiction.'

'You think Pon was fed misinformation?'

Tarrant shook his head. 'No, the Chinese had heard a similar story but had always taken it to be literal. They're only just slightly ahead of us on getting an actual location name, so my guess is that right now, they're as puzzled as we are.'

'Maybe it's apocryphal,' Brennan suggested, 'just some old spook's tale, kicking around intelligence agencies until someone was ready to believe it. It certainly wouldn't be the first time.'

'Maybe,' Tarrant said. 'But I'd think we'd see more variance between the version we heard and the version known by Chinese State Security if that were the case. No, we need to go to the source. As far as they can tell, the story started circulating after Master Yip Po's escape. Either he's still out there and can tell us more, or someone who knew him in his final years is. We need you to go to Harbin, Joe.'

Brennan waited outside the elevator bank for a ride down to the lobby. He'd managed to keep his temper with Jonah. It wasn't due to pragmatism; he just knew from experience that the deputy director was telling him the truth. If they had an asset who was both deniable and easy to work with, as well as speaking Mandarin, they would have gone to him in the first place.

And whether he liked it or not, he still worked for the Agency until they signed off on his departure. As a covert asset, no sign-off meant no reversion to normal employee status, which meant no pension. That left Jonah Tarrant in total control of his future, and Brennan didn't like that one bit.

The elevator doors opened. Carolyn wore a tan suit and white blouse. They looked shocked to see one another.

'Joe! What are you doing here? I thought they sent you overseas...'

'Yeah... I just got back this morning. I meant to call you.'

She looked hurt, and he knew it was precisely because of that. 'I understand, I suppose. I mean... you could have called, made time for us to have lunch with the kids at least...' She let the sentence drag, unsure of herself. So little of his life was his own. But he hadn't even made an effort.

'They've had me in debriefs and analyst interviews since this morning. You know how much I miss you all when I'm gone,' he said. 'It's the worst.'

'We miss you too. Josh made shortstop.' Their son had just started Little League baseball.

'That's awesome!'

'He wanted his daddy at his first game...'

'Carolyn...'

'But I think he'd settle for a game. Any game, pretty much.'

Brennan frowned and checked his watch. 'It's... nearly nine. Where are the kids?'

'They're sleeping over at friends. You're not the only one working extra shifts because of this North Korean thing.'

'I have to leave again right away.'

She didn't say anything immediately, and her

eyes drifted down to her shoes.

'Carolyn....'

'I knew what I was in for when I married you. I try to hang onto that, you know?'

She never made it easy. He'd long accepted that. He tried to see it from her perspective. 'You know I'm trying to get out,' he said.

'Try harder.' She realized as soon as it came out of her mouth that it was unfair. 'Joe... hon, I'm sorry, I didn't mean that.'

'I know.'

'If it's any consolation, Jonah's new assistant deputy seems to want you off this thing.'

'Really?'

'She invited me to lunch and was asking about whether you were still suitable for field work.'

'This would be Adrianne Hayes, I take it.'

'One and the same. She's actually pretty nice when you get to know her.'

'Trustworthy?'

She gave him a sly look, like he was talking crazy. 'Please... in this business?'

They both knew better. 'I guess not,' he said. 'Do me a favor: keep an eye on her, okay? The ones you start to like are the ones you have to watch out for; it's never been about making friends.'

She smiled gamely at that. 'Sure, uh huh. It would be easier if my best friend was home sometimes.'

He wasn't sure he believed her; and he knew that was the surest sign that they were in trouble. Brennan wondered when one of them would start fighting, trying to keep things together. But he wasn't sure that was what either of them wanted.

She nodded down the hallway toward the offices. 'Look, I have to go...'

'Next time, I'll call you as soon as wheels touch the ground,' he said. 'I promise.'

She knew he meant it.

But Carolyn wasn't sure that was enough anymore, either.

DETROIT, MICHIGAN

The alcohol hung upon the frontal lobe of Paul Gessler's brain like a wet sweater, every thought and action weighing more than it should, a general haze that kept things simple but made walking hard. Or, harder than it should have been.

He cursed them for taking his keys at the bar, making him stagger home. He swayed and shimmied his way along the sidewalk toward his neighborhood, the world around him moving indiscriminately, streetlights blurred streaks of white, the buildings on a slight angle.

Up ahead, a man came out of a restaurant. Gessler's enfeebled brain didn't immediately make the connection. Then he realized it was the little foreign man from next door. He felt a surly anger building again and clenched both his fists. He picked up his pace as best he could, given his balance problems. 'Hey!' he yelled from twenty yards behind. 'Hey! You!'

The man looked over his shoulder then frowned, doubtless put off by the loud and obviously drunken man stumbling toward him. He turned back to the sidewalk and kept walking.

'Hey! Don't you go anywhere!' Gessler yelled. 'You... you and me got to talk.'

The man looked back again before picking up the pace, his stride lengthening. Gessler wasn't having any of that and tried to match him, equilibrium his biggest challenge. 'I told you to fucking stop!' he yelled.

He staggered onward. After about a half block, the small man stopped and looked back. 'Leave me alone, sir, you've had too much to drink!' he yelled. He picked up his pace again.

'Fuck... fucking raghead,' Gessler muttered to no one in particular. The streetlights kept the midnight sidewalk just dim enough to dissuade too much traffic. 'Fucking talk back to me...'

He stumbled but managed to right himself. Then he picked up speed, half-staggering into a jog, like a zombie trying to make time, his vision blurred and bouncing with each stride. The man was closer, he could tell, looking over his shoulder as he began to run himself.

'You... you stop right there,' Gessler managed as they reached the turn to the crescent where they both lived. 'You... you better tell me what you got planned, Mr. Islamist...'

'Leave me alone, you foolish man!' the neighbor demanded. 'You don't think I see you, spying on me every time I leave my house? I am not even Muslim. I am Hindu. I am not even Arabic.' The smaller man turned to face him. 'I warn you, I will defend myself and I know how to do so!'

Gessler wasn't sure what to make of all that. His brain wasn't functioning at anything close to normal levels. 'You're fuckin' lying,' he snarled.

His phone began to ring.

Both men stood there in the dark, saying nothing, anticipating violence, the phone ringing in the background to interrupt at the most awkward time.

'Are you going to answer that?' the East Indian man said.

Gessler frowned again but somewhere inside it occurred that the idea was solid. He reached into his pocket and answer the phone. 'Yeah?'

He stood there with the phone to his ear, swaying in place for about ten seconds. Then he put the phone in his pocket and began to stride toward the East Indian man.

'Hey! I told you sir, I will call the...'

Gessler tried to walk right by him, but their shoulders collided, spinning each man a half-turn.

'Yídòng pàng lǚ!' Gessler yelled.

He kept walking, the East Indian Man standing on the sidewalk stunned, unsure of what he'd just witnessed.

Gessler reached his front door and opened it. He hung up his coat and emptied his pockets into the large ashtray on the telephone table, pausing for just long enough to fight off the brain fog of alcohol. Wallet, keys, coins, cigarettes, lighter. He took the first door to his right, into the living room, then the stairs up to the bedrooms.

His wife was sound asleep, although the radio was on, a rebroadcast of an old Paul Harvey episode. 'His name was Claude Dunkenfield,' Harvey intoned, voice caramel-thick, 'the boy who popped Pop on the noggin...'

Gessler didn't worry about waking her. It wasn't going to matter. He went to the closet and reached up to the attic hatch. He thought about the man on the street. Had he said something to him, unaware in the haze from the liquor that his 'cover' had consumed? He moved the hatch aside and reached up into the opening, feeling around until he felt the handle of the small suitcase. He pulled it down into the closet, then walked back out into the bedroom.

His wife Mary woke when he threw the case onto the end of the bed. 'Paul... what are you doing?'

He opened the case and withdrew the silenced pistol, then levelled it at her. She had just enough time to raise her hands to try to cover her face and to yell, 'Don't...!' before he shot her through the head, the gun's pop quiet, but far from the silenced air compression of movie silencers; instead it was more like a large balloon pricked with a needle, her body thrown back against her pillow. He strode around the bed, covered her face with half the pillow and shot her twice more, then went back to the suitcase and began to methodically double-check its contents.

The code words had been ingrained into him years earlier, the message easily decrypted on the fly: Fire is lit.

He needed to get going; he had a long drive ahead of him. On the bookshelf, the radio program was just ending, the famous announcer's voice echoing out like a ghost from radio's huckster past. 'And now...' Harvey intoned, '...you know the rest of the story.'

27/

DAY 11

LOS ANGELES

Zoey no longer looked forward to her short meetings with Detective Drabek. It had been two days since he'd been able to tell her anything important and she was starting to lose hope of ever getting answers. And life was complicated now: she'd had to move her few possessions in with Valentyna, because police had evicted her from their apartment, which was now a frozen asset.

She sat and stirred her coffee absently, beams of light crossing the vinyl cafe booth table from the large windows out onto the sidewalk. The homicide detectives had been particularly hard on her, grilling her for hours about Ben, their life together, the night he left, the case full of money... They'd spent almost as much time accusing her of being involved somehow, dragging up her prior arrests. In the end, they'd simply told her she could go, but they'd left her without dignity or information, or confidence.

The door to the cafe opened and Drabek walked in. He made his way to the booth. 'Sorry I'm late.' He hadn't sat down for more than five seconds before the waitress was by with the coffee pot. She poured him a cup and Drabek tried to smile pleasantly.

When she'd gone, Zoey slumped back against the booth's high back and tossed the spoon onto the table next to her cup. 'Yeah, well, that's about what I expected, I guess.'

'You're bitter about homicide taking over.'

'You told me it was going to happen. I guess I should have expected it.' Then she leaned forward on the table and eyed him seriously. 'Where were you yesterday? I called your phone three times.'

'I caught up to Ben,' he said.

She took a sharp intake of breath.

'It wasn't good,' he said, not wanting to get her hopes up. 'I spotted the car he was driving at a fleabag motel. When I came out, he was standing on the road with some grocery bags. He dropped them and took off on me, and then lost me in the neighborhood before I could get air support in.'

'How was he?' she asked. 'Did he look okay?' Then she realized what she was asking. She bit her lip for a moment and Drabek stayed silent. 'What am I saying? Did he... I'm sorry, Norm. That's pretty stupid at this point, isn't it?'

'Nobody's going to begrudge how you feel about all this right now,' he suggested. 'Anytime someone commits a crime, he or she victimizes the people they profess to care for, as well as the actual subject. Just keep this in mind: none of this is your fault.'

She knew it was true, but inside she still felt as if Ben had rejected her. It was foolish, and immature, but it was there. 'I shouldn't care about him still, I know. But none of this makes sense. It's hard for me to blame him when I don't recognize the man involved.'

That part got to Drabek. He'd spent a week talking to this woman, and she hadn't struck him once as a dumb bunny. This was a bright, caring individual. And there was just enough off about the guy -- from the missing parents to the gunshot in the condo -- that he didn't think she was imagining it. 'I think you have to consider that he might have developed mental health issues -- borderline personality disorder or worse, complete schizophrenia. Either way, he's a danger to anyone who crosses his path right now.'

'I have dreams about him,' she said, her eyes lowered to the table and distant. 'I have dreams of him shooting at me, and then it morphs, and it's you, and I can't get away and you shoot me down.' She frowned and looked up at him. 'I'm sorry. That's a terrible thing to tell someone.'

Drabek sipped his coffee. 'You need to stop worrying about how I feel, Zoey. I'm doing a job; this is your life, not mine. You need to look out for yourself; and don't worry about some dumb dream. If I had to spend a week dealing with serving members, I'd be upset too. Anyone would. Just realize, I'm not going to give up on helping you out with this, whatever the outcome is. I'm there for you kid, okay?'

He'd hoped that might comfort her, but it seemed to have the opposite effect. She awkwardly turned away slightly and rubbed the top of her head with her fingertips, as if struck by sudden embarrassment at the offer. 'You don't have to...'

'Sure, I do, and I've got my own reasons. You stop worrying so much and leave that to me. Try to find something to keep your mind off this stuff.'

That seemed to work a little. She smiled gamely. 'Valentyna has a cousin with a flower shop just off Crenshaw. She thinks I should go work there and just let the detectives handle this.'

'She might be right.'

'It sure doesn't feel right. I still need to know, Norm. I need the 'why'.'

DETROIT, MICHIGAN

DAY 11

The homicide scene had been busy all morning. The yellow police tape around the small home's front porch had already begun to sag a little, and neighbors around the small crescent continued to gather with family and friends at the end of nearby driveways and in front windows.

Det. Ed Kinnear lifted the tape and ducked under it before taking the wooden steps to the porch and the open front door. His partner, Det. David Underheath, was standing just inside the door talking to a tech.

'... basically within a few minutes, depending on heat loss,' the tech said.

Kinnear nodded to both and Underheath acknowledged him, then turned to the rest of the room, where another pair of techs were taking digital photos of footprints. 'Everyone, our problems are solved. Detective Kinnear has decided to start work for the day. A half hour after the rest of us, to be sure, but certainly, with his brilliance on scene...'

'Yeah, yeah, knock it off,' Kinnear said. 'Your legendary sense of humor can grate at seven-thirty in the morning when I haven't even had breakfast yet. What have we got?'

'Forty-year-old female; multiple documents identify her as Mary Elizabeth Alison Gessler, married, no kids. Shot once at short range, probably from the end of her bed, with a .40 calibre-ish slug, then twice more at much closer range through a pillow. A paperback was beside the bed, as if she dropped it.'

'Double-tap? A pro?'

'More or less. Can't see an amateur thinking to reduce spatter and sound with the pillow. The techs say the powder residue is cordite, so it's an older weapon, and there wasn't much of it. No reports from the neighbors canvassed so far of any noise.'

Kinnear peered at his partner. 'So who *is* this broad? She sure doesn't look like the type who makes bad guys with money angry.' And then the obvious second question caught up to him, as he looked around the room and remembered she wasn't single. 'Where was the husband when all this was going on?'

'No sign of him so far,' Underheath said. 'His vehicle's gone, and we found an open attic hatch in their closet. So maybe he grabbed something stored up there before taking a powder.'

'So he's our guy?' Kinnear suggested.

'Yeah... that bit is weird. The guy has a carry permit but it's because he hunts deer and target shoots. There's a rifle hanging on one of the kitchen walls and an empty gun rack in the garage. And everything we've found said he worked demolitions for a local construction company. We're not talking 'slightly off' the profile of a pro hitter, we're in a whole other ballpark. I mean, he has an expired membership card for a local militia, so we're not talking squeaky clean, necessarily. But nothing that explains what's in there...' Underheath nodded over his shoulder toward the bedroom door.

Kinnear walked by him and peeked around the doorjamb. The body was still reclined in bed, a pillow over her face. The techs were measuring the distance from positions along the edge of the bed to the victim's head. Kinnear tried to put himself in the shooter's shoes, see what he'd seen. 'She's reading, he comes in with the gun, she freaks and tries to cover up or shield herself. Pop, he shoots her once and the book falls to the floor. He walks around the bed, folds the pillow over her face....'

So it was planned and deliberate. That meant immediate passion was out of the question; this was no heated argument, no case of spousal battery gone wrong. The veteran detective walked back out to the hallway.

'Have we talked to the neighbors yet?'

'We've got a couple of patrolmen making sure no one goes anywhere, and so far there's only one who saw Gessler today, an East Indian gentleman named...' he flicked open his notepad, '... Pradesh Patel.'

It was a start, Kinnear knew, albeit not much of one. 'Perhaps we should go find out what Mr. Patel has to say, and whether he knows where we might find Paul Gessler.'

28/

BLAGOVESHCHENSK
FAR EASTERN RUSSIA

The night train from Ignatyevo Airport rolled into the aging station just before ten o'clock, its last stop. The old locomotive's steel wheels screeched under their load as it slowed to a halt. Its front lights shone through the darkness across the tracks and bolstered the muted glare over the platform. A handful of locals waited for colleagues, friends and family to debark.

The city lay in the heart of the Amur Oblast, a vast and verdant river valley that divided the southeastern portion of Russia from China, and its sister community, Heihe. In late summer it was warm, even at ten. Brennan looked out the carriage window as the car came to a halt, trying to spot his contact. Yuri Koskov was from Moscow originally and, at five feet ten and nearly three hundred pounds, stuck out somewhat among the smaller, Asian locals.

He walked over to greet Brennan as he got off the train, a nicotine-stained smile emerging from behind his full beard and moustache, his clip-on sunglasses flipped up to deal with the end of the day. He had a denim jacket on with a grubby sheep's wool collar, and a cap with the earflaps down, despite the warmth. 'It's a great time of year for a visit,' he suggested in Russian, before switching to Standard Mandarin. 'If you need a tour guide, my brother is capable.'

'I'm familiar with the terrain,' Brennan said. 'I carry a map with me everywhere.' He took the old Washington, D.C. road map from his pocket.

Yuri reached into his back pocket and took out a folded-up chart of his own, a road map of Vladivostok. 'That won't help you much around here,' he said in English.

'Sorry I'm late,' Brennan said as they covered the distance to the end of the platform, where short steps led to the parking lot. 'My route was convoluted.'

The Russian driver chuckled. 'Not to worry, my friend. I understand the rationale; there is no way you could fly directly to Harbin. Chinese security has facial recognition at all major airports.'

'And most of Russia...'

'But not in Blagoveshchensk, a place Muscovites forget exists, until there's a need for a political crackdown of some sort. It's because of a paranoid cultural tradition, you see, the belief that the ancestors of the Czarists, the White Russians, live almost exclusively out here now -- well, mostly in Harbin, but also here.' The man spoke quickly, then puffed on his cigarette. 'You want one?'

'I don't smoke.'

Yuri looked amused. 'Another sure sign you're not local.' They arrived at his car, an aging steel-grey sport coupe. 'Out here, you better believe everybody smokes; well... not always tobacco, but something.'

The socializing was mildly irritating. 'When do we cross?' Brennan asked.

'You get right to business, eh? Okay my friend, I get that. Get in.'

Brennan checked the back out of habit before climbing into the front passenger's seat. Yuri just barely fit behind the wheel. 'We go in two hours, just after midnight. My cousin Sergei...' he grunted slightly as he settled into his seat and looped on his seat-belt, '... he's going to handle everything on the other side for you. I'm told you have a cover already for once you get to Harbin?'

'There's a film director who was supposed to be shooting a documentary on the local Jews; he's been unfortunately temporarily detained due to a glitch in the U.S. We already look fairly similar once I'm wearing glasses and no one there has met him yet, so there's no one to vouch against my identity.'

'And it's not like Harbin is the middle of nowhere,' Yuri said, backing the car up, then navigating it out of the lot and onto the exit road. 'Ten million people, western amenities. They have two Pizza Huts now, and a really good Wal Mart. It makes all of this seem a little silly, really, having to smuggle people over.'

'The games politicians play,' Brennan said, 'when the rest of us are busy getting things done.'

The car followed a brand-new two-lane road adjacent to the Amur River. Grey apartment buildings and cement slab office blocks filled most of the left-hand side of the road. Then the road diverged, forking to the left and the right. They took the left fork, separating themselves from the view of the water behind older apartment blocks. The road began to break up in spots from neglect and the grass was muddy, dying. There was garbage strewn about, a cinder block lying beside the road without purpose.

"It is harder on this side of the border, you'll see,' Yuri said. 'The Chinese, they treat Heihe like it's the crown jewel of the fucking west or something. The road between it and Harbin is so smooth it's like glass, for six hours. Heihe's waterfront is like Las Vegas or EuroDisney over there, there's so much neon. New buildings, new roads, new shopping malls full of consumer junk. You'd have a hard time guessing which one was the Communist country these days.'

Brennan could tell what he meant. On the Russian side, it appeared as if development had stopped with the death of Yuri Andropov. The buildings were drab, square, dirty. Monuments to the revolution were flung around the town in small, barely used street corner parks. Along the waterfront, the massive anti-aircraft guns from a warship had been mounted to a column and pointed

244

across at the Chinese, as if in a show of obviously mythical dominance.

'The road right in front of the river basically constitutes the border,' the driver continued. 'It's closed to regular traffic and has cameras on it. But not to worry; where there is a will, as you Americans say... there is a dead man's possessions. No, I kid!' He chuckled at his own joke.

'Yuri, you seem like a jovial guy,' Brennan said. 'But this is serious business tonight. Right?'

Yuri dropped the playful look and took his eyes off the road for a moment to return Brennan's stare. 'Believe me, my friend, I know that better than anyone. You know, guys like me, we're a big help to guys in your type of business. And I know there's probably eight guys just like me in every city you go, so you bet I like your business, eh? Don't ever worry about me, my friend. I stay healthy by staying professional.'

'Watch out!' Brennan yelled. Yuri slammed on the brakes, the car squealing to a halt at a stop sign. In the cross lane, a police car pulled slowly through the intersection. Through the front passenger window, a dour officer watched them with a mix of suspicion and irritation.

They waited until it had passed, then continued on. 'Sorry about that my friend,' Yuri said. 'Try to look on the positive: I did not hit the police. That would have been bad.'

Brennan took an inward breath and held it for a few seconds to gather his inner tension, then exhaled deeply to release it.

It was going to be one of those nights, he could already tell.

DETROIT, MICHIGAN.

It had been more than twenty years since Det. Ed Kinnear earned his shield, and he liked to think in that time, his pragmatism and stoicism had made him an even-handed guy, and a fine judge of character.

Unless Pradesh Patel was a superb actor, the East Indian man was terrified. His eyes had been wide as saucers since opening the door. When they'd told him they were there about a homicide, he'd said, 'please, come in,' and gestured with a wave of his arm for them to enter his small rented house, but his face had said 'what the heck is going on?'

He'd listened to them explain that they felt he might be a material witness, and that he might have evidence that would help them, but it was obvious all he could hear was 'homicide' and 'police.'

'Mr. Patel, we're not here to arrest you,' Kinnear said as they sat across from each other at Patel's kitchen table.'

'I know nothing of any of this, I swear it!' he insisted. 'All I know of them is that he is a foul beast of a man.'

'How so?'

'He gets drunk very often, and he stares at me through his kitchen window and through the back door. Last night...'

'Yes?'

'We had an encounter, I suppose you would call it. He was following me from work or the bar or somewhere. Anyway, he was very intoxicated! And he kept calling me a Muslim.'

'Did he threaten you in any way?' Kinnear asked. 'Did he have any kind of weapon?'

The man shook his head. 'He did not have a weapon that I saw, but I felt very much threatened, yes.'

'Why?'

'Because he is a large man, and he was yelling at me in a most aggressive way. He was calling me a Muslim.'

'But that was all? He didn't do or say anything else?'

The man looked blank for a moment as he

thought it through. 'Well... there was one strange thing.'

'Sure.'

'He got a mobile phone call. He got a call, and he answered it, and then he did not seem interested in our confrontation any longer. He walked right past me... he did sort of bump into me, and then he yelled at me, but I did not understand what he was trying to say.'

'Because he was too far away?'

'No, it was in another language, I think something Chinese or maybe Vietnamese. I am not certain.'

Kinnear and Underheath stared at him with the same puzzled expression.

'What?' Underheath said, 'you mean, like, he was making fun of Chinese people, or...'

'No, I mean he was speaking a language. It was not a sing-song voice, if that is what you are inferring.'

'You're sure about that?' Kinnear asked.

'I speak five languages sir, and while I am not a professional linguist by any measure, I do know what it sounds like when someone is trying to make up words. This was Chinese of some sort, I am fairly certain of it; and the way he said it, it was an expletive of some sort.'

The two detectives gave each other the same puzzled look. Underheath asked the obvious question.

'Does that make any sense to you, Ed?'

Kinnear shook his head. The murder of Mary Gessler had just gone from puzzling to downright weird.

29/

KOWLOON, HONG KONG

The city lights glinted off the black water of Hong Kong Harbor just before midnight. In an apartment block overlooking the water, Daisy Lee stood with her arms crossed in indignation and gazed out of the floor-to-ceiling window.

'You realize that this is complete and total nonsense?'

The phone was on speaker, her handler's voice echoing over the line from Beijing. He was officious and pragmatic, a young man with his eyes on a long career. 'You're aware this channel...'

'Is being monitored at all times by PLA intelligence? Yes, of course. Right now, I'm too angry to care what the higher ups think of me.'

'You are handling this very unprofessionally, Daiyu,' he said. 'Chairman Yan was clear that his personal intelligence suggested Charlie Pang's source was somewhere in Hong Kong.'

'And after being here for two days, twisting a few arms and paying off a few other less-than-stellar individuals, it's quite clear to me that this is a deliberate wild goose chase. I'd like to know why.'

'Your instructions were clear. You were to investigate the Pang rumor, then wait for contact from a relief agent.'

'Xiaodang, you have always been straight with me...'

'I am just following my orders. And right now, you should be doing the same. Stay until your relief arrives. It has been two nights; I'm sure it won't be long.'

'And then what?'

'Then we'll find out when we're given more

instructions. Aiyah!' He sounded exasperated. 'Why are you being difficult about this?'

Why? Because something felt wrong about the whole trip, that was why. They all knew from the surveillance transcript that Charlie Pang's source was in Harbin. There had been literally no mention of another Hong Kong connection until the moment she left Mexico. So, she'd been sent on a time-killing wild goose chase; if it had been a matter of allowing her to save face while pulling her off the file, she might have understood. But Yan Liu Jeng was one of the highest-ranking intelligence officers in the nation; there was no reason for him to have made the call, or for him to have intervened with a 'personal source.'

But there was no advantage to sharing that with Xiaodang, whom she respected, but hardly knew on a personal basis. 'It's just the vagueness, that's all. You know I hate to operate in a vacuum. I'm used to hard targets, direct assignments,' she lied.

'Well, just relax. You know what? You should get some sleep. If they have you on the move, it probably won't be tonight, even if that's when they make contact. More likely you'll be flying out tomorrow morning to Macau or another assignment.'

'A good idea. Perhaps... perhaps you're right,' she said, selling it as effusively as possible. 'I am tired, after all. Good night, Xiaodang.'

'Goodnight, Daiyu.'

She knew as soon as he suggested she get some sleep.

It was the timbre of his voice, the meter. Something was off. He was a good handler, Xiaodang, but he was a lousy actor. That meant someone was coming for her, for reasons either political or professional. Either one could mean arrest, or detention; but more likely, given her own history, it would involve a bullet behind the ear.

Lee knew she had to prepare, get ready for visitors. They'd picked the apartment well; it had only two proper exits, with no balcony. If they'd ordered Xiaodang to contact her to make sure she was in place, it meant the exits were already being watched. There would be no easy way out.

So perhaps it was best to let them come, Lee decided. She crossed the living room to the bedroom door. Her suitcase lay open on the bed, the silenced pistol on top.

THE AMUR RIVER, FAR EAST RUSSIA/CHINA

The ferry approached the Chinese side of the river at a leisurely pace, passengers crowded on its top deck. They were all Russian; Chinese visitors to Russia had to go through a laborious visa process, so all of the traffic was one way. It was just as well; there wasn't much to buy in Blagoveshchensk except for black-market goods that had been bought in Heihe to begin with, the prices marked up to take advantage of those who couldn't or wouldn't cross the border.

But in the Far Eastern fronts of Siberia, Russian did not mean Caucasian. There were very few westerners present, aside from Brennan, Yuri, and Yuri's cousin, Sergei, who allegedly had great contacts in the Chinese city. According to Yuri, he was 'the most respected smuggler among the working class of Blagoveshchensk.'

Sergei was standing by the rail and nodded to his brother and Brennan to join him. 'See that light down there, near the shore? That's where we're headed. There's a customs office, but they allow free passage for Russians. It's swarming with cops, and they're looking for anyone out of place. But as long as we're with Sergei, we're okay.'

'Comforting,' Brennan said. He didn't trust Sergei as far as he could throw him. He'd been non-communicative, which was fine; but he'd also seemed nervous all night. 'Then what?'

'Then we drop you downtown. Sergei has some contact who knows everyone in the local black societies. If your guy disappeared in Harbin, they will know where, or nobody does. So we leave you with him, he takes you to Harbin. Then when you return, you call me on the phone I'll give you, we pick you up and take you back.'

'Both of you?'

He shrugged. 'Sergei has contacts at both borders; and on the Russian side they check a lot more closely. Me? I just drive. I'm your ride back to the airport. I get you back there, we get the rest of our bread, everyone's happy.'

The ferry pulled up to the dock. Both of the Russians inhaled their Winstons feverishly, the smoke billowing around in the wind. Sergei had his worry beads in one hand and was running them through his fingers, squeezing them each time for tension release.

'You two look nervous,' Brennan said.

'We're Russians,' Yuri said. 'It's our nature to be bleak.'

The passengers began to disembark.

'Where are we headed?' Brennan asked. He was getting nervous himself. The territory was too unfamiliar. He'd looked over maps of Heihe and tried to prepare but it was his first time with boots on the ground, and his unwelcome status had been made abundantly clear in Jonah's last meeting with the Chinese.

'Just keep your head down,' Yuri said. 'Once they see Sergei, they'll leave all three of us alone.'

'And if they don't?'

'Unless your Russian is going to get a lot better a lot more quickly...'

Brennan answered in Yuri's mother tongue. 'My Russian is just fine, Tovarisch...'

Yuri's eyebrows rose. 'You're full of surprises, my friend. We assumed you couldn't understand what we were saying. I'm exceptionally glad I did not sound like too much of an asshole.'

Sergei nodded that it was time, and they made their way down the gangplank to the docks. At the bottom, a policeman was checking papers. 'Let me do the talking,' Sergei said to Yuri in Russian. 'Keep our friend here quiet or the whole thing goes to hell.'

The policeman eyed them suspiciously but spoke rapid-fire Mandarin. 'These two are with you?'

'They are.' Sergei put his beads on the counter and fished in his pocket for the three passports. Brennan only worried briefly about how quickly his had been cobbled together; the forger in Tokyo had been a company asset for years.

'You should give us some notice for something like that. What if a supervisor was visiting for inspection today? We could all be in real trouble.'

'Point taken. But we're good, right?'

The man nodded gently but didn't look certain. He motioned toward Brennan. 'Who's this guy? I recognize your brother.'

'This is Leonid Shevchenko; he's from Kiev.' Then he leaned in conspiratorially. 'He's got a line on American smokes at decent prices, eh?'

That caught the policeman's attention. He looked directly at Brennan. 'How much for a carton of Marlboros?'

Brennan frowned. 'One carton?' He had to delay. He realized he had no idea how much cigarettes cost in Heilonjiang province.

Sergei interrupted, recognizing his predicament. 'Don't you give him that sixteen yuan bullshit; you give him the price you quoted me.'

'Ten yuan per packet,' Brennan told the policeman. 'But at that price, you have to order at least half a case, five cartons.'

The policeman nodded. 'Uh huh. When you're on this side of the river, just remember: I say what I do or don't do, and I say what you can do, or don't do. You remember that, you can make some good money here.'

Sergei interjected again. 'Don't worry, he knows the score, right Lenny?'

Brennan nodded vociferously, his gaze as wide and witless as he could manage.

KOWLOON, HONG KONG

It was after midnight when the electronic door lock on the apartment's front door clicked open. Lee had been dozing in the corner armchair, fatigued after a long day of travel and the anxiety of the anticipated visitor. She'd changed into all black garb, and was barely visible in the shadows. She flicked off the pistol's safety.

The door opened slowly, a head poking into the room. But rather than looking for the lights, the figure crept into the room. 'Lee!' the man whispered loudly. 'Are you awake?'

He crept around the corner of the room and toward the bedroom door. Lee caught sight of his face, moonlight streaming through the tall windows to partially illuminate his right profile.

Xiaodang.

She'd half-expected him, but still felt a pang of regret at what was about to happen. She knew he was just following orders, being the faithful, unquestioning public servant. He would have been told he had no choice, that it was essential to national security, that she'd gone rogue.

He leaned into the bedroom and saw the roll she'd placed under the cover. She rose even as he raised his weapon, quickly and silently crossing the carpeted living room, until she was right behind him. His hand was shaking slightly, his brow beaded with sweat. She wondered how long it had been since his last field assignment, if ever. Lee felt her sympathy for him rising; she pushed it down deep and tried to keep in mind what he was about to do.

Xiaodang gently squeezed the trigger. The report was loud, slapping their eardrums. The first shot was high and thunked into the wooden headboard of the queen-sized bed. The second two were on target, finding the hump on the pillow where Lee's head would have been, had she listened to his pleas to make it an early night.

As soon as he heard the sound of the impact, he raised the pistol toward the ceiling. 'You knew.'

'You made it obvious. Thank you for that.'

'If it makes you feel any better about this,' he said, 'I was genuinely trying to fool you, so that I could do my job.'

'Who ordered a cleanup?'

'Are you going to let me go?'

'You know that's not an option. But if you tell me what I need to know, I'll make it quick.'

'And if I don't?'

'I'll be required to convince you. I suspect a bullet through the front of your kneecap will clear the matter up.'

'It was Beijing.'

'I knew that already. Whose direction?'

'Yan Liu Jeng, I believe. At least, it came from one of his men.'

'He sent me here to get me away from Legacy.'

'He sent you here because you failed twice and caused an international embarrassment.'

She shrugged. 'To-may-to, to-mah-to,' Lee said. She shot him in the back of the head, the blood spatter hitting the far wall at the same moment that her former colleague's body hit the bed.

Lee moved around the bed and checked his pockets. He had a phone, papers, a spare magazine; nothing else that would likely help. Despite what Xiaodang had been led to believe, she knew they wouldn't just take out a failed operative. She might have been demoted, or even fired. But Beijing had no reason to liquidate. That meant someone was worried, worried that she was onto something in her pursuit of Master Yip Po.

That meant someone within the service had a tie to Legacy. It might even be Yan Liu Jeng himself.

And that meant she had no one she could trust.

She reached down beside the bed and picked up her suitcase, carrying it back to the living room.

Whoever was trying to shut her out had made a grave error in judgment, she noted, assuming she had poorer contacts in Hong Kong than Macau. She'd have a new identity within an hour, money transferred from one series of accounts to another before the bureaucrats were awake to follow up on Xiaodang's mission.

Lee looked out the window, the harbor busy even past midnight, flecks of white and red lights dancing across the ripples and swells of the water. Solving Legacy was about more than stopping a terror attack, now; it was about absolving herself, and proving to State Security that she was still an asset. To do that, she had to find Master Yip.

Behind her, she heard the electronic door lock click again.

30/

HEIHE, CHINA

They'd driven in the rain past the neon lights and office towers, to the other side of the city and an industrial park, mile after mile of factories, warehouses and storage yards, machine shops and barbed-wire fences. The streets were grimy and trash-strewn, unloved compared to the business-facing urban center, where Russian shoppers and Chinese entrepreneurs mixed in equal measure. Here the lights were lower, the shadows running deeper.

'Where are we going?' Brennan asked.

'It's not far now,' Yuri said. 'Sergei's guy is with the Black Cranes, a local gang. They control this area of the city.'

Brennan's hackles were up; he was accustomed to criminal contacts, but dealing with a Black Society was infinitely more dangerous. They would have the manpower, complete control of the meet, and any number of possible ulterior motives.

'I don't need to meet the whole gang,' he said. 'Just a source that will lead us to Master Yip Po.'

'Just relax,' Sergei said. 'Everything is good, my friend -- as long as you've got my money.'

They turned down a narrow laneway, the headlights doing all the work, iron gates and double garage doors coming briefly into view through the thickening darkness, then fading as they passed. Sergei slowed the car to a crawl and turned left, through an open double gate, into a warehouse yard. The place was surrounded by ten-foot corrugated metal fencing, topped with barbed wire and glass shards inset into concrete.

They parked and got out of the car. Brennan counted five cameras in front of the airplane-hangar-sized building alone. The front door was reinforced steel, designed to latch only from the inside so that there wasn't even a lock to pick. He counted nine cars, and assumed at least double that many men. *Pretty lousy odds.*

'No patrols? No guard posts?' he asked.

Yuri scoffed at the notion. 'They don't need them. No one messes with the Black Cranes and lives more than about an hour to tell of it.'

They walked up to the door and Sergei pressed the red button next to it. A moment later, a slot in the door slid open and a pair of eyes appeared. 'What do you want?' the guard asked in Mandarin.

'It's Sergei. Vincent is waiting to see me.'

Yuri whispered to Brennan. 'This is the part where I leave you to your business.' He handed the American an older-model flip phone. 'Dial the last number and that is me if you need anything, or when you want to cross back.'

'You're not coming in?'

'No man, no way. Vincent Gao ain't my a-number one fan, if you know what I mean.' He turned and headed back to the car. 'Sergei, are we good?'

'We are.'

'Then a good night to both of you.'

Brennan looked over his shoulder as Yuri made his retreat, the red taillights of the car disappearing around the corner. 'I'd have felt better about this if he stuck around.'

Sergei snorted, but didn't say anything.

The door clicked open. The guard leaned around the edge. 'He'll see you.'

The guard led them into an atrium, this time with two doormen, and yet another steel door. They kept an eye on the pair as they were led through the second door and into the building proper.

If Brennan had any expectations that Chinese mobsters would be more refined than their American counterparts, they were quickly put to rest. The place was part old-school video arcade, part lavish apartment. There were a handful of loveseat-style sofas, a couple of armchairs, a big flat screen on one wall, a pinball machine, and a kitchenette that was covered in debris. Black-leather clad gangsters in mirrored sunglasses lounged around with exotic dancer types under pink and orange neon, some sharing cocaine or opium, others groping each other. There was a white tiger pelt as a rug on the polished concrete floor, and electronic dance music thumped out of giant speakers in each corner of the room.

The Red Pole named Vincent Gao sat at the end of the room on a raised dais, on a clear plastic armchair that looked to Brennan like a prop from Battlestar Galactica. He absently wondered if the guy's butt was visible from the other side.

Gao made a gesture with his hand, a summoning motion, as if his visitors weren't worth the effort of speech. His face was cold and emotionless. 'This him?' he asked Sergei.

'I tell him 'if anyone in Heihe can find a person in Harbin, it's Mr. Gao,' Sergei said.

'Okay,' Gao said. 'Go on then, get out of here.'

'I still need to get half my mon...'

'Did I stutter?' Gao demanded. 'Get out, stupid Russian, before you try my patience.' The gang leader was probably in his late twenties or early thirties, Brennan noted; it was probably humiliating for Sergei. Or, it should have been.

'I'll pay you when we touch base again,' Brennan said quietly to the other man. 'Maybe you better listen to the man.'

Sergei nodded curtly and turned to leave. 'You have that phone...'

'Out!' Gao bellowed. A gangster in a charcoal suit and black dress shirt towered over Sergei. He grabbed him by the upper arm and led him to the door.

'That was my ride,' Brennan said dryly in Mandarin.

Gao's surprise was obvious. 'A gwai lo who speaks the language?' He turned to his men. 'That's like teaching a monkey to paint fine art.'

They dutifully laughed much harder than the joke deserved.

Brennan ignored it. 'I'm told you can help me find Master Yip Po.'

'Is that what you were told?' Gao reached down to the translucent plastic sidetable and picked up a huge joint from an ashtray. He lit it and took a puff, then let the thick white smoke billow about. 'Maybe Master Yip don't want to be found. Maybe there is no Master Yip. What do you want him for, anyway? You think you're the next action hero or something? Maybe he'll teach you Wing Chun kung fu?'

His friends chuckled again.

The vibe was getting tense. Sergei had assured him they were onside already. 'Can you help me or not?' he asked.

A chorus of ooohs circled the room, the gang amused at his disrespectful tone.

'Who the fuck are you anyway, white boy?' Gao asked. 'Sergei said you're some type of spy or something. Your shitty Mandarin accent says you're American. So, what're you doing all the way up in Heilongjiang province, sneaking around with lowly Russian dogs?'

'Hmmph. Sounds like Sergei and I are going to have to have a little chat about privacy.'

'And how do you think that is going to happen?' His supporters started chuckling again. 'Why would we help you? Or let you go?'

'Sergei paid you, right?'

'He did.'

'And...'

Gao shrugged. 'Life doesn't come with a guarantee.' More laughs from the peanut gallery. 'Maybe we hold you for ransom and until your people pay, we send them a piece of you each week. Or maybe we call Master Yip; he has some powerful friends, according to the rumors.'

'The rumors? So I'm guessing he doesn't give you a lot of face time.'

Gao's look soured. 'Maybe we just shoot you

tonight, then send pieces back to your employers anyway, see how much money I can make off your corpse.'

'Certainly not my favorite option.'

Gao smiled at that. 'Hey! Grace under pressure! I like you, Gwai Lo. Maybe I won't kill you at all. Maybe I just sell you to a slave trader.'

'Oh... that's never going to happen,' Brennan said. He'd already assessed the room; nine, one for each car. *Two beside Gao, one sitting on the back of the first sofa, two on the second to my right with girls; one behind the first chair left, attentive; the two beside me; and one at three o'clock in the armchair, his leg over the arm. Jacket bulges on a pair, the rest doubtless packing something in their waistband. A couple of katanas, ethnically discordant, one in the hands of the man perched on the edge of the first sofa, like a deadly walking stick. The other in its sheath of the thug at one o o'clock, standing behind the couch to the right.*

Too many. Brennan's combat skills were as honed as they'd ever been and turning forty hadn't slowed him enough to make him any less dangerous. But nine armed men, at least three already alert to danger? That was suicidal.

'Take him,' Gao said. 'But don't kill him! He's worth money.'

That evens the odds up a little, Brennan thought. The thugs on either side moved to grab his arms. Brennan ducked down slightly to throw off their grip, then struck fast and hard, his right foot driving into the side of one man's knee, his left elbow flashing backwards, the guard turning into it and taking the brunt to his throat, crushing his windpipe.

The first guard had collapsed holding his knee, screaming, and his co-workers were clambering to their feet. Brennan rolled to his right and swept his leg in a semi-circle, catching the katana-wielder as he rose from the couch, his feet flying out from under him. The American caught the sword before it hit the ground and pivoted, using his kneecap to spin on the smooth surface, the blade swinging in a wide arc that caught two more guards by surprise, slicing them open, blood spewing out onto the polished concrete. The sword's owner had recovered and tried to catch him from behind; but Brennan was ready, thrusting the blade backwards and through the man's torso.

The other swordsman was charging in, his colleagues abandoning their girls to join him. Brennan pulled hard on the sword as the man behind him dropped to his knees, dying. But it wouldn't budge, caught in the man's chest cavity like an axe blade in a partially chopped tree. The second sword flashed through the air, its owner swinging it with measured, fast cuts and thrusts, Brennan ducking and dodging each, rolling to his left, throwing a hard punch to the groin of the second guard and....

That was when the pistol came down on the back of his skull, and everything faded to black.

KOWLOON, HONG KONG

The lock clicked over. Lee ducked behind the corner between the hallway entrance and living room. She cursed herself silently for not replacing the slug she'd used to shoot Xiaodang.

The door flew open. She leaned around the corner and fired off two quick rounds, the suppressor muting the volume; but whomever had kicked open the door had also then stepped to one side, anticipating gunfire.

She went back into cover just as a figure obscured behind a pair of pistols leaned into the apartment and opened fire. Bullets whizzed by her and through the floor-to-ceiling safety glass. One caught the door jamb, breaking it and sending pine splinters into the air. Lee leaned back around the corner and got off two more shots, but the man was in cover again.

'We could do this all night, you know,' she said loudly in Cantonese. 'Assuming the neighbors haven't already called the police.'

'You want to give up now, Sweet Pea?' the man replied. 'Your American friend ain't here to save you this time.'

She was puzzled for just a moment; the hitman, from Macau. Tommy Wong. He leaned into the open door frame for just a second, and she fired her last round, but a split second too late. In a second, she knew, he would realize that the final click had been the trigger and an empty magazine. She needed to act.

Lee ran toward the apartment's entrance, but the gunman stepped into the opening before she could get there. She leaped into a jumping side kick, but the hit man blocked it with crossed arms, his stance wide, absorbing the force. Lee found her feet as she fell to the floor. She rose off the balls of her feet, pushing hard backwards, the flat of her back thumping down onto the hardwood even as Wong's pistols trained upon her, sliding backwards on the polished floor as he unloaded both weapons, the bullets thunking into the wood just millimeters behind her as she slid all the way to the windows.

Then both clicked empty, the triggers without resistance, the slides back.

Out of ammo.

Lee rolled right and found her feet.

'I thought I'd see you again,' he said. The man's suit was dark olive this time, but it was definitely Wong.

'That's funny; after I defeated you so easily the last time we fought, I assumed you would go back to wherever little bitches go to lick their wounds.'

'You know, there's a misconception about mechanics like myself, that we all enjoy killing people,' he said, going into a bouncy fight stance. 'But it's not true. I mean, I personally do, but not everyone is me. Correct?'

'Let's just get on with it,' she said.

He charged in with a flurry of punches, his stance wide enough to thrust both high and low. Lee slapped them away with open palms then tried to shoot Wong's knee, wrap him up in a hold before things progressed. But he ducked backwards, dropped low and shot out a hard, straight kick that caught her shoulder nerve cluster, deadening the arm slightly. She danced away then rushed in before he could react with a pair of overhead spinning kicks, the first blocked, the second catching Wong flush, her heel cracking across his jaw like a whip. Wong flew sideways in a half spin, his body crashing onto the sofa. Alertly, he shook off the blow and rolled over the top of the couch and onto the floor behind it before she could follow with a knockout strike.

She circled so that her back was to the hallway as she faced him. She expected him to do what most men did, and Wong obliged, assuming his size advantage would help. He charged in, trying to overwhelm her. Instead, she dropped in a perfect set of splits and thrust upwards with a closed fist, the impact catching Wong square in his testicles. He doubled over, grabbing at his groin with both hands, staggering sideways away from her, until he was in front of the giant window. Lee took two powerful steps and flew into a side kick. This time, Wong's hands were otherwise engaged, the blow striking him square in the ribs, breaking them. He crashed into the giant window, which was cracked badly from the two earlier gunshots, the glass splintering and disintegrating instantly, the hit man tumbling through, his scream audible for barely a moment as he plunged fifteen stories.

Lee ran toward the bedroom. She needed to grab her things and go; the police would be all over the building within moments, and now she had no doubt: someone within the security service had hired Wong and set her up. And they'd deliberately kept her away from Harbin and Master Yip Po.

She had contacts in Kowloon, good ones. Whoever set her up couldn't use official channels and that meant she could still travel, at least until she was tied to the two bodies at the apartment building. They'd use that as a pretense to have police pursue her. So she had to move quickly, she knew. There would be a flight to Harbin at some point in the next few hours, and she intended to be on it.

30/

BEIJING, CHINA

Yan paced his office nervously, waiting for the conference call to begin, his anxiety steadily building.

He'd never seen the other participants in person, and only knew that they were Chinese patriots, just like him. They were Communists, and they saw China's emergence in the modern world economy as the loathsome betrayal that it was.

He was as anonymous, in turn, to each of them.

They were each recruited by a man who remained in the shadows, funding their movement's growth and inevitable ascension to control of the Central Committee. And it was this same man who always debriefed and instructed him, always with a tone and air that suggested any misstep would cost him his place among the elites after the new revolution.

He knew their elusive leader would expect a certain confidence and stoic professionalism from him; but he was genuinely nervous, unsure of how things had progressed in Kowloon. He was supposed to have heard from Wong by now, and the silence felt like condemnation. And there was a rumor from their office in Heilonjiang that an American was snooping around Heihe, looking for the Black Cranes, Master Yip's Black Society in his youth.

For a man who had risen to his lofty position through calculated political alignments and coasting on the successes of others, he knew his involvement in Legacy was taking an enormous chance. He was a true believer in the cause, but he also recognized that in change lay the seeds of opportunity. His father, a party organizer from Shanghai who had known Mao personally, had been utterly ashamed of his son's silken guile and easy charm. He thought him a capitalist at heart. Perhaps, Yan thought, Legacy was a chance to prove his father wrong while still maintaining the power and lifestyle to which he'd become accustomed.

Or perhaps it was simpler; perhaps it was the opportunity to be immortalized in the annals of history, to ensure that, loved or loathed, he would be remembered.

A chime signaled that the call was coming in and he checked his posture, even though the caller would only see his face. Confidence was important in such situations.

As always, the caller was shrouded in shadow, his voice disguised. It was unnerving, but Yan knew that was the point. The man wanted to intimidate and control, and the politician knew the value of both, even if he was on the receiving end at times. They had spoken little about the details, beyond what the Shadow Man had taught him about Project Legacy, how to trigger it, and the massive, deadly consequences to the decadent west. In its wake would rise an army of supporters, recruited from across China over the course of two decades, he was instructed. China would need new blood at the top, and Yan was the perfect man for the job.

'Status report, Yan,' the leader asked without further greeting.

'We are into the second phase. I expect we'll see increased intelligence pressure from both sides, but there is no reason to believe any of our work has been compromised. The package will be in place on time.'

'And the opposition?'

'Chasing its tail. Our own agent has been sequestered to Hong Kong, and the Americans need our help to progress. There is...'

'What?'

'It's nothing, probably.'

'Don't waste my time, Yan...'

'There's a report of an American operative in Heihe.'

'Heihe?'

'Black Crane territory. As is Harbin.'

'Ah. And how are you handling it?'

'I'll be travelling there tonight on official business anyway. The timing is perfect. The Cranes will doubtless pick him up and, assuming they haven't killed him already, I can ensure he gets no closer to Master Yip.'

'And if necessary, you will have to consider our exposure, what with the revered one at large, even at his age.' Before Yan could protest the notion of assassinating Jiang Qing's favored servant and teacher, his contact changed the subject. 'What about Legacy? Do we have an operational framework in place?'

'We do. The final target is fluid, for obvious reasons, but we'll have plenty of time once we know what the political road is over the coming days. The third phase is prepared for any eventuality.'

Neither man ever spoke of the final stage, or the eventual fallout of their plan, the inevitable loss of life, the political discord. Neither preferred it; they just recognized the necessity of revolution when trying to reshape the world.

DAY 12

LOS ANGELES

'Tell me about the tattoo on the back of your left hand.'

The therapist's voice was calm and level, with

just enough of a tinge of interest to make her seem genuine. Zoey looked at the tattoo, one of nine on her hand and left arm, running all the way to her shoulder.

'Who is 'KMA'? the therapist asked.

The letters were oversized, in a cartoonish script, intertwined with marijuana leaves. It hadn't been one of her prouder moments, that tat, and it had hurt like hell, although the alcohol had helped. The small bones in her hand were bruised for a week.

'Not who, what,' she said. 'It stands for 'Kiss My Ass'. When I was seventeen, I thought that was edgy.' She'd been fired from a particularly dictatorial salon that morning, and had felt like shouting it to the world.

The therapist smiled warmly. 'You sound wiser in your old age.'

'Isn't everybody? I've got a few others that are as goofy, but more that I really love. Besides, the bad ones are like lessons you always hold onto.'

'That's a very positive outlook.'

'So I've been told. It's not really helping much right now.'

'Because of Benjamin?' the police therapist had access to notes on the case, within limits. The girl was suffering from social separation, emotional trauma, acute distrust of authority... it was a panoply of issues and a sure-fire recipe for anxiety, depression, and avoidant personality disorder.

'Because I can't find him and confront him. And as well as I thought I knew him, it's just one more sign that I really didn't.'

'Los Angeles is a big city...'

'But he's a creature of habit,' she said. 'He folds his socks, for crying out loud. It's just not possible...'

'That he killed someone?'

'Yeah.'

Zoey felt better for talking about it, but it wasn't because she expected the therapist to actually resolve anything. That closure wasn't going to come until she talked to Ben again. It was a familiar sadness, the same despair she felt when she thought about her childhood, her abusive father, her time on the street. It was a sense that no one really loved her.

'Do you have any friends or family out of town?' the therapist asked. 'A change of scenery can do wonders sometimes in this situation.'

She shook her head. She'd never had a real vacation, or gone on a long trip. The closest had been when Benjamin took her for a quiet weekend at a little motel in Santa Barbara. They'd walked along the beach, and had dinner on a patio at an Italian restaurant. And then back at the motel, she'd rocked his world...

'What about here in town?'

'I'm staying with a friend now. She's been really great. We didn't really know each other before this.'

'She's also a former dancer?'

'Current hooker.'

'Oh. And you're okay with that?'

'My life hasn't exactly been squeaky clean,' Zoey said. 'I try not to judge.'

'That wasn't my...'

'No, it's okay,' Zoey said. 'I understand that I don't really fit in with normal people. But a lot of them are not so nice on the inside, you know? I mean, there are a lot of people who look more normal than me, but when anyone gets in their way, they find out these people are crazy bad. Like, corporate executive types, politicians, gangsters...'

'Plastic surgeons?'

Zoey hadn't really considered it, the possibility that Ben had always been bad, had always had a secret side. The idea that the mild-mannered Jewish kid from... well, she didn't really know where from anymore... but the idea of him slipping away to cater to dark, hidden whims was absurd.

'Am I in denial?' she asked the psychiatrist. 'Is it possible to be so in love with someone that you can't tell they're a monster?'

Zoey walked back to Valentyna's apartment from the psychiatrist's office. At the first cafe with a patio, she decided to take a break for a cup of coffee. The session had thrown her, made her think about her own past, everything she'd had to go through to improve her life. Maybe what Ben really deserved was a punch in the nose. He had everything, and he was walking away, enthralled by something.

Or maybe someone?

It angered her that he could walk away without explanation, that he could try to hurt her. It angered her that she was angry, because she'd put the constant tension and explosiveness of life on the street behind her.

She thought back to the trip up the coast, just six months earlier. He'd acted like he was going to propose, or like maybe it was a scouting trip to find the perfect spot for them. They'd gone around town and tried the local restaurants, a few bars, a couple of days beachcombing, the walk under the stars, where he'd held her hands in his by the shoreline and told her that she was the only person who had ever made him feel like he could be himself...

Zoey took out her phone and pulled up a map of Santa Barbara. The Motel had been among several within walking distance of the beach. It wasn't fancy, but it was a clean room, and it was private.

That struck her as odd, though. She hadn't really thought about it until then, but Benji never worried about money like that. His fitness club, his car, their place, his clothes; everything was expensive and classy. At the time, the whole trip had been so romantic that she'd just put it down to him wanting a place as near to the beach as possible.

She checked the map again; there were resorts and first-class places within the same walking distance to the beach, a couple right on the coast, the ocean outside the back doors.

Then why that place, in particular? It was more anonymous; if they'd been having a fling, she could see it. But she'd lived with Ben for three months already by then.

Zoey wondered if she'd missed anything else that seemed strange or out of place. She felt anger and resentment welling up again at his betrayal. Why Santa Barbara? What else had he been up to? She resisted the notion of another woman, as petty as anything of that nature seemed in the current light; it wouldn't make sense to take her along anyway.

So... maybe it had just been what it was, a romantic episode in a relationship that seemed utterly real but was now utterly ruined.

She sipped her coffee. That motel, though...

Something wasn't right.

She took out her phone and hit redial.

He answered on the second ring. 'Drabek.'

'Norm? It's Zoey. I think I have something we need to check out.'

DETROIT, MICHIGAN

Det. Ed Kinnear hung up the phone and then pinched the bridge of his nose. He'd worked overtime for two days straight on the Gessler case but they were nowhere.

'Penny for your thoughts, partner.' Underheath was on the other side of the two-man desk behind his computer, looking up something and sipping on a Styrofoam cup of coffee.

'I don't get it,' Kinnear said. 'Cases like this, the guy has usually flipped out and he's either caught near the scene, or he's picked up fleeing after doing something stupid in traffic. If it were random, he just disappears. That I can see. But he killed his wife, and now there's no trace of him.'

'Credit cards come back?'

'Yeah, nothing. He last used his debit card at a cash machine two days ago. He took out twenty bucks right before visiting the liquor store down the street. The victim used hers the day before him to buy groceries. The credit cards haven't been touched in several months and the balances are near the max.'

'That means he has cash on him or no money at all.'

'He can't get anywhere without either money or a brash desire to rob gas stations, and we'd have heard about that by now,' Kinnear said. 'What have you got in terms of getting his profile together?'

Underheath hit a key on the PC to save something, then moved out from behind it to his desk proper. 'Pretty much what we suspected from the house. He's part of the American Independents of Michigan, a militia group. Going by its chat board, it attracts a lot of young, white, underemployed individuals, most of whom have no faith or trust in any political institution anymore.'

'And what do they do, these unhappy few?'

'Mostly they go off into the woods and shoot targets, then get drunk and complain about life.'

'Ah. Old school, then. They couldn't just go hunting like any other pissed off kids in the UP, could they?' Kinnear suggested.

'Apparently not. I cross-referenced a few of the members and about half of them have minor convictions for assault, drunk and disorderly, a few B-and-Es... A winning bunch. You get anything on him speaking other languages?'

'His former supervisor had a good laugh over that. It seems Mr. Gessler is a pretty racist guy. He's never been outside America, as far as anyone can tell. He's never applied for a passport. He's never even been to Canada and it's only a few hours away. I talked to a local neurologist...that's a brain doctor...'

'I know, Ed...'

'Anyway, he says there have been cases in the past of people remembering languages they'd learned as kids and then forgotten; and there have been cases of people developing foreign accents after a blow to the head or stroke. But they've never seen a case where a grown man spontaneously learned something as complicated as Vietnamese or Chinese.'

'Maybe we should revisit the little brown guy from next door. Maybe he was schtupping the wife,' Underheath suggested. 'Maybe that's why they had the confrontation outside. Gessler goes home and kills the wife, goes looking for Patel, Patel gets the drop on him...'

Kinnear looked at him curiously. 'What have you been smoking, exactly? The twenty-something East Indian engineer next door was sleeping with forty-something, five-foot-six, one hundred- and sixty-pound Mrs. Gessler?'

Underheath shrugged. 'It was just a thought.'

'It wasn't much of one.'

'What next, then?'

'Next, we hit up his former co-workers, his buddies, anyone called from the home phone. Then we wait. Something has to come out of either forensics or Mr. Paul Gessler making a mistake, or an appearance,' Kinnear suggested. 'Let's just hope he doesn't decide to shoot anyone else in the meantime.'

SANTA BARBARA, CALIFORNIA

The Palms Motel hadn't changed much since the Nineteen Fifties. It wasn't better off for it, but it gave the weathered, beaten-up overnight stop a certain charm. The sign, for one, was the same rotating piece of black-type-on-bright-yellow glass that had been there since it opened. It had been broken and repaired a few times, but it kept on turning with the same predictability as the seasonal ebb and flow of tourists.

Drabek rolled down the driver's-side window on the air-conditioned sedan and eyeballed the rest of the building. It had ten units, each beside the other.

Across the road was The International, an almost identical motel with a non-rotating yellow-on-red sign. It was perhaps ten years' newer, from the swinging sixties, and had the very bottom of an old billboard frame still attached to the longest part of the roof.

Neither motel would be mistaken for club med. But to Drabek's eye, they both looked okay, certainly as good as anything in Hollywood at the same price range.

'Yeah, okay, I get it,' he said. Zoey was in the seat next to him. 'I'm guessing these places don't get a lot of plastic surgeons away for the weekend unless the person next to them is someone other than Mrs. Plastic Surgeon.' He undid his seat-belt. 'Come on, let's go talk to the front desk. Maybe he's been back.'

The main office had been all drab wood paneling at some point, but someone had had the smart idea to paint everything white, and it was clean and cheerful. The front counter was glass and featured souvenirs and post-cards inside. Some of them were yellowing around the edges. Behind the counter, a curvaceous, large blonde woman with her hair in a bun and wearing bright pink sweatpants was talking to someone on the phone.

'... so she SLAPS the card down on the table and yells Bingo! Bingo!... and sure enough, she's grabbed the card off the table from the large, angry drunk guy who'd stumbled off to the bathroom. And just as she yells it, he comes back...' She noticed them waiting for her. 'Just a second, sweetie...' She looked at Drabek. 'Can I help you?'

'We sure hope so,' Drabek said. 'My name is Detective Norman Drabek, and I work missing persons. This here is Zoey Roberson. Her boyfriend is missing.'

The woman registered surprise, and some concern. 'Oh... oh dear.' She lifted the receiver again. 'Janice, I'm going to have to call you back, sweetie, this is important.' She hung up the phone. 'Now, what can I help you with, sir? Were you thinking maybe this fella was staying here? 'Cause, we only got the three guests right now.'

Drabek showed her the photo. 'You remember this guy?'

Her eyes narrowed and she peered at Zoey. 'I remember you now,' she said. 'I remember your tattoos. This is the guy that was with you, huh?'

Zoey's disappointment was obvious. If she didn't even remember Ben, then... 'He's not here?'

The woman looked sad for her. 'I'm sorry, hon, I really am.'

They walked back to Drabek's sedan silently. The sun was streaming down, cooking the asphalt and making the car uncomfortably hot.

'I'm sorry,' Zoey said. 'I really thought maybe there was something to this, that he had to have had some ulterior motive for driving us all the way up here...'

Drabek had counselled the families of criminals before. He understood the sense of shame, denial and confusion she was going through, and that she needed to know it wasn't her fault. 'Don't make the mistake of questioning everything in your relationship,' he said. She looked like she was going to cry and he felt awkward, unsure of how to comfort her. He patted her hand. 'Something obviously went wrong with Benjamin, but that doesn't invalidate what you had, or your feelings, or that it was something good. That's just hindsight messing with you.'

He started the car and backed out of the motel parking lot.

Across the road at the International, Ben Levitt hid behind the white lace drapes and watched as the sedan backed up and then pulled out and left. He'd scouted well and his diligence had paid off.

It looked like the same woman he'd seen at the condo, the woman he'd shot at. There was something achingly familiar about her, an almost primal sensation of belonging, as if she was family, or maybe someone he'd once loved. He tried to push it down, but it had surfaced on three occasions now and he was concerned it might jeopardize his singular pursuit of the objectives.

He shook it off and turned back to the room. He'd already packed his case and rented a new vehicle with his second new identity. In an hour, after eating, he would drive north, through Oregon and Washington State. He would cross the border and head toward Vancouver.

He would fly to Toronto and take a commuter to Baltimore, where Fire was slated to meet him in two days.

And the man wanted for the murder of Paul Joseph would disappear.

31/

DAY 13

HARBIN, CHINA

He heard the voice first.

'Wake him up.' The accent was dapper and English, tinged with a local dialect.

Brennan braced himself. He knew what usually came next. Sure enough, the stinging slap of a bucket of cold water hit him from up close. It went up his nose, and he spluttered momentarily from the sinus pressure, blowing out excess liquid and mucus.

He squinted. The room was dark, a warehouse again, but this time poorly lit. There was a set of stairs against one wall that led up to another room, suspended above the rest of the operation.

A Chinese man in a sharp, narrow-cut brown suit and bowler hat was standing a few feet away, leaning on an onyx, silver-tipped cane while two thugs in string t-shirts and track pants checked Brennan's wrist and ankle restraints. 'You sir, are in a lot of trouble,' he said in perfect English.

'You sir,' Brennan replied, 'have lousy taste in hats.' He looked around. 'And friends.'

The man looked incredulous. 'Come now, Mr. Brennan. While I don't mean to brag, I'm renowned across Asia for my style. When I go to a club, designers take note.'

'And cops too, I imagine.'

He smiled. 'I like you, Mr. Brennan. Anyone who can maintain a sense of humor and the absurd in your situation is either entirely insane or quite courageous. I shall guess the latter, given that Sergei informs us you are an American agent of some sort.'

'He's a very creative fellow, that Sergei.'

'He was actually quite loyal. We placed him under considerable duress.'

'Let me guess: I'm supposed to be James Bond or something?'

'Or something. Bond was British, after all...'

'You sound like you spent some time there. Oxford? Cambridge, perhaps?'

'London School of Economics, after a few years at Harrow.'

'Ah. So, old money then?'

'Some of the oldest in China.'

'Yikes.' Brennan kept the tone light and flippant, but that was genuine cause for concern. The oldest Black Societies went back centuries and were massive multi-tentacled organizations. Taking one on at any level was never wise.

'But, like any organization, we have business that must be taken care of,' the man said. 'My name is Benson Chu. Like all Black Cranes, I must produce, for the men above me, a certain amount of tribute each month.'

'I'm guessing there's a point at which this involves me,' Brennan said.

'Quite...' The man walked over with the cane over his shoulder, the image almost whimsical, as if he was about to break into a chorus of 'Singing in the Rain'. When he arrived beside Brennan, he lowered it to the ground and leaned on it once more. 'What to do, what to do... You know, there's a group from the State Security Ministry flying to the city to look for you today.'

'Word travels quickly for a big country.'

'These crazy kids and their internet.' The gangster smiled again. 'Of course, I'm certain I could negotiate a pretty penny for turning you over to them.'

'Doubtless.'

'So you concede your value, as an American agent?'

'No... I just think I'm pretty.'

That elicited a grin. The gangster paced with the

cane in a small semi-circle around Brennan's chair. 'Or, I could sell you to the Russians. You came in through their airport, so I'm sure they could find some espionage charge that would stick for a century or so. They pony up real money for information, the Russians; they might even look the other way while we move product across the border for a while.'

'That's really fascinating stuff. The world is your oyster.'

'Quite. There's one problem with both of those scenarios, of course: they don't account for Vincent Gao and his preoccupation with ending your life.'

'Really? What did I ever do to him?'

'Well.... you did kill five of his men and cripple another back in Heihe; one of those whom you so expertly disemboweled was his second cousin, and his ire is, we shall say, considerable at the present time. Fortunately for you, I outrank him. Barely. And I rather prefer the profit motive to revenge. It's so much more 'now'.'

'An ancient black society, but one that changes with the times?'

'Exactly.'

'And when you make a decision like this, do you ever consult the elders of the society? Say... Master Yip Po?'

'Subtle.'

'Thank you.'

The gangster rested one hand on the cane and put the other in his pocket. 'Now why would a Gwai Lo from... let me guess... upper New York State? Yes, I think that's about right... Why would a Gwai Lo from Buffalo want to talk to the Revered Master Yip? It could be for training, I suppose; from what I'm told about the fight in Heihe you can certainly handle yourself...'

'Thank you again.'

'...or it could be because he used to work for State Security in some capacity he has never discussed, and has technically been a wanted man for many years.'

'Could be.'

'He does not wish to speak with you, unfortunately.'

'You checked already? So efficient.'

'You were unconscious for nearly a day. After the fight in Heihe...'

'Where are we?'

'Harbin. After the fight in Heihe they gave you something to keep you calm for a little while, and you had a sleep. So any contact, any handler or associate you'd made arrangements with at the border? That's done, I'm afraid. There is no one coming to help you. And Master Yip has a standing 'no contact' order for almost everyone here.'

The words had barely left his mouth when a red light by the main door began to blink. A man leaned out of the upper floor office. 'Sir, we have a visitor. The alarm on the rear fence has been tripped.'

The man rested his hands on the cane again. 'Perhaps I spoke too soon.'

The warehouse property was dark and surrounded by a chain-link fence. There was so little exterior lighting that even in a relatively well-lit business park, it was hard to tell how many men were patrolling its asphalt grounds. A shadow moving off near the far fence, another near the rear-side door; a few more out front. There was a large parking area, and then lanes running behind the main building, presumably leading to a loading dock of some sort.

Daisy Lee counted six men so far; the number of cars alone suggested there were a few more inside. Her contact, an old listening station agent who'd retired to Harbin but had helped train her a decade earlier, had heard that the Black Cranes were holding an American. Given Brennan's habit of finding the people he sought, locating him might also mean locating Master Yip Po.

If there was a way to accomplish her goal without also saving him in the process, she sulked, it would be preferable given the trouble he'd caused her. But Lee knew she might have no support left at State Security, at least until she figured out who could be trusted; that made the Americans potentially valuable allies, assuming the end goal was uncovering Project Legacy. The idea of it consumed her, given the attempts on her life in both Macau and Hong Kong. Whatever it represented was a kind of evil, the type of adversary she'd hoped her career would focus on; she wasn't just going to walk away.

She scaled the ten-foot fence with ladder-speed; at the top, she threw her leather jacket over the barbed wire to cross unimpeded, then dropped down to the ground below.

Across the yard, a red bulb by the door of a second small building lit up and began to flash. That usually wasn't a good sign. She'd studied the fence and hadn't seen any sign of alarms but knew the greeting was probably for her. That meant it would be followed by guards, a lot of them. She sprinted into the shadows behind the main building. Any moment she knew a guard could round the next corner and...

There. She darted at him and before he'd fully turned the corner was on him, her elbow slamming into his throat, crushing his windpipe. The man collapsed and his rifle clattered to the pavement. She heard voices raised, men running. She moved to the corner of the building and peeked around.

Bullets pinged off the wall, chips of plaster striking her as she ducked back. Two at least on the one side. She had to assume the same on the other side of the building, which meant at least four gunmen closing on her. She looked around for another exit. The building's rear windows had bars over them. She jumped up to grab them and pulled herself cautiously to chest height. Her pistol was unclipped in a holster strapped to the outside of her thigh and the bars caught the butt. It tumbled to the cement below, clattering when it landed. She clambered onto the top of the bar cage.

She looked down at the gun but there was no point trying to get down there to retrieve it before the others arrived.

Above her was another window and another set of bars, but they were ten feet up. The only way to reach them was to try something dangerous...

She took the half-step back that the bars afforded, then leaped up on a diagonal, using the wall like a step to push off and up. It had to be timed perfectly or she'd push off too hard, miss the bars and fall twenty feet to the asphalt. Her hand reached out as she pushed off the wall, her fingers barely finding the bottom of the upper bars. She held on tight, flinging her other arm up, finding another hand hold and pulling herself up just as the men converged below her. She could hear them talking, confusion reigning. One of them looked up and she heard rapid fire warnings, guns swinging around to train on her just as Lee jumped up to grab the roof ledge. She threw her body over it onto the roof, then quickly found her feet.

A pair of skylights sat fifteen feet apart in the middle of the roof. She sprinted to the first. There was a sound coming from the roof's far corner, like someone stepping on tin.

A ladder. She was going to have company any moment.

Lee opened the first skylight, just as the armed guard reached the top of its ladder and reached up to open it himself. Her look was probably as surprised as his and for a split second, they stared at one another. Then the guard tried to unshoulder his weapon while holding onto the ladder. She slammed the skylight closed and ran over to the other. She could hear feet climbing the ladder up the side wall. Lee opened the skylight and this time the guard was prepared, his weapon pointed right at her. She threw herself sideways and tucked into a roll as the gun sprayed slugs into the night air.

Across the roof, a guard tried to climb over the edge from the escape ladder. She bolted over to it and planted a front kick in his chest, the man screaming as he plunged to the ground. Behind her both skylights had opened, and the guards were climbing out. She ran over to the first, pirouetting in a ballerina spin, her right foot in a wide, sweeping kick that knocked the man senseless. The other guard was up and onto the roof but before he could sight her, she jumped through the open skylight, grabbing each side of its ladder so that she could slide down its length to the floor below.

Before she could assess her surroundings, a blade swooshed through the air in a wide arc; Lee ducked backwards as far as she could, just millimeters under the razor-sharp sword. Instinct told her the strikes would be fast, direct, attempting to knock her off balance, and she kept going over backwards, a reverse cartwheel that took her a few feet from her assailant.

The room was dark but appeared to be a large office of some kind. The guard charged her, screaming for battle, the sword thrusting out quickly in repeated stabs at her torso, Lee dodging each adroitly then knocking the flat of the blade to one side with a slap, her other hand flying out to catch the swordsman in the mouth, staggering him. Angered, he charged her again, bringing the katana down in an overhead chop. Lee caught the blade flat between both palms, but she could feel his greater strength forcing it down toward her.

Behind her, another guard entered the room. Lee released her grip and spun out of the way, the blade coming down hard but finding nothing except air. She spun on her heel, a back kick catching her assailant in the spine and sending him tumbling forward, the sword thrusting right into the man who'd just entered the room. Before the shocked swordsman could withdraw it, she closed on him, grabbing the back of his head and his chin in each hand, spinning his neck hard to one side, feeling it snap and the man go limp.

She ran out of the office; a set of steel stairs led down to a football-field sized warehouse, but four men were at the bottom and climbing them. Going back to the roof was out; so was facing all four on a narrow stairway, even with the high ground. Guns were being drawn; she had to act quickly. Lee threw herself over the side of the rail, catching the edge of the metal walkway and hanging suspended. They began to rush up the stairs as she eked her way over to the bottom of the top step. She used the underside of the open metal steps as monkey bars, climbing quickly down hand-over-hand even as the guards yelled to back up and tried to stab her through the gaps. She dropped to the ground as the first reached her, gun arm extended.

Instead of seeking cover, she ran directly for him on a slight angle, making it harder to sight her, then at the last second dropped down and slid on the polished concrete, the sliding side kick slamming into the man's ankles, breaking them. He went down screaming, a gunshot fired off wildly, the bullet going through the corrugated metal roof.

There was a series of boxes on pallets, some stacked high, others low. They were grouped in the middle of the warehouse and Lee used them for cover, ducking in between the crates so that she was hard to see. At the back of the warehouse, a man was screaming apoplectically in Mandarin. 'Find him, or explain your transgression!'

The voice was familiar, but she couldn't immediately place it. Lee crept through the maze of boxes, looking for an opening that would allow her to see the back of the room and what was going on. The yeller was probably their Red Pole, she surmised, which meant that if she wasn't caught, someone would pay with a life.

The pistol came out of nowhere, the guard stepping out from behind a crate and putting the barrel against her temple. 'Don't move!' he ordered. 'You stay right there.' The proximity was a mistake;

even on a gun with a light trigger pull, she knew she could snatch the barrel and pull it sideways before he could squeeze off a round and she did so with cool precision, the bullet flashing wide and smashing through wooden crates, the volume of the shot in the confined area half-deafening them both. Still holding his gun hand wide, she threw out three quick jabs, each catching the guard on the chin's nerve cluster, his legs turning to rubber even as he lost consciousness.

She retrieved his dropped weapon, a knockoff of an older Colt. The sound alerted her first, a rustling behind her. She pivoted, gun hand raised, but her instinct told her to move instead and she dove to her left as the machine-gun fire ripped through boxes.

The same voice was screaming now, outraged. 'No guns! Don't damage the product, damn you!'

There had to be at least four other foot soldiers by Lee's count. She followed the tallest section of crates until she reached the edge of the storage area. The fist came from nowhere, flashing in from her right so quickly that she barely had time to duck backwards and out of the way. But it hadn't been aimed at her; instead the punch knocked the pistol cleanly from her left hand. Lee rolled forward, through a gap at the edge of the crates and into the open.

Her attacker was skilled, she recognized immediately. His stance was snake-like, loose and limber, like a Changquan disciple, or a varied stylist. Before she could further assess he took a half step before leaping into the air and flipping head over heels sideways in a 'chekongfan', a jumping side kick, his heel striking her shoulder as she tried to bob out of the way. Lee went down hard, landing on her tailbone. She ignored the pain and reacted on instinct, rolling backwards and coming up on her feet even as he stepped into a jumping side kick. Lee dodged sideways and he flew past her; as soon as his feet hit he cement he was turning back to face her.

His speed and skill were considerable, Lee

worried. Behind her, she heard a footstep. A shadow caught the corner of her eye and she ducked down, realizing someone had closed on her six. The blade of the butterfly knife found air and she reached down to grab her attacker's arm, yanking it hard over her knee, the bone breaking and the guard collapsing in screams. His associate didn't flinch, ignoring the man's painful plight and instead stepping in to deliver a hard punch that caught Lee flush in the side of the head, staggering her. Before she could regain her balance, he'd swept her legs out from under her. Then he was on her, trying to pin her to the ground with his knees so that he could choke the life from her.

Lee reached up with both hands, trying to pry the man's arms away. But his grip was like a vice and he was much stronger than her. She could feel her neck muscles giving under the strain of fighting strangulation. In desperation, she jabbed at both of his eyes with her forefingers, pushing until she felt a squishing sensation. He screamed in a terrible, high pitched wail and pitched over sideways, crying and bellowing.

Lee's training kicked in and she reached down to the prone man's waistband, pulling out a handgun. There were still the men outside, and there was still at least one guard inside unaccounted for...

The fine hairs on her neck stood up. She spun around, gun outstretched. The gangster was in a similar pose. He looked about eighteen years old. His hand was shaking.

'Look around you,' she said. 'Who do you think is more likely to miss right now? You? Or me?'

'Don't shoot him,' a voice requested.

Daisy cocked her head just enough to look past the slightly taller youth. The man walking out of the shadows was older, perhaps in his sixties. She recognized him immediately. 'Benson Chu.' Chu was one of the most famous Mountain Masters in China, effective head of the thousand-plus member Black Cranes. 'He is my grandson, and while he probably deserves his fate, I would rather like to see if I can turn his direction in life around.'

'And why should I acquiesce to your request when your other men have been trying to kill me for the last ten minutes?'

'Because if you pull that trigger, the other six men will gun you down where you stand.'

'And if I lower my weapon?'

'We will hold you with your American associate until State Security arrives. We have reached... an arrangement, shall we say.'

'Where is he?'

'In the other outbuilding, keeping a calm head. On the other hand, my grandson, Deng, is nine feet in front of you, shaking like a leaf in a strong breeze. My sister would be most displeased with me if I allowed you to blow his brains out. Now, lower your weapon. You have no chance of escape.'

Lee did as requested. At least they would be moving her halfway toward her goal; if past form told the tale, Brennan would know where Master Yip was located. If she could get it out of him and still leave him for State Security, even better.

The 'cell' was a powered down old meat locker at the back of the second building. Lee was escorted to the door and then shoved inside. The exterior lock clanked shut behind her.

'Oh goodie,' a familiar voice said from the opposite corner of the room. 'It's you.'

She turned and sighed. Joe Brennan was sitting on one of the two cots that had been set up as a makeshift sleeping quarters.

He wasn't going to be easy to deal with. 'Mr. Brennan. I'd like to say I'm surprised to find you here but, in all honesty, I'd almost expected it.' In fact, she'd been counting on it; but he didn't need to know that.

'From the way the guard was talking earlier,

we're both being sent to Beijing,' Brennan said.

'I wouldn't count on it. We're not beaten yet,' she said. 'And most of these guys aren't exactly what you'd call disciplined.'

'We're suicidally outnumbered. Short of the Mountain Master having a change of heart, I suspect we're about to become bargaining chips in the Black Cranes' ongoing quarrels with authority.'

'And all before you had a chance to meet with Master Yip Po,' she said.

'Before I had a chance to even find him.'

'Damn.'

He frowned. 'You haven't...'

'Not yet, no. I suppose I should have expected you to be useless in that regard.'

'You know, for a little girl who's had her buttocks spanked twice by yours truly, you sure do have a high regard for yourself.'

'No, I just know Americans. Nobody thinks more of himself with less reason to do so than an American.'

'And no one thinks less of everyone else with no reason to do so than the Chinese.'

'Then we've established that we don't like each other.'

'I think I got that message the first three times you punched me in the face,' Brennan said. 'But I thought our two sides had reached an agreement to help each other.'

'To share information and intelligence. Not to co-operate in all regards when it comes to getting that information and deciding what you may see.'

'And yet somehow, you not only aren't in a sharing sort of mood, you seem to be in the same trouble I am. Now how did you manage that, exactly? Why is Daisy Lee hanging around a Harbin meat locker at midnight?'

Before she could answer, the lock clanked open. The door swung to with a creak.

Daisy Lee smiled. 'I wondered if you were related,' she said to the new arrival.

Jackson Chu smiled back. 'He's my uncle. I assume you're talking about the Mountain Master?'

'You still owe me a life from Macau.'

'Yes, about that... you invaded our compound, killed our men and threatened my nephew -- his grandson.'

'It's a good thing you weren't there,' she said.

'And why is that?'

'Because I'd have been forced to kill you, too,' Daisy said, 'rather than just talking about it.'

He frowned as he undid her shackles. 'I rather thought we had nice chemistry, you and I.'

'Let's pretend, however, that you're a criminal, and that I work for State Security,' Lee said. 'We'll get along better that way, okay?'

From the corner, Brennan sounded fatigued. 'Are you two done with the charm initiative? Because if we don't get out of here soon, your beloved State Security will shoot all three of us, not just me and wonder girl, here.'

'Your gratitude for my rescue attempt is about what I'd expect from you,' she chided. 'I could have left you here to rot...'

'And why didn't you?' Brennan asked. 'Let's just examine that for a second. I know what my objective is. And I suspect it's the same as yours. But you're looking for me, which means you need my help. That means you don't have any clue where to find Master Yip Po, and neither does State Security.'

'Presumptuous, too!' she said. 'How much crasser could you be?'

He ignored her. 'Now, since the Black Cranes were planning to hand me over to State Security for a wad of cash, that must mean you're not here representing your branch of Chinese intelligence; you're on your own.'

'He talks too much,' Chu said. 'Are you sure I can't just kill him?'

'Not until I know what he knows,' she said.

'Either of you are welcome to try,' Brennan offered. 'But let me extend the idea a little here before we get to that: you came here on your own, without your department's support, which means there's someone there who either doesn't trust you, or who you think is a crook.'

'He really is annoying, isn't he?' Chu proposed.

'I'm just here to do a job...' Brennan said.

'Stuff like that doesn't help,' Lee added. 'But if you're asking, yes, I'm probably in a lot of trouble for coming up here. Some gratitude...'

'You weren't here to make friends with me, Lee,' Brennan said. 'You're just working the angles, same as I would do. Let's not insult each other's intelligence by suggesting it was altruism.'

'Fine. If not altruism, then at least a motivation to save lives, the same as you.'

'Well, I hate to disappoint you, but I'm no closer to Yip Po than you are.'

Chu looked quizzical. 'Master Yip Po? The two of you are here for the venerated Master Yip?'

'We are,' Lee replied. 'You know him?'

Chu nodded. 'He trained me as a boy. But I'm afraid the two of you have put yourself at considerable risk for very little reason; Master Yip fled Harbin many years ago. He is still in contact with the Black Cranes, of course...'

'Where?' Brennan demanded.

'I am not at liberty...'

'You owe me your life,' Lee said.

'And I am repaying you by helping you escape.'

'No, not for Macau,' she said. 'For now.'

'I don't....

'Simple: You can tell us where Master Yip is hiding, or we can hold you here until they turn you over to your uncle. Since he will almost certainly make an example of you by killing you, it stands to reason that if we choose not to turn you over, you once again owe me a life.'

Chu looked slightly horrified. 'That's...'

'Only fair,' Lee said.

'...pretty twisted,' Brennan replied with a smile. 'I like it.'

Chu peered at her suspiciously. 'You wouldn't really kill me after I tried to help you, would you, Daisy Lee?'

Her gaze back was flat and cold. 'Try me.'

'If it's any consolation, she lies a lot,' Brennan said. 'But just to be on the safe side, it might be better if you helped us instead.'

'He's a half day's drive from here. He receives a healthy stipend from the society but the pressure from the central committee over the years became too great for him to remain in the city.'

'Now was that so hard?' Lee asked. 'The next question is even easier: how are you going to get us out of here?'

32/

WASHINGTON, D.C.

HAY-ADAMS HOTEL,
AUXILIARY CONFERENCE ROOM

The Chinese weren't making life any easier, Jonah Tarrant had decided.

The meeting had taken a half-hour just to establish where the six-member delegation would sit. Now David Chan was making demands, and Tarrant had to be polite. Chan carried weight on both sides of the Pacific, with over twenty billion dollars invested in the U.S. economy to go along with his role as chairman of state security.

'Mr. Chan, what you're asking is already a considerable get in terms of budget allocation, due to the last-minute nature of the talks. But to add another detail of six men at such a late date...'

'It is not a discussion point, deputy director.' Chan was stoic and unemotional at all times. Strictly business. Tarrant found him slightly unnerving. 'We will have an additional committee delegate attending, Mr. Wen Xiu of the interior ministry...'

That caught Tarrant off guard. 'Wen...?'

'You are surprised because of our reputation for disliking each other, of course,' Chan said. 'But you must understand the gravity of these discussions requires his presence. Although North Korea is an international matter, we share a border, and therefore there are internal security considerations that must be weighed.'

'Certainly,' Tarrant said. 'The timing is short and...'

'And I have no doubt that you will be able to

accommodate the request, deputy director,' Chan suggested.

'If there was any way we could schedule these sessions at a later date...'

'But there is not, so it does not bear discussing,' Chan said. 'The launch has forced all of our hands and the Premier and vice-premier are both anxious to meet with the President and vice-president, to ensure that we are reading from the same page when we discuss these matters with PyongYan.'

'What about the public time, the meet-and-greet in New York's Chinatown? Surely that's something...'

Chan cut him off. 'The premier wishes for it to be clear that he considers past enmities between our nations to be just that, and that our spirit of openness will continue, despite any missteps either side may have taken in the past two years. One important part of that is engaging with Chinese people in America, and Chinese Americans. It is important that there be no suggestion of weakness in any manner...'

'Of course, of course,' Tarrant agreed. As much as the need to save face seemed paramount to the Chinese, his bosses weren't much better. They continually wondered about the political fallout of any decision, no matter how small. It amounted to much the same thing. 'We've kept it short but poignant; there's a motorcade through Chinatown to wave to folks, with the Premier's limousine directly behind the President's second security detail. The Premier will shake hands with Betty Wu, one of the city's oldest residents at a hundred-and-four at a seniors' home. That will be right before the start of the public session ..."

'Four vehicles back?' Chan looked worried by the arrangement. 'He may not like that.'

'Placing them adjacent to each other is out of the question, given Legacy. We don't expect anyone to get through our cordon – or to be even close, for that matter – but that's a bridge too far.'

Chan considered the options, a worried frown

barely creasing his brow for an instant. 'Acceptable,' he eventually said. 'But...'

Tarrant hadn't seen Chan pause before, or struggle for words. 'Chairman...'

'Off the record... I admit I must agree with your initial assessment. I asked them to reconsider, but the vice-premier has the premier's ear, and Wen Xiu in turn his.'

It was a surprisingly frank admission. 'You suggested waiting until Legacy has a resolution?'

The chairman smiled at that. 'That... would be taking openness a step too far, to discuss such matters. Let us just say that I share your concerns. But the vice-premier won't hear of it.'

He tried not to show any hint of satisfaction. But Tarrant liked Chan being off his game, perturbed. It was an advantage, a potential destabilizing factor. By the time the sessions kicked off in seven days, he might even be nervous enough to convince them to cancel the public portion of the visit.

At the very least, the retinue decision would cost Chan in his boss's eyes.

Tarrant gave his guest a rueful smile. *Destabilizing the central committee with his own failure? Maybe this summit won't be a total disaster after all.*

BEIJING

Wen Xiu was meeting with regional policing representatives in the hall of the interior ministry when Yan finally tracked him down. The chairman's call from Washington had not been a surprise and, as expected, the Americans had demanded the premier's motorcade be separate from their president's.

But more importantly, they had approved additional security for the interior minister to attend. 'Sir!' Yan called out as the scrum of officials began to dissipate. 'Sir... over here!'

Wen saw the bureaucrat frantically waving his arms from across the hall. He moved through the sparse crowd, making apologies and offering greetings in equal measure, until they were face to face.

'You contacted Chairman Chan in Washington?'

'I did, sir, yes. He indicated the Americans have approved your request, per the instruction of Vice-Premier Liu.'

Wen smiled at the attribution. 'Chan really thought he would have the Premier's ear alone for the entire trip, didn't he?'

'It is not for me to speculate...' Yan stammered.

'Oh, calm yourself! Our mutual dislike is no secret to anyone. The question you need to ask yourself, Yan, is who will be left standing when Legacy is complete?'

'They seem to believe they have the matter well in hand.'

'Who? The Americans? Don't make me laugh! As we speak, their best effort is somewhere in Harbin, being held for us by the Black Crane Society, ready to be delivered to us.'

'They are here?!?' Yan's alarm was evident. 'Surely the risk of exposure for sending field operatives – short-term players...'

'Apparently they think this Legacy issue is a substantial problem.' Wen almost snickered at the thought. 'But it will amount to nothing. A forty-year-old sleeper cell?' He looked at the younger man with what Yan supposed was an attempt at sage wisdom. 'It will come to nothing. It will be the modern equivalent of one of those Japanese soldiers on the islands, coming to light, blinded by the modern world, his war long over.'

'And... if it isn't? Yan asked, braving a contrarian stance. 'If Legacy is successful? What then?'

The older man shrugged, his eyes darting around the room to ensure no one was listening in. 'Then? There are many who believe our nation's new openness is a betrayal of sorts. There is a rural campaign underway, a misinformation effort via local internet boards, sent out from within our borders. It's probably the Russians. The rural poor are increasingly disillusioned that they are not receiving the same benefits from an open China as those in the cities. And they are legion. The administration will have to answer to them and many others… should they be embraced by the west so tightly that it chokes us all.'

Yan waited for a moment to see if the more senior man had any other profundities, before adding, 'I've emailed your travel schedule to your assistant and CC'd you.'

'Then our business for today is concluded,' Wen said. 'Thank you as always for your loyal efforts.'

'Of course,' Yan said.

The interior minister's assistant sidled up behind him silently, then led him away by the elbow to another meet-and-greet near the main doors. Yan watched them walk away then checked his phone for messages. He looked around the room cautiously, then switched the official government phone for another in his left coat pocket. He used a thumbprint to open its screen, then tapped the encrypted message app. Then he smiled and turned it off, placing the phone back in his pocket.

The message contained just two words:

'Water flows.'

33/

WASHINGTON, D.C.

Senior Agent Brandon Mah was waiting in Tarrant's office reception when the deputy director and his personal assistant returned. He had a young woman with him and he gave her a worried glance before standing to greet his boss; the badge said she was NSA, but she was familiar nonetheless.

Tarrant pointed at her quizzically. 'Ms....'

Mah intervened to introduce. 'Agent Jennifer Parnell, my NSA opposite number on Legacy. They've... requested that she have full access to our plans and be my field liaison.'

Jonah shook her hand. Her grip was firm, her expression confident. 'We've worked together before...'

She nodded. 'Your memory is exceptional, sir. I wouldn't have recalled it if you hadn't mentioned it.'

Tarrant's eyes narrowed and he peered at her, trying to place the face. 'But what was it, again...?'

'I was D.C. Metro Police back during the Evans case...'

The missing recruit. Tarrant had been a young analyst when Evans had jumped into the Potomac; her suicide had sent shock waves through the agency, which was under fire at the time for putting candidates under too much stress.

'Of course! You were the lead detective...'

'Second. That was my partner.'

'And a decade later, you're a senior agent with the NSA. That's impressive.'

'Thank you, sir.' She blushed slightly under the pale gloom of the fluorescent lighting.

Tarrant motioned toward the office. 'Come, let's talk.' His assistant leaned over to the receptionist and whispered for her to bring coffee.

The office remained spartan and impersonal after the death of Tarrant's predecessor. He hadn't felt right about it, not yet. Not having been the one who'd pulled the trigger. That he'd saved lives didn't really matter. It was a stark, harsh memory for a man who had never been a field agent and he bristled slightly every time he walked into the room. He gestured to the two chairs ahead of the desk while his assistant sat on a couch along the far wall.

Once he was behind his desk, Tarrant leaned forward, both hands clasped. 'Well guys... this one is a clusterfuck, to say the least.'

Mah crossed his legs, then tapped on his notepad with his pen. 'They wouldn't go for the idea of cancelling the motorcade?'

'They wouldn't even go for cancelling the meet-and-greet with the centenarian. Parnell, are you fully up to speed?'

'Yes sir,' she nodded. 'My superiors are equally anxious about this and frankly, we really just think it's asking for trouble given Legacy. They suggested I ask about the possibility of a last-second adjustment, perhaps a road closure or detour, something the public can quickly adapt to but that might upset anyone planning an attack.'

Tarrant's secretary interrupted with coffee, passing him a cup then offering one to each of the agents. Mah turned it down, but Parnell gratefully accepted the beverage.

'Cream and sugar?' the woman asked.

Parnell covered the cup with her hand. 'I'm fine, thank you.' She leaned in conspiratorially. 'A little lactose intolerant, to be honest.'

She was more approachable than Carolyn Brennan, at least. Tarrant thought the idea that the NSA would be able to keep something like a route change secret laughable. His own spies in her department had already filled him in on the idea. *The Chinese probably knew six seconds after I did, the way the NSA talks.* 'Not a likely option, right Brandon?'

Mah knew a political question when he heard it. Tarrant had no intention of annoying the leaders of China and every official in Texas simultaneously, not when their decision already incorporated the risks. On top of that, he still didn't like her being there. 'It would be highly unlikely that city police would be able to work with something like that and we need them on the day...'

'That's fine,' Parnell said. 'It was just a suggestion, of course. I'm just here to lend a hand.'

Tarrant nodded politely. *Sure. The NSA needs a scapegoat and it's either her or us, should something go wrong.* 'Well, don't you worry. Just follow Brandon's lead and keep in mind that he has final call on everything, okay?'

'Yes sir.' She couldn't help but frown a little as she said it. They were making it clear where she stood.

Mah listened stoically, but Tarrant got the sense he was happy the lines had been drawn. He got the sense he didn't like Agent Parnell very much.

HARBIN, CHINA

DAY 14

The limousine crashed through the chain link fence and reinforced gate, pieces flying in all directions, the metal shimmering like a cymbal as it scraped the asphalt.

It was after midnight, and the guard had been bored, barely paying attention, a cigarette hanging from his lower lip and his AK-47 resting across his stomach. The crash jolted him alert, and he looked around confused for a moment before slamming the red alarm button under the gate control's dash.

Near instantly, men began to flood out of the small compound's four large buildings.

In the warehouse, where a storage locker had

been turned into a makeshift prison, Jackson Chu poked his head around its door and motioned to the guard. 'What's going on?'

The young gangster looked nervous and barely old enough to shave. 'I don't know, Mr. Chu. No one is answering my radio hail. Should I...?'

Chu nodded vigorously. 'Go and help; I will take care of this pair for you, make sure they don't try anything while you're gone.'

The younger man bowed quickly. 'Many thanks, Mr. Chu. I am blessed by your leadership.'

Chu poked his head back into the room. 'Quickly! By the time they get the doors open and figure out there's no one behind the wheel...'

'The wheel of what?' Lee asked. 'What was that?'

'That was a Harbin Limousine Services stretch Cadillac breaking through the front gate. No time to explain: come on!'

They followed him out into the hall. But instead of heading toward the front door of the warehouse, Chu led them in the opposite direction. 'There's a back door to this place and my car is parked on the other side of it. There's also a back gate to this compound.'

'So we might have guards to deal with?' Brennan asked.

'Potentially. But I don't think so.' He opened the door and as he uttered the last word, the sound of machine gun fire split the night, a furious assault. 'The gentleman who wedged down the accelerator also left a tape playing on the back seat. Small arms fire, I believe he said.'

'Who owns the limo company?' Lee asked.

'Why... we do, of course,' Chu smiled back at her.

Brennan almost laughed. The Black Cranes were eviscerating a limo from their own firm.

They clambered into Chu's sports coupe. 'I'd advise everyone to buckle up,' he said. Then he stepped on the gas, hard. The car shot toward the rear gate. One guard had stayed behind, a thin man with wavy dark hair and a look of shock. He didn't even get a chance to train his rifle on them before the car smashed through the gate, bouncing on hard racing shocks out onto the street. He spun the wheel left, the back end sliding out, then straightened the car out as he punched the gas one more time.

'And where exactly are we going now?' Lee asked.

'Not that you could tell anyone,' Brennan interjected. 'Seeing as how you're cut off from help. Right?'

She gave him a hard stare. 'I imagine I'll fare better on my own in these parts than you would, Agent Brennan.'

Behind the wheel, Chu laughed. 'She has a point, American. You don't exactly fit in.'

'The question stands,' Lee put to him. 'Where to?'

'Now? Now we go find the venerable Master Yip... and then I no longer owe your friend Ms. Lee her favor, while you, in turn, will be beholden to me, Gwai Lo.'

'Great,' Brennan muttered. 'Because things were going so well already.'

BALTIMORE, MARYLAND

The church on the corner of Highland and Pratt had been there for over a century, back when Baltimore was a more prosperous port, and inner-city crime was a fraction of the modern problem it had become. Swaddled in red brick, with a copper steeple long turned green by age and acclimation, it had served a small-but-vital congregation since the Teddy Roosevelt administration.

Gessler didn't know anything about that. Now, it was just a target.

He leaned out the driver's window slightly and looked back across the street at it. Then he took in the surroundings, looking for obvious threats or impediments. He'd surveyed it over the weekend, trading off with Codename Air until they had a sense of the neighborhood, of whether witnesses would be likely at eight o'clock in the morning on a weekday.

In the back of his brain sat a faint, dull recognition that once, many years earlier, this place had been pivotal in his life. But none of that was needed. The mission was restricted to essential knowledge only. And Paul Gessler didn't need to know where he'd come from, or who he was, or why the place was important.

He just knew he had a task to fulfill.

He checked both directions before getting out of the car. He moved to the trunk and opened it, taking out the two bleach bottles full of fuel. It had been the other's idea to use those instead of standard red fuel containers, which would attract attention. He closed the trunk and walked across the road, checking around once more for onlookers.

The church's front door was open. He walked inside, frowning again at the strange familiarity. A front reception area led through to the main church hall, sets of pews divided down the middle, an altar on a raised dais at the front of the room, a pipe organ behind it. The place looked deserted.

He walked up the aisle. There was a door at the back, beside the stage. He didn't know how he knew to go there, but he was certain.

Before he could reach it, the door swung open. A short, stocky senior in a clergyman's robe closed it behind him, then turned and saw that he had company.

'Can I help you, my son?' he asked. The priest had to be at least eighty, Gessler figured.

The man looked emotionless, brooding or brutish... the priest wasn't sure which. But it was a tough neighborhood, and not much surprised him anymore.

'Are you Father Peter Fischer?'

'I am.'

The man put down the two big blue bleach

bottles. Then he reached into his coat side pocket and drew the small pistol. He reached into the other pocket and withdrew the silencer, then began threading it onto the barrel, realizing he should've done it before entering the church.

But the priest did not try to run. 'Are you going to rob me? We have very little here. Our congregation is humble, and the Sunday collection is very small.'

Something was nagging Gessler, a feeling of unease. He pushed it out of the way, as trained. But it returned. The man was familiar, like the building. He peered at him, trying to place the face beyond the photo they'd found online.

'Do... we know each other?' the priest asked. 'You seem like perhaps you recognized me.'

Gessler squinted, feeling a sudden pressure behind his eyes. He'd had one of the headaches already, when he'd first been activated and had tried to remember the little Indian man. It was something... something he wasn't supposed to know.

The priest had been studying the man's face. But suddenly, his eyes widened, his mouth held open in a moment of stunned surprise. 'I... think I know you,' he said, his voice quavering. 'My Lord in Heaven. You're him, aren't you? You're the Taylor boy... Donald, wasn't it?'

Another stabbing pain struck Gessler behind the eyes, this time radiating to his temples and burning a hole through the top of his skull. 'I... I don't remember,' he began to say.

The priest looked shaken. 'We were never supposed to meet. I... I'm shocked to see you.'

'Don't worry,' Gessler said. 'It doesn't matter anyway.'

He raised the pistol and shot the elderly priest through the forehead, the force taking the old man over backwards. He lay on the cold stone floor. his life ebbing away, his final moments filled with regret.

Gessler walked over to the prone man and shot him once more in the head for good measure, then in the heart. He unscrewed the suppressor and blew out some smoke, then placed it back in one pocket, and the gun in the other. Then he walked back to the bleach bottles and picked up the first, unscrewing it as he walked to the back office.

Unless the priest had been dishonest many years earlier, there would be no paper record of any of them. But they couldn't leave anything to chance. The office was comfortable, personal, with pictures of church groups on the walls, a single crucifix on the back wall the only decoration. He stared at it sullenly but without judgement for a few seconds, then went about his business, soaking down the furniture, the two bookshelves and the carpet. He poured a thin trail of fuel behind him as he walked back to the other bottle. He looked around the assembly room, then up at the ceiling. Wooden beams would help, he noted.

He began to soak down the pews to his left, splashing fuel on a half-dozen before the bottle was empty. Then he drew a strike-anywhere match, lighting it off the stone floor and tossing it into one of the bench puddles.

The pews were engulfed in seconds. Gessler waited until the flames began to make their way to the back office before making his exit. He'd checked the street for cameras or other surveillance but had seen nothing. Even the nearest streetlight intersection cam was more than four blocks away. He headed back to his car, leaving the bottles behind, not staying to watch the old building engulfed in flames.

34/

DETROIT POLICE, HOMICIDE DIVISION

'Anyone here order a well-done filet of Lutheran pastor?'

Det. Ed Kinnear approached the desk he shared with Dave Underheath, half-eaten sandwich in hand. He'd been working on a cold case from the Nineties, a new lead suggesting new suspects and real progress for the first time in years. Then he'd popped out to get a tuna on a kaiser.

'Really, Dave? While I'm eating my lunch?'

'Is it my fault you were out when the call came in?'

Kinnear sighed. 'Every damn time I leave...'

'Yeah, well, you missed a good one. I think you and I are going to be hitting the road. Someone at Baltimore P.D. spotted the all-points, noticed the similarity with a security camera shot.'

'Uh huh. That doesn't sound so good. What happened?'

'Someone decided to torch the Inland Protestant Church early this morning. Unfortunately, Father Peter Fischer, eighty-seven, was inside at the time.'

Kinnear frowned. 'He was still serving at that age?'

'Three days a week by agreement with his replacement,' the younger man noted. 'I guess his father had been the pastor before him, and so on, right back to his great grandfather.'

'Yikes. And now he's charcoal,' Kinnear said. The nature of the job made insensitivity and gallows humor a sort of stress release, to be summoned only around serving members. 'Local murder cops have leads?'

'Yeah... well, that's where things get really, really

interesting my friend. Because wouldn't you go and guess who showed up there this morning...'

Ed shrugged. 'I have a hundred-and-sixty active-but-cold cases to pick from dating back to Nineteen Eighty-Two. How many tries do I get?'

'Mr. Paul Gessler himself. Our friends in Baltimore already mailed me what they've got.'

'You don't say! Did they get a make on a vehicle?'

'Unfortunately not.'

'A witness, then?'

'Nope. A camera shot from inside the church office. The pastor had a 'nanny cam' installed in a crucifix on the wall behind his desk. They'd had some break-ins over the years.'

'No kidding,' Ed scoffed. 'In inner city Baltimore? Shocked, I am. Shocked.'

Underheath handed him a phone. 'Check this out.'

Ed pressed play on the video. The footage was grainy, low-res and black and white. But it was clearly Gessler, soaking down the office with gas. A few minutes later, flames crept into the room and the desk was engulfed.

'The metal from the cross protected the camera. The video was being recorded then erased each day automatically by an app on the pastor's phone, which was trapped under his body. The fire crew pulled him out before the place went up completely, hoping to save him.'

'Smoke inhalation?' Ed asked.

Underheath shook his head. 'A twenty-two slug from an older model Walther handgun, right through the forehead, just like the late Mrs. Gessler. The shot was so clean, the analysts managed to peg the calibre right off the entry wound. Then he shot him twice more once he was down.'

'Huh.' Ed stared at the still image of Gessler, looking at the crucifix blankly. *What the hell were you doing there, of all places?* He'd been a homicide cop for years, and there seemed no shortage of reasons for people to kill a loved one. But Gessler felt different. There was something way off about the whole thing.

'No idea,' Underheath answered for him. 'But things are getting weirder already. I checked with state records, and that got me making a few more calls. Mr. Gessler, it seems, was not born in the State of Michigan. Or the State of Maryland. Or, as far as we can tell, anywhere else in the continental United States. His parents registered no record of his birth, and there is no record that they adopted a kid.'

'Whaaat the Hell...?' Ed wondered. 'His identity is fake? How can that be? He's got records back to grade school in the state system.'

'Well, wherever they got him from, they didn't do it legally. They began registering him as a dependent in Nineteen Seventy-Four, listing his age as eighteen months.'

'And his folks? Do they seem like the baby buying types?'

'They've both been dead for a few years. Salt of the Earth individuals. Upstanding, even; they'd volunteered in their community for years, did missionary work overseas; bought Lions season tickets, even, which is its own fresh kind of Hell. The old man opened a contracting company, which he eventually left to his kid. It didn't take that kid long to run it into the ground.'

Ed just nodded affirmation, then stared at the grainy photo some more. What the hell was Paul Gessler up to? His father – or whoever Tom Gessler was – had been from Baltimore originally, so there had to be a tie. 'I think you're right,' he told the younger detective. 'We better talk to the captain and get back in touch with Baltimore P.D., then book a flight. Oh... and see if Baltimore has any motel recommendations.'

WASHINGTON, D.C.

Codename Water had chosen an out-of-the way

spot, in a parking garage attached to a suburban
outlet mall.

Ben flashed his cars lights once he saw her
approaching.

The woman in the dark beret and stylish brown
overcoat looked around cautiously before climbing
into his vehicle and closing the door.

'This parkade has non-functioning cameras on
this level and at the entrance,' she said without so
much as introducing herself. 'There's no chance of
your vehicle being spotted. But use the second
identity to purchase a used sedan before the two of
you leave. On the possibility that Fire has been
spotted or identified, he should travel in the backseat
and keep low until you're at the target zone.'

'The priest has been taken care of,' Ben said.
'The afternoon newscasts pegged it as a suspected
electrical fire, so they know it's a homicide and are
trying to keep the details out of the press.'

'He was not compromised?'

'We performed a full sweep of the street and
church over the weekend and there was no evidence
of any cameras or surveillance. I suspect it was
completely clean.'

'Good,' she said. 'Fire is essential to the objective.
Have you obtained everything you need?'

'I have.'

'And you've run the system?'

'I have not, not yet. I'll wait until we're a little
closer. Even with a well-disguised trail, any
geolocation they turn up would give them D.C. and
New York, and that would get someone's attention.'

'Fine. You know the security best. The list I
messaged you is still good. Any one of those five will
be present, and none are using proper care with their
email. You'll phish them?'

He nodded. 'As a first effort. It usually works, if
the email is skillfully constructed. In the event that it
doesn't, the fact that three of five ignore using
encrypted message apps...'

She understood. Each of them had been trained

to continue educating themselves, filling in the required skill sets as the years passed. Air's skill was computers, hacking, although he was also fully trained in field medicine and small arms. Once he had compromised his target, they would be able to ensure that no one above her rank introduced any last-minute surprises. 'Is Fire performing optimally?'

'I believe so. His anger seems sufficiently suppressed for now. He... mentioned an incident...' Ben had considered not raising it, but his training was thorough. 'He had an altercation with a neighbor in Detroit...'

She frowned. 'You should have alerted me to this earlier.'

'It's nothing...'

'It has the potential to be a wild card, so it is definitely something. Whether it's something we shall have to handle? That's another question.'

Ben nodded agreement. 'I'll keep you informed if anything comes of it. You're heading there tomorrow?'

'Contact me when you're ready,' she said. 'Fire's contact in New Jersey is in place?'

'He is. He does not know we're coming however, as you suggested.'

'Good.' She opened the car door and got out, then walked toward the mall entrance. A moment later, Ben started the car, backed it out of the spot, and drove away.

35/

A VALLEY SOUTHWEST OF MAINDUHEZHEN, INNER MONGOLIA.

Brennan woke to the morning sun creeping across the car's windshield, the bright light shining through his closed eyelids. His head hurt, dreams of being caught again by the Black Cranes fading away. The car was on a bumpy surface, like a country road. Chu was still behind the wheel.

The American looked back. Lee was asleep on the rear seat, slumped under the window. 'Where are we? What time is it?' he asked Chu in Cantonese.

'It's just before eleven, and we're southwest of Hulunbeier, in the Inner Mongolian Autonomous Region. It's the last major stop before the Mongolian and Russian borders,' Chu explained.

Brennan looked out the window. They were on a plain, in what appeared to be a vast valley, low-level mountains – or perhaps very large hills – surrounding them. The fields were filled with wild grass at chest height, though the area around the road was scrupulously maintained. 'It looks like Idaho.'

'Doubtless, like Mongolia, a hub of culture and refinement,' Chu said sarcastically, his English perfect and tinged with an upper-crust accent.

Brennan stared at him judgmentally for a few seconds. 'You know, Mr. Chu, you're kind of a snob.'

'Discerning, my good man, discerning,' he said. 'There's a difference.'

'It's true.' Lee had woken up, and she leaned forward, so that her head was between the two front passengers. 'Jackson doesn't care if you're rich and snooty or poor and basic, so long as he can get his hands on your money.'

'And if that isn't the true spirit of egalitarianism, I don't know what is,' Chu replied.

'That's also true,' she said. 'He really doesn't.'

'Very funny, Ms. Lee. Nonetheless, I'm the one helping the two of you, against my own better judgment.'

'And out of the goodness of your heart?' Lee's tone was snide. 'Please, Jackson! If word got around Macau that you have a heart...?'

'I know, my reputation would be ruined.' Chu reached down to the center console under the armrest and retrieved a brown-filtered Dunhill cigarette from a gold-and-scarlet pack. 'No... as I said, Mr. Brennan shall owe me a favor of equal or lesser value, to be determined, as we bargained back in Harbin.'

'What else?' Brennan said. 'That's a nebulous reward at best. You're assuming we even make it out of the country. You're taking a hell of a risk for not much chance of a return. I'm guessing your father back at Black Crane Central is going to want to tan your hide.'

'Oh... I imagine he'll want to do worse than that,' Chu said. 'But... I have a personal stake in this matter, this... 'Legacy' situation, whatever it may be.'

Lee's attention perked up. 'And what might that be?' She'd been a poker player for long enough to keep her tone light, though she was sure it was making the smug American smirk again.

'I had a cousin, a dear friend to my brother and uncle. He was a superintendent with the Hong Kong Police, and tasked with interviewing your colleague in Kowloon, Mr. Brennan...'

'The raid. The two men shot in the police station the same night.'

Chu nodded but did not elaborate. 'And so now we are here, enjoying the banal beauty of a place no one goes and a road no one uses.' He flicked his cigarette ash into an ashtray mounted under the stereo.

'Aiyah!' Lee bickered. 'Lower a window if you're

going to smoke those terrible things.'

'Apologies,' Chu offered. 'But I've been good so far. That was only half a pack since we left Harbin last night.'

'You're practically the surgeon general of the middle of nowhere,' Brennan offered. 'And about that... are we heading somewhere in particular?' He glanced out the window again. They hadn't seen another vehicle for miles, the same fields of long, fallow grass passing endlessly.

'You wanted to meet Master Yip? This is where we need to be. He's ancient. He doesn't have a phone, and he doesn't stray into the city often.' Then he glanced toward the back seat. 'Did either of you bring some money or something?' He'll expect some tribute of some kind.'

'Brennan?' Lee asked.

He looked back with a withering glance. 'You're a multi-millionaire poker player and you want me to pick up the tab?'

'You can expense it,' she reasoned. 'I'm not supposed to be here, remember?'

'Maybe... I'm not even sure where here is...' Brennan began to say. The car crested a swale in the land, the road running up and over a steep hill. As they reached its summit, he got a view of the valley ahead.

The town was a few miles away, but even at distance something was different about it, off from everything else he'd seen in Asia. It was just a few buildings and streets, but it almost felt...

'Heads up,' Chu said, breaking his concentration. The driver gestured toward the bottom of the hill a few hundred yards ahead. 'There's a checkpoint up here.'

'A checkpoint?' Lee leaned forward again. 'Why on Earth would there be a checkpoint in the middle of nowhere.'

'Well... that's the thing. Master Yip lives in what was once an official nuclear test zone.'

Brennan's head swiveled quickly to his left.

'WHAT?!?'

'I... may have neglected to mention this earlier,' Chu said.

Lee took a deep breath, as if trying to shed the weight of his omission. 'You may indeed.'

'If it helps, Master Yip has always insisted the warning was greatly overstated for political reasons.'

'Probably not,' Joe said. 'Background radiation has a tendency to stick around for... oh... millions of years.'

Chu shrugged. 'I've been here a few times. I've never had a problem.'

'Yes, Jackson,' Lee said, 'but that's because you have poor impulse control, like most criminals, and are of ill health generally, because you smoke, drink and sleep with whores.'

'Also all true,' he admitted.

They reached the checkpoint and he slowed the car to a halt. A white-and-red gate barred the road, extending from a booth.

'What now?' Brennan asked.

'I don't know, to be perfectly frank,' Chu said. 'Master Yip always knew that I was coming and met me here.'

Lee seemed unimpressed. 'Because... he didn't want to bother you, or because there's nuclear waste past this point?

'As I said... I don't really know.'

The booth's rear door opened and a boy walked out. He was perhaps ten, in shorts and a faded old t-shirt, a pair of simple sandals on his feet. He shielded his eyes from the morning sun as he checked them out; then he walked over to the bar and lifted it, leaning his slight form on one end as the other rose and unblocked their path.

The boy walked around the front of the car to the driver's side and made a motion for Chu to lower the window.

The boy spoke rapidly in an accent Brennan could not follow. Chu nodded, then turned to his passengers. 'Master Yip will meet us. He is in the last house, at the end of the main street, according to the boy.'

'I didn't get a word of that,' Brennan admitted.

'Ulanchaab Baarin,' Lee murmured. 'It's a local dialect. They forced us to learn it at the academy and I think I've used it exactly once.'

'Oh yeah? When?'

'About six seconds ago.'

The boy walked back to the booth and re-entered it as Chu did up his window. The Black Crane boss pulled the car back onto the road. The asphalt ribbon continued for another mile before dipping into a gulley and banking to the left in a long 's' turn. As the Infiniti exited the last turn, a sign on the left side of the road grew nearer, until it was the size of a small billboard. The colors had faded to muted shades over time, but the picture under the type was still visible, a Middle American kitchen scene from the Fifties, a mom with curls and pearls pouring milk on her boy's cereal while a pipe-smoking dad in a brown waistcoat looked on approvingly, over the top of a newspaper.

Splayed across the sign in a Disney-ish script were the words "Welcome to Plenty, Montana!

'What the actual fuck...' Brennan began to mutter, before Lee hushed him.

'Shhh... Slow down, Jackson! I'm trying to read the second line,' she said. 'Home of the world's largest bison, Matilda. Population 1,412. A family kind of place!'

Brennan turned slightly to face her as Chu stopped the car. 'It doesn't make any sense, does it?'

Chu was nonplussed. 'Didn't your government also set up fake towns to see the effects of their weapons tests? I imagine that's precisely what this is.'

Lee shook her head. 'No, Brennan's right; this doesn't make sense. The test towns were clapboard, false fronts and streets, and the building were generally razed in any blast. And all of China's sites on that scale are well-documented in reports to international nuclear regulatory bodies. This place looked like a pristine town from two miles away...'

The car carried them up the other side of the gulley and over a small hill. Brennan saw the sign before anyone else, coming up on the left, a spindle of rusting iron with bubbled and peeling off-white paint, shooting up from the long grass; on top, an oval logo was stained with bird dung, holes punched through its glass veneer by the ravages of weather and nature. But he could read the '76' logo underneath the mess, and see the clear plastic shelf, where oversized numbers once relayed the cost per gallon of motoring to locals.

Behind it, above the top of the long grass and weeds, they could see the top two-thirds of a building. 'Lee...is this what I think it is?' Brennan asked.

'If I had to guess, I'd say it's a petrol station,' she replied. Then she saw his annoyed reaction. 'But I'm guessing you were asking about the town. And I suspect we're both thinking the same thing.'

'Would one of you perchance enlighten me?' Chu asked. A row of houses began to appear on both sides of the street, grass grown up above head height, held back at the roadside by temporary fencing that fronted each property. It appeared to have been tacked up after the fact, perhaps to protect the road and make it easier to maintain. The homes were boxy, two stories, with sloping tile roof and siding, front pillars suggesting there was a porch back there somewhere.

Halfway along, the buildings changed to low rise brick, only a few fully visible over the grass. One had a Pepsi-Cola sign still visible above where the front door likely was, raised letters on the front fascia declaring 'Brookman's Pharmacy.' Another had large white script painted on the side. 'First Bank of Plenty. Deposits. Savings. Security. FDIC Insured.'

'Oh, sure,' Brennan said. 'Even out here, they're too big to fail.'

'What on Earth is going on?' Chu asked, slowing

the car down again, exasperated. 'Why is there a picturesque American town in Inner Mongolia?'

'It's a training town,' Lee said. 'Whether it was the Soviets or us, I'm unsure. This area was closely aligned with them until the Sixties, even as a de facto province of China. This is definitely more their kind of thing, and that pharmacy looked like it was from the Fifties...'

To their left, a rusted vehicle fronted one of the properties. The body had corroded and collapsed into itself, perished rubber laying on the road around the wheel hubs. On top was the tell-tale pair of ruby-red cruiser lights. 'Straight out of *Adam 12*,' Brennan said. 'That must've been the police station.'

'It looks like there are a couple of blocks of houses on each side behind the main street, but that's about it...' Lee said.

The road dipped once more, revealing another small valley just ahead of the hill leading out of the town. It was only a half-mile across, if that, but was just deep enough to look down from the road above, to see the top of a building the size of a football field. On the property next to it, a church steeple poked out of the overgrown field.

'Any guesses?' Chu asked.

'A school,' Brennan said. 'If I was driving into an actual Montana town and I hadn't seen one yet, that's what it would be.

'Whatever it is, it's the last building at the end of Main Street,' Lee said. 'Park the car, Jackson. Let's see if we can find the venerable Master Yip, and finally get some answers.'

Master Yip Po occupied the school office, fifteen or twenty feet from the front doors and off the main hallway. He had a cot stretched out along one wall, an oil lamp on an adjacent side table providing gloomy illumination. He was sitting at his desk when they arrived, a wizened, tiny man with a bald scalp, white mustache and goatee, and a pair of wire rimmed glasses. He ran his finger across the pages of a book, the tips tracing the lines of text so that he could follow it.

Then he heard them approach and his head tilted up slightly, cocked to one side. 'Jackson?' He said before they'd announced themselves. 'Is that you?'

'Yes, Most revered Master...'

'I knew that smell was familiar.' The old man turned wrinkled his nose once more. 'My eyes have almost failed me now. Who are your friends?'

'They are government agents, Master.'

'One American, the other Chinese. They also smell... unique. Why are they here?'

'They require details on a project called 'Legacy,' Master...

His reaction was immediate, a worried look, a frown that suggested senility... or perhaps just sincere regret. He looked down at the book. 'It... is about time, I suppose. Eventually, someone had to utter that word. This world has become one in which it was inevitable.'

'What is it?' Daisy asked. 'Forgive my forwardness, Master Yip. I am with the intelligence service. You trained my mentor.'

'Ah!' he smiled for the barest moment at the notion. 'The service. I am glad it is one of our own...'

'Well... not entirely,' Brennan interjected in Mandarin. 'I am Joseph Brennan, an American.'

The old man nodded. 'That is also not surprising, given everything.'

'We know so little,' Brennan said.

The old man struggled to rise, pushing himself to his feet using the desk as a brace. He straightened his belted robe and used his left hand to feel his way from the desk to the wall, then to the other side of the room, helping his failing vision. A filing cabinet stood against the whitewashed concrete, next to a sink and two old red-and-white metal drums. He reached down to the third drawer and haltingly pulled it open, rummaging around inside for a moment before withdrawing a stack of old film reels in metal containers. Four were locked with clips, the other in a simple carboard box. He removed it from the pile, then placed the others back in the drawer.

'Wait...' Lee asked. 'The other films; those containers...'

'They are very old,' Yip said. 'They are my most prized possessions.'

Brennan walked over to the drawer and opened it again, picking up one of the containers. 'Who is 'Lan Bing'?'

Yip averted his eyes, staring rigidly at the floor.

'Jiang Qing,' Lee said. 'It was the name she used before politics. You knew her in the west as 'Madame Mao'.'

'The wife of Mao Zedong?' Brennan didn't hide his surprise. 'She was a film maker?'

'An actress,' Yip said, his gaze distant, reverent. 'Our most talented and beautiful. An ideal mother to our nation.'

'How old are they?' Chu asked. 'I thought her acting career was long ago.'

Yip confirmed it. 'They are from before the war. One, the reel marked 'Doll's House' is the only known copy in existence.'

'Oh yeah... I get it,' Brennan said. 'They're made from an old material, very unstable and unsafe, so they had to be stored carefully.' He nodded toward Yip, who held the flat carton in his arms. 'What about that one?'

'I watched this many times over the years, until my projector bulb broke. I did not wish to bother anyone for another. Now, I am afraid I could not see it well enough to watch, even if it was possible.

He handed the reel to Lee. She was puzzled. 'I don't understand.'

The old man took a deep, cleansing breath. 'Legacy was our last hope,' he said.

'Our?' Lee asked. 'Who is 'our', exactly?'

'The Followers of Jiang Qing and her crusade for

pure Maoism. Those of us who wished not to reform Communism but to save it. To bring egalitarian oneness to all mankind. Those who foresaw humanity's need for a perfect, communal order, led by its most brave and fervent.' His voice became sturdier when he said her name, as if he'd gained a measure of strength and confidence just by uttering the words.'

'What's on the film?' Brennan said. 'What happened here, old man?'

'At one point, there were many films, and tests, and reports. This was just one day, a picture of life when things were... better here.'

JUNE 19, 1985

'PLENTY', A SPY TOWN IN INNER MONGOLIA.

Dorian Fan rose to the morning sun streaming through the Taylor family's guest bedroom window. He got up and looked out at Main Street.

It was busy, people coming and going, cars parked further along, in front of the local businesses. He smiled. It was like something from a Jimmy Stewart movie, a slice of American pie.

The Taylors drove him to the school to meet with Principal Anders and Mr. Shou, the administrator. The building sat at the end of Main, a white concrete bunker on one story, the size of a large supermarket. They found a parking space between the teachers' cars, in front of the flagpole. The Star-Spangled Banner fluttered in the breeze.

Anders met them at administration, just past the front doors. 'Mr. Fan, sir! It's so good to finally meet you!' he gushed. 'Mr. Shou has told us so much about you.'

Fan sized the man up as he extended a handshake. He could've been the school head in any

American television program, balding, conservatively dressed in tweed sports jacket, sweater, shirt and tie. 'I understand I will have a chance to meet some of the recruits today?'

'Absolutely, sir, yes! Come... let's walk.' Anders led them down the hallway toward the back of the building. They passed a flight of stairs to the basement, then three classrooms, a gym across the hall. It was small, but functional, and about what he'd expected for a town of a few hundred folks.

'You're going to be really pleased, I suspect,' Anders said as they strolled. 'We have seven remaining at this point. But there are three in particular we plan to use as the core of Legacy.'

'And they're ready?'

'We believe so, yes. The process of stripping away their identity then rebuilding it to suit our ends has been psychologically devastating to most of the children. But we had nearly a dozen who placed in the final round of suitability, and these were the three that stood out, as you'd requested.'

He pushed open the rear door to the school and they walked back out into the sunshine. Behind the building, the field was filled with students lined up in three rows. An instructor in a black robe was teaching them wushu kung fu, the students precisely copying a series of stances. The three students who made up the front row moved in synchronicity as they negotiated each pose and stance. Fan recognized one immediately.

'That's the Taylor boy, Donny. Correct?'

'Indeed. He is our blunt object. A muted intellect, angry, strong, fearless, lacking much in the way of empathy or remorse.'

'His test?'

'We had him rape and murder his mother.' Anders said it perfunctorily, as someone might do assessing the speed of a mail room delivery. 'He took to it with zeal while under our control and remembered nothing of it afterwards.'

Fan turned and studied the man for a few

moments. Anders was an interesting specimen himself, also the son of a missionary from the Midwest who'd spent years in China. He seemed utterly psychopathic, but quite functional and capable. 'And the other two?'

'The boy, Christopher, will be our technical specialist. He can already strip an engine down in no time, perform field medicine, pick a lock in seconds... Oh, and he is a 'hacker'.'

Fan frowned. 'A what?'

'He has been taught to write code for IBM and Apple personal computers, and how to break into protected government and university computer networks. He will be a digital thief, of sorts, as we predict rapid growth in this social area, particularly in America.'

'And the girl?'

'Amelia Sawyer. She has an ingrained need to take control in the absence of good parenting for both her and her sibling; it makes her ideal as our handler. She's receiving extensive tactical training and her loyalty while under sway is absolute. Our intent is for her to become an expert in surveillance, intelligence gathering and law enforcement. She will be our eyes and ears with the government, a double agent.'

Fan felt his anxiety build. He rocked on his heels slightly, hands behind his back. 'Wonderful, wonderful!' he said. 'Shou has led you well. Now... before we speak further, I must meet with Master Yip Po. Is he available?'

'He looks forward to it, sir,' the principal reported. 'He is most proud of his students. Come...' He motioned with his hand for them to head back into the building.

They walked back toward administration, students passing them in the hallway as if it were any other day in the small town.

The program had taken nearly three decades to establish and cost millions. Soon, more people would wonder about the diverted funds, the cooked books.

Fan thought back to the encounter with Mah Xiao. He felt a genuine pang of remorse and regret. The young administrator had been a loyal public servant and a good man, outside of his perverted proclivities. It would take quite some time, if ever, for authorities to tie his murder to the missing funds and back to his more illustrious associate.

By that time, Fan knew, Shou's surgeon friend would do his work. Fan would be unrecognizable, as able to blend into the background as just about any kid from a town like Plenty.

36/

TODAY

A single tear traced a lazy track down Master Yip's cheek. 'It has been some time since I watched the film. But, more concisely, it is a slice of what life was like here for the children. And for us, of course.'

'You cared about them,' Lee said.

'Strangely, I did,' Yip said. 'I mastered such emotional distractions many years earlier, I believed.'

Brennan didn't care about the sentiment of the thing. 'You mentioned there were eleven children left in the program when the film was shot...'

He nodded. 'But only three were selected from the eight who finally qualified, the three best: Amy, and Christopher, and Donald.'

'You remember their names?' Brennan asked. He couldn't believe their luck.

But the old man frowned and shook his head. 'Just their given names, their 'Christian' names.'

'It's something,' Brennan said to Lee in English. 'It's not much but it's something.'

Daisy looked pensive. 'That story doesn't explain how this town came to be here, or the children and their parents.'

Yip nodded sagely once more. 'The parents themselves were the children of Missionaries. Once, until just after the Second World War, there were more than a thousand from the west in China, and they had many offspring, many of them illegitimate. Others were added from orphanages sympathetic to China after long-time missionary work. Once their children were separated from them, in the Fifties, many of the parents never returned to America; they were killed, their bodies disposed of, their children raised by proxies as the first generation in "Plenty."

"They didn't try to leave, constantly?" Chu

wondered.

"They were being brainwashed, using isolation techniques and hallucinogens. An early core belief was that the town was in a quarantined nuclear test zone, and unsafe to leave." Master Yip's head dipped once more in silent shame. 'Times... they were very different then. We had a naïve desire to repair the world.'

'By taking choice from children and turning them into killers,' Brennan reminded. 'No amount of time will make up for that. What happened to the others?'

Yip pursed both lips, fighting off more tears. 'When the program was dissolved, there was no reason to keep them here. And there was no more money to come. I was instructed to... remedy the situation.'

'By Dorian Fan?'

He nodded again.

'And how were you expected to do that?'

The old man said nothing, but his unease was obvious. 'This was very long ago...'

Chu sounded worried. 'Master?'

Yip continued to avert his gaze. Then he sighed once and placed the film carton on his desk before motioning toward the door. 'Please,' he said, 'follow me.'

He led them to the end of the main corridor, propping open the rear exit so that it would not close after them. He led them out behind the school, where two large, overgrown fields of wild grass preceded the hill that overlooked Plenty. But just ahead one field had been kept neatly mowed. There were no gravestones, or crosses. Just a series of rocks, evenly spaced. Brennan began to count them mentally, pursing his lips anxiously and blowing out a slow whistle. 'There are...'

'Four hundred and seven,' Daisy said. 'Four hundred and seven markers.'

Yip nodded gently. 'One hundred and eighty-two adults... two hundred and twenty-seven children. The markers were... for respect. They are not each buried there. There... there was a pit...'

Brennan felt the anger welling inside. He tried to push it down. He'd seen bad things, in tinpot dictatorships where mass graves spotted the countryside, and in industrial zone disasters, where corporations ran roughshod over local health and dignity. But the idea of the frail old man callously executing so many kids? He thought of his own kids, playing.

He drew the pistol from Chu's belt before the other man could react, placing it against Yip's temple. 'Say your last, you sonuva...'

'No!' Chu demanded. 'Don't shoot him, please!'

'You heard what he did! And he's told us all he can. Tell me: explain to me how something like this deserves to exist, to call itself human!?'

'You owe me a life!' Chu barked. 'Master Yip helped raise me...'

'One life for four hundred and seven?' Brennan spat.

Lee had been silent until then. 'He's right, Brennan. You cannot shoot this man; you cannot just perpetuate the violence here.'

Brennan stared at the withered, tired old face. Then he shifted his gaze to the nearby field. *They didn't even get proper burials...* He cocked the pistol. 'Kiss your ass goodbye, you psychopathic...'

They heard the shot a moment after the bullet whistled by Brennan's head and buried itself in the wall behind them. Brennan looked up toward the hill.

'Sniper!' Lee yelled. They ran for the back door... but the elderly trainer dropped to his knees behind them.

Chu was about to go through the door when he turned and saw him. 'Master Yip!' he yelled. 'Please...'

Instead, the elderly man remained on his knees. Then he looked back at the young gangster, a placid look upon his face. The bullet caught him square, entering through one temple and blowing out the other side of his skull, the venerable master pitching forward, dead instantly.

'No!' Chu exclaimed.

Brennan grabbed his arm and pulled him inside. 'We're sitting ducks out there,' he said, slamming the door behind them. 'Do you have any more weapons?'

'Other than the gun you took from me?' the distraught criminal asked.

'After what he did, the old man got off lightly,' Lee interjected. 'And if there is any life after this one, you know he will not be judged kindly. Weapons, Chu! The sniper won't be alone.'

He shrugged. 'Nothing. Just the gun.'

'Daisy, check the front, see what we're dealing with,' Brennan said, bolting the back doors. 'Jackson, come with me.'

'What are we doing, exactly?' he said as Brennan led them back to the administration office.

'Getting ready.'

WASHINGTON, D.C.

10:22 P.M.

Water would not be there, Gessler knew.

He parked on the rear side of the Denny's restaurant just outside the city, among the overflow of vehicles from the patrons gathered for breakfast. Then he rolled down his passenger window to get a better look at the rest of the lot.

The rear door to the restaurant opened and Air walked out. He was shorter than Gessler imagined. He was certain they knew each other well, that once they had been close. But he couldn't recall why. That part of the past was gone now. He flashed his headlights once, then turned off the engine. His contact looked both ways then crossed the lot and opened the passenger door to climb in.

'We have a complication,' Air said.

'What?'

'A witness, in Detroit. He called the police. I've been monitoring their channels and feeds. They have an all-points bulletin out for your arrest.'

The man on the sidewalk. He didn't recall what happened, but Gessler knew there had been a confrontation. 'What now?' he asked.

'This was anticipated as a potential challenge and will change little. We stay on plan, but we travel separately. I'll handle the issue in Mexico and meet you in New Jersey. You drop in on your internet associate. Obviously if you're compromised at any time...'

'I have my capsule,' Gessler said. 'Water is ready?'

'Water is already on scene, taking care of the preliminary approach. The plan comports perfectly to our requirements. Great favor has been passed to her by our handler, Master Fan, who wishes us the best of luck.'

Gessler's expression shifted at the mention of Fan's name, a sense of wonder settling in, an unreserved enthusiasm. 'He said that?'

Ben nodded. 'She said to tell you that he mentioned you personally and his great appreciation for your efforts.'

It had been many years since he'd even heard Master Fan's name, years of lying in the dark, hearing but unheard, empowered but powerless, waiting to shed the illusion that swaddled his presence in shadows and half-truths, waiting for his purpose. But the feeling of pride was still there, the feeling that there was nothing else on Earth quite so important as fulfilling Master Fan's wishes. His pride swelled and he felt a confidence that had been absent since his awakening, a certainty that soon Jiang Qing's Legacy would seed a new dawn.

A new world.

BEIJING

DAY 15

The State Security Committee had been fully gathered for more than ten minutes but the meeting still had not come to order. Instead, the low murmurs of tested allegiances filled the room, as allies conferred and tried to get a sense of what their opponents were thinking.

Yan watched them stoically. The only opinions that mattered at the end of the day were those of the two faction leaders: the chairman, David Chan, and his opposite number, Wen Xiu. Both were back in the capitol for just two days, then scheduled to fly to New York with the premier. But the committee meeting was unavoidable; word had filtered across the agencies that an American was loose and operating somewhere in Helionjiang Province.

It took two more minutes before Chan banged the gavel and called the meeting to order. 'Gentlemen, we face a crisis of confidence at the worst possible moment.' Around the semi-circular conference table, the murmurs renewed with abandon. 'Gentlemen, order!' Chan demanded, banging the gavel twice. When it had quieted, he continued. 'It does us no good to ignore the reality that we have an unwelcome presence in China, in the form of an American intelligence agent working on Legacy. Unfortunately, it appears he is receiving aid from one of our own, as the briefing Undersecretary Yan distributed indicates.'

'Perhaps if the Chairman had followed the initial recommendation...' Wen Xiu began to interject.

But Chan cut him off, banging the gavel again. 'Order! If the Interior Minister would be so kind as to follow the rules of the committee and wait to be recognized, it would be most appreciated. Now... as I said, we must address this situation; but we must do

THE GHOSTS OF MAO

so delicately, and without leaving the Americans any suggestion that Legacy is a Paramount issue. The talks next week in New York offer us a rare opportunity to help directly shift the course of American policy with respect to North Korea and the United States' role in patrolling the Sea of Japan and the Yellow Sea. I am open to suggestions.'

'Chairman...'

'The chair recognizes the Interior Minister. Now, Wen, what is it that required such an outburst?'

Wen counted silently to five before answering, reigning in his desire to spit fire at the ever-manipulative Chan.

'With the utmost respect to the chairman – and with my thanks to the vice-premier for ensuring I was included in the visit – we have only one option: we must find this agent and his associate, Ms. Lee, and we must eliminate them before they take any findings across one of our many borders. Should Legacy succeed – and if what we have pieced together is true, this summit is a prime target – the damage could be multiplied by any notion that we knew in advance of what was going to take place. We must prevent any connection from being made between Jiang Qing's insanity and modern, competitive China. Surely the chairman, a man of far greater wealth than any of his countrymen, recognizes that most of all.'

The committee muttered on mass once more. It was nothing less than a veiled threat to his mandate as the committee's leader, Chan knew, a challenge that he 'put up or shut up,' as the Americans liked to say. He waited until the noise had subsided somewhat. 'The learned minister is no doubt aware that I personally approved his request to come with us to America and I commend him for his bravery, given what seems a certainty on his part that Legacy is a grave threat. I am not so certain, from what we have so far seen, that such is the case. However, I share his concern about any... misinformation that the American and our rogue operative might decide to disseminate in the west... if not his histrionic expression of such. My understanding from our last briefing is that the same criminals interested in handing the American over have promised to recover him for us?'

Yan stood and bowed to the chair and vice-chair. 'They have, sir. The Black Crane society has eyes and ears all over Northern China...'

'As do we,' Wen interjected. 'Surely we are not leaving such an important matter to a gang of thugs?'

'Once again, Interior Minister...' Chan said almost laconically, 'you disrespect the committee's members and work when you do not follow rules of order.'

'Mr. Chairman, this is not a small matter, but one of considerable...'

'Order!' Chan barked, banging the gavel again. 'Or I'll end the meeting now and we can discuss your conduct at a state disciplinary session.'

Wen sat back down and was quiet, crossing his arms in an almost child-like defiance.

'Of course, we will martial other resources,' Chan offered. 'But we will do so quietly, while the Black Cranes can make as much noise as they like without any of it being connected to our responsibilities. And we shall attempt to arrest this American and find out what he knows; your zeal to eliminate him worries me and strikes me as short-sighted, Wen. Perhaps this individual can offer us real insight into how Legacy remained active or was once more triggered.'

'Yes, but... Mr. Chairman...' Wen began to implore.

'Enough!' Chan reaffirmed. 'Mr. Undersecretary, ensure our assets in the Northern cities are put on alert to their presence. And make it clear to the Black Cranes that we want both agents alive, if possible.' He turned and gave Wen a stare that was as close as he would get to conciliatory. 'But that either way, we need results. And we need them now.'

After the session had broken up, Yan paced the

worn red carpet to his office, not looking into each office as he passed, instead deep in thought. In a sense, he knew, the meetings were a form of high farce, politics masquerading as good intentions. Most of those in the room were there by family connection rather than high achievement, and rarely offered much else beside muttering. At least Wen and Chan's battles were backed by purpose, even if their true intentions were often shrouded in secrecy.

Once at his office, he closed the door behind him, removed the encrypted phone from his side pocket then hung his suit jacket on the hook. The room was becoming cluttered, he realized, the wall-length bookshelf full and magazines finding new homes in small piles ahead of various volumes. He walked behind the desk and sat down, then opened the phone app.

'Your suspicions were correct, if that meeting is any evidence,' the man in the shadows observed. 'He is going to be a potential problem for the entire trip unless we can get him to drop Legacy inquiries entirely.'

'His authority makes him dangerous, sir... Perhaps we should deal with him pre-emptively in some manner.'

'As I was forced to do so many years ago, you mean? No, let's not repeat that mistake. Once you take a man's life with direct impunity and involvement, you place a target on your back. In this case, it would be exceedingly large and exposed. The plan was designed to accommodate this sort of distraction.'

'Then I shall meet you in New York,' Yan said. 'And when the Black Cranes deliver our spies?'

'Ensure that does not happen,' the shadow man said. 'Ensure they take care of Mr. Brennan and Ms. Lee permanently. And bury whatever's left deep; the sooner both are forgotten, the better.'

37/

'PLENTY', AN ARTIFICIAL AMERICAN TOWN IN INNER MONGOLIA.

The men approaching the building from the front were all young, probably hired from the slums of Hulunbier. Chu peeked through the thick glass on the front doors as they worked to get Brennan's preparations in place. The plan seemed utterly mad, but Chu had to admit he couldn't think of any alternatives.

The band of criminals was twenty yards away, having parked up the hill. The sniper had probably called them, filled them in on what they were facing. 'I don't recognize any of them,' Chu said. 'If they're Cranes, they're not from Harbin. My guess is they put a bounty on us. My uncle would prefer me returned alive, but I'm not entirely sure, given the circumstances, that he wouldn't decide to make an example of me.'

'Come on, quickly!' Brennan called to them from the stairwell to the basement, halfway down the corridor.

Lee finished up, slapping her palm on the door to make sure her work held tight. 'There!'

They ran back to the stairwell and joined him. 'This is either going to work beautifully, or we're in it deep,' Brennan said. 'Either way, when they come in hard, I'll be running for whichever door looks most open, so keep up.'

They'd bolted both sets of doors. Brennan had noticed the metal twenty-gallon drums by the filing cabinet in the office. The opportunity was there.

They'd just needed a couple of minutes, and it had taken their opposition that long to settle on a plan of attack. By Chu's count they had five out front and at least one coming down the back hill. They'd figured on at least one more car, out of sight, so maybe four more on top of the first six.

And they had fourteen bullets in total, which meant adapting.

'Are you sure about this, Brennan?' Lee asked. 'If we'd piled more objects in front of the doors....'

'They would still get through eventually. They have us completely outnumbered and outgunned. Can you think of an alternative?'

She looked at Jackson. 'Can you negotiate us out of this?'

'That's very amusing,' Chu said. 'If you recall, they didn't ask questions first when that sniper appeared on the hill. No... no, I don't think that's going to happen.'

'If we get out of this...' Lee began to say.

'You'll concede I'm better at this than you?' Brennan suggested.

She sighed. 'Men! I was going to say '... we still have to get across the border, find someone to fly us to safe territory and get what little information we have back to our people.'

'You sure know how to take the fun out of a last stand,' Brennan said.

The doors at both ends of the hallway began to thump inwards. 'Here they come,' Chu muttered.

'It looks like they're going to try and overwhelm us from both sides at once,' Brennan said. 'Be ready, this could happen quickly...'

'I hope you're right about this, Gwai Lo.'

The front doors burst open, splintered wood from around the lock spraying the hallway as the men crashed through. Brennan leaned around the corner and carefully sighted the small pile of film in the corner, on top of the drum, behind the right door. He squeezed off two shots in rapid succession. The bullets struck the top of the drum, the sparks hitting the ancient nitrocellulose film. It flared like old photo flash paper, then hit the fumes of the barrel, the flame shooting into the container.

The thundering blast came just as Brennan leaned the other way, firing off two more shots. The second explosion was a split second later. The highly flammable film flashed, blew the barrels, which ignited the developing solution poured around the base of each door... which lit the remaining film, taped to the doors and walls at each entrance. The initial blast took out six of the ten men. The ensuing wall of flame that shot up caught the remaining four men, their clothes slick with burning chemicals, the screams loudest from the three at the back door.

They didn't have time to wait for a clearer path. 'Let's go!' Brennan yelled. He sprinted up the steps, then turned left toward the front doors. Lee and Chu followed him. He stopped in front of the administration office and reached down to peel the ancient, crusted doormat off the floor. 'Get behind me!' he yelled over the cacophony of burning wood and cracking glass. He flung the mat over his head like a cape and hood and they huddled behind him. Brennan stepped over the burning men and pushed past the flash fire, his shoelace catching. They shoved the doors open and burst outside, Brennan tossing the burning mat to one side. Lee spluttered and coughed up chemical smoke.

Chu was on all fours still as Brennan rose and turned. The school looked like it was made of concrete but there was evidently enough wood inside to act as kindling because it was going up quickly, flames licking the roof.

'The other film!' Chu said. 'The film of the spy program. He left it on his desk.' He stumbled to his feet and began to head back toward the school.

Ahead of him, the doors burst open once more. The gangster who stumbled out was engulfed in flames, one arm outstretched as he burned to death, squeezing the trigger almost blindly. He got five shots off before he emptied the magazine, two striking Chu in the chest. His eyes rolled back and he collapsed to his knees, then coughed up some blood, before slumping to the ground.

'Jackson!' Lee yelled. She began to run back to his prone body as the flaming gunman continued to click the trigger on the empty weapon. Brennan raised Chu's pistol and shot his killer once through the head, the man collapsing on the school steps, his corpse still burning.

Somewhere inside the school something blew, the explosion tearing a hole through the roof, concrete chunks showering the ground behind them.

'He's gone!' Brennan yelled. 'And we might be right after him if we don't go now!'

She looked at the Black Crane, immobile in a widening puddle of his own blood. Then she turned and ran back to the car with Brennan. He started it as she climbed in.

'What now?' she demanded.

'The Cranes won't have been satisfied with leaving this to local thugs. They'll have more men coming up from Harbin. We need to get across the border. Their reach is limited in Russia, and I have contacts who can make new arrangements for us.'

He stepped on the accelerator.

'What do you think?' she asked, pushing away the guilt over ignoring Chu and getting back to business. 'The target wasn't implicit, from what he told us...'

'There are three highly trained, deadly assassins on the loose in America, and someone is pulling their strings,' Brennan said. 'They talked about the program creating a new regime in China, with Fan at the top. To do that...'

'They would have to get rid of the old one. I believe we know who their target will be,' she agreed.

'They're going to kill the premier of China,' he said. 'And it's going to look like Americans were responsible.'

38/

DAY 15

NEW YORK, NEW YORK

David Chan watched CIA deputy director Jonah Tarrant saw into his steak, the cuts quick and precise, the morsel just enough to be worth a few chews.

He even eats efficiently, Chan thought, *like he was bred to handle bureaucrats and other stifling incompetents. I like him.*

The hotel had closed off the revolving dining room at the delegation's request so that the two men could have a private meal. The premier and vice-premier weren't to arrive for two more days, but the logistics of the trip, the security and the sessions demanded that the men actually running things be ahead of schedule.

'I find it odd that we find ourselves here,' Chan said, to break the silence. 'Do you not?'

Tarrant swallowed, then patted his mouth with a cloth napkin. 'In what sense?'

'The entirety of it, really. After all, this sudden need for our two nations to make some decisions about the region... it came about because of an action by North Korea against Japan. And yet, once again, it is China and America who are going to the table to talk.'

Tarrant seemed non-plussed. 'With great power... you know the saying.'

'Certainly. There is always the underlying social issue of whether something is right or wrong, of course. Perhaps that is what fascinates me, that two countries with no immediate role in the issue at hand are the ones to reach such a decision.'

Tarrant finished his meal and put down his knife

and fork. A waiter appeared from nowhere instantly and removed the plate. 'Thank you,' he told the man, before turning his attention back to Chan.

'I'm only interested in how we got here, Mr. Chairman, inasmuch as it relates to China's international obligations. While North Korea is the nation breaking international law, neither of us is foolish enough to believe that Dictator Kim would do so without alerting your country first.'

'An alert is not a request,' Chan stressed. 'You may be assuming too much, with respect to our input.'

'Then we would have common ground,' Tarrant said. 'Surely, if he's willing to fire a warning shot with a nuke and do it *without* China's express permission, he's willing to risk just about anything.'

Chan knew there was logic in it. But he also knew that China's dossier on the Korean leader was complete; he was rabidly opposed to dying himself. There was no delusion of real religious or spiritual significance, or any nonsense about 'ascending' this life to something else in Kim's belief systems. If unleashing nuclear weapons meant his own death and his nation's destruction, the intelligence experts were convinced, he would not take that step.

It was just as easy, and politically beneficial, to allow the North Korean leader to think his decisions went unchecked. It was plausible deniability on a global scale.

'Your own intelligence, I am quite certain, tells you that Kim does not ask for our permission. But neither does it suggest he bares any ill will toward China. Ultimately, we must be responsible for our own citizens, not the machinations of an unstable man. We are, however, quite willing to negotiate our assistance with Leader Kim, should the United States be willing to make some concessions.'

Tarrant wasn't sure what to make of the man. Of all the senior Chinese politicians willing to push for positive, economically driven change, Chan seemed the most approachable, the most aware of how important it was to co-operate. He was Harvard educated, rich, and had made a career of standing against any notion of slipping backwards to more authoritarianism. It wasn't as if China was exactly lacking in social controls.

But he still seemed ruthless on the Korea issue, regardless of the lives at stake.

'Chairman...'

'Mr. Tarrant, please do not think me ignorant of American intentions or of the benefits that global trade has offered both our nations. But we cannot simply override an internationally recognized nation-state, regardless of our influence there. And, as you say, he is unpredictable. And we are much closer to him than you are. There is no great willingness among my colleagues to abandon our cautious support for the regime, if only for the fact that it keeps his crosshairs squarely elsewhere.'

'So, better Japan or America, than...'

'The people I represent? Yes, I'm afraid so. And as that hesitancy to confront him puts us in much the same boat as your nation, our only influence comes through his belief in our alliance.'

But Tarrant knew there was another card China could play. 'You could do one thing for us that would make us more willing to bend on trade.'

Chan felt his pulse quicken. This was it: the deal, the point of either man being there, possibly in them even existing. He'd come to love the deal; that sense of a win, even in small percentages but best when it was a big one. 'I'm listening.'

'China has helped North Korea invest its ill-gotten gains around the globe. Much of that money was sourced from online theft and fraud, along with outright theft from other nations, piracy both electronic and actual.'

'We're acutely aware of the problems they cause online,' Chan agreed. 'Then... you would like us to stop helping them spend their money and lose our cut? I'm afraid...'

'To the contrary,' Jonah said with an assured

smile. 'We'd like you to help them invest much, much more.'

And of that, Chan was unsure what to think. He wasn't surprised often in life – ever, really. It was an odd sensation. 'Explain.'

'The reality, sir, is that our intelligence suggests Legacy makes your colleagues in the Chinese leadership as nervous as you. You're all rich men, capitalists in charge of a non-capitalist system. And you all have investments here. If the chairman was so heavily invested in America...'

'He would be loath to attack it.' Chan allowed himself a small smile. 'Of course with the economic embargo it can't be direct. You'd have to backdoor any such investment through a partner...'

Tarrant smiled and Chan realized his intentions. He really did like the young American. He seemed devious and charming, both highly flexible skill sets.

LOS ANGELES

Det. Norm Drabek hesitated for a moment before rapping on the smoked-glass window, just above the gold-embossed words 'Capt. Forrest Dean.' Then he turned the doorknob and opened it a crack. 'You wanted to see me, cap'n?'

The heavyset Dean looked up from his iPad, then set it down on the desktop. 'Yeah, come on in for a minute, Normie. Close the door there, too.'

Drabek closed the door. That was never a good sign.

'Am I in trouble, cap?'

'Grab a seat there for a second, okay?' He gestured to the two chairs ahead of the desk. Drabek sat down in the right-hand one.

'Okay, what's up?'

'Normie, I'm placing you on leave for two weeks, effective immediately.'

'What?! You're suspending me!!?'

'Norm! Now... just relax, okay? It's not an official suspension, and you won't get a knock on your file for health issues. It's technically administrative...'

'What the hell, Forrest!? Thirty-six years on the job, I get pulled?!? For what?!?'

'I told you again and again, you had to stop interfering in homicide's work on the Joseph case and give them what you had. But you're obsessing about helping this young woman, and I think we both know it's because of your daughter.'

'Forrest, buddy...

'No, no getting around this, no playing the 'old friends' card, Normie. You need a break, and you know it.'

'But Captain, the suspect in this case, this Ben Levitt guy... I'm telling you, there's something really weird about this guy...'

'He left a man dissolving in lye in a bathtub. I was pretty damn sure there was something wrong with him before I called you in here.'

'He yelled at someone in Chinese,' Norm said. It was the weirdest factoid he had, and just throwing it out there, he figured, might give the senior man pause.

It did, for a couple of seconds. The captain wasn't sure what to make of that. 'Chinese?' Then he realized that if he didn't know about it... 'Have you passed this on to Terry Cummins yet?'

Ah, hell, Drabek thought. 'Not as of yet. I just found out about it.'

'Uh huh. Just.'

'A couple of days ago. Look, Forrest...'

'Two weeks. Do I have to take your shield and your piece? And be honest with me, damn it! We've worked together for nearly thirty years.'

Norm shook his head. 'I'll play it straight. No official business.'

'Uh huh,' Captain Deen replied, unsure if the word 'official' should make him nervous.

Drabek was eight feet out the division's front doors when his phone rang and Zoey's number came up. It gave him an immediate warm sensation.

'Norm! I haven't seen you in three days...'

'I know, kid, I know. You're not going to have to worry about that for a couple of weeks...'

'Eh?'

'I got suspended. Well... sorta. Anyway, they put me on leave. I think it was heat from Terry Cummins in Homicide....'

'You're kidding me. They didn't...'

'They did.'

'But... what about Ben? What about us finding him first, finding out what happened to him? He could be hurt, Norm! He could have a head injury, or an aneurysm or something...'

Drabek didn't buy it. Levitt was working too deliberately, too purposefully. He couldn't tell her that, not yet. She obviously hadn't fully accepted yet that he was a bad guy. Or that she wouldn't fix him. 'Look... Just because I can't work it officially doesn't mean we can't still make calls, chase a few things down. I'll call you tonight and we'll get together and go over everything again, okay?'

She sniffed a little, like she'd been gently sobbing. 'Okay, Norm.'

After she hung up, Drabek headed to the small adjacent parking lot. His aging Chrysler Lebaron looked sad and unstylish, a twenty-year old boxy piece of reliable frugality. He sighed a little as he climbed into it, feeling the weight of his years on the job and the frustration of never being able to just give it a rest, to give up the threads of a case. He wondered just what it was that had made him that way.

His phone rang again.

'Normie? It's Pace.'

His partner would've already been told, Norm knew. The captain did things by the book. 'What's up Jeff? You calling to commiserate or make fun of me?'

'Never, partner, never! I figured while you're off having your little vacation you'd be keeping an eye on that, uh, 'other matter' that has Terry so interested...'

'Oh yeah? You got that right, I guess.'

'So you'd probably be interested to know that Baltimore P.D. put an all-points out for a Homicide suspect this morning, some guy who killed a priest and tried to burn down a church.'

'I would? I hate to tell you, young man, but I've never been that religious and the closest I've been to Baltimore was rewatching *The Wire* last year.'

'Yeah, yeah... that's not the interesting part.'

'Feel free to skip right to it...'

'Well, based on a somewhat odd witness description, I called the investigator, and the same guy is a person of interest in a homicide a day earlier in Detroit. The interesting part, Mr. Impatient, was that he yelled at a passerby in Chinese.'

'That... sounds awful familiar.'

'Uh huh. Too much so, given that he's already shown up in two cities out there.'

'I think you might be onto something there, young master Pace.'

'I think I might.'

'Give me the number,' Norm said, feeling a surge of adrenaline. 'Fuck Terry Cummins in his fat pedantic ass. I'm going to catch this fucking guy; I'm going to catch him if it's the last damn thing I do.'

39/

THE ERGUN RIVER, RUSSIA-CHINA BORDER

The passenger train from Blagoveshchensk to Irkutsk operated under an ancient agreement that allowed it to save hours of travel time. It continued using tracks that had once belonged to the Soviet Union but now lay within Inner Mongolia, under a special agreement.

There was a customs check at Daxing'anling Prefecture, then hours of uninterrupted mountain and valley scenery before it snaked its way to the bridge at Shiwei, the small village that spawned Genghis Khan and that had once been the center of a great Mongol empire, now just a sleepy river port and tourist stop.

It had taken Brennan and Lee half a day to get to the town across backroads and through stretches of trail that cars hadn't seen in years. But Chu's Infiniti, though not built for it, had admirably handled the task. Now they were parked near the river, just out of sight of the customs office, waiting for the train to appear on the horizon.

Lee was engrossed in something online, using a 'burner' phone purchased in Hulunbier.

Brennan was taking in the scenery. The whole place reminded him of Alberta or Montana, foothills and rolling hummocks, and vast plains. Most of the locals were horsemen, it seemed, and there were majestic animals covered with bright blankets grazing in paddocks all around the village. Shiwei itself seemed sprung from a Rocky Mountain fairy tale, all log cabins and rustic designs. It was the kind of place he could see retiring in with Carolyn, having a small ranch...

Carolyn. The kids.

He hadn't thought about them in days. That

wasn't a good sign. That was the business, typically, with everything external to the mission being set aside. But it had been so long, so many years of making everything else secondary. He knew how much she'd come to hate it, and wondered if she could still really love him.

'Aiyah!' Lee griped. 'Who translates this stuff?' She had the government's official Shiwei tourism page open. 'Later many Russians and Chinese inter-married, creating plentiful moving love stories.' Huh? Who talks like that, outside of Japanese video games?'

'If the lousy English is our biggest problem, this is all going to go just fine,' Brennan said.

'You still haven't explained what we do after we get to Irkutsk and catch a plane,' Lee said, breaking herself away from the phone. 'Assuming we can get past customs...'

'It's a big enough center for Jonah to wire us the money and contacts I need. I get us the paperwork and we buy tickets. Russia's free now, remember. As long as we have Russian passports, that's not an issue. The question is what we do with you once we get there.'

'And where is 'there', in this context?'

'Home. D.C.'

The notion surprised her. What was he suggesting? 'I can't do that,' she said.

'Why not? It seems like the sensible move. We need support, we need to get this information to the right people. And you know I didn't understand half of what the old man said.'

'But it's Washington, D.C., your capitol. Langley, Virginia is not far away. The optics...'

'You're not exactly in your superiors' good books as it is, Daisy. Am I wrong?'

It wasn't that simple, she knew. There was the longer term to consider, if she even had one. 'I can't go with you. It would be tantamount to defecting. Or it would be seen as such, given that someone in the ministry has a kill order on me. I have to find a way to clear this up with my paymasters, first.'

Brennan knew he wouldn't convince her otherwise, not without Jonah demanding he try to turn her. And that was a task he most definitely did not want. 'Fine. But from here to Irkutsk, you fill me in on what the old man told you. When we get there, I'll get you a new Chinese passport...'

'And an Australian one, also,' she said. 'I may need to keep moving in the region for some time before this is resolved.'

'You realize there's a good chance they'll just send a hit squad after you, to make sure the next time?'

She'd told him about Hong Kong during the drive. 'I know. But they may have yet more information, and I have managed to take care of myself in the past. If someone in the ministry has this much desire to keep me from 'Legacy', it is possible the entire plan continues to have government support, in some respect, despite the passage of time and the changing of our culture. Perhaps uncovering that link would be sufficient to restore my honor.' The contempt in her tone was considerable, Brennan noticed, and understandable.

'Do you have some way to be reached, in case we need to fill each other in? There's no telling what you're going to stumble across...'

She nodded. 'The Venetian Macau casino. There's a pit boss there, Nancy Tong. She has an emergency dead drop for me.'

A dead drop was old school spy craft, a bin or box or other quiet public location where something could be dropped and, typically, the drop marked in some way to show there was a delivery. With no contact between the two parties and complex signalling sometimes used to disguise locations, Brennan had used a few of his own over the years. 'Fine. Look, Lee...'

'Don't! Don't get all sentimental on me, Brennan. You saved me from that hitman, I saved you from the Black Cranes. We'll call it even.'

'Well...' Brennan said, counting back with his index finger as he thought it through, 'technically the film strips were my idea, so I saved you again back at Plenty. And I'm providing you the paperwork. So that's two...'

'Brennan:'

'Yes, Lee?'

'Shut up and enjoy this lovely sunrise. The train will be along any minute.'

They would hop it when it slowed on the bridge, ride it past the tiny, understaffed and disinterested customs post, and then stow away or, if necessary... buy a ticket.

Once in Russia, everything would become easier, Brennan knew. *Well... aside from preventing a major assassination and diplomatic disaster, of course.*

A few miles away, the train's whistle sounded loudly across the river valley.

MANHATTAN, NEW YORK

Agent Jennifer Parnell stood next to the veteran Secret Service liaison Lloyd Dobler, as he gestured at the busy city street beside them. He'd been going over the same point for twenty minutes and it was getting frustrating, because she knew she didn't have the authority to override her bosses, any more than he had the President's ear.

'It's a bad route, Jen,' he whined.

Jesus H, dude, shut up. He'd been calling her by her first name, truncated, for five days and it was driving her crazy. But Parnell insisted on keeping her cool and remaining professional.

'The president stands to be exposed to potential crossfire from one of these alleys or adjacent tall buildings on at least five separate occasions between leaving the conference center and Chinatown. It's just unacceptable when we aren't even being given a rationale for this route by the Chinese...'

He kept droning and Parnell tuned him out. She couldn't help it; the week had been a whirlwind and she was mentally fatigued.

A limousine pulled up to the curb, a long, square, navy blue Lincoln. It had diplomatic plates and an American flag on a front-headlight stanchion. The back door opened and CIA assistant deputy director Adrianne Hayes leaned out. 'Agent Parnell: a few moments of your time, if you please.'

Hayes made Parnell more nervous than all the men in the agency combined. She was a ferociously political animal who'd managed to claw her way to the top of the CIA from virtually nowhere, a state school graduate with no Washington connections who'd nonetheless taken to the intelligence game like a big cat in a field of drowsy gazelles.

She climbed into the limo, Hayes shuffling across the seat. Deputy director Jonah Tarrant occupied one of the jump seats opposite them. 'Jennifer,' he said.

'Sir.'

'You've had a chance to speak with the Chinese?'

She'd been about to glance at Hayes, wondering why she was suddenly in the loop. But she managed to hold off. Hayes had no role or interest in the security detail in the weeks prior. Now she was in Manhattan in person?

'Yes sir, ma'am. The head of the Chinese security detail, Po Lei Wei, insists they have had no credible threats other than what we've already been told of Legacy. We've kept a close eye on him, and he has spent minimal time in contact with the traveling delegation, who are in... I believe... Nigeria this morning.'

Hayes' gaze burned a hole through her, reading her every expression. 'The guy on the curb, the secret service liaison...'

'Dobler.'

'He seemed pretty upset by something...'

'With good reason,' she said. 'This route is a nightmare to defend, let alone pass off as relatively secure.'

'Where are the worst spots?' Hayes asked. She leaned in as she said it, as if she was genuinely curious, and not just senior management being patronizing. 'Say... the side streets either way? Chinatown? The route from the conference center?'

'More likely the buildings downtown, if you're talking about a sniper,' Parnell said. 'For anything bigger like a grenade launcher or RPG, they'd want some space around them. So... yes, the side streets are a considerable risk. We've had some help to block them off...'

'Jennifer was trying to reach an agreement with city police and fire,' Jonah noted. 'They want to take part anyway, but we need them on call. This way, they can do both.'

'And ideally station a man at every one of them?' Parnell asked. She knew the additional request would seem extreme on top of a half-dozen fire trucks and a dozen police vehicles.

'Not a chance,' Jonah said. 'They're not even staffing the trucks, for the most part, just giving us drivers, spotters, some extra hands if necessary. We've already leaned on the NYPD hard for route help.'

'What about asking the state police to kick in...?' Parnell suggested. 'After all, our involvement is already saving them...'

'Again, not a chance,' Adrianne interjected. 'We've already racked up too many favors owed and the budget can't sustain that sort of prolonged additional manpower. Not over a parade, even with a perceived threat like Legacy.'

'Perceived?' Parnell sounded surprised.

Jonah shrugged. 'We still have very little other than a fifty-year-old rumor about a plot by a woman who's been dead for twenty-five. We haven't heard from Brennan in nearly a week...'

Hayes could see the younger woman worrying. 'Don't sweat the details too much, Parnell,' she counselled. 'This is what we do. The Asians... they have their own ways. Even though they're visiting us, we're still sort of just along for the ride.'

ANNANDALE, VIRGINIA

The drive from the airport to Annandale was quiet, although after being away for so long, Brennan was happy to let the car radio and a few familiar voices on NPR fill the void.

He was happy. Not ecstatic, or joyful, or anything quite so out of character; but he was finally getting to see the kids. It had only been two weeks, but it felt endless, not knowing how they were doing. He knew it was just instinct, that Carolyn would never allow anything to happen to them.

But that didn't prevent his sense of disappointment and guilt at not being there, again.

He pulled the car into the driveway of their modest bungalow. Carolyn wanted something bigger, in town. She was willing to wait until the kids were grown, because as sleepy as the suburbs were, they were also safer and generally healthier. But then, she insisted, they were moving to the Beltway proper.

He pushed the negative thought away, filing it for the future under arguments that could wait until much later.

At least for now, he was home.

He opened the front door on the second try, then picked up his suitcase and walked in. Carolyn had installed a keypad lock but kept cycling three different codes. It irritated him way more than it should, he knew. There was near zero chance that in the in-filled, upgraded subdivision any crook would bother targeting their modest property.

"Hello? Carolyn? Jessie? Josh?"

But the house was silent. He checked his beaten old Seiko wristwatch; but it was one-thirty on a Wednesday, with school not back in for a week.

They'd probably gone with friends for brunch,

Brennan figured. Something like that.

He'd tried to call her from Moscow, then again from the airport, but got her voice mail. For obvious safety reasons, he never carried the kids' cell numbers and contacts.

He put his case down by the door, vowing to unpack it properly this time. Then he crossed the carpeted upper tier of the step-down living room to the kitchen. If they'd been home recently the coffee pot would either still be on or warm, because his wife's caffeine addiction was predictable.

But it was cold, the remaining half-cup looking black and stale.

His phone rang.

"Brennan."

"Joe." It was Jonah Tarrant. "I didn't want you to get home and worry about Carolyn not being there."

"Explain."

"The NSA wanted her down here in New York on Legacy."

Carolyn wasn't an operative or handler. There was only one reason to put her in the firing line.

"Goddamn it, Jonah... where are my kids?"

"Look, just relax, okay? They're with your wife's friend Ellen McLean. The NSA wants a full debrief on China. They figured we might have a difficult time convincing you to come down without also being operational..."

"So they're blackmailing me into it by manipulating my wife, is that it? And you're letting them get away with it?"

"Joe... look, you know how complicated these political issues can be. But I'm on your side, my friend; you can count on that."

He wasn't quite sure how to respond at first. It felt as sincere as a Christmas card from the tax man. "You're a real piece of work sometimes."

"We do what we have to do. That's always been how the game is played."

"My kids aren't pieces in a game..."

"I'll expect you down here later today."

And then the odds-on choice for America's next CIA director hung up.

BALTIMORE, MARYLAND

Det. Ed Kinnear got back from the fire inspector's office at just past four in the afternoon, meeting Underheath at the Southeast District station. The old red-brick-and concrete building was a piece of stark Seventies architecture, like someone had stuck law enforcement inside a school gym. Inside the glass double front doors, past the front desk – where a duty sergeant looked bored taking complaints and waiting on street folk – the old, beaten-up hardwood floors led into the rear detectives' bullpen. It was just a handful of desks, a dais, a chalk board. A couple of pin boards on the wall, a television in one corner.

Det. Dante Green was updating a handful of uniformed patrolmen on the suspect description, as Underheath looked on, hands on his hips as they patiently got instructions.

They were still working on the assumption that Gessler was somewhere in the area. Kinnear had his doubts.

Underheath saw him and nodded his way.

Kinnear returned the gesture. 'Any word from our L.A. friends yet? They should be in town by now.'

'They're caught up waiting for the girl's bag at the airport, I guess.' Underheath didn't sound impressed by the potential connection.

'You get any sense of what they have to offer?'

The young detective didn't like to admit it, but... 'No, not really. The old guy, Drabek; he was real curt...'

That made Kinnear chuckle. By the time a Homicide dick reached their vintage, a little gruffness wasn't uncommon. 'I made a few calls to a couple of guys from the MC who work out in La-La land now...

Drabek's the real deal. Solid rep, big-time closer in homicide for years. I guess he had a death in the family and had to slow down some, so they stuck him in missing persons.'

'The girl, she thinks Gessler might be her missing boyfriend, right?'

'Benjamin Levitt, a plastic surgeon and amateur website building enthusiast. And another lucid babbler of Asian languages.'

Underheath fairly radiated skepticism. 'You're kidding.'

'I never kid about work, you know that. Unless there's free beer involved, and even then only to fool the likes of you into leaving it for me. Anyway, I guess he doesn't match the description, and it sounds like he killed some guy around the same time Gessler was stumbling around Detroit like an ass. So now we've got two of them.

'So why're you so hot on this? I mean, two guys who speak Asian languages...'

'Both wanted for seemingly unmotivated homicides, both out of the blue, both out of character? And in the same week? No, no, young grasshopper. Coincidence this, I think not.'

Underheath frowned. 'Was that an attempt at Yoda, or the old teacher from *Kung Fu*?'

'Eh... little of both, I guess. Anyway, I don't believe in coincidences. I had them send over the mugshot of the guy they're looking for, this Levitt guy, yesterday when Drabek first called.'

The Baltimore detective finished with his charges and they quickly left the bullpen, heading for the station's rear exit. Then Green walked over and joined them. 'I sent your mug over to my friend at Thurgood Marshall; she spent most of last night going through security cameras from the last five days at all gates where flights were deplaning from the west coast.'

'And?'

'Nothing,' Green admitted.

'Ah hell,' Underheath muttered.

352

'But...then she kept going, and despite having barely slept, spent most of this morning checking flights from Canada, just in case he slipped the border. And...'

'Let me guess: Vancouver?' Kinnear suggested.

'Most astute, my Detroit brethren. He got in four days ago.'

'How are your hotels about sharing info...?' Underheath suggested.

'Ptth... you have got to be fooling. Not a chance. They play the privacy card real tight without warrants, so we won't be fishing through their camera footage. But we're circulating the photo to front desk staff, gas stations in the areas near hotels and motels. Maybe we get a hit.'

One of the duty officers from the front desk poked her head into the room. 'Detectives Green and Kinnear et al: we have some guests here for you.'

'Send them on in, thank you,' Green answered.

Drabek was about the leathery old soul Kinnear had expected, his shirt collar too big for a neck shrinking with age, his tie loose at the knot. The girl looked like she'd walked out of a rock concert crowd or something, her arms tattooed heavily, a nose ring hanging from her septum, bangles in each ear.

Drabek reached in to shake hands first. 'So...' he said. 'I guess our suspects have something in common. This is Zoey Roberson; like Mrs. Gessler, as you described it, Ed. Her guy took a shot at her, too. Unlike in the case of Mrs. Gessler, our suspect missed.'

Kinnear nodded approvingly. 'Well that beats the hell out of the alternative.'

'I hate to disappoint you before we even start talking...' Zoey suggested, '... but I'm as baffled as everyone else as to what's going on.'

Kinnear kept nodding but the smile had faded somewhat. 'Good to know,' he said. 'Let's get started by you going over everything you can tell us about your boyfriend. Okay?'

40/

NEW YORK, NY

DAY 16

The limousine that picked Brennan up at JFK airport didn't bother sending the driver inside to meet him. Instead, Jonah timed their arrival perfectly, somehow, the stretch vehicle pulling to the curb just as he stepped out of the arrivals lounge.

The back door swung open. 'Agent Brennan.'

Brennan had only met Adrianne Hayes a handful of times. He didn't like her. She reminded him of the clandestine service's former deputy director, the late David Fenton-Wright. 'Ma'am.'

He climbed into the spacious back-facing jump seats. Jonah Tarrant was sitting beside her.

'Nice of you to finally join us, Joe,' Jonah said. 'We got your encrypted send from Irkutsk.'

'You're a real bastard, Jonah. You know that, right? How dare you involve Carolyn...'

Jonah shrugged. 'Not my call, my friend. She's NSA now.' But they both knew it was a lie, and his decision to sell it as sincere made Brennan that much angrier.

'Right. After this is done...'

'I know Joe, we're going to have to talk. Look... we caught a major break yesterday. We got a call from Baltimore PD on three homicides in three different cities. The prime suspect in two of them is a Paul Gessler of Detroit. We believe based on his background that he is the child from Dorian Fan's brainwashing project. Donny, I believe was his birth name.'

'The sociopath.'

'Apparently so, though from your intel we have to assume that if the other two ideal candidates were similarly indoctrinated, they're every bit as dangerous. And it appears the other name we have — a plastic surgeon named Benjamin Levitt—has already proven that out. He killed a man to steal his identity, right after being activated a week ago. His significant other, unlike Gessler's, survived to tell us about it.'

'Can I talk to her?'

He ignored the question as if unasked. 'There's the third shooter to consider when you're on route. The girl in your story, Amelia. They'd identified three as ready, according to your source in the village. Our tactical assessment is that all three were probably trained in a variety of commando and black ops techniques but that each likely had a specific operational identity and objective, as well. Gessler is the muscle, trained in explosives, quick with a pistol, utterly remorseless and unlikely to break, bend or snap at the wrong time. Given how easily Levitt took over Paul Joseph's life, he'll be handling the technical stuff. He's probably well-versed in computers, security, and finding ways for them to breach defenses. That leaves a third person.'

'The trigger man or a distraction?' Hayes suggested.

'Possible,' Jonah agreed. 'It's all purposeful behavior, useful regardless of what might have changed with the passage of time. We need to keep in mind this idea was hatched forty-plus years ago.'

'An insider,' Brennan said. 'She'll be an insider. If you had decades to wait, potentially, and you needed to infiltrate a country's security infrastructure, would you do it all from the outside? Or would you bring someone up through the system itself...'

'A mole,' Hayes said. 'With us?'

'It sure as hell wouldn't be the first time,' Jonah

said. 'We all know any agency is only as good as its individuals, and we employ a lot of people.'

'Well... we can narrow it down by gender, to start, if the other two are Donny and Christopher; we're looking for a woman,' Brennan pointed out.

'Probably,' Jonah said.

'Maybe,' Hayes proposed. 'As you reported, the old man's memory was incomplete, weak, unsupported by much more than some old film reels he looked at occasionally. We have to be alert to the possibility that there were numerous other kids trained there -- maybe another male assassin, for example.'

'So we're looking for an orphan. Has someone run down background on everyone cleared —' Brennan began to suggest.

But Jonah cut him off. 'Gessler's background had been carefully concealed so that he appeared for years to have been the Gesslers' birth son. This was probably agreed to by the adoptive parents as a condition of buying the child on the black market. With his father's temper and history of spousal abuse, there would have been no way they've have been granted a baby through official channels, even back in the Seventies. Not without someone screwing up, anyway. It happens, but not in this case. So, we can't even go by that.'

The reality hit home. 'Then... it could be anyone,' Brennan reasoned. 'How many people have official security passes along the route?'

Hayes looked at her boss anxiously, which Brennan took to be a bad sign.

'Forty-three, including the Chinese,' Jonah said.

The agent's head sunk. 'So this is a turkey shoot, potentially.'

'If the target is the Chinese Premier? Yes, that's about the sum of it,' Hayes said. 'We have the utmost confidence that the President will be well-protected by his detail, but the Premier insists on riding in an open-top convertible, an Americanism he has always admired, and he apparently believes the idea of a plot from within his government to be absurd. Given how many potential rivals he's purged, I'm not sure if he's right, or if an attack is just about inevitable. Either could be true.'

'Open-top... that's madness.' Brennan said. 'Jonah, we can't possibly be allowing...'

'This is way above our pay grade,' the deputy director said. 'The Chinese are looking for trade concessions at these talks, in exchange for their help in convincing the North Koreans to disarm. At least, that's the message from David Chan, their security chairman. But he's the only real progressive capitalist on this panel. So getting firm commitments on that front hinges to some degree on keeping him happy. And he can't risk alienating the Premier...'

'Utter. Insanity.'

'I know, Joe, I know. But, as I said, the NSA, police and FBI will have nearly three dozen agents in the crowd, all along the route.'

'And where do you want me?'

Tarrant and Hayes looked at each other quickly.

'Joe, the Chinese are aware you were in their country. They don't want you there; neither does the NSA. They want to debrief you and the girl, Zoey Roberson. And then they want you on ice until this is done. That's it.'

'You're kidding me. You dragged me here, away from my family, and now you're pulling me off this?'

'You know full well you'd have preferred to stay in D.C. anyway,' Hayes suggested. 'Be thankful you don't have to spend an hour on your feet, jogging behind limousines.'

Tarrant was more conciliatory. 'I'm sorry, Joe. I know you'd either want to go home or see it through. But we'll get it done as soon as we can. We've got a room for you at the Hyatt, alongside the girl and her detective friend from Los Angeles...'

'Uh huh. I risked my ass to figure out what Legacy was for you. I've been halfway across China and back. And now...'

'Now it's time to put your feet up for a few days.

Enjoy the legendary Big Apple hospitality.'

'Sure, Jonah. I'll just relax and wait for my debrief, then. Because that's what I've been known to do in situations like this: nothing. Just relax.' He crossed his arms, looking defiant and irritated as the limousine made its way downtown.

SEOUL

The barbecue house was packed with patrons, its front open to the street, the rows of bamboo and wicker tables, filled by four or five people, perhaps a hundred in total. The restaurant's signs were all in Korean, and there were only a couple of western faces in the place, Lee noticed.

A smell from the kitchen of ginger and onions reminded her she hadn't eaten lunch yet. It had taken three days to get word to her old training school partner Jin Hu that she was in the South Korean capitol, as Hu lived and thrived on the city's black market underground; and this where her old friend had insisted on eating.

At least she made herself obvious when she finally arrived, crossing the restaurant to join Lee at a back table. A smuggler and information broker, Hu was still a tomboy into her early thirties, her hair spiked and dyed green, a shoulder bag slung across her back like a rucksack, a string tank top over shorts.

Halfway to the table, between the sitting patrons, Hu stopped and pulled out her phone. She resumed walking, tapping a text even as she negotiated her way around the furniture and customers as if they weren't even there. Then she ended the message and glided into the seat across from Lee.

'Daisy, baby, what's happening!' She offered Daisy a fist to bump. The agent did so, feeling a little silly in the process. 'Long time no see, stranger! You miss me?

'Of course!'

Hu took out a packet of Benson & Hedges 100s and lit one, blowing smoke up into the steamy rib shop air. 'I was beginning to think you forgot about me.'

'How's the capitalist high life treating you? By how hard you are to find, you must be doing well for yourself...'

Hu shrugged. 'I do okay. I spend a lot, to be honest. You see the new small-form factor case from In-Win?! I have to have it, you know? I don't even have a PC build going right now, but... I never was good with money the way you are. Spend a lot, make a lot. It all works out.'

'I guess.'

'So what's the dealio, Daisy Duke? Why's a big shot poker player-slash-secret agent slumming with yours truly? I mean, I know I'm pretty to look at and all, but Skype is a thing now...'

'I need some intel. Of the 'dubiously sourced' kind, thus the weird circumstances.'

'Hmmm, really? Are you sure the kill order out on you had nothing to do with it? Because I hear someone high up in the ministry wants your head on a plate.'

Damn. Lee had hoped word hadn't gotten around yet. 'For the time being, sure. But you know how these things tend to go. One day you're sipping champagne...'

'And the next day you can't get a cup of water.' Hu grinned. 'I never realize quite how much I miss your company until I see you again for the first time in a while.'

'And I you!' Lee squealed with enthusiasm. She meant not a word of it; Hu had been the college friend with mental issues, a good soul buried under years of emotional problems. Their last year of college had been a rollercoaster of helping her avoid jail, expulsion and social pariah status.

Still... the part about her having a good heart underneath it all was true, Lee had always believed.

'But... as you guessed I'm not just here to be social.'

'Do I sense some of that government largesse coming my way? I mean, assuming they don't kill you before you get a chance to pay me. You know... you can pay me in cool spy stuff, if you want. Like, a car with revolving plates. Or a motorbike with machine guns. Maybe a cool weapon in a secret stash that I can spring on someone when cornered; a fountain pen gun or something?'

'You know that stuff is all make believe. Anyway, I need you to be focussed! My contacts in Saigon insisted the man I'm looking for is in the DPRK. You have contacts there, the business intel network you sell data from, to the Norwegians and French among others.'

'My, my! You are well informed these days, Daisy Duke. Still, that must mean what you're looking for is Hella hard to find. That means I can charge you a shit-ton of money for it.'

'Hu...'

'I've got this wicked new set of handlebars I've been eyeing. What is it, anyway?'

'I need the location of Duk Su-Ree, personal plastic surgeon to the former supreme leader, Kim Il-Sung.'

'Huh. You don't want much, do you? He's an insider, a trusted friend of the Kim family. That's some dangerous data to be tossing around in these parts. What's he to you?'

'The important question to you, old friend, isn't why or who, just how much.'

'With those terms? Ptth! A hundred thousand dollars. No less.'

The value of Fan's identity could be incalculable, Lee knew. She didn't really have a choice, even facing the prospect of paying it herself. 'Done.'

Hu's surprise was momentary before her business instincts kicked in and she tried stoicism. 'Done, just like that, huh?

'When and where?'

She looked around and snorted. 'Hnnh... Not

here, that's for damn sure! Too many criminals in this place. Feels unsafe or something. Tonight in Myeong-Dong. We'll get a lobster tail at the booths by Club Clio.'

That was about as public as things could get, which meant some risk, but much more likely there would be too many civilians around for a firefight, no matter how much someone in Beijing wanted her dead. 'Eight o'clock?'

'Be there or be square, Daisy Duke.'

But at Eight o'clock, Hu was not there.

Daisy Lee waited while the lobster cook eyed her suspiciously. She was in a business casual dress, and hardly looked the part of the enterprising young lobster tail thief. But he couldn't be sure, evidently.

That, or business was slow, and he was hoping she would eventually actually buy something.

Her phone rang, the number blocked. 'This is Daisy.'

'It's me. Sorry, my associates are very careful. They wanted me to be sure you'd show up alone.'

'How long have we known each other?' Daisy asked indignantly.

'Relax! Relax, Daisy Duke. Head two blocks west and one south. You're looking for the money exchange on the corner, near the Chad Keane leather store. I'll be out front.'

The call ended. Daisy stared down at the phone. It had caught her off guard. If it was anyone else, she'd assume someone was luring her into a trap. She didn't know Seoul that well, after all.

She also didn't have much of a choice. Hu probably knew that. *I wonder if she's trying to shake more money out of me.*

Lee walked the two blocks casting wary eyes around her. The streets of the district were brightly lit pedestrian thoroughfares with minimal through traffic, electronic store fronts open late, backlit cosmetics models draped in gems, decked out for the luxury luggage next door.

The money changer's shop didn't fit the surroundings, with a peeling old wood sign that suggested it had been there since before the economic revival turned the district into an eastern take on Rodeo Drive. Hu stood outside with her hands shoved into the pockets of a big coat, warding off the cool fall air.

'Why here?' Daisy asked, before her friend could greet her. She scoped the surroundings to try and peg down an answer. The road ended at a 'T' junction, meaning one fewer exit, but that was about it.

'It's quiet but still public, still safe,' Hu said. 'You bring my money?'

'I brought you bitcoin for half the amount. You get the second wallet when I'm clear and the information is confirmed. That way, if I do clear my name, there's at least a chance the ministry will refund the 50k.'

Her old friend frowned at that but it was clear she didn't have a choice, if she wanted to get paid at all. 'Fine. Pak has been living in Sonbong, a town in the northeast, along the ...'

'Along the border with both Russia and China. Plastic surgeon to all sorts of interesting individuals, I'm sure, from such a strategic location. That's where the uranium mines are too, I believe.'

'You want to visit a hot zone, sweetie? This one's as hot as they get. You head to housing block k-3. Its official name is 'Benevolent Home to Children of the Wise Father,' but the locals just call it 'three.' Apparently, they're not big on sentiment.'

'You got a unit? I assume this is one of those thousand-unit mega shitholes, like in Pyongyang.

'I do not, but my guy said he thinks seventh floor.'

'So... all I have to do to talk to him is break into the most heavily fortified nation in Asia, make my way to its northernmost point, get into a town unseen and unreported despite thousands of soldiers, police and guards… and then make my way through seven stories of concrete bunker filled with some of the party's most loyal drones.'

'Yeah… yeah, that's about it. Easy peasy, as the Brits say. You see that place there?' Hu nodded down the 'T' junction, a narrow one-lane road heading northwest.

'Sure. You mean the metal gates?'

'Uh huh?'

'It looks like some kind of government deal.'

'It's a nursery school for rich types. All kinds of high-end security.'

'Okay. So?'

'They close at four. After that… the street is kind of deserted…' Hu's voice had dropped a notch in volume, and Lee realized the woman had stepped back, out of her peripheral vision. She turned quickly, just in time to see the store's metal door close behind Hu, the bolt sliding into place. Lee ran over to it and yanked on the handle. But inside, metal security shutters were rolling closed.

That was why she picked this spot. It's great for an ambush.

Lee heard the motorcycle engines before she saw them, three in a 'v' formation heading down the one-way road. There were a few pedestrians using the small stretch, and they stumbled out of the way, warned by the noise as the machines roared into the intersection, riders' arms extended, ready to…

Her body went to work before her mind had even caught up, recognizing the threat. She turned and ran, taking two strides before diving head-first through the glass front door of the bookshop next door. Bullets strafed the front of the buildings, tearing the books to shreds. Lee hit the floor inside, confetti and wood chips hailing down. She rolled to one side, behind the front display shelves, drawing her Heckler & Koch pistol as she came up in a crouch. There was a thin sightline, just a narrow gap through the door out to the street; but one of the riders had parked right in sight, and she squeezed off three shots toward his center mass, the man crashing to the pavement. Bullets strafed the books again, a woman at the counter behind her going down, crying out from a wound to the leg. The roar from the machine pistols continued for another second before both riders emptied their clips. They ejected them and began to load new ones. In the background, Lee could hear police sirens. She knew she might not survive another barrage, but any help still sounded blocks away.

The men resumed strafing the building, the roar from both guns deafening, drowning out the distant klaxons. Lee popped up once and sighted the first rider, emptying three of the last five shots in her clip to make sure he went down. His partner leaped from his bike and ran toward the front door, covering himself by unleashing another half clip on route. Lee sprinted for better cover, toward the back of the store, between the racks as the bullets pinged around her, puncturing paperbacks and magazines.

She crept around the end of the displays, keeping her head low. He'd stopped firing and was trying to figure out where she was. She could hear him slowly pacing down the rows, heading her way. She glanced down at the H&K, with just two shots left. She didn't have a chance against the man's MP-5, she knew, unless she could get the drop on him or...

Get out. Get out of the confined space. Her instinct kicked in as the man opened fire. The MP5's insane fire rate meant that if he just sprayed that corner of the store, he'd likely hit her before she could get clear, and Lee sprinted toward the left wall, praying the place was as old and flimsy as she thought. She leaped into it shoulder first, the rotten old drywall giving way like tissue paper, old wooden studs behind it cracking as she punched a hole straight through to the money changers'.

Lee hopped to her feet from her back. Hu was astonished, but she still had the presence of mind to reach for the back of her waist band. But Lee was quicker, her hand raised in a flash, a single shot ringing out, the bullet slamming into Hu's chest, knocking her off her feet. Lee turned in the same motion and fired, just as her pursuer stepped through the hole in the wall, the shot catching him square in the forehead. He dropped to his knees, then dropped his gun, clattering to the ground, before slumping face down, a pool of blood gathering quickly around his head.

Lee ran over to Hu. She was still alive, gasping for air. The gurgling made it sound as if she'd punctured a lung. The area of the wound suggested the slug had found her heart.

I guess she still has one after all. Lee leaned down. 'Why, Hu?'

The other girl coughed, fresh, crimson blood spewing out of her mouth as she tried to clear her throat to talk. 'Intel is intel. Business... is business. Sold you him... sold them... you. Like... my uncle's store?'

'You want me to call an ambulance? I don't think they're going to make it in time...'

Hu shook her head as well as she could. 'Don't got anyone else except uncle... have a drink on me sometimes... okay? Be... nice to be remembered.'

The sirens were really close now, Lee thought. She looked around the room as Hu breathed her last. At the front register, a wizened old man, tiny, had been standing in the corner of the room the entire time, shaking like a leaf, his hands up. He could see that his niece was dead, and despite his offer of surrender, tears streamed down his angry face.

Lee rose and headed for the door. There was no percentage in sticking around to answer questions. The dead would have to lay where they left themselves.

41/

BEIJING
DAY 17

Time had become a factor, and as Yan waited for the files from the ministry's mainframe to copy over to the encrypted drive, he looked out his office door, to the long, marble hallway. He'd given his secretary the day off, and his researcher, Jun, was at lunch.

The department expected him on a flight to New York. Instead, when he arrived at the airport, he would lose his assistant, then depart for his already planned bolt hole in New Zealand. Like his mentor so many years before, he hoped to be out and gone, with Beijing just a memory by the time his deception was discovered.

The ghost of Jiang Qing was on his side.

He'd spent the morning sending 'go' codes to a fleet of bank officials, draining the ministry's 'supplemental' field agents' fund and his own accounts in one fell swoop, some thirty-two million dollars being converted into cryptocurrency at one end, then back into cash via new anonymous corporate shell bank accounts in Panama, Switzerland and Malta.

Once the file transfer was complete, he'd have enough information to ensure they'd won the intelligence and online information war before the power struggle for the nation had even begun. And he'd have every remaining shred of written evidence in the government's databases that Legacy or Plenty, Montana ever existed.

The hallway was empty. He waited a few minutes, dreading an appearance, but it stayed vacant and quiet, save for the odd echo from elsewhere in the aging building. Even something as innocuous as the wrong person taking a bathroom break and wondering what he was doing could be his downfall, Yan knew.

But it seemed as if he was on his own, most people away for lunch. He skittered back to his desk and checked the file progress. It was at ninety-seven percent.

Just a few more seconds...

He watched the bar, immobile for what seemed an eternity, the tiny clock icon spinning away. *Come on, damn you, hurry! Why is this taking so long...!?'*

The bar clicked up one more notch, the number switching to ninety-eight percent, then quite quickly ninety-nine...

And then it froze again.

DAMN IT.

He felt his stomach flip and absently held an arm across it, the rumbling unpleasant, as if his appetite sensed his anxiety and decided it needed the comfort of familiar food.

One hundred percent. The bar hit the end of the line, the clock spun for a few more seconds.

As quickly as it disappeared, he was dragging the little drive icon into the trash and ejecting it, yanking the memory stick from the USB port and on his feet...

His desk phone rang.

The call display said it was coming from Wen Xiu's mobile.

He hung his head. *Not now. Anytime but now...*

Yan knew he couldn't ghost the call. But if he answered it, there was no telling how long the minister's request would delay him. If they checked the security desk log, they'd know he was still in the office at the time...

To hell with the log, he decided. *By then, I will be out of the country and gone. And to hell with Wen Xiu.*

The desk phone's first line continued to flash orange as he pocketed the USB drive and headed for the door.

SONBONG, A SMALL CITY IN THE NORTHEAST, DEMOCRATIC PEOPLE'S REPUBLIC OF KOREA

Sonbong was a town out of place and out of time, the buildings largely dating to the post-war reconstruction, before drab authoritarian utility took over the nation's architecture. Mottled, muddy pink stucco mixed with teal concrete-and-brick, grey cement, and factory smokestacks. Giant cranes that leaned out in parallel precision across the open waters of the port mostly dated to when the Soviets used it as a Sea of Japan staging base. They were rusted, immobile, but undaunted in their solemn guard duty, refusing to bend to the ravages of nature and the passage of time, undefeated and unbowed by the demands of commerce, but useless to it all the same.

The city was the only 'economic free zone' in the entire nation, a place where, under a watchful eye, goods and services could be bought and sold between government-approved merchants and free-market capitalists. Of course, large volumes of additional product moved off the books at the same time.

Their clients were principally from Russia and China, although some Americans, Canadians and Scandinavians also operated in the town. One of Lee's contacts in the casino industry had met Anna Choi when helping to set up the first such gaming establishment– not open to North Koreans, of course, mostly forbidden from even visiting Sonbong. Choi worked in Sonbong as a trade ambassador for a Chinese manufacturer of voltage regulators. She'd been recruited nearly a decade earlier, but rarely used.

She was small, delicate. She watched Lee from a few feet away as the agent stood at the hotel room window and spied her target through binoculars.

Duk Su-Ree was fat and successful, which was a rare situation in which to find one's self in the DPRK. The plastic surgeon's midsection was expanding, but so was his bank account, and his penthouse flat had a lovely balcony that overlooked the Sea of Japan.

Lee hadn't seen many fat North Koreans, beyond the obvious candidate. She watched Duk sit and read placidly, a glass of wine on the table next to him.

'He seems harmless enough,' she said, lowering the spyglasses.

'He probably is,' Choi said. 'It's his connections that make him dangerous, not the man himself. Well... his connections and his skill with a scalpel. He's made and remade faces for the regime's criminals and agents for two decades, like his father before him.'

'Just as his father did for Dorian Fan,' Lee said. 'If anyone knows what happened to Fan, whether he died or passed on a mantle to someone else...'

The smaller woman sighed. 'Good luck. He almost never leaves his place, except to go down to the casino... unless you're thinking that would be the place...'

Lee shook her head. 'No, unfortunately not. While taking him at cards like a Bond villain is appealing, the reality is that the same consortium in Macau with whom I sometimes work also owns the place here, and there's every chance I could be spotted by someone who recognizes my alter ego.'

'Problematic.'

'Absolutely. But when isn't it?' Lee smiled knowingly, and Choi felt a surge of confidence. She'd been in the grimy, struggling port town for long enough to know that she wanted to be anywhere else. Perhaps a successful mission would get Beijing's attention and they'd finally pay her out, let her move on from working undercover; clear the record of any notion she cheated on her trade certifications.

The lights flickered twice, then cut out. The air conditioner slowed, the constant drone fading to silence as the apartment was plunged into blackness.

They both listened for a few seconds, the only sounds through the open window of some cars down below and the creaking rustle of the cicadas. 'Blackout?' Lee asked.

'Rotating, sort of. Regular, about every six hours. The local political radicals – the underground movement, weak as it is – believes the blackouts are being caused by the power draw from a construction project just outside the city. Officially, they're expanding an oil-fired power plant. Unofficially, the radicals think it's some sort of uranium enrichment facility. I wouldn't inquire too deeply, however; they've also reported seeing some of our boys visiting.'

'Central committee?'

'Army.'

They were quiet again. Across the road and a block away, the light flicked on in the surgeon's apartment.

'Four minutes,' Lee said.

'He has a backup generator, I imagine,' Choi noted. 'Probably diesel. The Russian have a direct pipeline, embargo be damned. The more affluent locals have manual diesel generators. They don't switch over automatically, but they're push-button, easy things to operate.'

'He doesn't have a maid or houseboy or something?'

Choi bristled a little. 'As you know, I only changed rooms yesterday at your request. I haven't had a chance to figure that out yet.'

'How long have they been building?'

'Going on three months. We have no notice of how long it's going to take.'

That was good, Lee thought. It meant the blackouts wouldn't end any time soon. 'What does he do about companionship?'

'He's seen around town with a couple of 'friends', whom everyone assumes are his lovers. They're not officially sanctioned, of course. But it wouldn't be enough for any sort of leverage anyhow; they give him more room to move than that.'

Then the prostitute routine was out. 'That building: what's on the first and second floors?'

'Residences on the second and third, a nursery school on the ground floor. It's usually closed by four in the afternoon.'

'He'll have some sort of bodyguard, I take it...'

Choi nodded. 'I never see him but I believe there's someone else there, most of the time.'

'Does he live in the apartment?'

'I can't say for certain. He almost never leaves the building, so he's either in the same unit or next door. But I don't suppose they'll be expecting any problems, not really. Duk's been here for a long time, I understand. When are you going to...?'

'Tonight,' Lee said. 'The clock is running down.'

42/

MANHATTAN, NEW YORK

The agent had been over her statement six times. Zoey felt her anxiety rising again, the tension throughout her body, her muscles tightening as they sat across from each other in the tiny hotel suite living room.

'Ms. Roberson, you mentioned that he'd never used a firearm before, to your knowledge. Did he speak with anyone unfamiliar in the weeks just prior...'

Drabek interrupted from his spot next to her on the sofa. 'Is this really going anywhere?' he asked the NSA man.

The agent leaned forward and shuffled his papers nervously. 'Mr. Drabek...'

'Detective, please. I worked damn hard for that shield.'

'Detective Drabek,' the agent said, over-enunciating his title, 'as you are well aware, there are always small details that get left out or missed...'

'Yeah, but I haven't missed anything, and I haven't left anything out,' Zoey insisted. 'Look, I don't see why we can't just go down there...'

'You know that's not possible, Ms. Roberson,' the agent said. 'A civilian with a tangible link to our suspect could prompt even more unpredictable behavior, or simply put your life at considerable risk...'

'That's my decision,' she said. 'It's my life.'

On the sofa nearby, Brennan was flicking through local channels. The noon news had a piece on the parade, just two days away, the excitement ratcheted up in the city's large Chinese expatriate community. 'You can argue all you want, he won't listen,' Brennan suggested. 'He's programmed to stick to his objectives.'

The interviewer looked his way. "At the National Security Agency, we take our responsibilities entirely seriously.'

Brennan paid him no attention, continuing to channel surf, but muttering in a mock voice, 'At the national security agency, meh meh meh meh meh meh...'

'Excuse me?' the Agent said loudly.

'Don't mind me,' Brennan said. 'Go back to your deeply important work.'

The agent shot him an irritated glance, then turned back to Zoey. 'Forget whether he spoke with anyone, then. Did he exhibit any skills that surprised you, anything out of the ordinary...'

Brennan piped up again. 'He means like computer skills, or languages, or an uncanny sense of perception to when someone has had enough...

The NSA man was getting sick of the quips. He already bore a heavy grudge against his colleagues at the CIA; Adrianne Hayes had been his mentor, and they'd poached her. 'Agent Brennan, I understand your suite is down the hall. Perhaps you'd like to wait there until we're ready for your statement.'

'Huh. So... next month sometime, then?' Brennan suggested. And in spite of everything, it made Zoey smile a little.

SONBONG, DEMOCRATIC PEOPLE'S REPUBLIC OF KOREA

Duk Su Ree knew that he had many blessings to count. He sat in his favorite armchair, looking out toward the Sea of Japan, his book on his lap, a nice glass of wine on the stand beside him. He'd gone in for a while to have some dinner, a decent piece of fish cooked by the restaurant in the nearby hotel. Then he'd gone over appointments for the next month, gratified that his calendar was fairly empty.

Duk was his father's son, most happy when counting his earnings. He was a great believer in taking what he wanted from life, and had managed to do so while maintaining strategic alliances with China and North Korea. True, there were multiple intelligence agencies who wanted to end his life; after all, he'd given new faces to a score of notorious terrorists alone in the decade prior. But they weren't going to risk an international incident. On the rare occasion that he pined for a place more sophisticated, he could always slip across the border to China and take a weekend excursion flight to Hong Kong or Sydney.

But he'd reached age sixty, and that meant it was time to start considering getting out of North Korea. He'd socked away money for decades in Swiss and Bahamian accounts. Either country would also make a fine new haven, he'd decided.

He just needed to lay low for a few more months; put his feet up, read a few books. It didn't need to be complicated and, given that he could potentially release data on their many false identities as payback, he didn't expect the DPRK to chase him there.

Or his father's enemies, for that matter. He knew little of the old man's work, but had followed in his footsteps, leaving a trail of blackmailed clients and dangerously satisfied customers across five continents. He knew his father had worked for the state security service, and that his files – though mostly coded gibberish – were valuable enough to keep them from coming for him, for fear he would release them.

He had two boyfriends, both young and enamored of his power. Soon, he would have a proxy purchase his new home, and leave the world of international treachery and deceit behind him for retirement.

Life could hardly be better, he decided.

The lights flickered twice, then cut out, ceiling fans slowing, air conditioning dying. Duk sighed.

That was another reason to leave; the standard of living in the DPRK had never been high class, but the side distractions were becoming deplorable. He got up, wandered over to the sideboard and found his flashlight. He followed its beam across the living room and into the kitchen, then through it to the small store room where his generator was hooked up.

He flicked the power on, then held down the start button. It would only take a couple of minutes to build up enough charge for everything to return to normal.

Duk wandered back to the balcony. *Now, to get back to my book...*

The chair turned suddenly. The woman sitting in it was small and wiry. She wore black, form fitting clothing. 'Beautiful evening, isn't it Dr. Duk?'

He frowned. 'How did you get in here? The front door...'

'Was carelessly left open by a departing tenant. Apparently they feel the city is fairly safe for that kind of thing.'

'And my front door...?'

'The alarm went down when the power went out. You need to build in a failsafe.'

'Hmm. I shall have to speak to the manager. Who are you, and what are you doing in my flat?'

She rose. 'My name is Daisy Lee, Dr. Duk, and I believe your father used to work for my employers.'

Shit, it's the Chinese Secret Service. His eyes scanned the room, settling for a moment on the desk near the door.

'Don't bother,' Lee said. She held up his pistol by the trigger guard. 'It hasn't been serviced in a long time – or cleaned. I was probably doing you a favor by keeping it from backfiring on you.'

'Are you going to kill me?'

'Possibly. That depends on a few things.'

'Such as?'

'You must have expected we'd come for you at some point, doctor. I need your father's files. I need anything and everything he had on a project called 'Legacy'.'

Duk couldn't contain a small smile. He knew his father had worked on Madame Mao's masterpiece, her grand project. But that was all that he knew. Even an exhaustive reading of his notes had revealed little, beyond the identities of some of those involved. 'You are going to be sorely disappointed if you expect me to help,' he said. 'And surely the secret service is aware that they have... responsibilities to high-ranking party members, some of whom have used my services to cover their own tracks.'

He judged that she was like most party members: terrified of offending anyone above her. Throwing around his weight a little might put her off. Instead, her smile disappeared, and her face took on a blank, emotionless countenance. 'Understand me, doctor, and make no mistake: if you don't produce what I need, any leverage you have will be of little use, after I remove your hands and your eyes.'

For the first time in longer than he could remember, a chill ran up the aging surgeon's spine. 'I... will attempt to provide what you want,' he said.

'Your files...?'

He nodded to the left. 'In my study. Everything is on paper still. I don't trust digital records.'

'Wise,' she said. 'Lead on.'

He turned and took her down the main hallway, toward the front door. Just before it, he opened a door to his left and entered. Lee stayed close, to ensure he didn't try to grab a weapon of some sort.

Instead, he went directly to the filing cabinet by the back window. Lee surveyed the room; it was cluttered with stacks of papers, files, old magazines. The bookshelves were stuffed with titles, mostly in Chinese and Korean. Duk unlocked the top drawer and reached in. 'He only kept the most important details about the project...' he said as he turned back toward her.

Lee glanced back toward him, cursing her carelessness in the split second it took the leads from the taser to reach her, the electrodes pricking her skin, the current staggering her with a moment of intense muscular cramping as her limbs locked up and she toppled over.

She tried to move, but the effect was too intense, lactic acid seizing her joints like an unoiled machine. She tried to speak, to say something, but the bottom of the man's shoe came crashing down, slamming into her face, her head caroming off the floor, darkness and unconsciousness settling in.

MANHATTAN, NEW YORK

'Tell me what the hell I'm doing here, Ed.'

They sat at a small table in a diner, the place mostly empty. For the first time in a week, he'd asked Zoey to give him some space to breathe. His job was probably gone, or hanging by a thread at best. They'd been shut out by the feds. And the girl continued to have no closure.

So like any good cop, he called another cop to talk about it.

'You're trying to do the right thing,' Kinnear offered. It was late in the evening, and the Baltimore cop needed sleep. But it hadn't taken him long to realize he liked Drabek, foolish nobility notwithstanding. 'But none of this is on you, Norm. You're just doing the right thing by her.'

'Thank you for not adding 'because of your daughter'. That gets a little old.'

'You said she'd passed...?'

'Yeah. Yeah, Nicole. She overdosed four years ago.'

'I'm sorry to here that.'

'We... my ex-wife and I ... we tried to get her into rehab a few times. I was gone a lot when she was a kid. I wasn't there when it mattered, I guess...'

'So, with this girl...'

'Yeah. Yeah, something like that. She's a good

kid, Ed. She was on the street for years before she met this guy, and she thought she'd found someone who was finally there for her, and then the son-of-a-bitch takes a pot shot at her.'

'She seems convinced he's redeemable in some way.'

'I don't think that's it,' Drabek suggested. 'I think maybe she knows quite the opposite. But it's not closure unless you see the person, unless you have a resolution.'

'Then you're staying here until this is done?'

'The feds are putting us up in a suite until after the parade. They want us under a watchful eye, I guess, in case we say something publicly or Zoey tries to act out or something.'

'Maybe that's a good thing?'

'What? How'd you figure?'

'I mean... she's a wildcard, right? And if she's out at the parade and something actually happens, at least you don't have to worry about her snapping and taking off after the guy or nothing.'

That annoyed Drabek, but he held his tongue as best he could. 'She's not like that. She's not flighty and stupid; people look at the tattoos and the piercings and how upset she is by this, and they see what they want to see. But she's a smart, resourceful, resilient person. She's gotten this far in a world that crapped on her for thirty years solid.'

'I didn't mean anything by it,' Kinnear offered. 'Just that maybe it's better she sees this guy taken in on TV, you know?'

'Yeah... sure, I guess.' But it was true. If there was one thing Drabek admired about Zoey – one trait he wished Nicole had shared – it was her toughness. She probably would go down to the route and try to spot him; she probably would jump in and get involved if anything happened. 'I'm just going to look out for her until we get back and I can find her some help. You know, lining up a job and a place to live.'

'Does she have family? Maybe after Saturday there's someone she can stay with...'

'Man... she has nobody. I mean, no one. To have this happen to her...' Drabek paused for a second, angered but resigned to the reality. 'To go through years of abuse, rape, forced into prostitution...'

'Jeez...'

'Yeah.'

'Your CO is cool with all of this?'

Drabek looked up from his coffee cup, surprised. 'I thought you knew: officially I'm not here. This is vacation time for me.'

'You're kidding. They're making you...'

Drabek shrugged. 'You do what you've got to do to get the job done. Am I right?'

Ed tipped his coffee cup the other man's way in a salute. 'You are indeed, my friend. You are indeed.'

43/

SONBONG, NORTH KOREA
DAY 18, JUST AFTER MIDNIGHT

Lee's head hurt. Her eyes fluttered open despite the pain, the sharp light from a desk lamp near the far wall not helping.

'Ah, good. You've rejoined us,' Duk said in Mandarin. He had a man beside him the size of a refrigerator box. 'This is Mr. Kim, and he takes great pleasure in causing pain. I'm not a professional interrogator, by any means. And I just had the most delightful manicure. Instead, when I can't get an answer from you, Kim is going to break something.'

'Not character, I hope,' Lee offered. 'Because if he starts a song-and-dance, I'm leaving.'

'Good! It's good that you can laugh. It will probably the last time, so you might wish to... savor the sensation.'

'What, exactly, are you expecting me to tell you?'

'Who you really work for, for one. Your colleague, Ms. Choi, was rather surprised to discover you are no longer employed by State Security. She was rather incensed that you tricked her, and was quite happy to share that fact with me. But that means you must be working for yourself, or for someone else. I doubt it's the former; you're too young to know anything about Legacy other than the vaguest of related instructions from a handler...'

Behind him, the gorilla-sized bouncer continued to grin wickedly. 'Is he mute or something?' Lee asked. 'If you tell me he owns a bowler hat that cuts off statue heads... again, I'm out.'

'Don't mind his stoicism. He's Scottish. You know how they can be,' the doctor deadpanned.

Great. I'm being tortured by Joe Wong. Maybe he'll do a tight five before he lets the walking outhouse loose. Behind her back, Lee's fingertips sought out the knots holding her wrists tight, but they were out of reach. The ropes had no give, but at least they'd been stupid enough to tie her hands behind her instead of strapping her down. That meant there was a chance. She just needed to get the gorilla out of the room.

'My throat is like sandpaper,' she said. 'Do you mind if I have a glass of water?'

'I do. I do mind,' he said placidly, as he reached down to pick up a hypodermic and a bottle from his desk. 'I'm well aware that you and your colleagues are trained to seize any kind of advantage you are given. So I don't intend to let you go anywhere, not until we've chatted.'

'What's in the syringe?'

Duk stared triumphantly at his oversized helper. 'You see! She's totally professional. The drink request didn't work but she doesn't attempt to oversell the lie. She just moves on. If we didn't plan to kill her and feed her to the sharks in the Sea of Japan, you could learn something from her, Mr. Kim.'

For the first time since she'd awakened, the bodyguard reacted, grunting slightly.

'He really likes to talk one's ear off...' she proposed.

'Oh... he manages to get his point across in other ways. I've tried to tell him that breaking a man's spine by popping one vertebra at a time doesn't work, because the man's paralyzed after the first two. But he never listens.' He stuck the needle into the dispensary bottle's rubber nipple and drew clear yellow fluid into the syringe. 'This is just a little something to loosen your tongue. And who knows... perhaps after I'm done with you Mr. Kim will loosen you up a little as well.'

'That's why my mother wanted me to marry a doctor,' Lee suggested. 'You're a class above.'

Duk's phone began to buzz and he checked its

screen. 'I have to take this. Shan't be long!' And then he strode out of the office.

The bodyguard didn't move, eyes locked on her, grin persistent. She tried to turn her left hand, to pinch it together tightly so she could slip it out of her bonds. But she couldn't get enough leverage. 'Your employer is deceiving you,' she said to him, the fluent Korean surprising the large man enough that he raised his eyebrows. 'He didn't tell you I speak Korean so that he could speak Mandarin with me and you wouldn't understand our conversation.'

His expression had shifted from jovially psychotic to just dour in a split second. 'Shut up!' he barked at her. 'Don't speak to me unless I ask you to.'

'He called you an ape and a fool,' she said, 'who is only good at breaking things.'

He didn't answer right away, considering the notion for a split-second. 'You lie,' he said. 'Doctor doesn't have a reason. No reason to say that.'

'He said after he was done with me, he'd let you break my legs, as that's the only thing you're good for.'

Lee needed him to turn around, even just for a few seconds. 'He said he has a file on you in which it says your parents were basically apes, too. He nodded toward the desk drawers when he said it, so maybe you can check for yourself.'

The guard didn't move, but he didn't say anything, either. He glanced quickly over his shoulder at the desk. 'You lie,' he repeated, this time less certain.

'I'm not going anywhere. I'm tied to a chair. So... look for yourself if you don't believe me! Aiyah!' She gave her best performance of 'exasperated.'

The goon looked over his shoulder at the desk again. Then he eyeballed Lee. Then he looked back at the desk again...

As he turned his head the second time, Lee threw her left shoulder back as far as it would go and wrenched upwards, dislocating it from its socket with an audible 'crack'. He turned quickly.

'What did you do?'

'Top drawer, fool! It's right there!'

He turned again. She held her shoulder back, the acute angle turning her bound-but-limp forearm at the wrist until her hands were almost back-to-back. The pain in her shoulder was excruciating, but it had created enough play in the rope to wiggle her right hand free.

The bodyguard opened the top drawer. 'There's nothing in here,' he said. Behind her, she heard the office door swing open again.

'Now,' Duk said as he strode over to the chair, 'where were we?'

Lee's hand shot out from behind her with lightening speed and precision, snatching the hypodermic from his hand as soon as the doctor was within reach, then plunging it into the side of his neck. Duk screamed, the piercing shrink accompanied by him stumbling backwards as he flailed at the needle to pull it out.

Mr. Kim turned and charged her as Lee scrambled to clear the ropes with her one good arm. Her feet were still bound, but she rolled away from the chair just in time, his sledgehammer fists shattering it. Duk stopped stumbling backwards, the syringe withdrawn but the serum kicking in, a dazed look overtaking him; he sunk to his backside and sat against the wall.

Kim turned and charged, Daisy rolling to one side again, her shoulder throbbing from stabbing pain. She reached her other hand over and yanked hard, down and in, popping the shoulder back into joint with a pained grunt of her own.

He was deceptively quick for such a big guy. As she turned, Kim grabbed her long black hair and slung her sideways, tossing her into the rolltop desk. She slid off and as he ran at her again, reached over and yanked the file drawer wide open, the Korean running face first into it. He staggered back a step and Lee threw herself into a leaping side kick, heel catching his solar plexus, knocking his wind out.

Kim stumbled into the wall but quickly righted himself. He went for the pistol inside his jacket, but she danced ahead, a sweeping round kick catching his wrist and sending the weapon flying.

In close, Lee kneed him in the groin, took a quarter-turn, and spun into a sideways elbow strike to his throat. But the big man merely turned his head, her blow catching him in the side of his tree-trunk thick neck. He smiled and laughed as she rained blows down upon him. Even catching him square in the face was like a mosquito trying to swat a person, the strikes doing no damage.

He threw a roundhouse punch, missing by a mere inch as she leaped backwards, then ran out through the office door, into the hall. He ran after her and, as he reached the doorway, the office door slammed hard into his face, staggering him once more. She kicked him in the groin again, this time putting everything behind it, catching one of his testicles. Kim's face contorted in sour agony, and the second his eyes closed she was on him, hammering him with fast, solid punches to the jaw, face and throat. He staggered back and she hit him again, and again, and...

The last shot caught him on the submaxillary ganglion, a cluster of chin nerves known to put many a boxer to sleep, no matter how big the man. The giant's legs folded underneath him and he crashed, glassy-eyed, to the floor. Her kick caught him square in the jaw once more, knocking him unconscious.

Daisy slumped to the floor, exhausted, the pain in her shoulder an almighty throb, like someone hitting it with a hammer from the inside.

Duk was still on his backside, even more glassy eyed than the now sleeping foot soldier. 'What's happening to me...'

'You took the full dose of whatever was in that vial. Are you dying?'

He shook his head slowly, haphazardly, like a besotted drunk. 'Don't know. Only... supposed to take small dose...'

'Hmmm. How unfortunate.' If the drug was anything like traditional 'truth serums' it would simply make him more susceptible and open to talking. Whether anything he said was reliable was another matter. But it was worth a try.

'Your father's files. They're not in the desk, are they?'

He shook his head slowly.

She rose and moved over to the bodyguard, retrieving the rope Duk had used to bind her and using it to secure him. He lay on his stomach, and she pulled one of his shoes off, then bent the leg up at the knee. Then she tied one end of the rope to his big toe. She bent his left arm behind him, then tied the other end in a sheath knot that pulled his thumb back and down, so that the string between toe and thumb was taut from tension.

'What...?' The stoned doctor looked confused.

'There are incredibly painful nerves between the thumb and forefinger, as well as between the big toe and the arch of your foot. With proper application you can immobilize someone for as long as you like by tying them together. Any movement on his part will be...uncomfortable.'

Kim stirred, groaning slightly. Feeling his arm pulled behind him, he tried to pull it free... then screamed, a piercing, unmanly shriek that sounded like someone was flaying skin from his body. He stopped pulling and was audibly panting from the stress of the moment.

'See?' Lee smiled at the doctor. 'Now, what I'm going to do to you will be so much more painful if you don't' tell me where your father's files are located. Can you imagine having two of those bonds attached, one to each foot and hand simultaneously. I'm not sure a man could survive the agony. I rather think his heart might explode.'

Even in his drugged state, Duk recognized the implications. He gestured sloppily toward the far wall and a painting, a copy of a Dutch master. 'Safe,' he said.

'What's the combination? Quickly; I can affect the same method of torture with a shoelace, in case you're wondering. I don't need to go find another rope.'

SOUTH AMBOY, NEW JERSEY

For the sixth time that week and the umpteenth-thousandth time in thirty years of living in South Amboy, Pearl Vincent walked her Yorkie-Terrier cross Scooby down Henry Street, trying to keep a brisk pace. She'd had her hip replaced two years earlier, but Pearl considered herself lucky to still be active at sixty-six, and she had no intention of giving up her beloved companion.

So walkies were a must. But every time she got to that one corner, she got an uneasy feeling.

Except for on this day.

For the first time, the white stucco house with the narrow, tinted windows was quiet. No booming country music; no drunken loudmouths sitting on the front patio under the fluttering flag, drinking tallboys, yelling insults at her.

Normally, she had to rush by with Scooby, and they'd mock her, maybe even throw an empty beer can in her general direction, albeit never with enough weight to reach the curb. *And thank Goodness they were too stupid to figure that out,* she thought, as she maintained their pace and her peripheral vision remained glued to its front door.

What was it the one had yelled last time? 'Sand flea.' That's what he'd said. 'Hey, Sand Flea: just what kind of nigger are you?' he'd called out.

She hadn't heard that kind of talk since she was a little girl, in the Fifties, back when her family name was still Vahabzade, and her parents were newly arrived in America, fleeing the Shah of Iran's hit squads. But she knew well enough to not react, to not feed their notion that they were important just because they hated people different from themselves.

She was almost past the house when the strange silence struck her. Yes, it was preferable. But it was odd, to have something so intrusive and loud suddenly disappear. A loss, albeit a good one. Pearl wondered if the house would go up for sale. She looked down at Scooby. 'What do you think, Scoob? Would my daughter want to buy a house around the corner from her mom?'

Scooby looked up with baleful eyes.

'Hmmm. Uh huh, that's kind of what I thought, too. Come on, sweetie. Let's get going again. When we get home, I'll get you a biscuit, okay?' She knew she wasn't supposed to spoil him, but Scooby was nine, and a little overweight, and he still fell asleep in her lap like a puppy.

From inside the home, the man at the front window stayed slightly back from the curtain gap, watching the woman and her dog. He'd seen her once before, when he'd staked the place out three days earlier.

'Problem?'

Gessler turned around. Codename Air was exacting, always on top of the situation. Gessler didn't like him, but he had no idea why. He didn't remember Donny Taylor, or Christopher Platt-alias-Ben Levitt, or any of it. But he knew in some other place, he'd have hit Air just for asking a question.

'No, I don't think so. One of the neighbors was keeping an eye on us. But given the nature of who lived here and her complexion, that's not all that surprising.'

The firefighter who'd lived there – a man befriended and 'catfished' online by Levitt through his white supremacist militia group – was still technically there. Gessler had slit his throat and left him to bleed out in the upstairs bathtub and had yet to realize the tub was stoppered. With the door closed, the man was beginning to smell, despite the powerful extractor fan.

As Levitt had predicted based on their online talks, the man had an extensive arsenal of weapons in the home, dutifully stored away in a locker. Levitt picked its lock in under a minute. The C4 explosive and detonators were a positive surprise, he'd noted, a little old but still usable. They'd amended the plan as a result. They knew they were expendable if it meant Dorian Fan's glorious ascension. They would trap and ambush the convoy as planned, then detonate the C4 while making their escape. The combination of the noise, smoke and damage would finish off any stragglers in the Chinese premier's retinue and provide cover.

'What time does Water arrive at the trigger point?' Gessler asked.

Levitt frowned. He already felt unnaturally nervous around the bigger man, like an old score hadn't been settled. 'You're supposed to be clear on everything by now. You should know the plan backwards and forwards.'

'I'm just double checking.'

'She'll be there at ten forty-five, bringing up the rear of the procession, well back from the target car. She has one secret service agent accompanying her. By the time the target reaches us, she'll have dealt with him and be about two blocks back, closing off their safety valve.'

'And the papers, the arrangements? You had no problem phishing the identities...'

'Completed, I told you,' Levitt said, trying not to show annoyance. 'We'll show on the duty roster as loans at the station house, while my online friend will show as off sick. Water has contacted the appropriate senior managers to let them know they're getting some help for the day. We begin shift at Battalion Forty at six, exit the facility with you driving at seven-forty-five, in place on route by eight-fifteen.'

Gessler nodded. 'Then we're ready.'

Levitt nodded once. 'A glorious new dawn awaits.'

44/

SONBONG, NORTH KOREA

Anna Choi slept soundly, despite her treachery.

After all, from her perspective, Daisy Lee was a traitor herself, a rogue agent using Choi's employer as cover for her own activities.

When she'd received the call from the surgeon, she'd initially been terrified of discovery. But Beijing not only didn't care, it wanted her to cozy up to Dr. Duk, find out how many people he held files on, and where.

And so, she'd had one more glass of wine and then gone to bed, secure in the knowledge that Lee would no longer cause anyone in the strange little city problems.

She awoke to the click of a hammer being cocked and the press of cold metal against her temple. 'Don't make a noise, Anna Choi, or you'll be having tea with your ancestors...'

'Lee? Lee... Thank... thank goodness you're alive...'

'Oh, don't even bother. He was crowing about your deception for an hour.'

'Did you...?'

'Hmm? The surgeon? No, nor his bodyguard. But they'll both be wishing they had more friends unless someone stops round soon, as they're both quite immobile. I imagine they're both rather hungry. Now, you and I are going to go for a little drive...'

'It's... it's very early. There will be checks, cars being stopped. It's before the end of the curfew, technically.'

'Then I'd advise you to avoid them. My Korean is better than yours, Choi, and if that happens, you officially become my 'captor' until the matter is taken care of. One way or another. Imagine what some pissed off yahoo DPRK soldiers would do to a kidnapper at five in the morning, after a long shift. Now... get up and get dressed.'

Five minutes later they were in Choi's aging Mercedes, pulling out into the first light of day. 'Where are we going?' Choi said from behind the wheel.

'The plant you mentioned. The upgrader. I want to see it.'

'Why?'

'Not that it matters to you, but it may be relevant to peace talks in which China is currently involved. It's possible no one there knows it's an enrichment facility. It's somewhat relevant to the subject at hand.'

It took them ten minutes to get to the old, cracked road that led to the waterfront refinery's front gate. 'Keep driving past it, but find a parking space within sight,' Lee commanded.

The smaller woman did as she was told.

At the parking spot, Lee got out of the car and moved behind the cover of a nearby rock outcropping. She pulled out her binoculars and sighted the facility's front door for focus, then panned around, trying to take in everything.

Then she slowly lowered the binoculars, her expression worried.

'What?' Choi asked, coming up behind her.

Lee pointed to the center of the complex. 'That is an oil-fired electrical plant, yes,' she said. 'But that building next to it isn't. Those two towers are for cooling radioactive cores. This is a uranium enrichment facility. And it looks like it's close to coming online.'

She headed back to the car, motioning with her pistol for Choi to stay where she was.

'You're leaving me out here?'

'I am. They'll either find you here and shoot you or you'll make your way back into town. Either way, it's more of a chance than you gave me.'

Lee rolled up the window and threw the car into

drive. She had a boat to meet at the port in twenty minutes. It would take her to Posyet, where a charter pilot with a float plane could get her back to the south.

Dorian Fan's true identity had shocked her. The parade and conference were less than a day away. She needed to get the surgeon's information to Brennan, before Legacy could complete its terrible task.

BROOKLYN, NEW YORK
DAY 19

Drabek sat on the hotel room sofa and watched the two news anchors discussing the parade from their perch, halfway along the route. The city was making a big deal of the event, 'A Day of Peace' according to the television sponsors.

'This is excruciating,' he said.

A few feet away at the other end of the sofa, Brennan leaned back and took a sip from his coffee cup. 'What? The commentary? Or the fact that we might be about to witness a terrorist attack on live television and can't do a damn thing about it.'

Drabek gave him a less-than-appreciative glare. 'Pick one.'

Zoey was sitting in the armchair to their right, her feet curled up under her. She was leaning on her hand, bracing her chin, her other arm draped protectively over her mid-section. Drabek figured she looked like a kid being left out of the school play or something. She looked like she might cry, even though he knew that wasn't going to happen. She was sturdier than that.

He turned his attention back to the television. There was something bothering him, still, but he didn't know what, some piece of information, some clue or pointer, stuck at the back of his mind. He just couldn't quite put it together, but something about the parade itself was off.

He nodded Brennan's way. 'You still have that map that Mah gave you?'

'Sure.' He got up and walked over to the bedroom, returning a few seconds later and handing Drabek the folded sheet of paper.

Drabek spread it out on the coffee table. The route was simple enough to monitor for a well-organized squad. That wasn't it. And they'd managed to eventually convince the Chinese not to allow an open-top car but rather window waves. A sniper from above would have that much more difficult of a time with an already acute angle. He looked at the guidelines underneath for travel speed and anticipated stops, choke points along the route.

But he still couldn't see it.

'What's bugging you so much, anyway?' Brennan asked. 'You're fidgeting like a child.'

'Something...' Drabek shook his head. 'I don't know. Something about the route is off.'

'I drove it yesterday at the same time as you,' Brennan said. 'I didn't spot anything. Mah's an expert at these and he didn't spot anything.'

'I know, I know...' The stress hit him and Drabek closed his eyes, then ran his fingers through his hair nervously. 'I just... Gah! Something's off. When you get the feeling, it's never wrong. It's a warning...'

Brennan shrugged. Then he leaned forward and sighed, recognizing he was being a jerk for not taking the veteran cop seriously. 'Here, let me look again.'

'I'm getting a coffee,' Drabek said, rising to walk to the kitchen.

Brennan stared at the map, tracing the route with his finger, looking at the various cross streets and side streets, where the most dangerous intersections might be. 'You know they'll have people all along each block as well, right?' he said more loudly, so that Drabek could hear him in the kitchenette around the corner.

'I know, I know,' Drabek said. He leaned out of the kitchenette area and poked his head toward the front hallway to the door. 'Hey Mike, you want a coffee?'

The NSA man guarding the door leaned in. 'Don't mind if I do?'

Drabek walked over and handed it to him, then went back to his own cup.

Brennan ran the route backwards, then went over to the desk and found his laptop. He put it down next to the map on the coffee table. He opened a browser and pulled up an overhead of Manhattan, then zoomed into the same area. He looked at the high-res image of six-to-eight blocks of real estate. Then he checked the route again.

Drabek was right. Something was off.

And Brennan also had no idea what it was.

'You know... you might be onto something here,' he said.

Drabek looked around the corner but remained standing, sipping from his cup. 'Is that good news or bad?'

'Probably the latter, in the bigger picture,' Brenan said.

'So what is it...?'

'That the thing: I don't know either. I can't figure it out, but something is off.' He stared at the two images like a kid with a Spot the Differences puzzle. 'I'm just... not seeing what it is.'

Zoey looked worried. 'Should we talk to the NSA guy? Maybe call your boss?'

Brennan waved the idea off. 'I've been in worse situations than this and he's ignored them. We need something specific.'

He went back to the two maps, poring over the page and screen.

Drabek signaled silently to Zoey with a head nod. She got up quietly and walked over to the kitchenette.

He held a finger up to his lip. 'Keep it quiet.'

'What's up?' she whispered.

'We're a half hour from downtown Manhattan, but the traffic tie ups today mean it'll take me an hour to get down there...'

'You're GOING??' she muttered.

'Shh! Keep it cool, okay? The guy at the front door? He's going to get really sleepy in about ten minutes courtesy of some Rohypnol...'

'You roofied the guard?'

'I have to go down there and catch this guy, Zoey... if he's even there. If this is even a thing. I can't just sit here.'

'Then I'm going with you. You have no more authority here than I do, and I need to know... I need to see him, Norm!'

'No! I can't put you in danger...'

'It's not up to you, damn it! Just for once in my entire life, the hard decision is going to be mine to make, not someone else's. Not yours. Not theirs. Not Benjamin-whoever-you-are-goddamned-Levitt,' she hissed.

'OKAY!' he said, trying to keep it low. 'Okay. Just... follow my lead. Head back to your chair for now. I'll hang here until I see the guard go to sit down. Then you make an excuse if need be to Brennan and follow me out. Okay?'

She nodded, then returned to the armchair.

Brennan had switched the internet screen from overhead satellite view to another map of downtown Manhattan and was comparing the street layouts without any distraction. Again, there was nothing obviously wrong. He looked up at the television; the news had switched to a story about wild animals showing up in the suburbs, looking for food. *Have to feed those twenty-second attention spans*, he thought ruefully.

He went back to the maps and traced the route again.

'I need to pee,' Zoey said, getting up and walking off.

Brennan went back to his work. The NSA's map had been taken from official sources, so there was no reason to think it inaccurate. On top of that, both Mah and Parnell had walked the route twice the night before, each covering one side of Canal Street, auditing the position of every cop and vehicle, to be damn sure there were no surprises.

And yet there was something...

Wait...

It was on the fringe of his thought process. But instead of straining to remember it, Brennan let his experience take over, blanking his mind, going to darkness so that his passive thoughts had free reign.

There. His attention shot back to the web map, and he went back to the overhead satellite image, then zoomed in.

There, a block from the turn onto Broadway, by the meet-and-greet. He went back to the official plan map again. It showed the south intersection with Cortlandt Alley as closed to traffic, blocked off by a firetruck with the number designator ENG-201. He traced his finger back up the blocks. Four other closed intersections were blocked with fire trucks, eight more in total, before police representatives took over. But the alley was the only one-way approach.

Each of the other firetrucks had a much smaller number: ENG- 15, ENG-18. The largest other was ENG-24.

He frowned, not knowing anything about the fire department's systems. It didn't necessarily mean anything. Brennan switched to an internet browser and plugged the numbers in, along with 'FDNY' and a few other search terms.

A map listing came up. He opened it, and tags showed the location of each of the 'Engine Numbers' for various stations. All of the lower numbers were from Manhattan stations. But the larger designator, 201, was from Brooklyn.

Why? Why would they borrow a truck from another borough when they're only blocking of a small portion of the route? Maybe it was just triage planning, he thought, borrowing the least-busy engine...

But it was a loose end, something that felt off. The higher number was probably what had tweaked

Drabek, too. He was just too upset to realize it.

Then... how? How would they get...

An inside man.

They'd anticipated an insider, someone in law enforcement with good access to the mission's parameters and objectives. The old man's story suggested a woman, the grown Amelia, from the fictional town of Plenty.

He looked at the plan again. Parnell and Mah were bringing up the rear. Parnell had made the arrangements with city emergency services. It had been her idea, although endorsed happily by Mah.

Brennan pulled out his phone and frantically dialed Jonah. It rang through to his voicemail. 'Jonah, call me now, it's urgent. It's Joe.'

Damn it. He dialled another number.

Adrianne Hayes answered on the first ring. 'Mr. Brennan. To what do I owe the distinct honor...'

'Cut the bullshit, okay Adrianne? We have a Clear and Present Danger, an emerging threat. Can you get a message through to Mah...'

'Brennan, I'll thank you to watch your language. Okay? I'm your superior, not some greasy informant in one of your third-world dives. Show some damned respect.'

Oh, God, fuck you and your politically correct bullshit right now, you pencil pusher... 'Adrianne, there's a glitch in the plan. There's a flaw, a choke point they may have compromised....'

'You really think you're something, don't you, Brennan? You act like some flawless avatar for truth and justice, a modern-day James Bond or some such bullshit. But the fact of the matter is, you're a government employee, mister, just like me. And this is not your assignment.'

'The plan...'

'I went over the plan myself, and with Agent Parnell. She's highly decorated and extremely competent, by the way, and you could learn a thing or two from the way she handles herself.'

'Adrianne, you have to listen to me; we know

there's another shooter, and the old man, he said it was the girl...'

'Who?!?'

Oh goddamn it. She hasn't even read my debrief. Goddamn you for promoting a political shark, Jonah. I saved your life, you little bastard. 'Amelia, the third assassin, is still unaccounted for...'

'Brennan, you have officially lost your mind. I'm hanging up now. Don't call me back! Once today is over, I'm going to call your Director of Human Resources and request a full psych eval...'

'Oh... fuck you.' He hung up, frustrated.

There was no other choice. He checked the time. The parade was already under way, and perhaps forty minutes from the block in question. If he and Drabek rushed, they could make it down there before any attack could take place. All they'd need to do was get by the guy at the door.

'Drabek, get over here for a second,' he called out.

There was no reply.

'Drabek!'

Then he realized the girl, Zoey, hadn't returned. *She'd said something a few minutes earlier when he was concentrating on the map, what... she was going to the bathroom.*

He got up quickly and looked around the corner, but there was no sign of Drabek. 'Zoey!' he called out.

Damn it. He jogged over to the front door and opened it. The guard was still in the metal folding chair the hotel had provided, but he was leaning against the floral wallpaper, snoring gently, a half-spilled cup of coffee tilted over in his lap.

Brennan closed his eyes and held his breath in for a second. He'd let them skip out without noticing. And he knew exactly where they were headed.

45/

MANHATTAN, NEW YORK

The delegation was on schedule. The parade route into Chinatown was lined with well-wishers, protestors, curious tourists, thousands of people held back on each side of the road by makeshift cordons. Police were doing a sterling job of keeping the crowds controlled.

Agent Jennifer Parnell signalled a thumbs up to her CIA counterpart, Brandon Mah. He was in an office above the donut shop across the road. The four blocks making up the end of the route between The Bowery and Centre Street represented the last opportunity someone would have to stage a ground attack. After the meet and greet, they would continue on at speed down Broadway; but the parade would be slowed after turning off The Bowery and onto Canal. Airspace was free and clear.

Their job was simple: in twenty minutes, the procession would pass. There were seven limousines, police cars ahead and behind, four motorcycle cops rolling beside the secret service, and twelve agents assigned to run with the lead car and the Chinese delegate car, two vehicles back. Once they'd passed, Mah would lead his team of Parnell and two plain-clothes police officers as trailers, ensuring no one attempted a last-moment diversion or ambush. Her NSA colleagues had the twenty-minute section up to her location, and the police and secret service were handling the first section, starting at Seward Park and East Broadway.

'Are we good?' Mah's voice crackled to life over her earpiece.

'Yeah, smooth sailing so far. The drones are reporting nothing suspicious from the overhead look either. It looks like this all might have been much ado about nothing, chief.'

Mah held his tongue. He wasn't a suspicious man, but he'd been an agent long enough to know the operation wasn't over until everyone was home safe. 'Just keep watch, keep your ears on for any alerts. Another half-hour and we can all breathe a little easier.'

He looked down through the floor-to-ceiling window in the empty dentist's office. She was looking up, wearing aviator sunglasses to go with her olive green dress suit. She stuck out like a sore thumb as a fed, he figured. Not that it would probably matter much. Any action by Legacy's sleepers would be brutal, direct and rapid. No one would be sneaking around thousands of people, drones, security.

Mah had been an agent for more than a decade. He trusted his instincts. And something about the woman just rubbed him the wrong way. He knew she had a hell of a resume; she'd worked on the disappearance of Sarah Evans, the agency recruit that had turned out to be a suicide a decade earlier, when Parnell was still a D.C. cop. And she'd been receiving commendations ever since. Her retraining scores were out of this world, the type even he was jealous of; and she had American parents, which meant less pressure.

Maybe that was it, he told himself. Maybe he was just jealous that someone was getting ahead even more quickly than he was. Adrianne Hayes certainly loved her work.

On the far side of the street, just inside the cordon, Parnell shielded her eyes from the sun's glare. She wondered whether Mah had family in China, how they felt about all of it. The constant animosity between two peoples.

There was something wrong in any man who would betray such a glorious cultural legacy, she thought.

Across the street, one of the plainclothes officers from the NYPD gave her a thumbs up and flashed a quick, wry smile under his short, clipped brown moustache. He probably thought that was cute; she smiled back. No point in worrying about him; they'd all be gone by the next day, assuming the exit plan proved viable. Air had seen to that. He'd followed her instructions perfectly. Now, all the woman once known as Amy Sawyer had to do was wait. She was like Water, fluid-yet-constant, in control and yet capable of unleashing anarchy. And she was quite certain that a glorious new dawn was just fifteen minutes away.

The cab hit heavy traffic ten blocks from their destination, slowing to a halting crawl, horns sounding on the one-way street as multiple lanes tried to make progress.

'What do you think?' Zoey asked Drabek. 'Would it be quicker now if we just got out and ran?'

'We're still more than a mile away, there's people all over the sidewalks...'

'What if you don't figure this out before we get there? What then?'

She had a new edge of panic in her voice, Drabek noticed. She was taking the entire threat too personally, as if she was responsible for Ben's behavior. 'Then we do the best we can: we find Mah or Parnell and we warn them, we tell them something's wrong with the route.'

'Parnell then,' Zoey said. 'She mentioned she used to be a D.C. cop. before she joined the NSA.'

'A little sympathy goes along way. Okay, Parnell it is, if we can find her,' Drabek agreed.

The cab crawled ten more yards then slowed to a halt again.

'This isn't going to work,' the detective said. 'It'll be tomorrow by the time we get to Chinatown.' He pulled out his wallet and handed the driver two twenties. 'We're getting out here, okay?'

The cabbie shrugged, then looked at the meter. It read twenty-one-twenty-five. 'Hey...wait! I owe you...'

But the door slammed behind them and the pair were off, pushing around the sidewalk crowd.

Six blocks away, Brennan's route was cut off by the closed streets. He dumped the red compact rental at the curb and made off on foot. When he got to Grand and Clinton, the last of the cars in the entourage had already passed.

He checked the cross street. He was eight blocks from Chinatown and behind, but the convoy was moving very slowly. He took off on a run, dodging other pedestrians, trying to make good time.

From an adjacent building, an NSA agent saw a man running through the crowd, upending people. He had an open-neck shirt and three-day stubble, a wild look on his face. The agent tapped his radio microphone call button.'

'Yeah, ah... Eagle Seven to Papa Bird; Eagle Seven to Papa Bird...'

Its speaker crackled to life. 'Go ahead, Eagle Seven.'

'Yeah, we've got a runner of some sort... sketchy looking guy in aviators, top two buttons on a grey shirt undone, sleeves rolled up. He's pushing people aside, knocking them over. He's probably just a drunk or a pickpocket who got caught or something, but...'

'Roger that, Eagle Seven, we're responding with two on the ground. Papa Bird to Ground 2, come in Ground 2.'

'Roger that, Papa bird, reading you.'

'Ground 2, we've got a runner on your side of the street coming up on your block. You want to put him down hard, please? He's probably just a sneak thief or junkie or something, but we want people seeing how safe it is out there today, okay?'

Brennan had to slow down, the foot traffic too dense to keep shoving his way through. Chinatown was only a couple of blocks away. He checked his battered Seiko wristwatch; the procession was on schedule and he was keeping pace with the last car, at least. Over the crowd, he could see the heads of the dozen secret service agents surrounding the lead vehicles.

The plainclothes officer seemed to come out of nowhere; one second, Brennan was looking over the onlookers, and in the next, someone was grabbing his upper left arm, trying to pull him aside.

'Hey! Hey, buddy! Slowdown!' the plainclothes officer yelled, trying to immobilize him by twisting his arm behind him.

A second officer stepped forward, baton extended. 'Just cool it, guy...' he suggested.

Brennan dropped low, his body weight wrenching him from the officer's grasp. He swung his left elbow out in a semi-circle, hammering the cop in the groin.

As his partner stepped in to strike, the agent's left fist shot out, catching him flush in the side of the knee, the interior cruciate ligament tearing, the cop yelping as he stumbled to the ground.

Before anyone could intervene, the agent was upright again and back into the crowd, the two cops lying prone on the sidewalk as the onlookers gathered around and wondered what they'd somehow missed.

SCARSDALE, NEW YORK

From David Chan's suite at his country club, Jonah Tarrant watched the parade on the massive flat screen that had risen from the floor. Chan was a few feet away in a leather armchair.

Adrianne Hayes sat next to the CIA man, waiting for her opportunities. She knew Jonah well enough to know that eventually, he'd leave an opening to be embarrassed, something that might make his position available to the right ambitious individual. He lacked the self-control to be a great director of Central Intelligence, but that was obviously his intention.

'So far so good, deputy director,' Chan said with a broad smile. 'It seems that all of this has been, as I suspected, blown terribly out of proportion.'

Tarrant's instincts said his opposite number was wrong, that there had been too much traffic, too much activity. But so far, the day had gone smoothly, he had to admit. 'Let's hope that's the case, Mr. Chairman.'

'Please... I grew up here. It's David.'

'Fine.' Tarrant suppressed a little smile and a profound sense of internal satisfaction. There was no immediate benefit in letting the man know how much he admired him. Chan was the heaviest of political hitters, a man with the wealth and authority to perhaps one day rule his nation, should he get enough capitalist reformers on side. And Tarrant harbored ambitions of his own. Former director Bush had set the template for how a man from the service could make the sideways move into the senior political ranks. His own family was just as connected, just as old money. He'd been a Skull-and-Bones man at Yale, just like the Bush boys, and long before his moment of heroism, five years earlier, in taking out an armed colleague, he'd been an effective fundraiser for the Young Republicans. 'Call me Jonah, David. If nothing else positive comes of this weekend, at least we can establish a mutually beneficial working arrangement, something that helps both our countries.'

He'd thought about leaving it as a question, seeing how Chan would react. But the man's hospitality suggested pushing ahead.

Chan smiled politely. "Of course.'

Tarrant's phone rang. 'Jonah Tarrant.'

'Sir, my name is Claude Boetcher, and I'm the federal agencies liaison down here at JFK...'

'Yes, Mr. Boetcher... I'm surprised to be getting this call directly... were you able to talk to my assistant...'

'Sir, no... it's not like that. They patched me over

from your building in Langley...They said you'd want to talk to me directly.'

'Okay... what can we help you with today sir?'

'We've got a woman down here who was caught trying to enter the country on a stolen passport. It got flagged by CBP and we took her into custody. She almost broke loose – broke an air marshal's nose and knocked out his front teeth in the process. He's pretty mad about that...'

'Sir... the woman?'

'Yes sir! Anyway, she seemed pretty desperate to talk to you or a 'Joseph Brennan'. She identifies herself as 'Daisy Lee', said you'd know what she meant. She doesn't have a scrap of legitimate identification as far as we can tell, and the really weird bit on top of all of it is she doesn't have any fingerprints; they've been removed. So, when she mentioned the CIA I figured she might be telling the truth and was not just some kook.'

'You made the right call sir. Hang on for just a moment.' He lowered the phone and looked over at Chan. 'Looks like we've landed one of yours at the airport on bad papers.'

Chan frowned. 'Really? I wasn't aware of anything like that going on during our visit...'

'It's Daisy Lee, the woman was working with Brennan. Shall I have them cut her loose?'

Chan gave it some thought. 'Hmmm... she was apparently with him when he visited the site of Legacy. She might have valuable intel.'

'True.'

'On the other hand, some of it may be China-centric or specific, and not for foreign ears. Would you be terribly offended if we took her off your hands and debriefed her in private? In the spirit of the day, we'll certainly share anything about Legacy, although...' he nodded toward the television, '... it certainly seems so far as if Madame Mao's only real legacy is to be a forgotten political figure.'

Jonah gave him his broadest smile. Nothing fazed Chan, it seemed. 'That's fine, fine.'

'I'll have someone from our New York consulate run by and pick her up.'

Two birds with one stone, Jonah figured. If Legacy had any legs at all, Chan would want to use it to further their co-operation, and in the meantime, Joe Brennan had no reason to potentially upset any apple carts.

Everything was going perfectly.

MANHATTAN, NEW YORK

Drabek held Zoey's hand so that they wouldn't get separated in the crowds. They'd made good time, staying ahead of the parade.

Zoey had butterflies in her stomach but was determined not to show them. She kept peering through the mass of bodies and heads, looking for gaps, hoping to catch a glimpse of Ben. She didn't even know if he'd look the same. She couldn't believe it still mattered to her, but for some reason, it did.

'Stay sharp, kid, we're getting near the end of the parade route,' Drabek said, speaking up so she could hear him over the din. He kept looking for signs of Parnell and Mah but feared they'd already passed them. 'There's an old school up here that's been converted to offices for a few years and there's a seniors' center next to it. I guess the Premier is supposed to meet some centenarian from the old country...'

Zoey remembered the CIA agent, Brennan, bringing up their effort to cancel that part of the Chinese leader's trip. She chewed on her lower lip nervously as they continued to elbow their way through the crowd. It was hard for her to understand how anything in a world so harsh could be so important as to risk all these peoples' lives. If word ever got out that they'd known about a terrorism threat...'

She lost herself in the thought for a moment.

Perhaps that was the best thing to do, once everything was over. Perhaps she needed to tell her story to a newspaper or TV station. She thought of Brennan's boss, Jonah, and the hatchet-faced woman who followed him around, Adrianne. They didn't seem to care about any of the people involved in their little drama, just the political fallout. *Maybe they'll give a damn about the rest of us when they're the ones being judged. Maybe seeing their names in headlines would teach them some humility.*

She realized she'd lost herself in thought and almost stumbled over a small child. 'Sorry!' she told the little boy as she straightened up and they resumed their pace. She looked across the throng.

She only saw him for a split second, but she could have sworn...

'Ben! He's here!'

Drabek stopped short. 'What?! Where?'

She looked back across the road. 'That direction. For a second I thought...' But there was no sign of him. 'He must have moved into the crowd...'

'Are you sure?'

She wanted to say yes, but Zoey knew nothing good had ever come from being full of shit. And she knew she couldn't be certain.

She shook her head. 'It was just a glimpse.'

Drabek looked across the road, trying to see what she might have seen. There were just as many onlookers over there. He tried to peer through the same gaps. There seemed to be a thousand different faces, but none familiar. The side street was blocked by a city fire truck.

He looked back down the street; the President's limousine was just a block back, crawling ahead slowly as the crowds waved their miniature Star-Spangled Banners. 'If we try to skip the cordon, someone will just nab us on the other side,' he half yelled. 'Maybe this is as far as we get...'

Zoey let go of his hand and moved through the crowd, toward the old seniors' center. It had three wide front steps. She used the extra foot-and-a-half to look over the crowd once more.

Drabek joined her. 'Any sign?' he said, looking up at her.

She shook her head. 'Nothing. I don't know, I guess... I guess maybe I imagined it.'

Her face was lined with tension, and Drabek felt the urge to reach out. He grasped her hand like a knowing grandparent and shook it a little. 'Don't worry, kid. You don't owe anyone a damn thing.'

For a few scant seconds, Zoey felt a warm glow run through her. She hadn't felt like that much lately, as if there was someone who cared. She looked toward the back of the convoy. 'I still can't see... Norm! I see... I think it's Parnell, back at the end of the block. She's leaning down for something... Damn it. I lost sight of her.'

Ahead of them, the crowd's cheers swelled. A kid six feet from the steps said, 'Look, Mom, look! It's the President!'

At the end of the retinue, Mah and Parnell followed the last limousine, their two plain clothes associates just inside the cordon, within reach of the onlookers. Parnell kept Mah in her peripheral vision. The last cross street before the senior center, Lafayette, was approaching.

They were far back and the onlookers were ignoring them, their stares toward the front of the convoy. She glanced both ways quickly; the plain-clothes officers were watching the crowd and the vehicles as well, not what was going on behind them. Parnell reached into her suit jacket pocket, then broke her stride, changing direction to angle her way over, next to Mah.

'What are you doing?' he demanded, not changing his volume, aware she could hear him clearly though the earpiece. 'We need to cover both sides properly.'

'No, we don't. Look!' she said, pointing ahead and

to the left. Mah's head's turned and she withdrew her hand from her pocket, quickly slamming the hypodermic syringe into the side of his thigh. He grasped at it, took one shocked look at her, then stumbled forward, grabbing at his chest.

'This man, he's having a heart attack!' she yelled toward the crowd. A few turned their heads back to look at them, a buzz building over the man lying in the street. Parnell knelt next to him. The plainclothes officers were nearly half a block ahead already, and no one was stopping the onlookers who climbed under the cordon and gathered around.

Mah looked up, his eyes wide and terrified, staring at his assailant, his vocal cords paralyzed along with most of the rest of his body, including his lungs. He felt them shudder to a halt, then seemingly disappear, the air no longer able to reach them as he began to asphyxiate.

'Someone get a doctor!' Parnell yelled, standing up. The other people kneeling didn't rise with her, and the last thing Mah saw before he lost consciousness was the NSA agent striding toward the intersection ahead.

46/

Levitt and Gessler sat in the cab of the truck, shrouded from the sun, the vehicle's big diesel engine idling. If Water was on schedule, she would be pulling barricades from each corner across the last intersection. The crowd would be gathering behind the last vehicle, blocking off retreat.

He reached down under the seat and pulled out a touchscreen pad. It held a video image. He clicked a few on screen settings and the image switched to the other camera. Each gave him a high corner view of the final two blocks. The signal might be picked up by a security sweep, he knew, but it would be too late.

Levitt watched the crowd swelling as people from further back moved toward the seniors' center. Enough got out of the way that he could briefly see the two wooden barricades, people assuming the block was closed now to traffic and milling across the makeshift pedestrian concourse. 'She's in place,' he said. 'The lead vehicle is approaching. We are go.'

Gessler stood on the gas and the fire truck lurched to life, pulling forward with surprising acceleration. It immediately struck several pedestrians, scattering them to the side like bowling pins. The crowd began to scream but the men inside the truck couldn't hear them and wouldn't have noticed anyway. It crossed into the road and blocked it, cutting between the Chinese Premier's limousine and its protectors, one car ahead.

Both men leaped out of the cab wearing flak jackets, each carrying a modified AK-47. They strafed the limousine with gun fire, disabling its tires, the armor-piercing rounds beginning to carve holes into the vehicle's plating, its bulletproof windshield quickly spidering. Gessler turned and leaned into the truck, and when he turned back was carrying a long metal tube. He mounted it on his shoulder and sighted the limousine.

Levitt turned, gun fire ringing out behind them as the two plainclothes officers tried to intercede. Parnell had told him what to expect and he swivelled to each in turn, gunning both men down with a quick, accurate burst of fire. The limousine ahead was trying to back up, guards beyond it trying to remove the barriers that closed off the street, but unable to get through the stampeding, panicking crowd. Shrill screams filled the air.

Gessler depressed the trigger and the launcher roared, its payload rocket shooting out in a perfect line, finding the underside of the limousine. The rocket blew, and the Premier's limousine flew skyward, flipping over backwards end-to-end, pedestrians struck by thousands of pounds of flying steel, blood spewing across the asphalt.

Brennan heard the explosion and saw the car flip from two blocks back, screaming chaos overwhelming the crowd, people running in all directions, knocking each other down, uniformed officers heading the other way, toward the danger. He didn't dare draw his pistol, not without them knowing him. But he had to get there, he knew, and his feet pounded the pavement as he shoved people aside.

Ahead, a balding man dropped what looked like a rocket launcher beside the fire truck that blocked the road. Then he unslung the assault rifle from his shoulder and began to take out the onrushing police officers with precise, methodical aim.

Men were trying to crawl out of the limousine, all black suits and white shirts, sunglasses. Bodyguards. The man with the assault rifle lowered his aim, strafing them, their bodies convulsing as the shells tore through them.

Ahead, through the smoke, Brennan could see another man heading in the other direction, toward the President's limousine. His rifle was held high as he walked, his aim swinging from one secret service agent to the next, picking them off methodically before most could even level a weapon.

Levitt. Brennan ran past the first shooter along the sidewalk, drawing his pistol from the back of his waist band. But before he could line the man up, he saw the muzzle flash to his right, felt the 'thwip' of the bullet pushing air past his left ear. He turned to the source and fired, aiming 'center mass' in the rush of the moment.

Parnell collapsed, the bullet passing between her rib cage, chipping bone before puncturing her lung, her gun clattering to the pavement. She clutched at the wound as blood began to gurgle up her throat, pouring out of her lungs with each breath. 'Fire...' she wheezed. 'Help... me. Help... me, Donny...'

Gessler paused from his assault, freezing for a split second. He stared down at her, but there was no flicker of emotion, nor recognition that he'd known Amy Sawyer since they were little kids together, so long ago. He stared just long enough to retrain his sights and put a bullet through the prone agent's head.

Then he went back to his task, the limousine eviscerated, the barrage impossible to survive.

Brennan shut out the noise and panic around him. He lined Gessler up for a head shot and slowly squeezed the tr...

'Sir, drop the weapon! NOW! DO IT!' the voice came from behind him.

"I'm CIA! Agency!' Brennan yelled.

'Drop it, now, or I'll shoot!'

Goddamn it, not now!

In the block ahead of the fire truck, the President's limo sped down the street, out of the line of fire. Whether Levitt saw it or not, Brennan couldn't be sure; but the man who'd once been a caring young soul named Christopher Platt was in trouble, without cover and outnumbered. He ran, infantry style, back toward the old school, firing behind him to clear his egress. Gessler spotted him and followed, bullets pinging off the building's façade as the agents and police tried to take them out. The sidewalks had cleared, terrified members of the public out of range. Both men put shoulders to the door, and it burst inwards.

Drabek saw the vehicle speed out of the alley almost immediately and realized just as quickly what had been wrong with the map. He grabbed Zoey's arm and pulled her behind him, up the stairs and into the seniors' center. He couldn't be sure the truck wouldn't explode, and it was the nearest cover.

Gunfire erupted, partially drowning screams from the parade goers. Inside the lobby of the seniors center, the gathered elders hit the floor when the first bullet shattered a front window.

'We need to go out there!' Zoey screamed. 'If Ben is out there, I have to see him. I have to know…'

'No way!' Drabek asserted. 'There are more than thirty federal agents down there and you have no protection from bullets.' Then he turned to the rest of the room from his kneeling position and said, 'Everyone stay calm, I'm a police officer. Stay low and stay inside. Don't go near the windows. Are we clear?'

The silence suggested everyone had the message.

'If he sees me,' Zoey went on, 'maybe he'll snap out of it; maybe it'll make him pause or break the hold someone has on him.'

'Just stay put!' Drabek insisted. 'Jesus H, Zoey, he tried to kill you already! The man is brainwashed, out of it.'

'He loves me. I know he wouldn't hurt me, Norm. That's why he missed! Don't you see, that's why he didn't shoot me. Because he's the only person who ever…' Her expression was miserable, overcome with doubt and pain. Then she bit her lower lip a little, her nostrils flaring from sharp intakes of breath, small signs that her indignant side was kicking in.

Zoey jumped to her feet and ran for the door.

'Jesus Christ!' Drabek's middle-aged muscles ached as he picked himself up off the floor and ran after her.

SCARSDALE, NEW YORK

The afternoon had fallen into ruin. They'd been scheduled to leave at noon, get to the conference just after one. Instead, Tarrant found himself in the back of Chan's limousine, heading back to the city.

'What the hell happened?' he barked into his phone.

'It's chaos down here, sir,' the agent at the scene told him. 'We've got bodies everywhere, two suspects, both loose. The Chinese Premier's limousine was destroyed, it doesn't look like anyone made it.'

'How? How did this happen?'

'We... I don't know, sir. This vehicle, a fire truck, it just came out of nowhere...It cut the limousine off for an attack.'

'We had all the side streets closed, blocked off...'

'We missed something, I guess...'

'YOU GUESS? Find out what the hell is going on and call me right back.'

He ended the call.

'How bad?' Adrianne asked.

'The Premier's vehicle was destroyed.'

They both shifted their attention to Chan, anxious at his potential response. But the man was smiling placidly. 'Okay,' Tarrant asked. 'What the hell is that about?'

'The Premier is perfectly safe,' Chan said. 'The man in the limousine was his double.'

'Excuse me?' Tarrant couldn't believe what he was hearing.

'The risk, your preparations. It all became too much to accept. And so a last minute decision was made to replace him with his public double. It is not an uncommon practice, Jonah. As you're well aware, your own president has...'

'I understand that. Why didn't you tell us? It might have led to fewer lost lives...'

'How? The public expected a parade. There would have been one. There still would have been an attack. The difference now is that both of our leaders are protected...'

'And dozens of our citizens are dead!' Tarrant exclaimed. 'We've lost officers, agents, good people, over nothing...'

'But your objective – to ensure the Premier and President were not assassinated – has been achieved,' Chan said. 'Given how brutal the attack seems to have been, you should be proud of the work...'

'GODDAMN IT!' Tarrant exclaimed. Then he chastised himself internally for losing his cool. 'That's not goddamn acceptable.' He began dialing his phone. 'I'm calling JFK,' he said to Adrianne. 'We need to take Daisy Lee into custody immediately and find out what else she knows before these people silence her.'

Chan gently shook his head. 'These people? Anyway, it's too late for that. We picked her up about ten minutes ago. But, as I promised, we will share anything pertinent....'

'The way you shared the switch? I don't think so,' Tarrant accused.

'In any case, she has already revealed to us that our interior minister, Wen Xiu, is the man formerly known as Dorian Fan. He will be arrested the moment his delegation is back at the hotel...'

'Okay, but he'll be arrested by us,' the deputy director insisted. 'If he's behind this, he'll pay for what he's done here, first, before you get a crack at him.'

Chan remained unfazed by any of it. 'He has

diplomatic immunity, deputy director...'

'Typically waived in the case of felony capital offenses, and mass murder...'

'We shall not be waiving any of his rights until he has had a trial at home, in our country,' Chan said. 'Lee has evidence directly from the man whose father performed Fan's plastic surgery...'

'And...?'

'And that is all that we need.' There was no percentage in discussing the nuclear plant with the Americans, Chan decided. They would figure out what it was soon enough.

'Adrianne, what's the Premier's handler saying?'

Hayes hung up on her call. 'They're incensed, of course. The conference is off. He won't go ahead with a pair of assassins on the loose, even with the so-called ringleader arrested.'

Chan's face sank. 'That is terrible news. This was our... our finest opportunity to affect real change in the region; to deal with Kim's threat and further our openness to the world...'

'I have agents with grieving families to worry about,' Tarrant snapped. 'My commiserations if your political plans have been derailed.' He leaned over the partition to the driver's cab. 'Step on it, will you? Break the goddamn speed of sound if you have to, just get us there!'

CHINATOWN, MANHATTAN

'I said DROP. THE PIECE. DO IT! NOW!!!' The officer screamed at Brennan, whose hands were up, the pistol trigger guard enabling it to dangle from one finger.

A girl ran past in a blonde blur. It took him a second to realize it was Zoey. 'Jesus H, call Brandon Mah! Call Mah, he's our security liaison for the event...'

'I'm giving you a three-count sir, then I'm going

to drop you, I swear it!' The young cop was getting nervous, not wanting to shoot a man from behind.

Drabek ran past, trying to keep up with someone more than twenty years his junior. He turned and followed the girl into the old storefront that had once housed the school.

'The guy who just ran past, he's a cop, like you. His name's Norm Drabek, he's working this...'

Behind him, the cop pulled the trigger of his service revolver, the rapport deafening both men for a few moments, hearing replaced by a high-pitched whine as the bullet tore through Brennan's thigh. He slumped down to the ground, weight on his opposite hip, the pain from the slug chipping bone excruciating.

'STAY DOWN!' the cop yelled. 'Stay down or I will shoot to kill!'

Instinct and field training kicked in. Even though he was in agony, Brenna swung his other leg out in a harsh kick, taking the young cop out at the ankles, the officer tripping and falling, his gun clattering out of reach. The cop tried to frantically right himself, but before he could do so, Brennan leaned over and slugged him in the jaw with the pistol butt, dazing him.

The agent pulled himself to his feet. The thigh was bleeding badly but the pain was a burning numbness, like a small area of flesh had been flayed from his body, rather than the searing agony of a broken femur. The blood wasn't spurting, which meant he'd missed the main artery. He pulled off his shirt, his torso sweat-soaked in the afternoon sun, then tore a long strip of cloth from it. The cop began to stir, trying to shake off the blow. Brennan leaned over again and pulled the pen from the kid's top pocket, using it to twist the tourniquet tighter, cutting off any blood flow, then looping it under the cloth to stay in place.

'You're... under arrest...' the cop tried to say.

Brennan ignored him and began limping toward the old schoolhouse, changing out his magazine on route and cocking the Heckler & Koch at the ready.

Zoey charged into the building, the door ajar, barely hanging off its hinges. The entryway was a half-landing, with short staircases up and down. She listened for long enough to guess the tromping footsteps were above them and took off again, taking the stairs as quickly as she could.

Drabek stumbled into the building right behind her, his pistol drawn. 'Zoey, wait! Stop!' he called out. But the girl wasn't listening. He took the stairs two at a time, adrenaline willing him on when tired muscles protested. He looked up between the railing and caught a glimpse of her on the second-floor stairwell.

Above her, someone leaned over the railing and opened fire. Zoey yelped and jumped backwards in fright, but Drabek wasn't as quick. The bullet caught him in the shoulder and he cried out, grunting from the pain, dropping to his knees, his revolver falling to the steps beside him.

Zoey glanced down over the rail and saw him, saw the blood pooling around him. 'NORM!' She turned back and ran down the flight, crouching beside him. 'Norm, are you okay?'

He was wincing from the pain, cupping his hand over the bleeding gash. 'It's just a flesh wound; hurts like a mother. I'll live. Kid, listen... you can't go up there...'

But Zoey Roberson had been listening to other people tell her what to do her entire life. Even when they cared, her life still always seemed to come down to someone else's choice. Ben Levitt had broken her heart, he'd tried to kill her and now he'd killed other people. She felt a malice in her that she didn't know had been there, lurking deep down, and she knew what she had to do.

Zoey grabbed the pistol and made her way back up the stairs. Behind her, Drabek called out for her to stop.

But she didn't listen. Ben was going to pay for what he'd done. He wasn't going to hurt anyone else.

47/

Brennan looked around the corner of the door then entered the building, quietly pushing the door closed behind him. He found his cell phone and texted the only person who he knew would definitely be somewhere nearby.

A few miles away, Jonah Tarrant's phone buzzed. He looked at the text on the screen. 'Two gunmen left, cornered in old school. Send backup.' He switched to the phone app and dialled for help.

At the school, Brennan crept up the stairs. The place was a two-up, one-down three story, from the early part of the Twentieth Century. Its floors and walls were concrete, and faint, random sounds echoed around the cavernous stairwell, not voices, just bass frequencies and air being pushed around; enough to know they were up there somewhere.

He turned the corner to the second floor and saw Drabek on the landing above. 'Where?' he said simply.

Drabek nodded up the stairs. 'She followed them up there.' Downstairs, they heard the door swing wide open. Jonah had gotten the message to officers on scene, it seemed. 'Wait for them,' Drabek suggested.

Brennan shook his head. 'She's in danger. Send them up after me.' He took the stairs gingerly, trying to keep his normal gait, to not limp or let the pain in his thigh overwhelm him. At the top landing, a corridor stretched nearly the length of the storey, past rooms that might once have been dormitories. It appeared to stop short of the back wall, a larger open entrance suggesting it emptied into one larger chamber.

He could hear voices as he crept down the hallway, pistol extended. '...don't understand. I checked the connections and leads myself,' Gessler was saying. 'There's enough C4 in that thing to level a building.'

'It's not working,' Levitt hissed, a clicking noise suggesting he was trying a button. 'If the truck doesn't blow, we're trapped in here.'

Water's plan had been ingenious; a sewer access juncture started just past the point where the truck was to blow. It would've taken out any remaining law enforcement and opened up their escape route. But the C4 wasn't firing. 'I thought you were supposed to have expertise in this,' he accused.

'It was improvised,' Gessler snapped at him. 'You knew that. I told you the leads looked crimped this morning! I'm doing good this time!'

Brennan peeked around the corner. Zoey Roberson was lying prone, unconscious, Drabek's pistol a few feet away from her. She was partially face down, like she'd been hit from behind, probably as soon as she ran through the door. He leaned fully around the corner and lined up Gessler, letting the trigger work, anticipating the gun's kick. The shot caught the man in the side of the head, through his temple, a fine red mist spraying the wall past him as Gessler slumped dead to the ground. Levitt turned, cell phone in hand. His pistol was on the table next to what looked like some sort of transmitter or range booster, and he reached for it.

'Ah! Ah, ah, ah... steady now,' Brennan said, limping into the room, pistol at the ready. "You won't make it before I take the shot, that I guarantee. And from this range, I will not miss.'

Levitt stared at him like a cornered animal, his eyes alert with anxiety. Then he glanced at the pistol again. Then at Brennan.

'Don't...!' the agent managed to yell as the other man grasped for the pistol grip. Brennan squeezed the trigger.

And it jammed. 'Oh, shit,' was all that Brennan could mutter as Levitt grabbed his gun and wheeled to fire. The sound was explosive once more, deafening, and Brennan flinched, his eyes closing in an involuntary wince, anticipating the sting of the fatal shot.

But it never came.

He opened his eyes.

Zoey was standing next to him, Drabek's revolver at arm's length. By the table, Levitt was clutching his chest at the entry wound, looking down at the blood flowing through his fingers. He looked frightened, puzzled by what was happening, as if snapped back to something resembling reality. Then he dropped to his knees, his head bobbing slightly, muscle control disappearing. 'But...' he muttered. Then he looked her in the eyes, and his were alone, and frightened and tear-stained. They belonged to Christopher Platt, a boy long forgotten by anyone who should have cared. 'I'll be good,' he implored 'I'll be good. I promise.'

He pitched forward into the growing puddle of blood. Zoey dropped the gun and her hands went to her face as she realized what she'd just done. She ran over to him and cradled Ben's head on her lap, and she held the man she loved, sobbing, her tears flowing freely.

48/

Jonah Tarrant's intervention allowed them some peace a day later, after the interviews. He tapped some contacts and found a house a few miles upstate, along the Hudson River, in which everyone could decompress until the investigation was complete.

The conference would go on, he'd told them. The loss of twenty-three lives meant that a day of mourning would be announced by the President. Then they would get back to the business of trying to prevent nuclear war.

But Zoey wasn't thinking about any of that. She sat on a cedar bench along the home's wrap-around deck and looked down at the river. Or perhaps, past it. She couldn't get her mind off Benjamin and the fact that, to her, he'd been as real as anyone. She knew he'd died the moment he got that fateful phone call, two weeks earlier. But that didn't make it any easier to take. He was gone, forever, but she would always want him there.

'You okay?'

Norm had his hands in the pockets of his brown corduroy trousers, looking worried. But that was par for the course. She was long past the point of fearing another motive, or that he viewed her as pitiable. He just cared. 'I know I will be, eventually. But all I can think about is that moment when he died, and he knew he wasn't supposed to be there. He just seemed trapped and confused, and alone. And... I don't know; I guess I've been there. I know how that feels... and then to die at that moment, when you feel the least loved, the least connected.' She looked up at him, years of pain etched into the small lines and wrinkles. 'That's a horrible way for someone you love to go.'

He sat down next to her. 'Yeah. I've always kind

of figured Nicole must have felt alone, or unloved, or unworthy. There were things I could've done differently. I could've considered them more... my family, I mean.'

'She made her decisions, rational or not. You didn't force her...'

'No, but I didn't help, either. And I'm her... I was her father. That was my job, more than any other. Those kids... the ones in China. From what we can tell, their parents were roped in, drugged, brainwashed themselves. They didn't make their children into killers, they just made a terrible decision to trust the wrong side, the notion that it was a force for positive change...'

She snorted a little at that, then apologized. 'I'm sorry, that's insensitive. But really, I'm beginning to wonder if there will ever be a right side.'

Brennan was standing in the doorway to the living room. 'Probably not,' he said. 'It's human nature to pick a side, join a group. We need a tribe to protect us. We need the strength of numbers. But sometimes, we pick the wrong group, the wrong idea. And we stick with it because the group makes us feel safe, like any other animal. The difference is that we can do better. It's inherent, but it doesn't stop us from bettering ourselves. What you did yesterday... you probably saved hundreds, possibly thousands of lives. A crimp in a wire broke the connection to a detonator they were going to use to blow up about sixteen pounds of C4 explosive, over a road that contained a major natural gas trunk line.'

Zoey's mouth dropped open a little. 'I didn't know...'

'Neither did we. So even though the loss of life was brutal, and unacceptable, and as unnecessary as that goddamned parade, while the politicians were busy making the world worse, you were making it better. And the Ben you remember, the one you fell in love with? He was a surgeon. He would've appreciated the Hell out of that.'

Then he walked back inside.

Zoey's head dipped again but there was a tiny hint of a smile, and that made Det. Norm Drabek smile for the first time in longer than he could remember.

MANHATTAN, NEW YORK

The Grand Ballroom at the Plaza Hotel was an opulent architectural gem, an expanse of marble floor, a gigantic crystal chandelier suspended from wisps of wrought iron, pillars and arches ringing the room, inset tray carvings between the arches and the ceiling. It could've been lifted from Paris' Belle Epoque, the great artistic era. Daisy Lee gazed around it with admiration, the tables beginning to fill, guests drifting over from the adjacent room's cocktail party.

'Just... beautiful,' she said with a little sigh. 'I'd seen it in movies but it's not like in person.'

Brennan gave her a sideways glance. She had a black cocktail dress on and he had to remind himself for a moment that he missed his wife and kids, because the dress was working overtime.

'Well, you earned this,' he said. 'I know you don't give a damn about official thank yous, or commendations, or any of that crap...'

'Speak for yourself!' she scoffed. 'I want my job back when I get home. Without getting a little credit in this whole mess, that wasn't going to happen. Plus, we get an official banquet and the Premier of China has to say nice things about me. This is absolutely lovely.'

They walked over to their assigned dinner seats, their position nearest the long head table and dais, where the two leaders would speak after the meal. Norm and Zoey were sitting together whispering. They both smiled when Brennan and Lee announced themselves.

Then Zoey leaned over to them and whispered. 'I feel really out of place! They loaned me this dress and it's worth more than most peoples' mortgages. And the diamond, too.'

'They rented me the monkey suit as well,' said Drabek, who had a snazzy looking Fifties-cut black tuxedo on with a narrow bow-tie. 'The shoes are pinching my damn toes.'

Lee tried a rough head count but lost track. 'There must be a hundred people here, at least,' she said.

'Yeah,' Norm muttered, 'who knew negotiating disarmament had to cost a thousand bucks a plate.'

The PA system crackled to life and people's attention shifted to the dais. The mayor gestured to his right and said, 'Ladies and Gentlemen, the Premier of China and the President of the United States.' A recording of 'Hail to the Chief' began to play as the delegates were led from the side anteroom to the table. The President and his foreign guest were put right next to each other, their wives on either side, followed by wives of the mayor and deputy-mayor.

It took a minute before all eighteen seats were filled. 'Okay!' the mayor announced, once everyone was seated. 'Let's eat!'

Brennan was skipping dinner, which was off his high-metabolic diet cycle of small meals, every two hours. He looked around the conference room. David Chan had the last seat at the head table on their side, and Brennan noticed him staring right back. He did not look happy to see him. Brennan flashed him a smile, but Chan just turned his attention back to his food.

What a piece of work, the agent thought. Like all of his ilk. *Selfish, vain, arrogant. He'll probably be their next premier. And could I honestly say we'll be any better of with whoever we pick?* Rubber chicken dinners always made him uncomfortable. He hadn't had to attend one in years, not since the SEALs. But nothing had changed. *Wealthy people on a free ride, no sense of dignity about what had just happened, no solemnity. No genuine feeling.*

Nonetheless, he knew, in a few minutes they'd all be called up to that front table, and they'd get a hearty Presidential handshake, and they'd all smile and be grateful just to be recognized, no matter how little, in the long run, actually changed. For folks like Zoey and Drabek, who didn't get sucked into some international drama every six months, it was probably thrilling. But for Brennan, it was sound and fury, signifying nothing.

The only thing that mattered would be what happened at the conference itself. Anything that protected Japan and South Korea from nuclear annihilation, that made life better for average people. That he held onto, a rationale for the madness. A human connection.

After the dinner and ceremony had concluded, the dance began, the President leading the Chinese first lady in a waltz, other guests joining in after a few steps.

Lee noticed Zoey had drifted away from the activity, toward the back of the room. Drabek had disappeared outside, potentially for a cigarette, though he'd claimed twice already that night that he was 'done with the damn things.'

She walked over to join the other woman. 'You should be trying to enjoy this,' she suggested.

Zoey offered a game smile, but there was no doubt the grief was making it hard for her. 'Yeah...yeah, I guess. They told Norm they're looking into a government job for me. Apparently, I showed 'great resilience in the face of extreme circumstances', or something.'

'It's something,' Lee suggested. 'It's one small positive out of this. A win. I'd take it.'

Zoey nodded but her heart wasn't in it. 'All my life I've ended up alone. I sometimes wonder if I'll eventually lose the ability to keep trying, or to really love people.'

'Brennan said something about you being a street kid... I grew up on the streets of Hong Kong...'

'I don't want to talk about that stuff, okay?' She said it sternly. 'My past is done. I'm going to try and move forward. Revisiting old wounds...'

'Okay,' Lee said gently, annoyed at herself for making the girl feel worse. 'But you're not going to end up alone. You do have friends.' She spotted Brennan hovering near the arches, crowd watching. 'I'm going to go talk to Brennan; want to come?'

Zoey shook her head. 'I'm good. I just... I guess I need to think about things is all,' she said.

Brennan nodded at Lee as she walked over. 'She looks like she's struggling.'

Lee nodded. 'As you know, this is not a world in which civilians thrive. She seems to be in quite a lot of pain.'

'At least she's got Drabek. He really dotes on her, doesn't he? You think he's...'

'What? A dirty old man?' Lee scoffed. 'No, Brennan. Do you always think the worst of everyone?'

It was probably a fair question, he knew. But he didn't like Lee thinking she'd won one. 'It's kept both of us alive more than once, hasn't it?'

'Yes, keep hanging onto the notion that I need your help in that regard,' she suggested. 'If it makes you feel more manly and secure, then all the better.'

'Manly and...' He blew off a little steam, then cut off his testy reaction early. 'Never mind. It's the job. It's always about... hey: speaking of which, did you sit down and think this whole thing through yet? I mean, puzzle out how everything went down?'

She shook her head. 'Not my department. They'll be debriefing us both until the next millennium though, I rather imagine.'

'It's just... the whole thing with the surgeon... something's wrong with that.'

She gave him a hard glance sideways. 'You mean the intel I risked everything to obtain from North Korea? That 'something'?'

'Yeah. Wen Xiu is a nationalist of the first order, but the man used to be a university professor.'

'So?'

'So he wrote three volumes on the excesses and mistakes of the cultural revolution, volumes accepted by the government as canon, and work that absolutely eviscerates the legacy of Jiang Qing. I mean, he made her an even worse monster than she was. I get that being a government minister is a great cover for taking over a government; but if you were going to do it for ideological reasons, in the name of Madame Mao... why would you spend three decades prior to that shitting all over her legacy?'

Lee frowned. She didn't want to consider it, but he had a point. 'That... is something I had not considered.'

'Neither had I, until I looked the guy up. The cover would've been just as good without attacking the woman he supposedly believed in.'

'You think I've gotten it wrong, don't you? You think he's not Dorian Fan.'

She sounded apprehensive, and Brennan hoped it was over the risk, not the loss of face. 'I... don't know. I'm a lot less certain than our respective bosses, that's for damn sure. And if we don't have him, he's a threat to world security every moment he's free. And if they're wrong about that, what about the old man's tip, the three students. Perhaps there were others.'

Lee nodded toward the head table. 'They don't seem to be too worried.' The President and Premier had both taken their seats and were chatting like old college friends, even as most of the room milled around on their feet. A Secret Service agent stood behind each of them, and she'd spotted at least eight more in plainclothes. 'They look as if they're rather taken with each other.'

'Birds of a feather,' Brennan suggested. He nodded over toward David Chan, who was standing near the doors to the hallway, a scotch and soda in hand, observing. 'He doesn't seem as happy.'

'I get the sense he takes a certain pride in things going the way they're supposed to. He planned much of this and it went to absolute ruin, until Americans intervened. I suspect he's happy about Wen, though...'

Brennan frowned. 'Why? I thought they served on the state security committee...'

'They were friends many years ago, when rising through the party. But Chan's business successes and wealth made him unpopular with the more traditional communists. Wen felt betrayed, apparently. They've fought hammer and tong ever since.'

'Huh.' Brennan tried to trace a line from Chan's gaze to the head table. Sure enough, he seemed to be studying his nation's Premier the way a lion watches an unaware gazelle at a drinking hole. 'I wouldn't want to be the people ahead of him these days...'

Then he frowned again. Zoey had wandered over in Chan's direction. She hadn't tried to, but she'd caught his attention nonetheless, eyeing her from a slight side-rear angle as if she were a model in a men's magazine, tilting his head to study the curve of her buttocks in the tight evening gown. 'And... he's a dirty old man, too,' Brennan said with a sigh. 'Humanity sucks.'

A few yards away, Norm Drabek took a load off and, while no one was looking, took one of the rented dress shoes off under the table, then the other. Then he rubbed his aching feet. What was it about age, he wondered, that made a man's feet hurt? He'd walked a beat as a twenty-something straight out of the academy. Surely that would've been worse on them than a few days of running around New York.

He scoped out the room, trying to get a sense of how the others were doing. Brennan and Lee were standing by an arch near the back of the room, just behind and to his left. The agents looked ill at ease.

His gaze followed the crowd along the wall to the door, where Zoey was chatting with David Chan, the billionaire. She looked sheepish and embarrassed, and he had a scotch tumbler in one hand, like something out of an old Playboy Club shot. Drabek felt a surge of irritation at the man's interest, a parental concern for the way he was looking at her.

Then he caught himself and felt foolish. If she'd proven anything, it was that she could take care of herself. She'd been so strong and resilient, despite what she'd been through. Sure, when they met, she'd been frightened. That's what had attracted him to help, like he couldn't for his daughter. Like he couldn't for Nicole.

But then, ever since that first day, Daisy had found the strength. Nicole had never been able to find that resilience. That toughness and bravery. He blamed himself. They'd given her a good home, a loving mother who was always there even when he wasn't. Compared to that, Zoey had had nothing, a street kid. But she was resourceful, clever, strong, with an inexhaustible will...

He looked at her again, then down at his socked feet, his toes wiggling in glorious freedom. Then he looked at her again as she chatted with Chan.

It seemed... wrong.

Not morally so, though losing Nicole had sometimes made his thoughts and feelings meander in that direction. Instead, it just seemed... off. He'd met dozens like that in his time as a cop, abandoned children, forced to hustle and make it on their own, often from abusive homes. There was always trauma under the surface, wounds that rendered them vulnerable at the worst possible occasions.

But not Zoey. She'd always acted like her past was only skin deep.

Brennan slugged back the last of his scotch but didn't take his eyes off Chan. He'd sidled up to the girl and they were talking closely. He glimpsed Drabek, seated, out of the corner of his eye and wondered whether he was getting uncomfortable.

Chan leaned in to say something to the girl, whipping off his glasses and chewing on one ear piece like some sage professor, or something; for a man of his age, Brennan thought, the entire display was nauseating.

They were only about a dozen feet away, he gauged. He considered throwing a cocktail weenie at the man, just to throw him off his 'game'. They were standing under the lights in front of the main doors, the girl's white skin and tattoos seeming even more starkly contrasted against his tuxedo and...

Brennan squinted. Chan had something behind his right ear; it looked like...

A scar. A large, vertical scar. The kind someone might have after plastic surgery. He whispered something to Zoey, and she nodded once, then turned. She began to walk directly toward the head table.

Something's wrong. He could feel it in his bones, though no one else seemed to notice. The dance floor was packed as she approached it. What had Lee said, about the possibility the old man was wrong? Or perhaps, even, lying to them – he had been a devotee of Madame Mao, after all. What was it Master Yip had said, that the little one was the saddest of them all.

'The little one,' he said out loud.

'Eh?' Lee replied.

'It's her.'

'What's her? What are you babbling about now, Brennan?'

'Becky, the other girl! The little girl in the story, Amy's sister. We forgot about Becky.'

'You're saying... what?'

'Zoey. She's the assassin. Not the other two, not Parnell. They were just ghosts, just sleepers sacrificed to put her in the perfect position. The perfect false flag...'

Lee looked around frantically for a secret service agent. She covered the ten feet to him and whispered loudly, to avoid any panic but still trying to be heard over the group of young delegates laughing in a group, next to him. 'I need you to radio your men by the head table, there may be an attack.'

'Pickup what?' the man yelled over the group. 'Miss, if you could speak up... Sorry...' He held up a hand, a voice coming through the radio. Then he turned back to her, 'You'll have to give me a moment, ma'am, my superior needs to speak with me...' He began to shuffle toward the other side of the room.

'Aiyah!' Lee exclaimed. She turned back to Brennan and shook her head that she couldn't get through to the man.

'Tell your people!' he called back. He nodded across the room and she saw the group of four Chinese secret service, sitting together quietly.

Brennan looked back to the dance floor. Zoey had begun to make her way through the mass of swaying partygoers. He saw her dip low for a moment, as if retrieving something from the floor, but lost sight of her. There were too many bodies, and she was a small woman. He began making his way over, pushing people aside, increasingly frustrated. In the midst of the dancefloor he saw a glint of chrome; he reached into his back waistband, then realized he didn't have a piece; they'd been individually patting down every single guest at the main doors in the wake of the incident. The only people carrying were secret service agents and a few cops.

Cops.

He looked over at Drabek. He was standing, despite his stockinged feet, staring in the same direction as Brennan. Then he looked over and caught the agent's eye, then shook his head. He wasn't local law enforcement, so he wasn't armed. They reacted in tandem, both running for the crowd, shoving dancers aside. The PA system blared a folky polka, a lighthearted group song. 'GUN!' Brennan screamed into the crowd, his voice drowned out by a chorus of three claps, everyone joining in.

Zoey was just yards from the head table. She stood tall, drawing the pistol from hip height, extending it, Brennan too far to react, screaming in vain as she sighted the Chinese Premier, his face frozen in shock and surprise. The crowd swayed in front of Brennan at just the wrong moment, his line of sight cut off, the crack of each gunshot echoing off the ballroom walls.

The crowd screamed on mass, people peeling away from the dance floor, panicking at the scene. Most of the head table were on their feet. Brennan saw movement to his right.

It was Lee, her right arm extended, pistol in hand even as the Chinese security agent behind her pawed at her to get his weapon back.

Zoey lay on her back in a pool of blood, her head cocked awkwardly to one side, her torso twisted ungracefully at the waist. Her face was placid other than the small trickle of blood running from one corner of her mouth, her blue eyes wide open but vacant, free finally of the burden of life. When she was still Becky Sawyer, she'd been the fastest girl her age. But it had still never been good enough, never enough to save them from the monsters who lurked down the street. And after that, there had never been a real moment, where she was herself. Just a parade of identities, biding time, fitting in, learning skills, chief among them how best to manipulate hearts.

Brennan looked over at Drabek, expecting him to rush over to her. But he just stood there, arms at his side, shoulders slumped, weighed down by the sort of sadness that can rob a man of his soul.

EPILOGUE

LANGLEY, VIRGINIA

Brennan watched through the one-way glass as a colleague debriefed Drabek. In the three days past, they'd already gone at him for some twenty hours. It was like Tarrant personally blamed the veteran cop for letting her get so close.

'How's it going in there?'

Speak of the devil. 'Jonah. He's holding up. How much longer is this going to go on?'

'Until we're damn certain he knew nothing. They finally got something more recent on 'Becky Sawyer'. Remember that trainee who disappeared, Sara Evans...?'

Brennan was stunned. 'Mike's star pupil?'

Tarrant nodded. 'Plastic surgery. They were going to leak her identity to the Chinese and American media; no one would believe that she wasn't an undercover assassin once a prior tie to the agency was established.'

A piece clicked into place. 'Parnell,' Brennan said. 'She investigated the case for the D.C. police before going over to the NSA. She helped her stage the suicide as soon as she was officially accepted for employment, which was why they waited until the very end of her training. What are you going to tell Mike? Or Drabek's people? The version in the papers will be expounded on over the coming weeks...'

He shrugged. 'Then they'll figure it out on their own, if they're worried. I have no beef with the detective, Joe; we just have to be careful, that's all. I'm not going to ruin his career, if that's what you're worried about.'

'It was.'

Tarrant looked hurt. 'Really?'

'I wouldn't put it beneath you, after how some of

this went down. You know David Chan was responsible for all of this, that he's the real Dorian Fan, don't you?'

'Of course. And officially, none of that is true. Officially, the Chinese will not be embarrassed by a rogue terrorist in their ranks into revisiting their own past; officially, he will be caught insider trading and executed for his crimes. Wen Xiu will have to resolve his issues without our help, at the Premier's personal request, as he is quite tired of the man. And we will receive their help in 'convincing' the Kim regime to dismantle their new nuclear reactor at Sonbong. But unofficially? Well... I guess that won't matter much in the end either.'

Tarrant turned and began to walk down the hall, back toward the elevators. He was younger than Brennan but the agent noticed his shoulders had begun to stoop even as his waist grew, like the weight of the world was beginning to drag him down. 'Hell of a business, this, Jonah...' he offered.

But the deputy director wasn't listening; his phone had begun to buzz. He drew it quickly from his pocket and answered. 'Jonah Tarrant. Uh huh...' After a few moments, he turned the corner, and disappeared from view.

Brennan turned back to the window. One of the two agents handling the debrief was standing, his sleeves rolled up, gesticulating wildly like he was angry or irritated by something, or maybe just frustrated. Drabek was shrugging nonchalantly, as if none of it mattered anyway.

'Hey... Joe!'

He turned. He recognized the young man with the clipboard but couldn't remember his name, giving him a finger point. 'It'll come to me.'

'Adam! Adam Karas, from logistics. Your kid and my kid play Little League together.'

'Oh... oh, yeah. Good to see you again.' He didn't really want to small talk but Carolyn wanted him to try being more sociable, more polite.

'Speaking of timing, we were just talking about

the New York thing and how it started with that Korean nuke.'

'Yeah...'

'So there was a story in the paper this morning... here...' He fished through the papers attached to his clipboard until he reached the clipping. He handed it to Brennan. 'Yeah... I guess that Fisherman who almost died, a Mr. Fujiwara or something... he had a grandchild this morning! They got a cute shot of him with the baby by his boat... here...'

The photo was close cropped, the elderly fisherman holding the newborn in his arms, his white beard neat and trimmed for the occasion, the undershirt freshly cleaned.

The baby was tiny, born prematurely to his twenty-year-old granddaughter; but it was happy and smiling, its mouth open in a tiny oval, tiny fat fingers grasping for air and context, its blue eyes looking up at him, full of wonder and love.

For a few moments, Brennan's world felt right again.

THE END

ABOUT THE AUTHOR

Ian Loome is a former Canadian journalist. He grew up in Africa in a communist dictatorship and spent weekends playing tennis against KGB and East German Stasi officers. He has lived around the world and covered stories ranging from executions and homicides to global politics and light features. As an author, he wrote Shadow Agenda in 2015. The global spy thriller garnered impressive reviews and reached Amazon's spy thriller best-seller list. His second novel, the Mafia action-drama Old Wounds, was released in August 2018.

Ian can be contacted at lhtbooks@gmail.com

Made in the USA
Las Vegas, NV
05 January 2023

65063056R00256